W9-CMO-163

DISCARDED

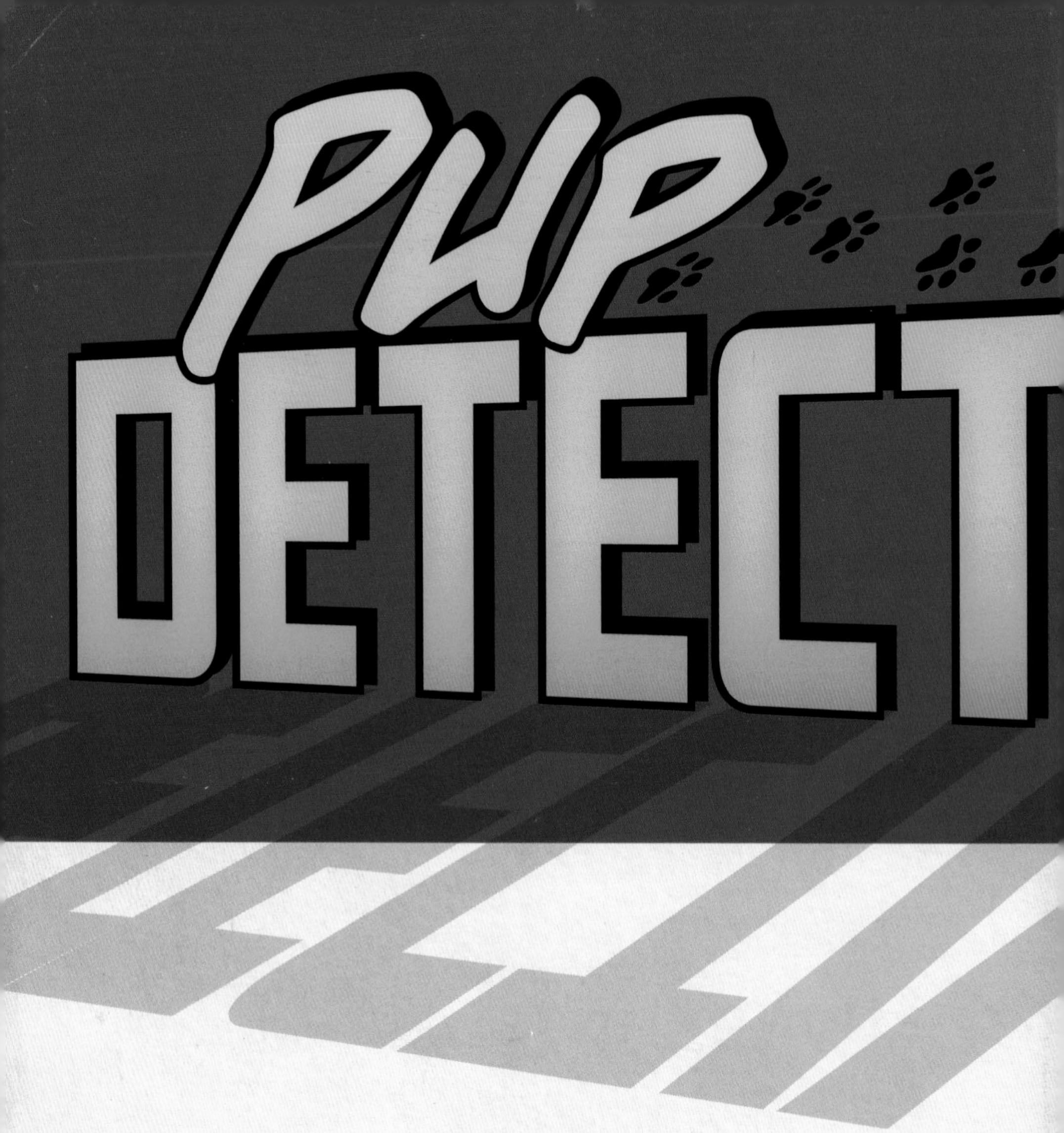
PUP
DETECT

IVES

THE SOCCER MYSTERY

Written by FELIX GUMPAW
Illustrated by WALMIR ARCHANJO
at GLASS HOUSE GRAPHICS

LITTLE SIMON
NEW YORK   LONDON   TORONTO   SYDNEY   NEW DELHI

THIS BOOK IS A WORK OF FICTION. ANY REFERENCES TO HISTORICAL EVENTS, REAL PEOPLE, OR REAL PLACES ARE USED FICTITIOUSLY. OTHER NAMES, CHARACTERS, PLACES, AND EVENTS ARE PRODUCTS OF THE AUTHOR'S IMAGINATION, AND ANY RESEMBLANCE TO ACTUAL EVENTS OR PLACES OR PERSONS, LIVING OR DEAD, IS ENTIRELY COINCIDENTAL.

LITTLE SIMON
AN IMPRINT OF SIMON & SCHUSTER CHILDREN'S PUBLISHING DIVISION
1230 AVENUE OF THE AMERICAS, NEW YORK, NEW YORK 10020
FIRST LITTLE SIMON EDITION JUNE 2021
COPYRIGHT © 2021 BY SIMON & SCHUSTER, INC.
ALL RIGHTS RESERVED, INCLUDING THE RIGHT OF REPRODUCTION IN WHOLE OR IN PART IN ANY FORM. LITTLE SIMON IS A REGISTERED TRADEMARK OF SIMON & SCHUSTER, INC., AND ASSOCIATED COLOPHON IS A TRADEMARK OF SIMON & SCHUSTER, INC. FOR INFORMATION ABOUT SPECIAL DISCOUNTS FOR BULK PURCHASES, PLEASE CONTACT SIMON & SCHUSTER SPECIAL SALES AT 1-866-506-1949 OR BUSINESS@SIMONANDSCHUSTER.COM. ART BY WALMIR ARCHANJO AND JOÃO ZOD • COLORING BY WALMIR ARCHANJO, JOÃO ZOD, LELO ALVES, HUGO CARVALHO, ADJAIR FRANÇA AND IZAAC BRITO • LETTERING BY MARCOS MASSAO INOUE • SUPERVISION BY MJ MACEDO/ANCIENT BLACK • ART SERVICES BY GLASS HOUSE GRAPHICS • THE SIMON & SCHUSTER SPEAKERS BUREAU CAN BRING AUTHORS TO YOUR LIVE EVENT. FOR MORE INFORMATION OR TO BOOK AN EVENT CONTACT THE SIMON & SCHUSTER SPEAKERS BUREAU AT 1-866-248-3049 OR VISIT OUR WEBSITE AT WWW.SIMONSPEAKERS.COM.
DESIGNED BY NICHOLAS SCIACCA
MANUFACTURED IN CHINA 0321 SCP
10 9 8 7 6 5 4 3 2 1
LIBRARY OF CONGRESS CATALOGING-IN-PUBLICATION DATA. NAMES: GUMPAW, FELIX, AUTHOR. I GLASS HOUSE GRAPHICS, ILLUSTRATOR. TITLE: THE SOCCER MYSTERY / BY FELIX GUMPAW; ILLUSTRATED BY GLASS HOUSE GRAPHICS. DESCRIPTION: FIRST LITTLE SIMON EDITION. I NEW YORK : LITTLE SIMON, 2021. I SERIES: PUP DETECTIVES ; 3 I AUDIENCE: AGES 5-9 I AUDIENCE: GRADES K-1 I SUMMARY: "WHEN A BELOVED TEAM MASCOT GOES MISSING JUST BEFORE A BIG SOCCER MATCH, THE PUP DETECTIVES ARE CALLED IN BY THE PRINCIPAL TO CRACK THE CASE!" – PROVIDED BY PUBLISHER. IDENTIFIERS: LCCN 2020027933 (PRINT) I LCCN 2020027934 (EBOOK) I ISBN 9781534478695 (PAPERBACK) I ISBN 9781534478701 (HARDCOVER) I ISBN 9781534478718 (EBOOK) SUBJECTS: LCSH: GRAPHIC NOVELS. I CYAC: GRAPHIC NOVELS. I MYSTERY AND DETECTIVE STORIES. I DOGS–FICTION. CLASSIFICATION: LCC PZ7.7.G858 SO 2021 (PRINT) I LCC PZ7.7.G858 (EBOOK) I DDC 741.5/973–DC23. LC RECORD AVAILABLE AT HTTPS://LCCN.LOC.GOV/2020027933. LC EBOOK RECORD AVAILABLE AT HTTPS://LCCN.LOC.GOV/2020027934

CONTENTS

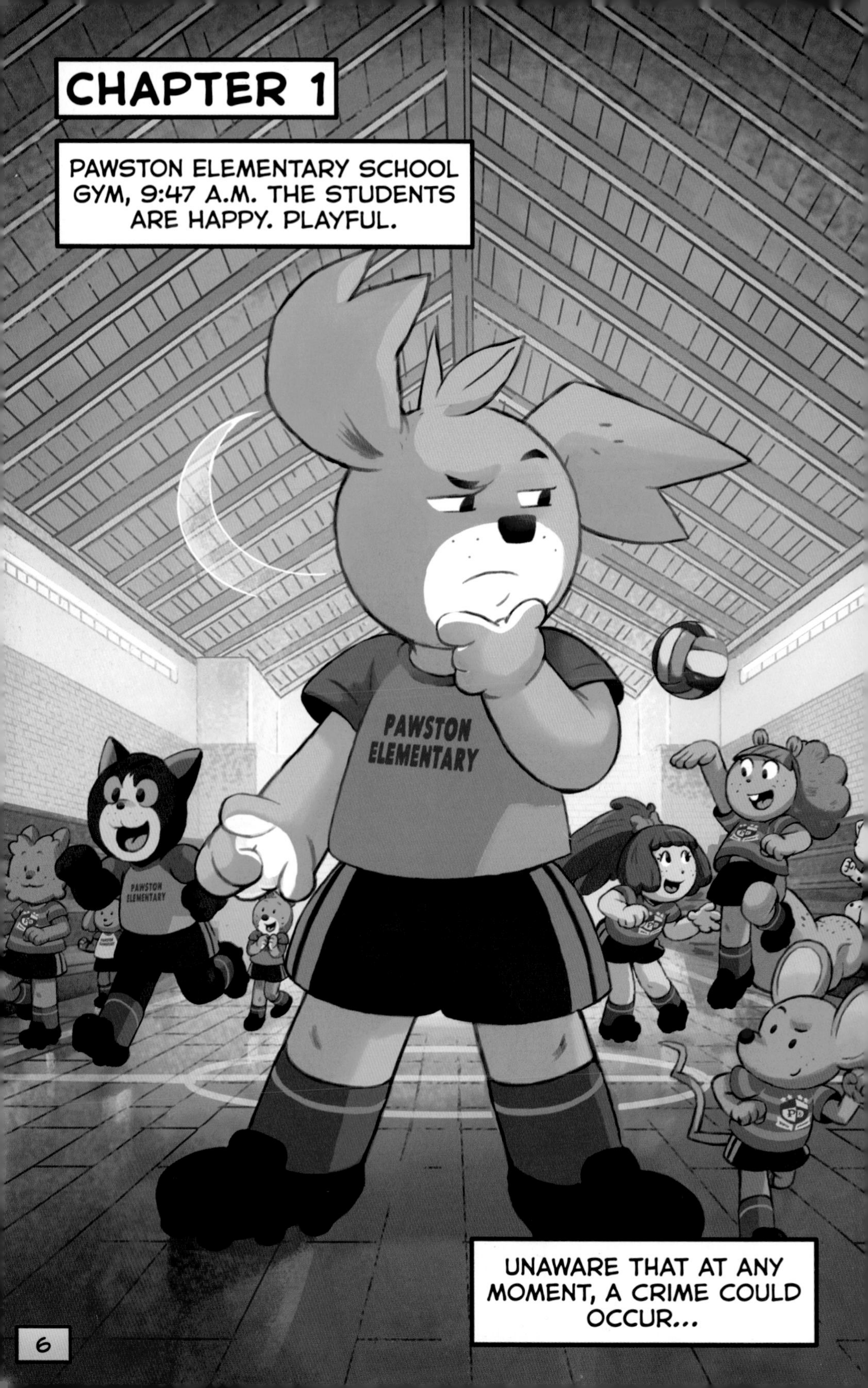
CHAPTER 1
PAWSTON ELEMENTARY SCHOOL GYM, 9:47 A.M. THE STUDENTS ARE HAPPY. PLAYFUL.
PAWSTON ELEMENTARY
PAWSTON ELEMENTARY
UNAWARE THAT AT ANY MOMENT, A CRIME COULD OCCUR...

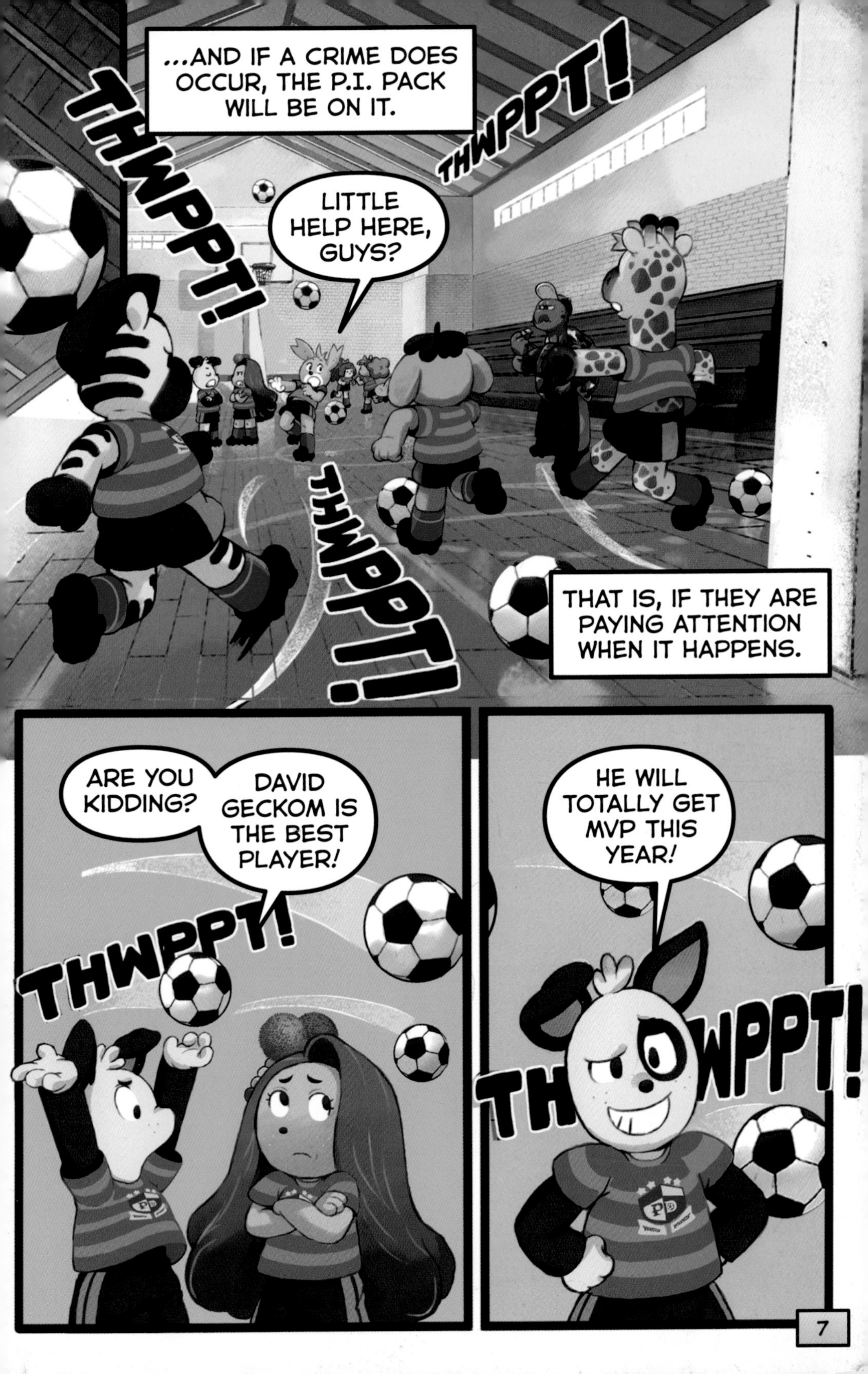
...AND IF A CRIME DOES OCCUR, THE P.I. PACK WILL BE ON IT.
THWPPT!
THWPPT!
LITTLE HELP HERE, GUYS?
THWPPT!
THAT IS, IF THEY ARE PAYING ATTENTION WHEN IT HAPPENS.
ARE YOU KIDDING?
DAVID GECKOM IS THE BEST PLAYER!
THWPPT!
HE WILL TOTALLY GET MVP THIS YEAR!
THWPPT!

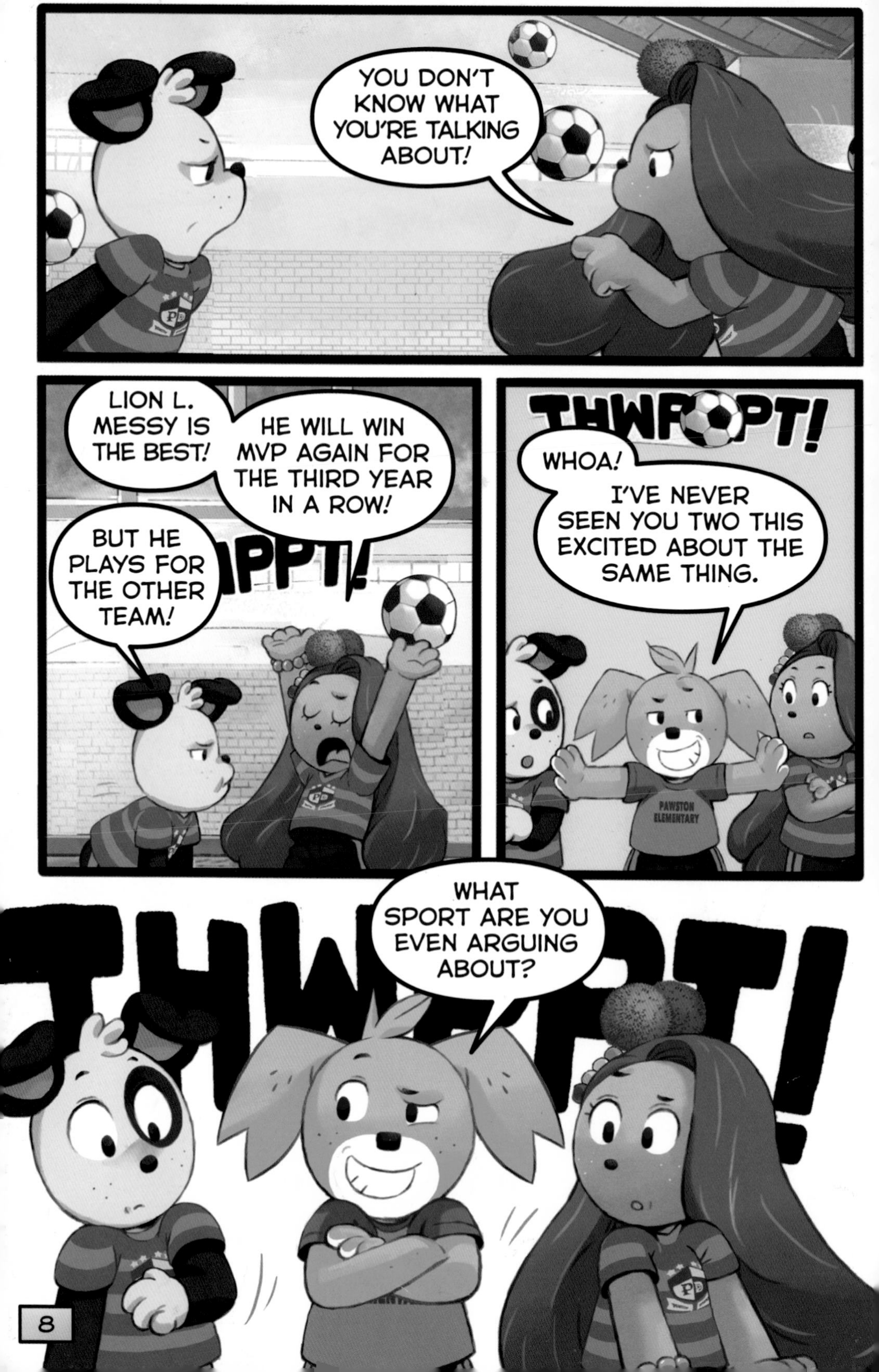
YOU DON'T KNOW WHAT YOU'RE TALKING ABOUT!
LION L. MESSY IS THE BEST!
HE WILL WIN MVP AGAIN FOR THE THIRD YEAR IN A ROW!
BUT HE PLAYS FOR THE OTHER TEAM!
PPT!
THWPOPT!
WHOA!
I'VE NEVER SEEN YOU TWO THIS EXCITED ABOUT THE SAME THING.
PAWSTON ELEMENTARY
WHAT SPORT ARE YOU EVEN ARGUING ABOUT?
THW PT!

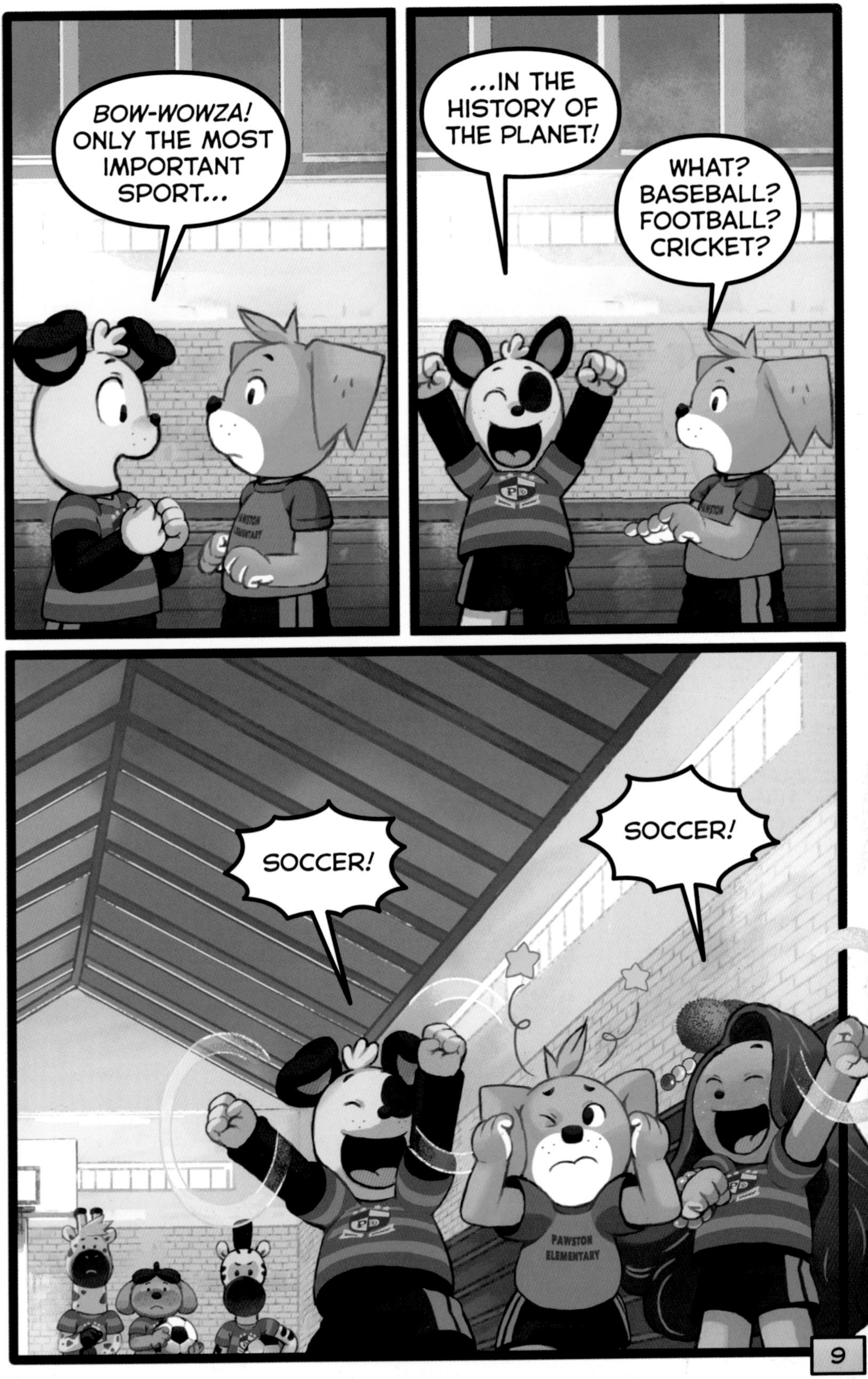
BOW-WOWZA! ONLY THE MOST IMPORTANT SPORT...
...IN THE HISTORY OF THE PLANET!
WHAT? BASEBALL? FOOTBALL? CRICKET?
SOCCER!
SOCCER!
PAWSTON ELEMENTARY

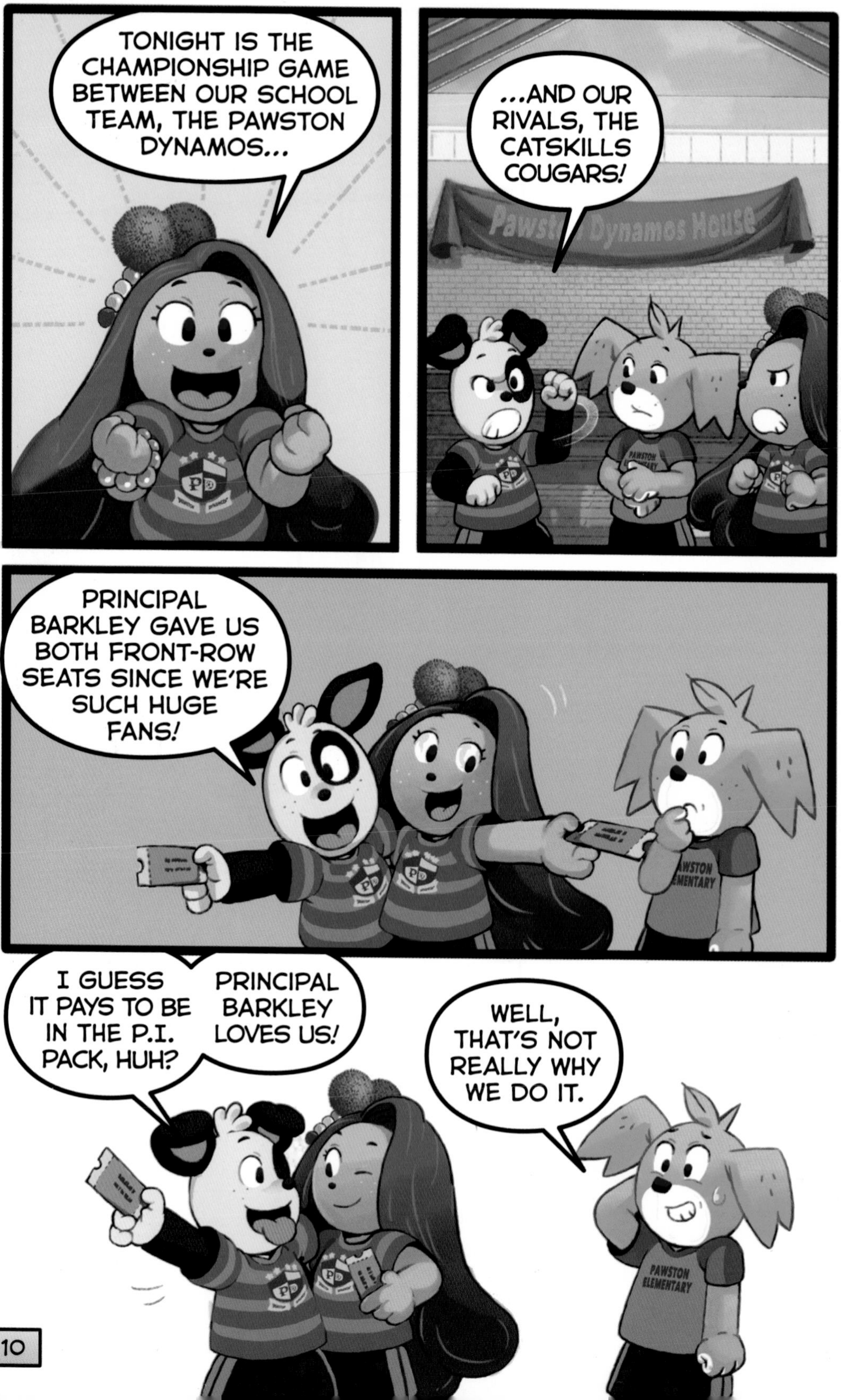
TONIGHT IS THE CHAMPIONSHIP GAME BETWEEN OUR SCHOOL TEAM, THE PAWSTON DYNAMOS...
...AND OUR RIVALS, THE CATSKILLS COUGARS!
PRINCIPAL BARKLEY GAVE US BOTH FRONT-ROW SEATS SINCE WE'RE SUCH HUGE FANS!
I GUESS IT PAYS TO BE IN THE P.I. PACK, HUH?
PRINCIPAL BARKLEY LOVES US!
WELL, THAT'S NOT REALLY WHY WE DO IT.
PAWSTON ELEMENTARY

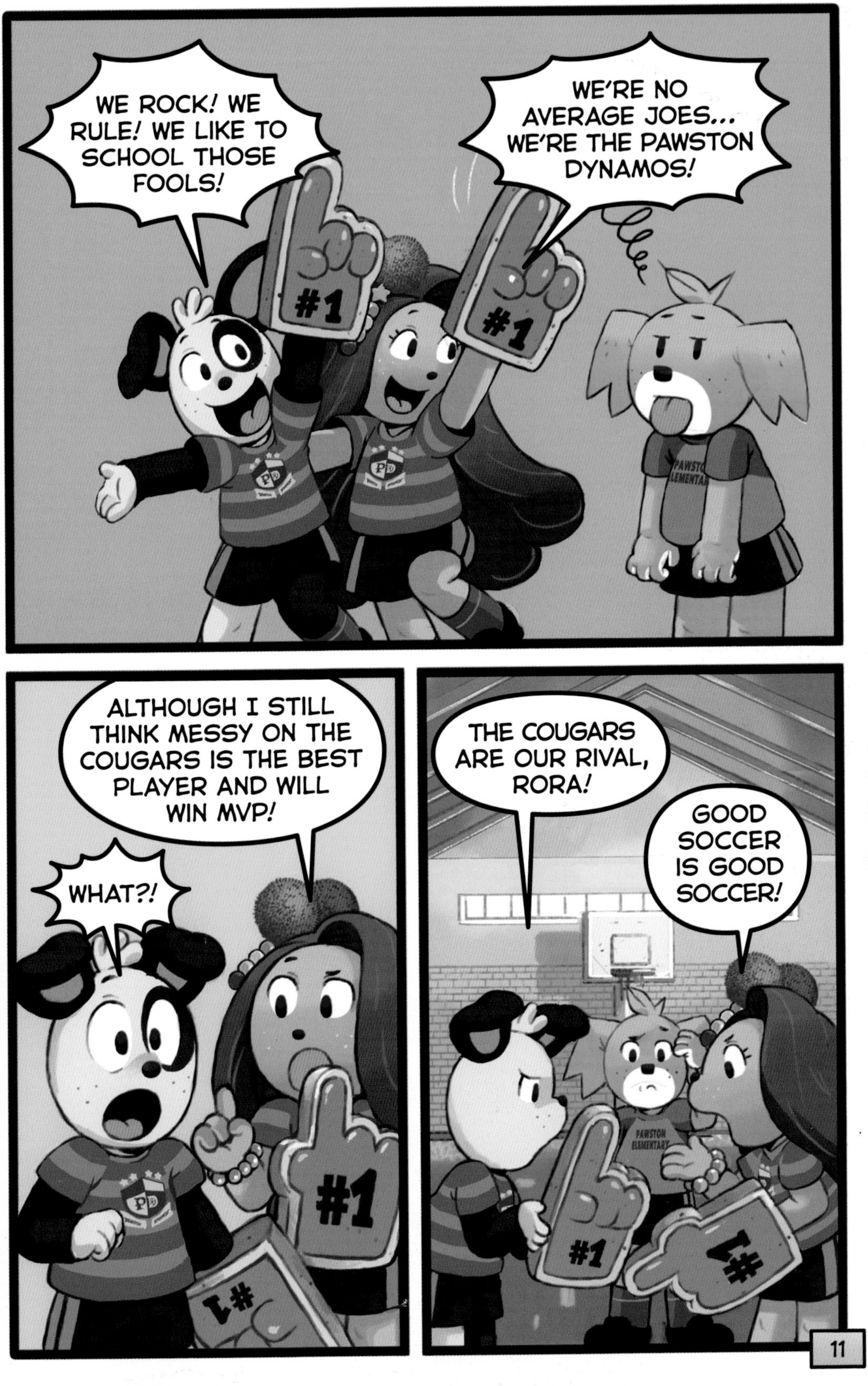
WE ROCK! WE RULE! WE LIKE TO SCHOOL THOSE FOOLS!
WE'RE NO AVERAGE JOES... WE'RE THE PAWSTON DYNAMOS!
#1
#1
PAWSTON ELEMENTARY
ALTHOUGH I STILL THINK MESSY ON THE COUGARS IS THE BEST PLAYER AND WILL WIN MVP!
WHAT?!
#1
THE COUGARS ARE OUR RIVAL, RORA!
GOOD SOCCER IS GOOD SOCCER!
PAWSTON ELEMENTARY
#1

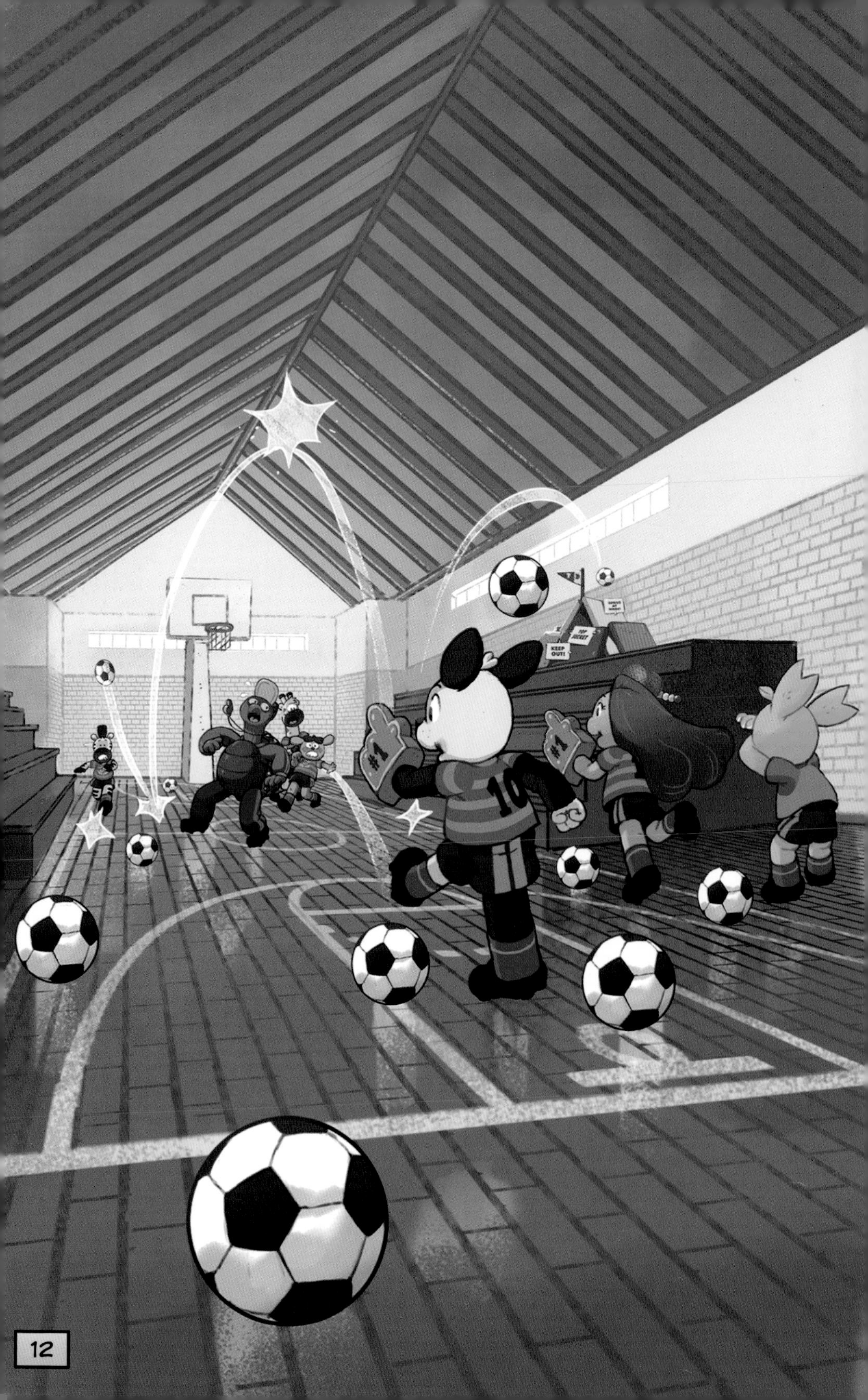
TOP SECRET
KEEP OUT!
10

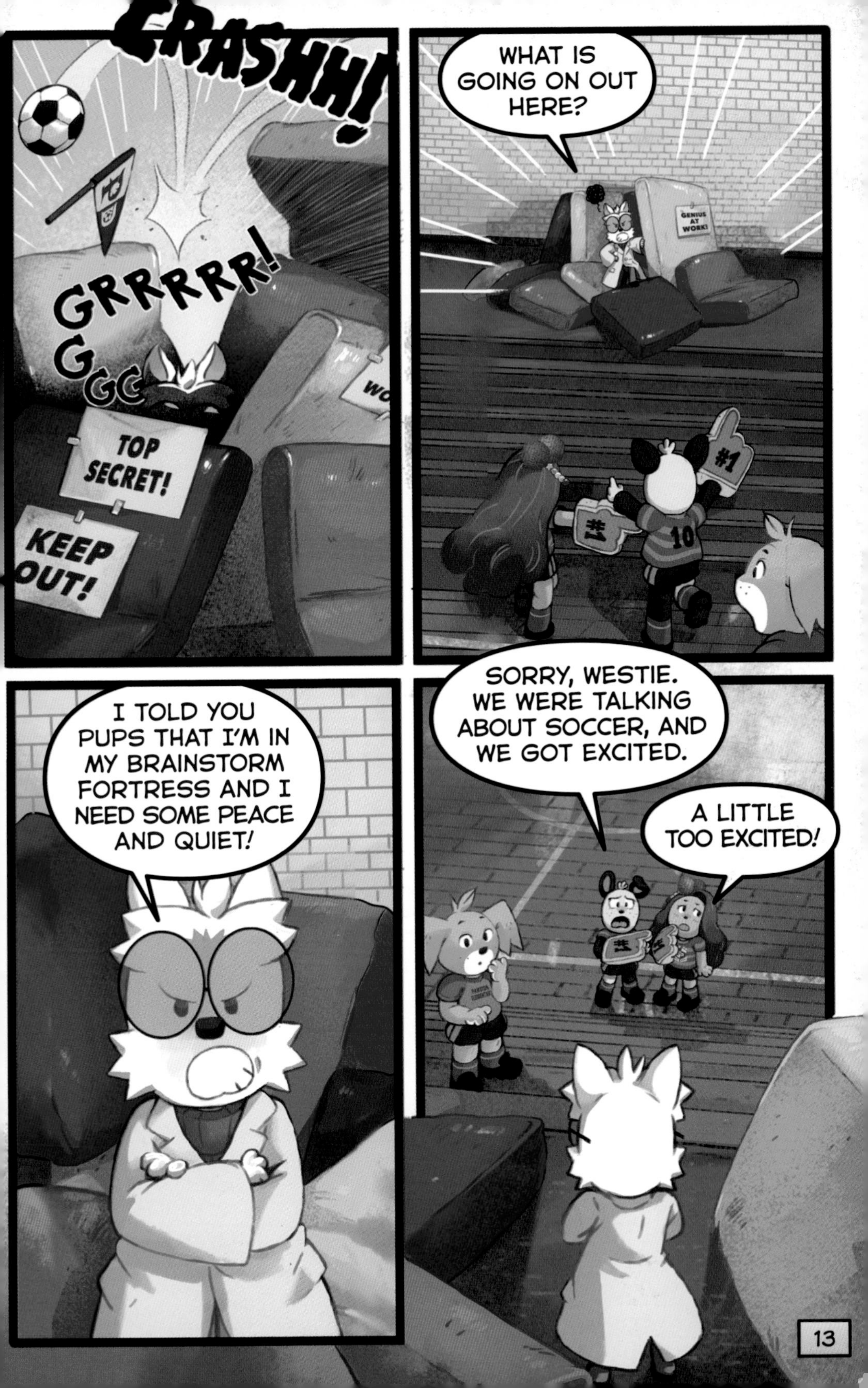
CRASHH!
GRRRRR!
GGG
TOP SECRET!
KEEP OUT!
WHAT IS GOING ON OUT HERE?
GENIUS AT WORK!
#1
10
I TOLD YOU PUPS THAT I'M IN MY BRAINSTORM FORTRESS AND I NEED SOME PEACE AND QUIET!
SORRY, WESTIE. WE WERE TALKING ABOUT SOCCER, AND WE GOT EXCITED.
A LITTLE TOO EXCITED!

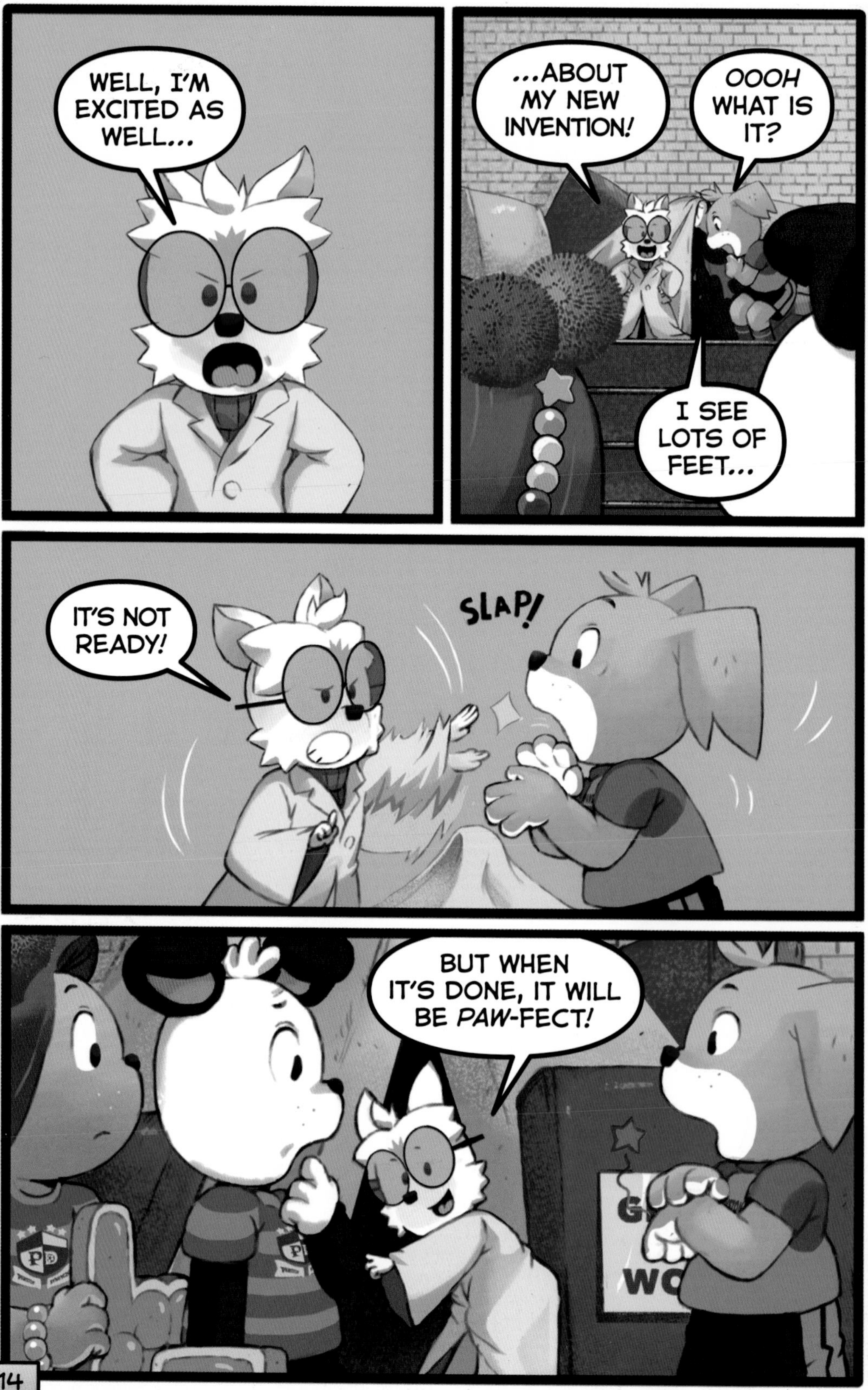
WELL, I'M EXCITED AS WELL...
...ABOUT MY NEW INVENTION!
OOOH WHAT IS IT?
I SEE LOTS OF FEET...
IT'S NOT READY!
SLAP!
BUT WHEN IT'S DONE, IT WILL BE *PAW*-FECT!

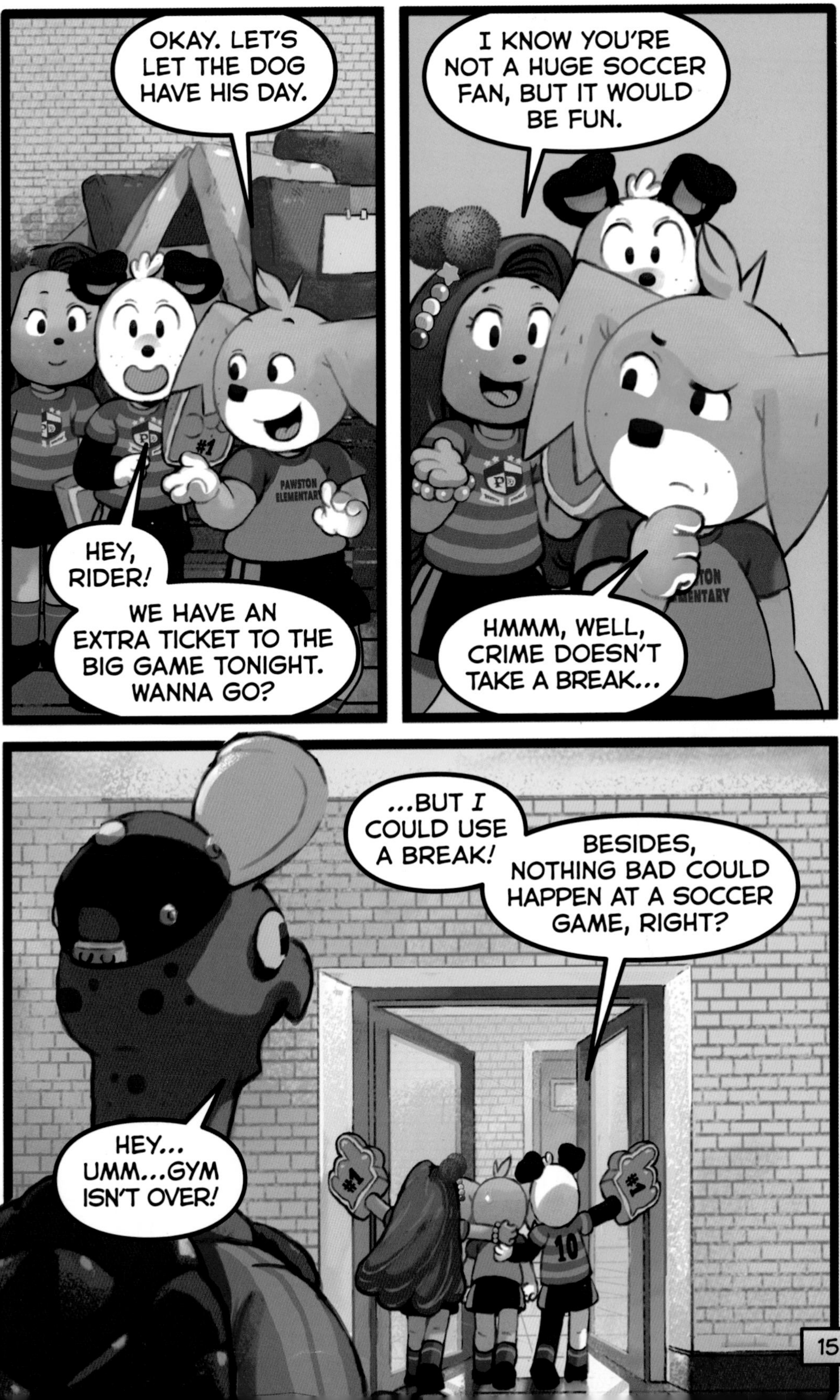
OKAY. LET'S LET THE DOG HAVE HIS DAY.
HEY, RIDER!
WE HAVE AN EXTRA TICKET TO THE BIG GAME TONIGHT. WANNA GO?
I KNOW YOU'RE NOT A HUGE SOCCER FAN, BUT IT WOULD BE FUN.
HMMM, WELL, CRIME DOESN'T TAKE A BREAK...
...BUT I COULD USE A BREAK!
BESIDES, NOTHING BAD COULD HAPPEN AT A SOCCER GAME, RIGHT?
HEY... UMM...GYM ISN'T OVER!

CHAPTER 2

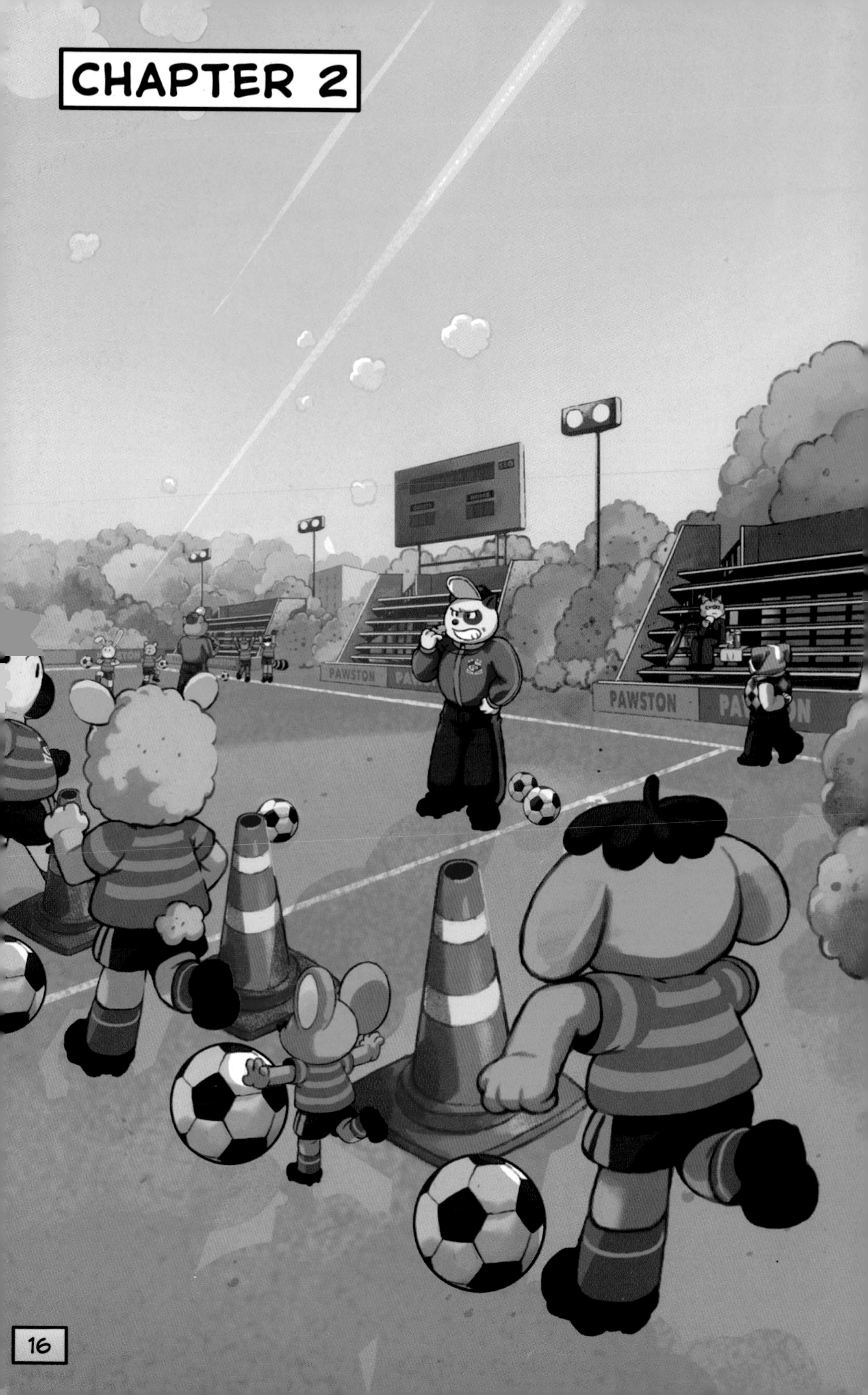
PAWSTON
PAWSTON

HELLO, MATTY MEOW.

ENJOYING SOCCER PRACTICE?

IT'S NICE TO SEE OUR NEWEST STUDENT SHOWING SOME SCHOOL SPIRIT.

EXCITED FOR THE BIG GAME LATER?

YESSSSSS, WELL...I DO LOVE SSSSSSSOCCER.

BUT I'M ROOTING FOR PAWSSSSSTON'S RIVAL, THE CATSKILLLSSSSS COUGARSSSS.

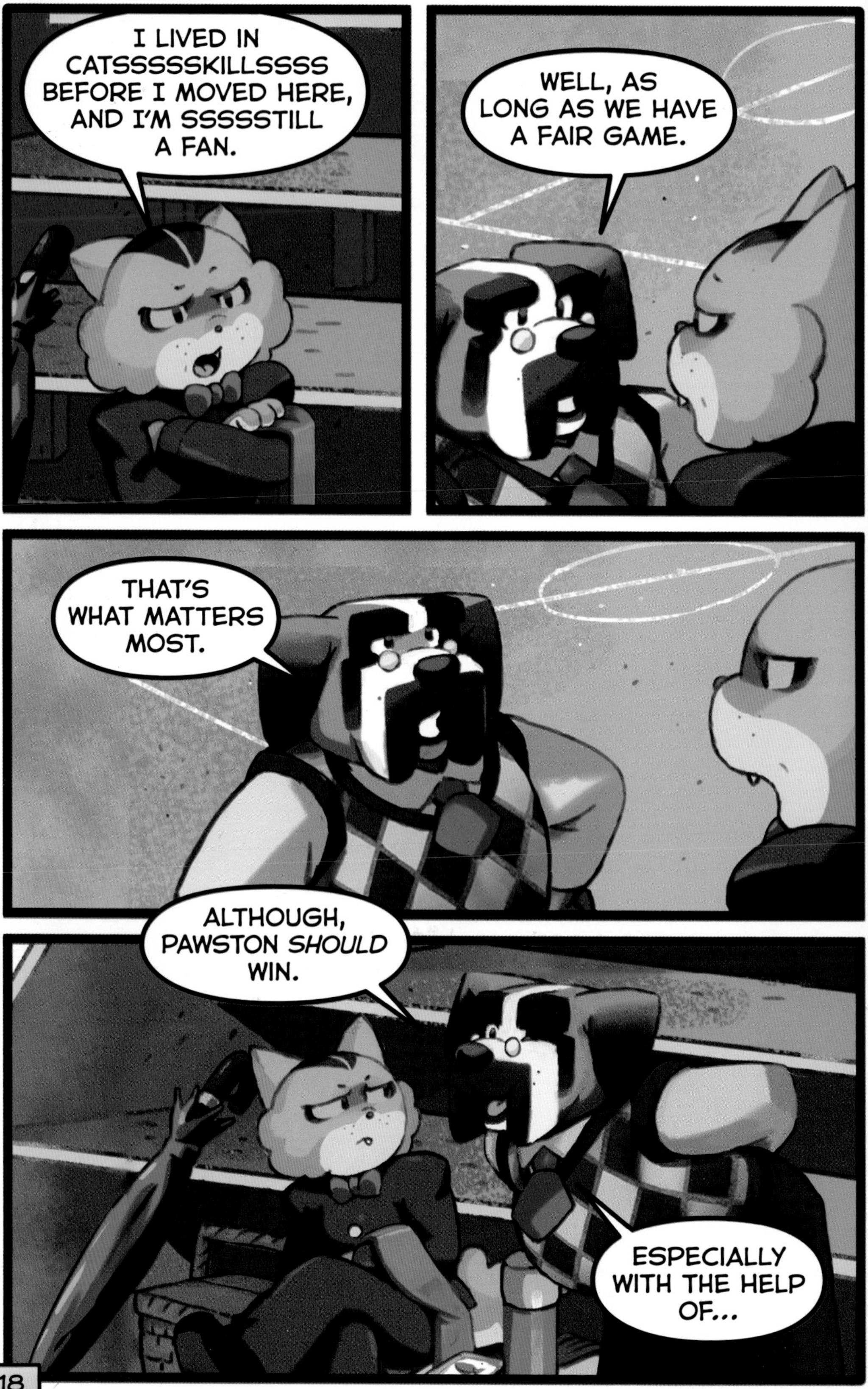
I LIVED IN CATSSSSSKILLSSSS BEFORE I MOVED HERE, AND I'M SSSSSTILL A FAN.
WELL, AS LONG AS WE HAVE A FAIR GAME.
THAT'S WHAT MATTERS MOST.
ALTHOUGH, PAWSTON *SHOULD* WIN.
ESPECIALLY WITH THE HELP OF...

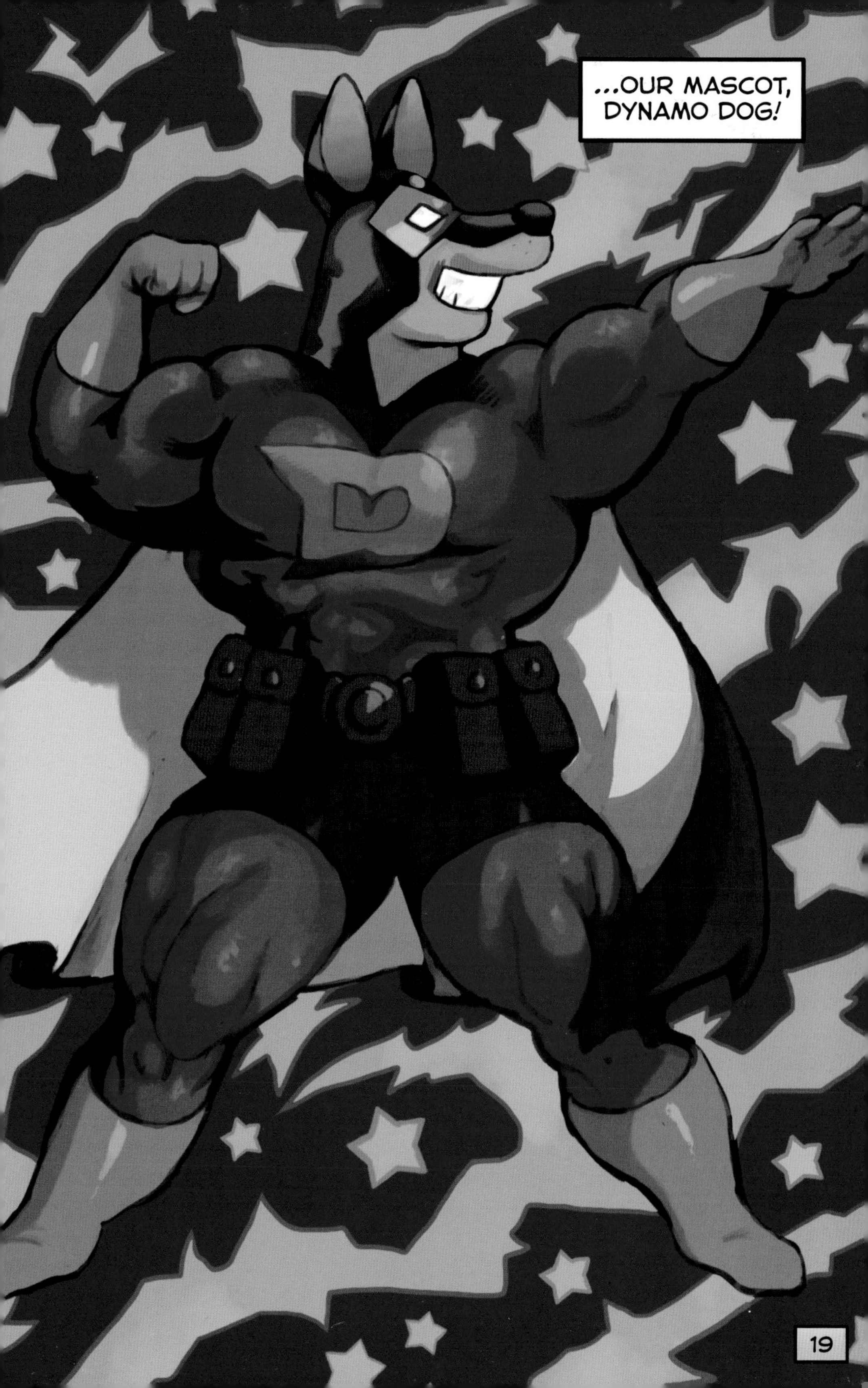
...OUR MASCOT, DYNAMO DOG!

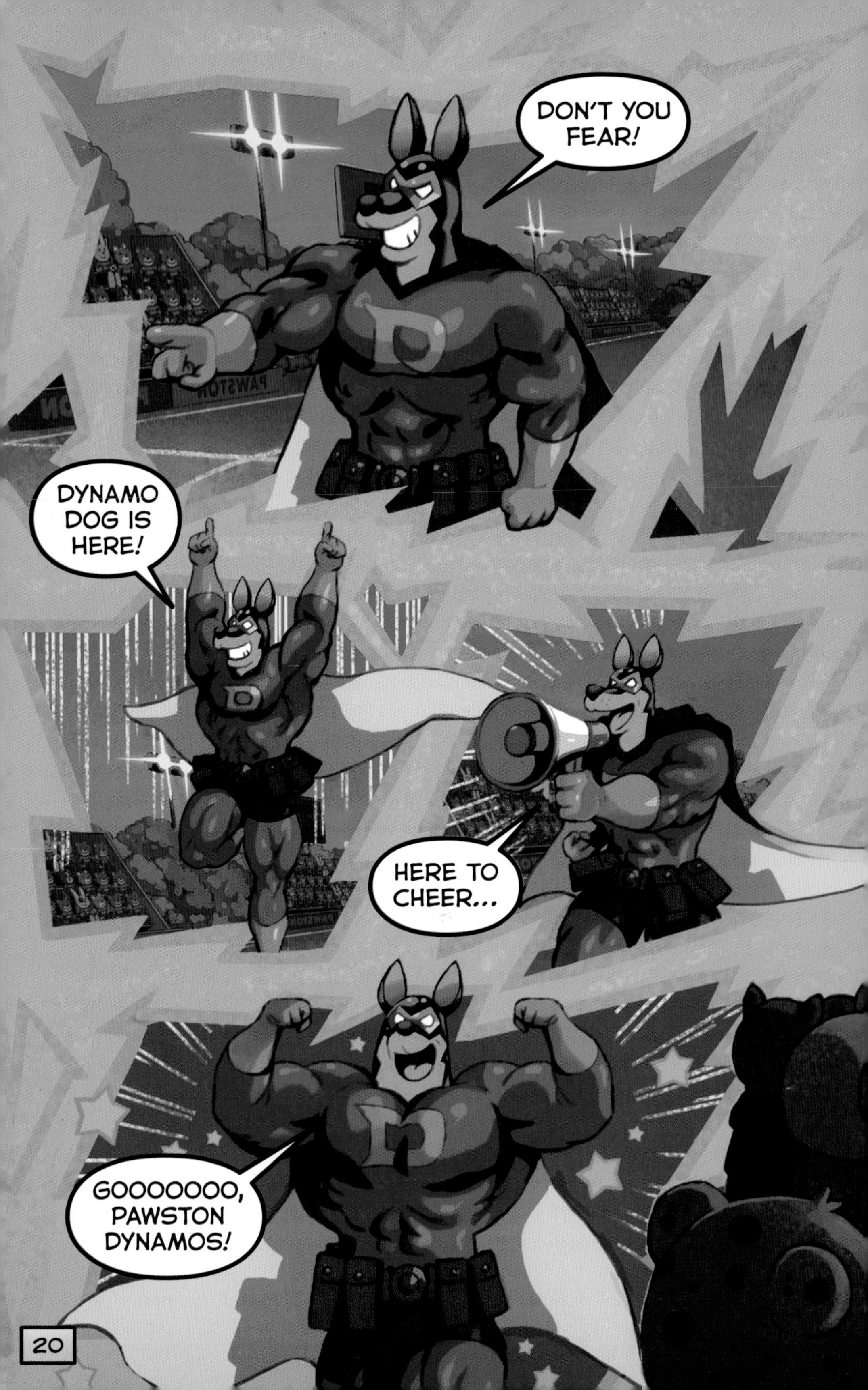
DON'T YOU FEAR!
DYNAMO DOG IS HERE!
HERE TO CHEER...
GOOOOOOO, PAWSTON DYNAMOS!
PAWSTON

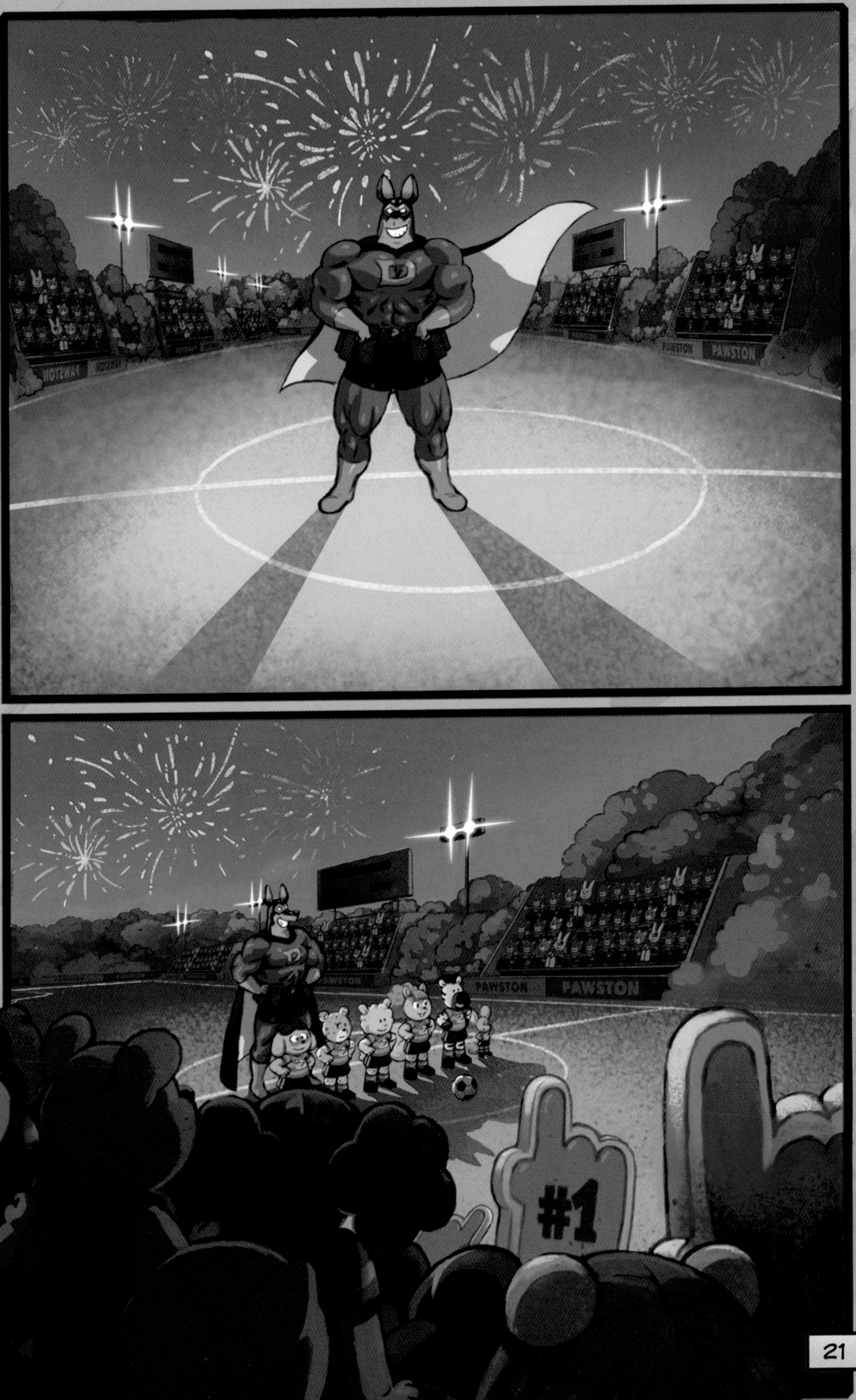
PAWSTON
PAWSTON
PAWSTON
PAWSTON
#1

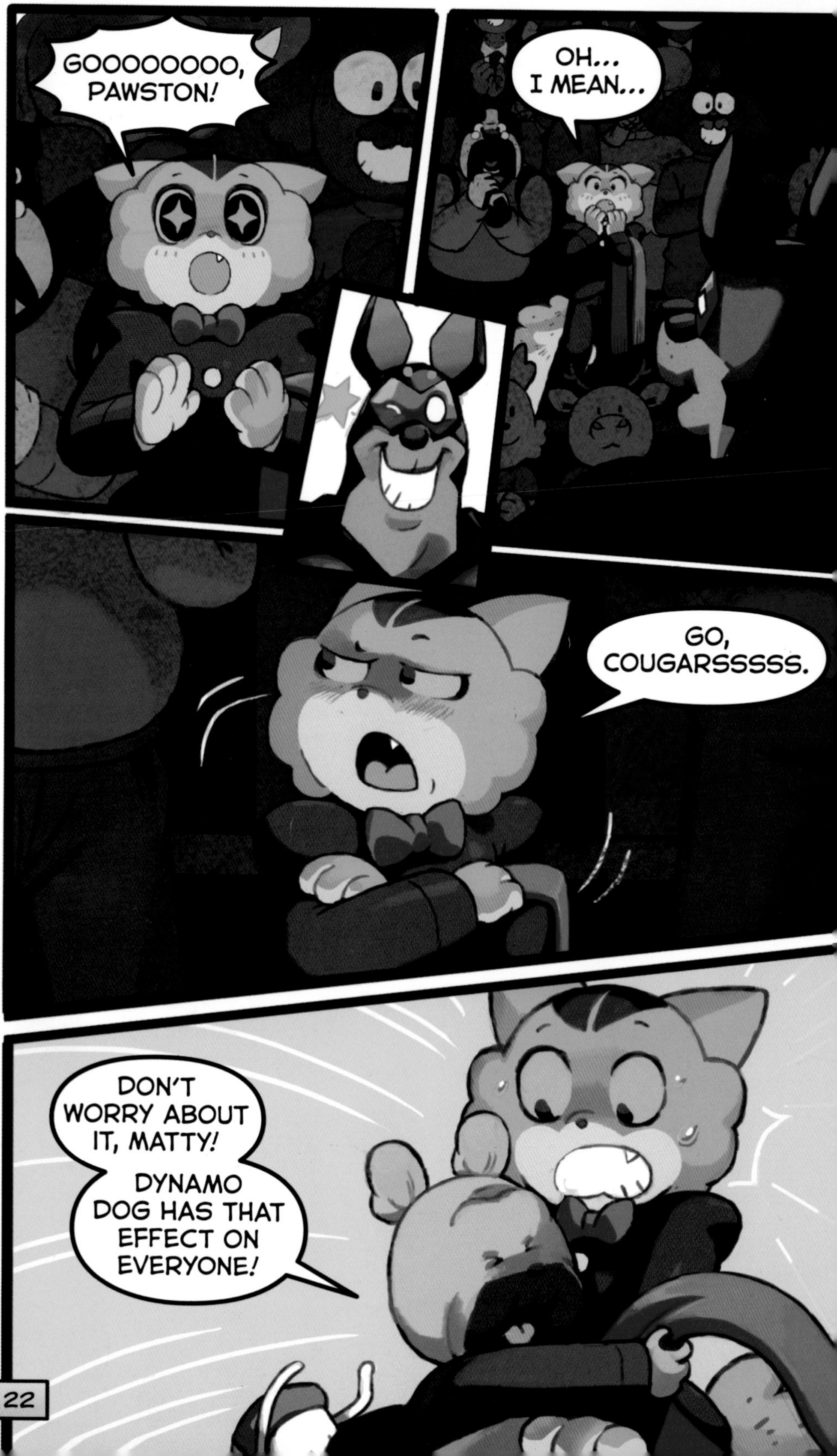
GOOOOOOOO, PAWSTON!
OH... I MEAN...
GO, COUGARSSSSS.
DON'T WORRY ABOUT IT, MATTY!
DYNAMO DOG HAS THAT EFFECT ON EVERYONE!

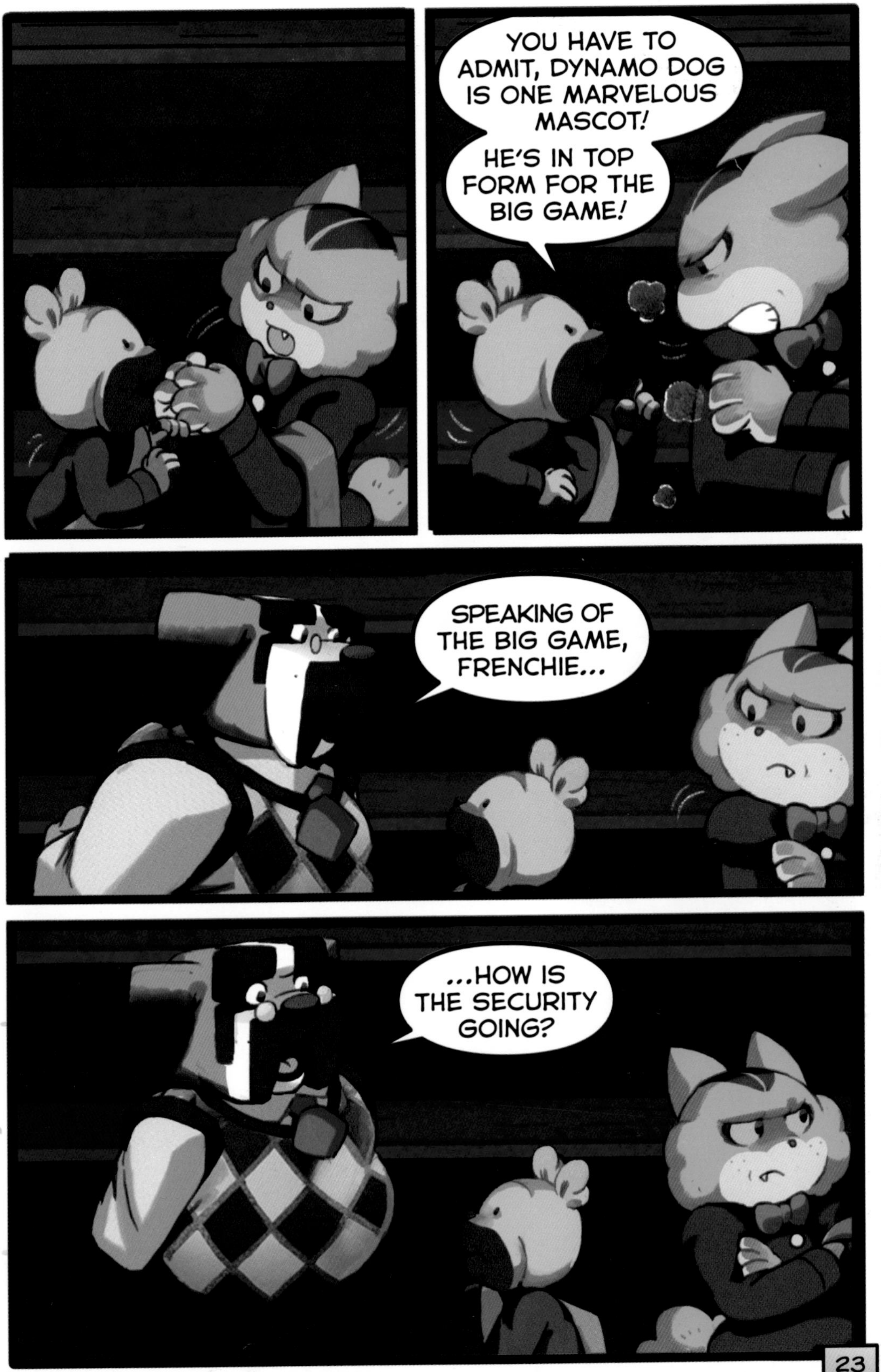
YOU HAVE TO ADMIT, DYNAMO DOG IS ONE MARVELOUS MASCOT!
HE'S IN TOP FORM FOR THE BIG GAME!
SPEAKING OF THE BIG GAME, FRENCHIE...
...HOW IS THE SECURITY GOING?

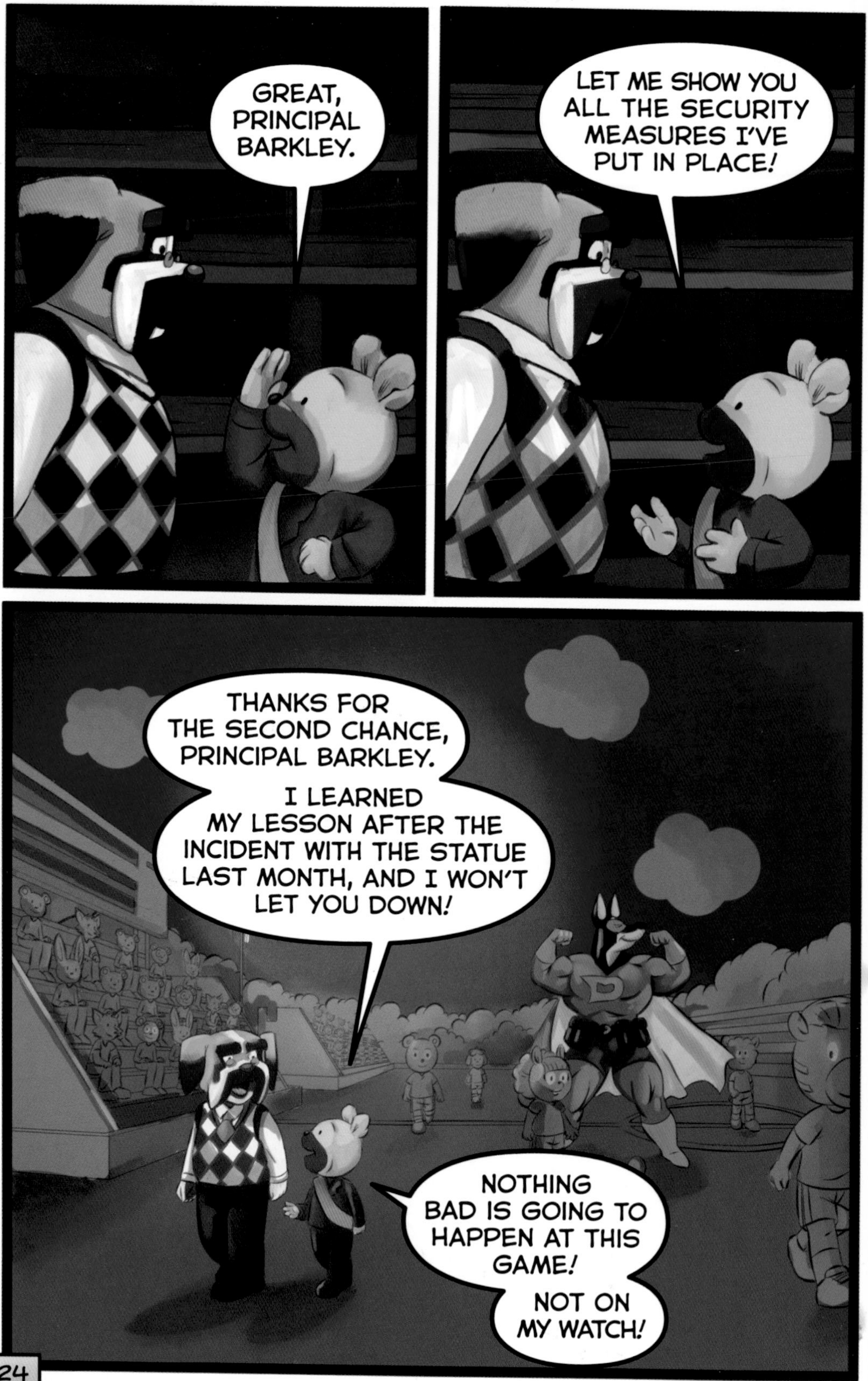
GREAT, PRINCIPAL BARKLEY.
LET ME SHOW YOU ALL THE SECURITY MEASURES I'VE PUT IN PLACE!
THANKS FOR THE SECOND CHANCE, PRINCIPAL BARKLEY.
I LEARNED MY LESSON AFTER THE INCIDENT WITH THE STATUE LAST MONTH, AND I WON'T LET YOU DOWN!
NOTHING BAD IS GOING TO HAPPEN AT THIS GAME!
NOT ON MY WATCH!

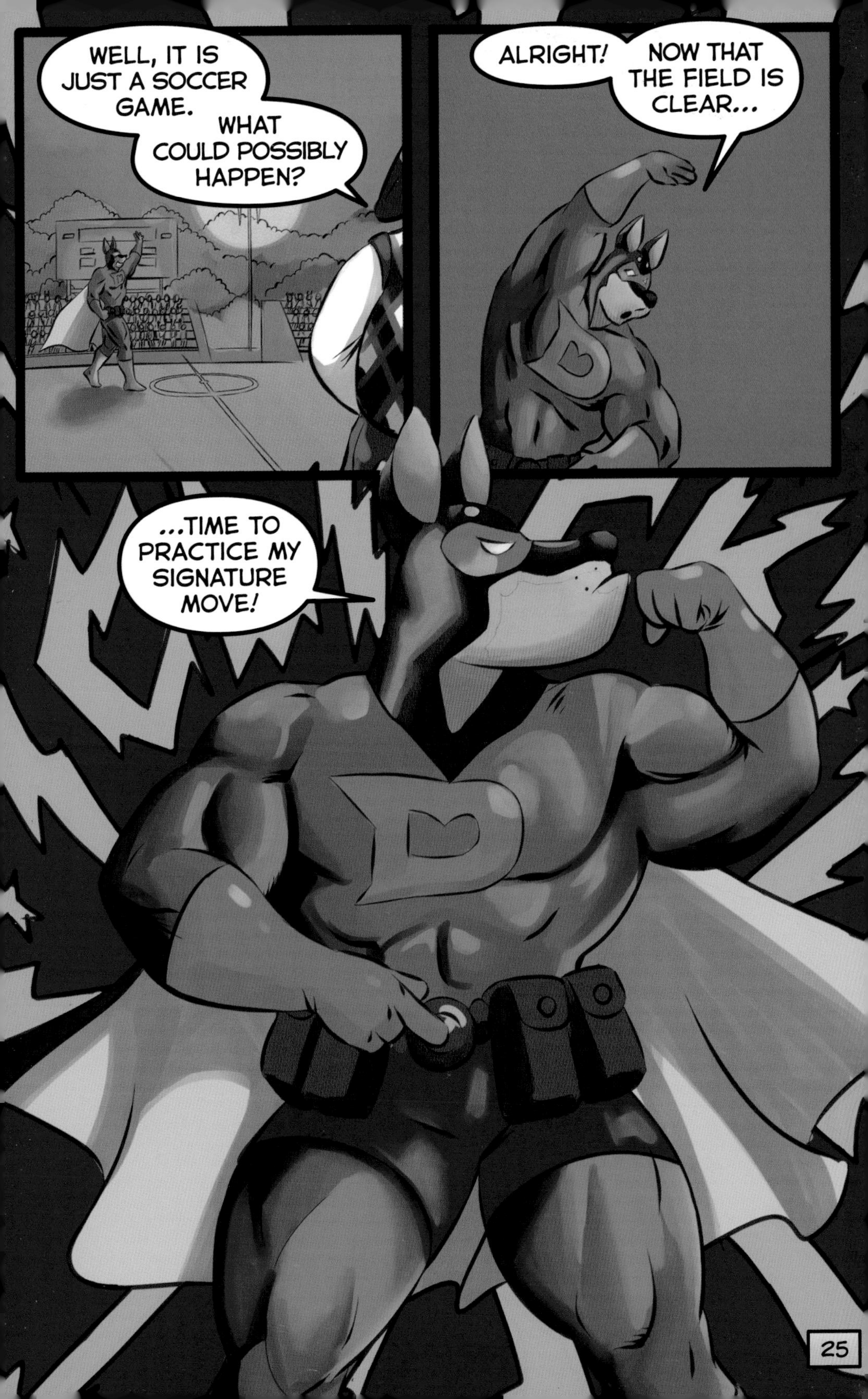
WELL, IT IS JUST A SOCCER GAME.
WHAT COULD POSSIBLY HAPPEN?
ALRIGHT!
NOW THAT THE FIELD IS CLEAR...
...TIME TO PRACTICE MY SIGNATURE MOVE!

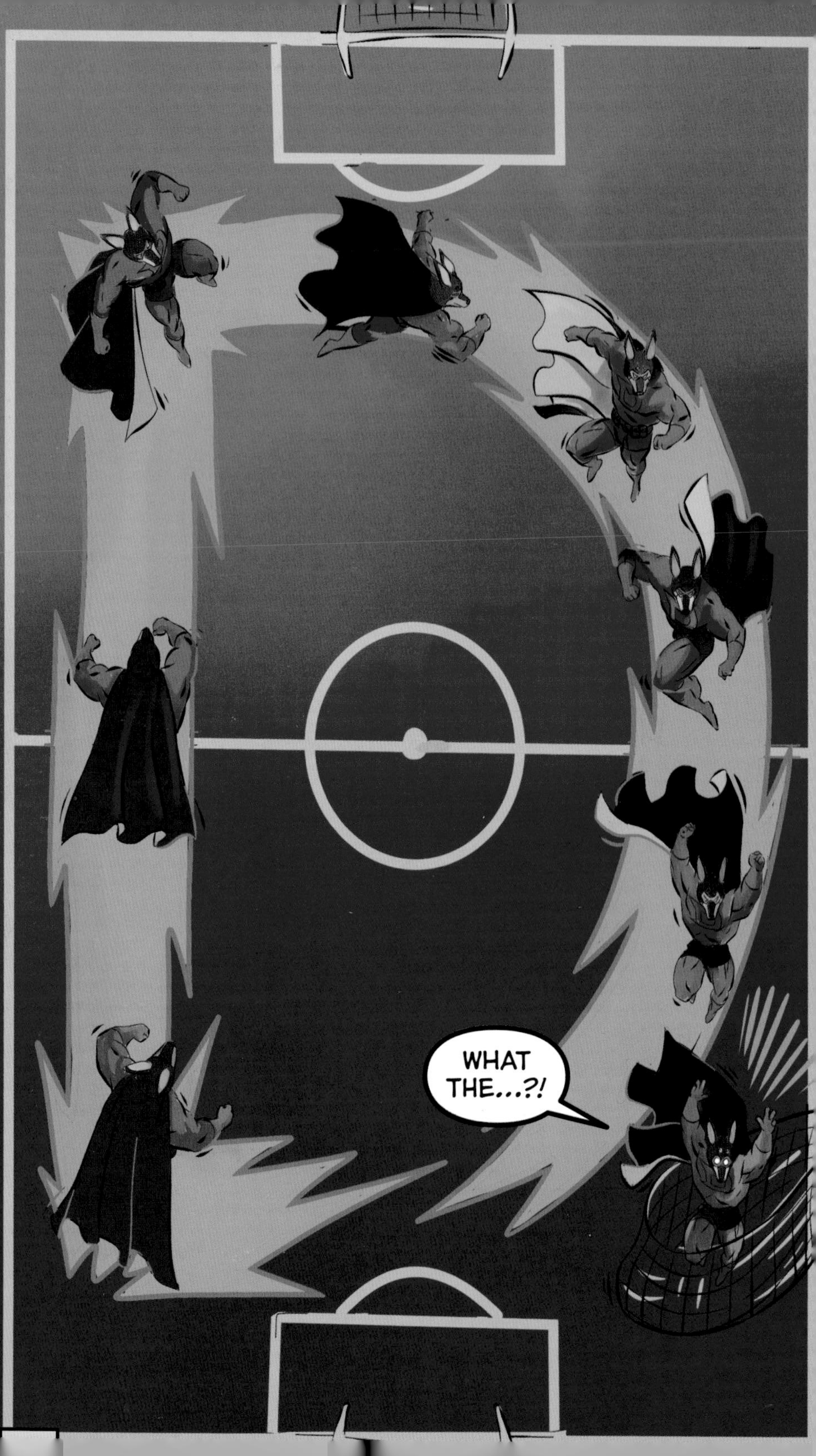
WHAT THE...?!

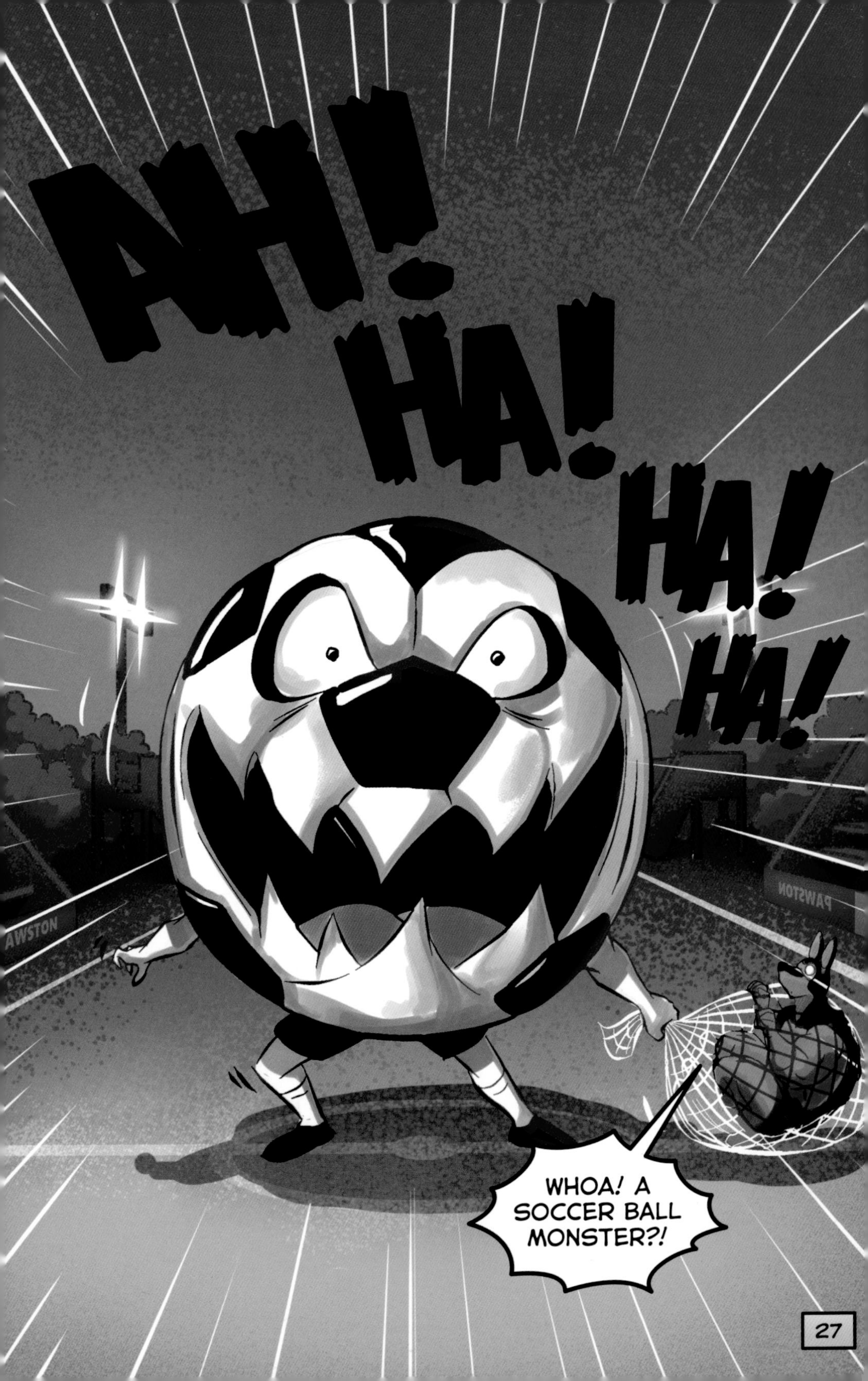
AH! HA! HA! HA!
PAWSTON
PAWSTON
WHOA! A SOCCER BALL MONSTER?!

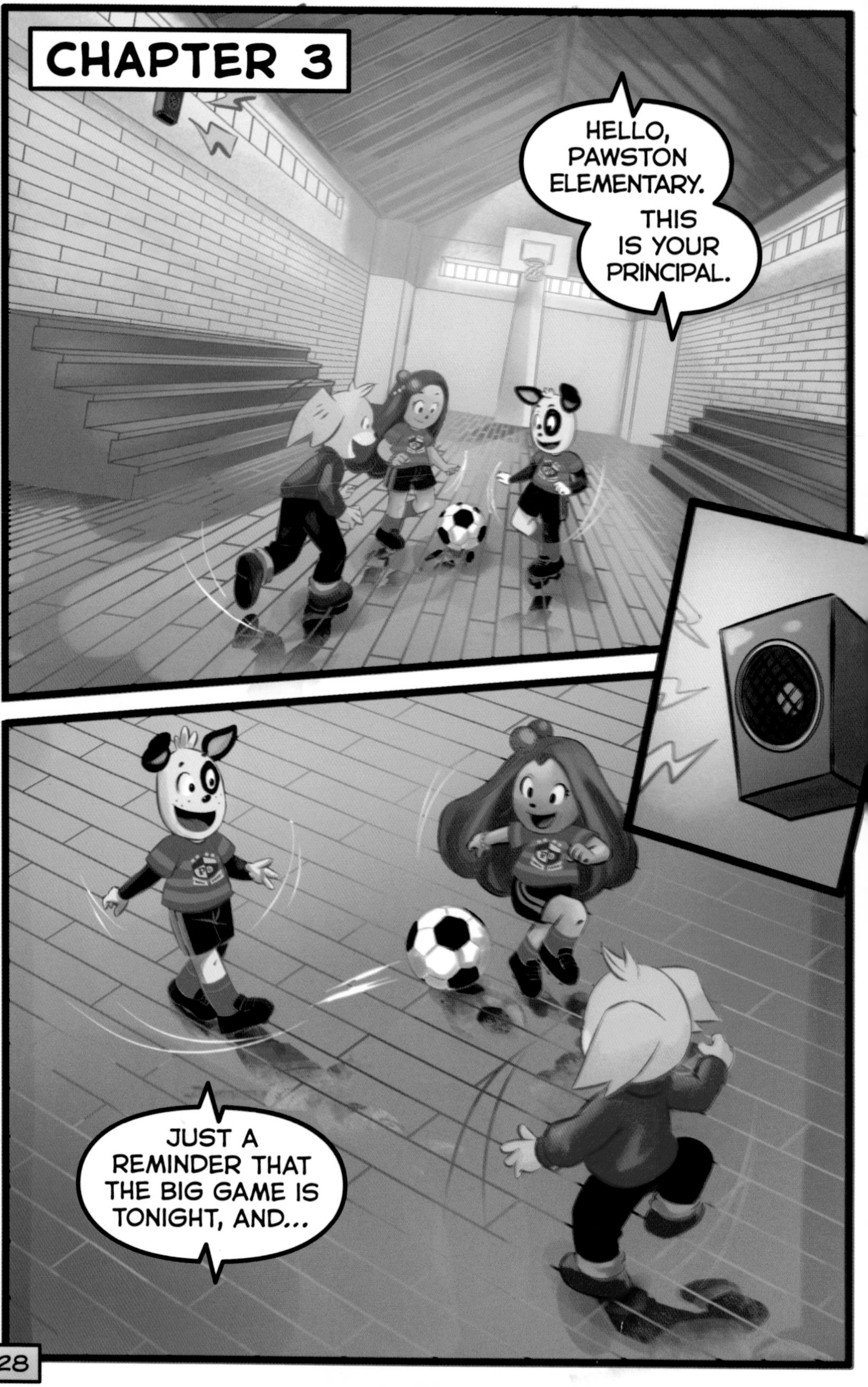
CHAPTER 3
HELLO, PAWSTON ELEMENTARY. THIS IS YOUR PRINCIPAL.
JUST A REMINDER THAT THE BIG GAME IS TONIGHT, AND...

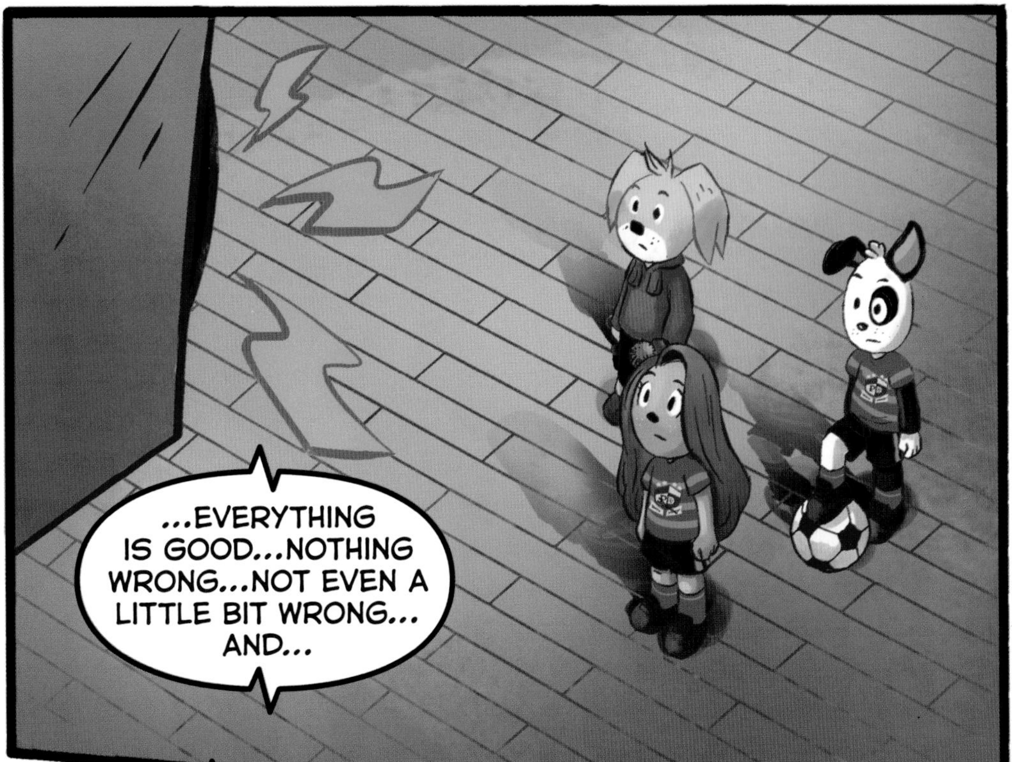
...EVERYTHING IS GOOD...NOTHING WRONG...NOT EVEN A LITTLE BIT WRONG... AND...

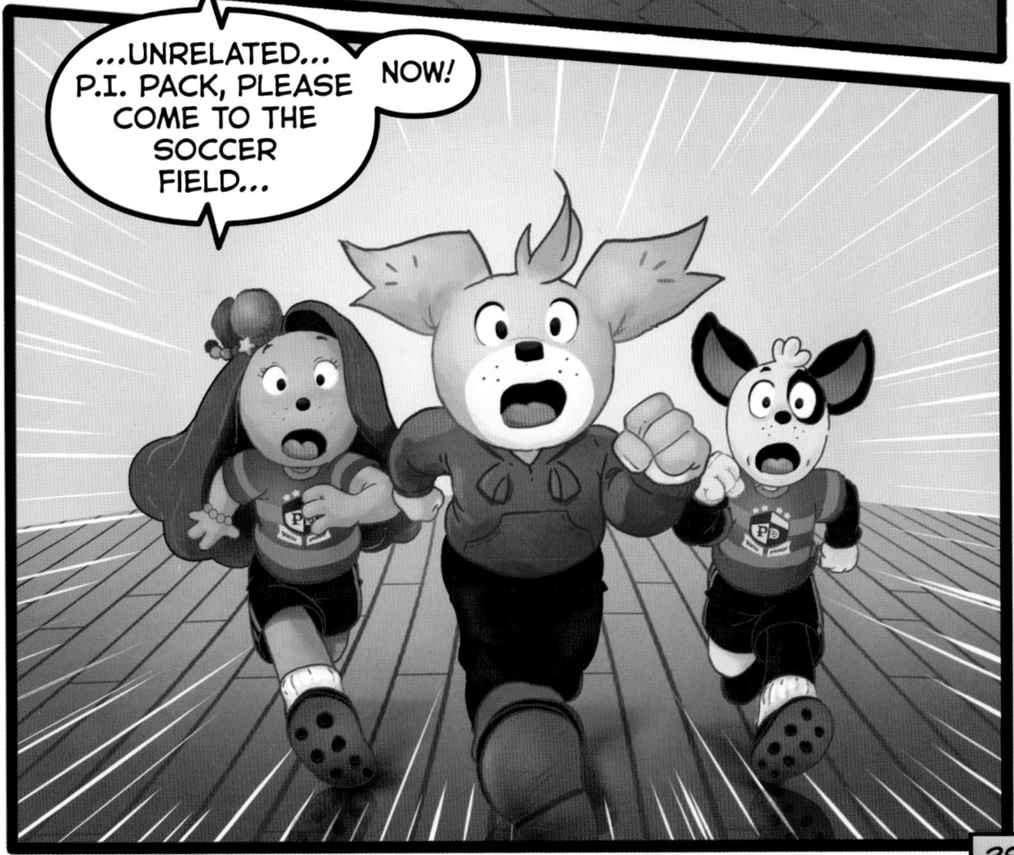
...UNRELATED... P.I. PACK, PLEASE COME TO THE SOCCER FIELD...
NOW!

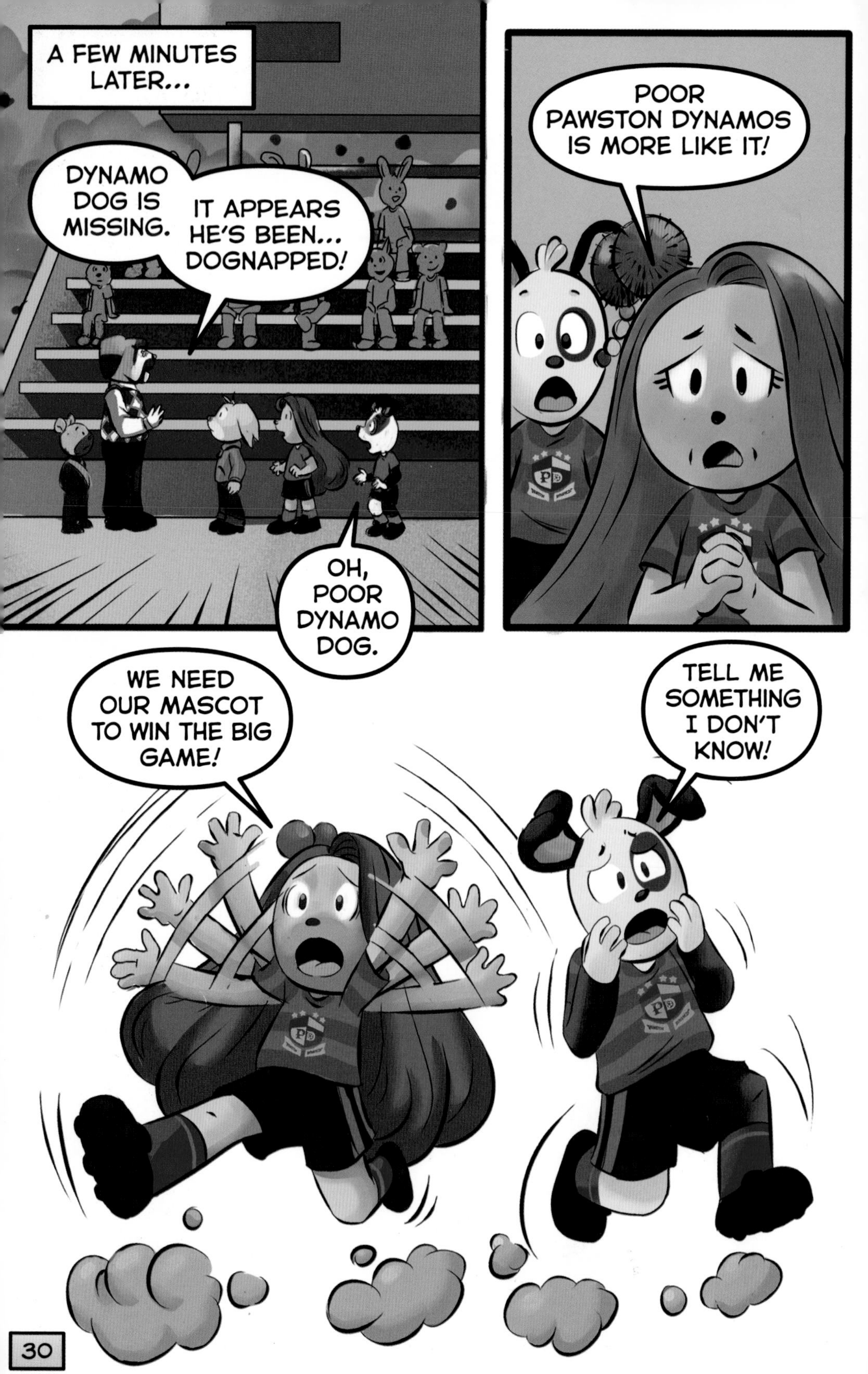
A FEW MINUTES LATER...
DYNAMO DOG IS MISSING.
IT APPEARS HE'S BEEN... DOGNAPPED!
OH, POOR DYNAMO DOG.
POOR PAWSTON DYNAMOS IS MORE LIKE IT!
WE NEED OUR MASCOT TO WIN THE BIG GAME!
TELL ME SOMETHING I DON'T KNOW!

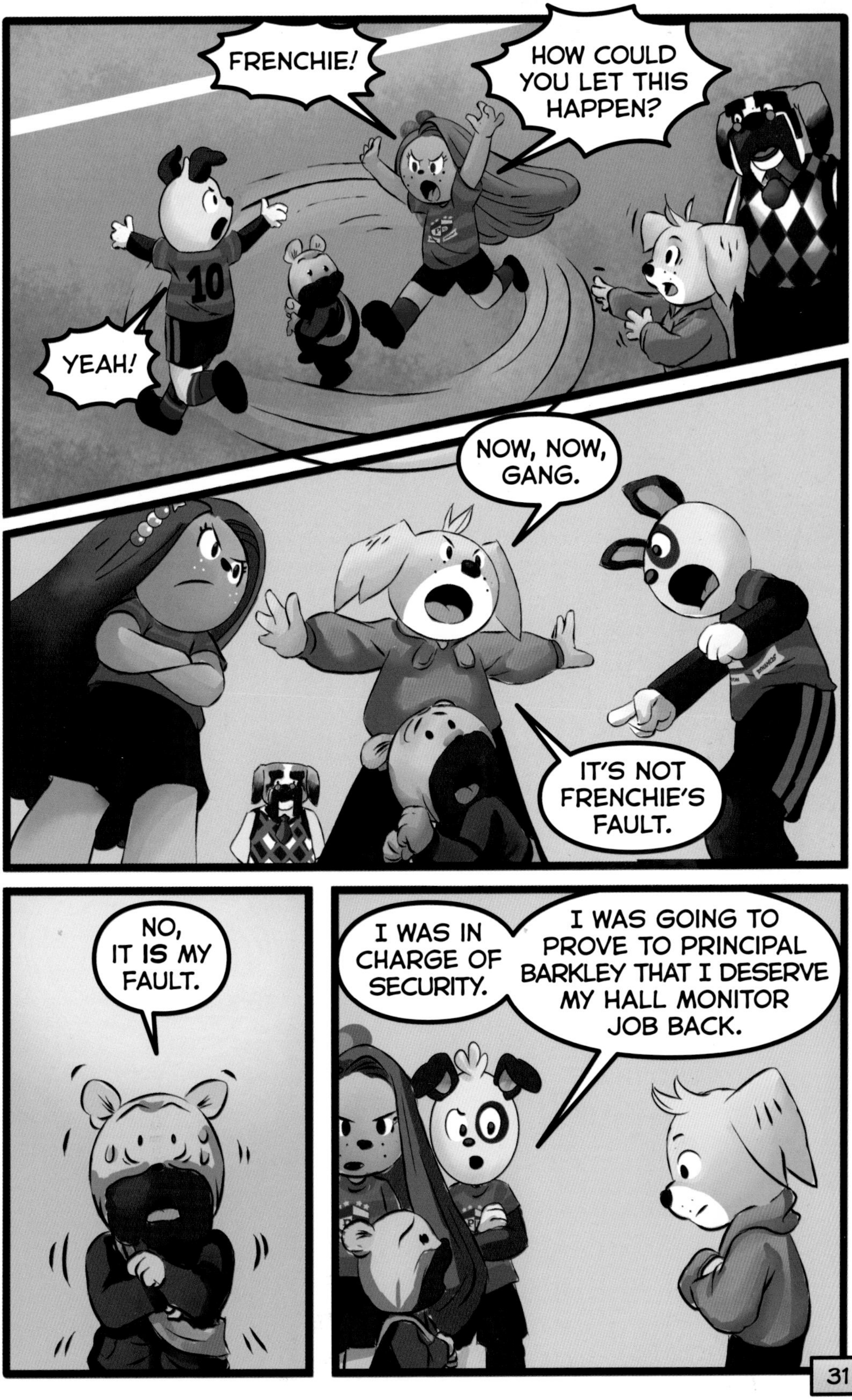
FRENCHIE!
HOW COULD YOU LET THIS HAPPEN?
YEAH!
NOW, NOW, GANG.
IT'S NOT FRENCHIE'S FAULT.
NO, IT IS MY FAULT.
I WAS IN CHARGE OF SECURITY.
I WAS GOING TO PROVE TO PRINCIPAL BARKLEY THAT I DESERVE MY HALL MONITOR JOB BACK.

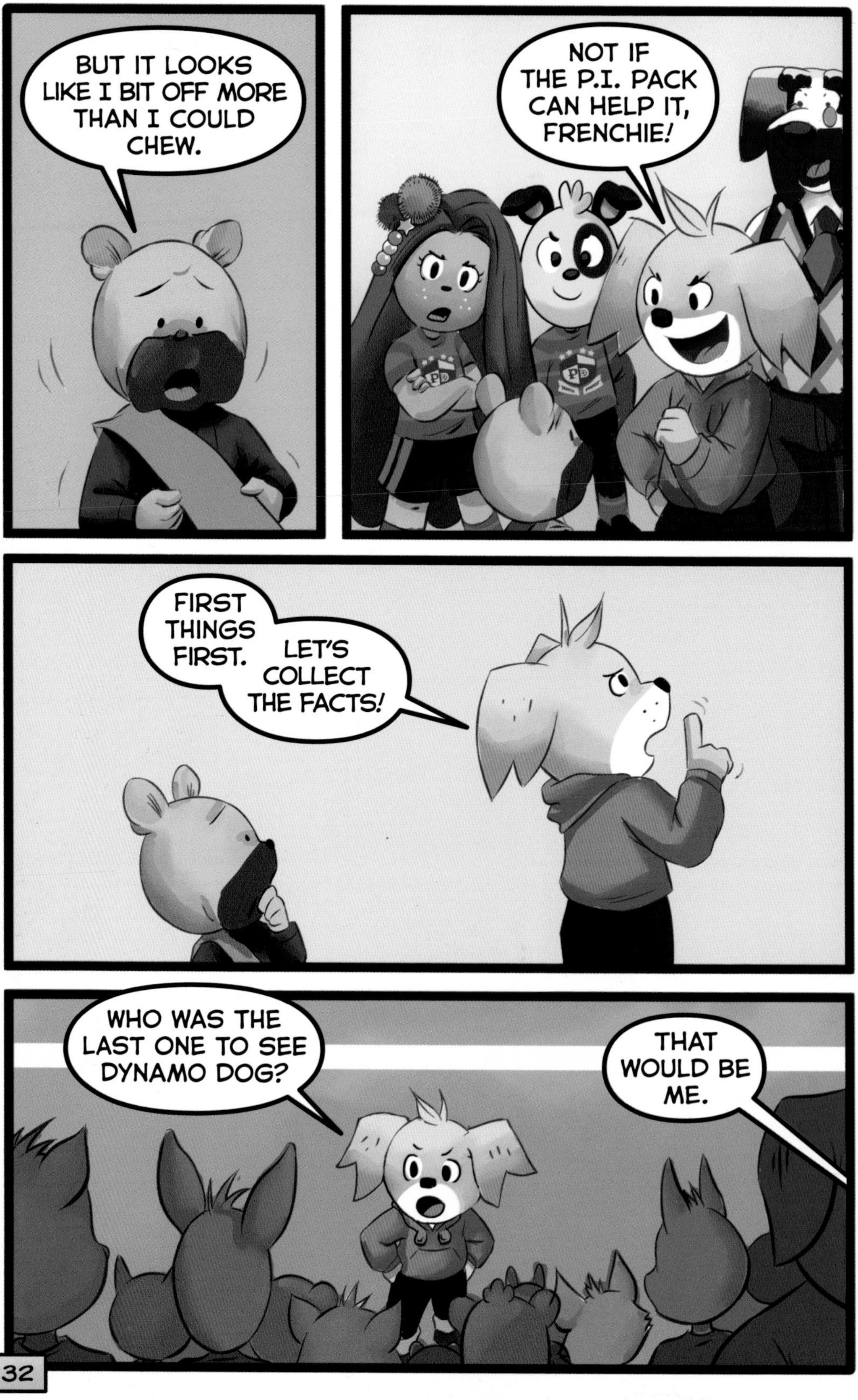
BUT IT LOOKS LIKE I BIT OFF MORE THAN I COULD CHEW.
NOT IF THE P.I. PACK CAN HELP IT, FRENCHIE!
FIRST THINGS FIRST.
LET'S COLLECT THE FACTS!
WHO WAS THE LAST ONE TO SEE DYNAMO DOG?
THAT WOULD BE ME.

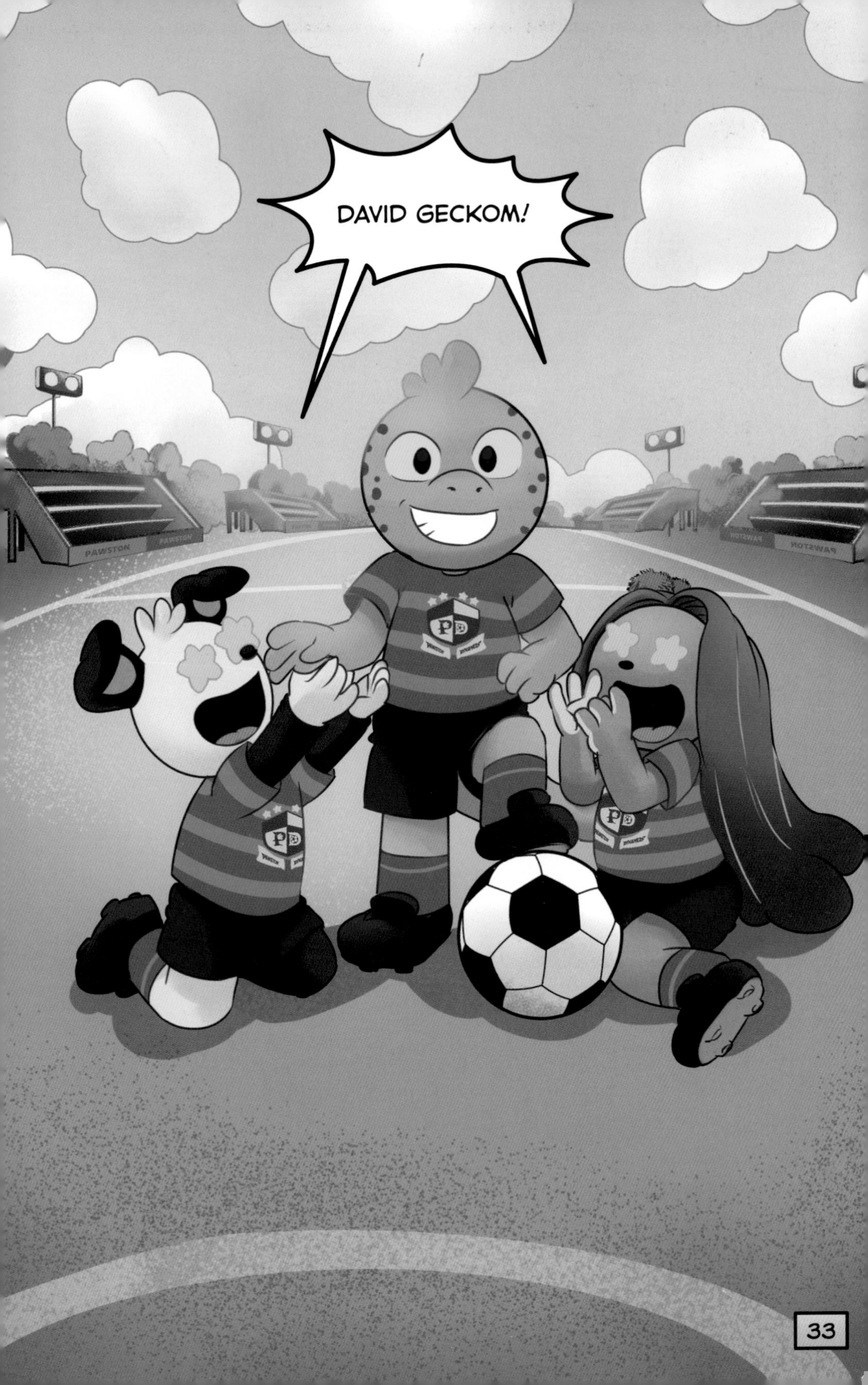
DAVID GECKOM!

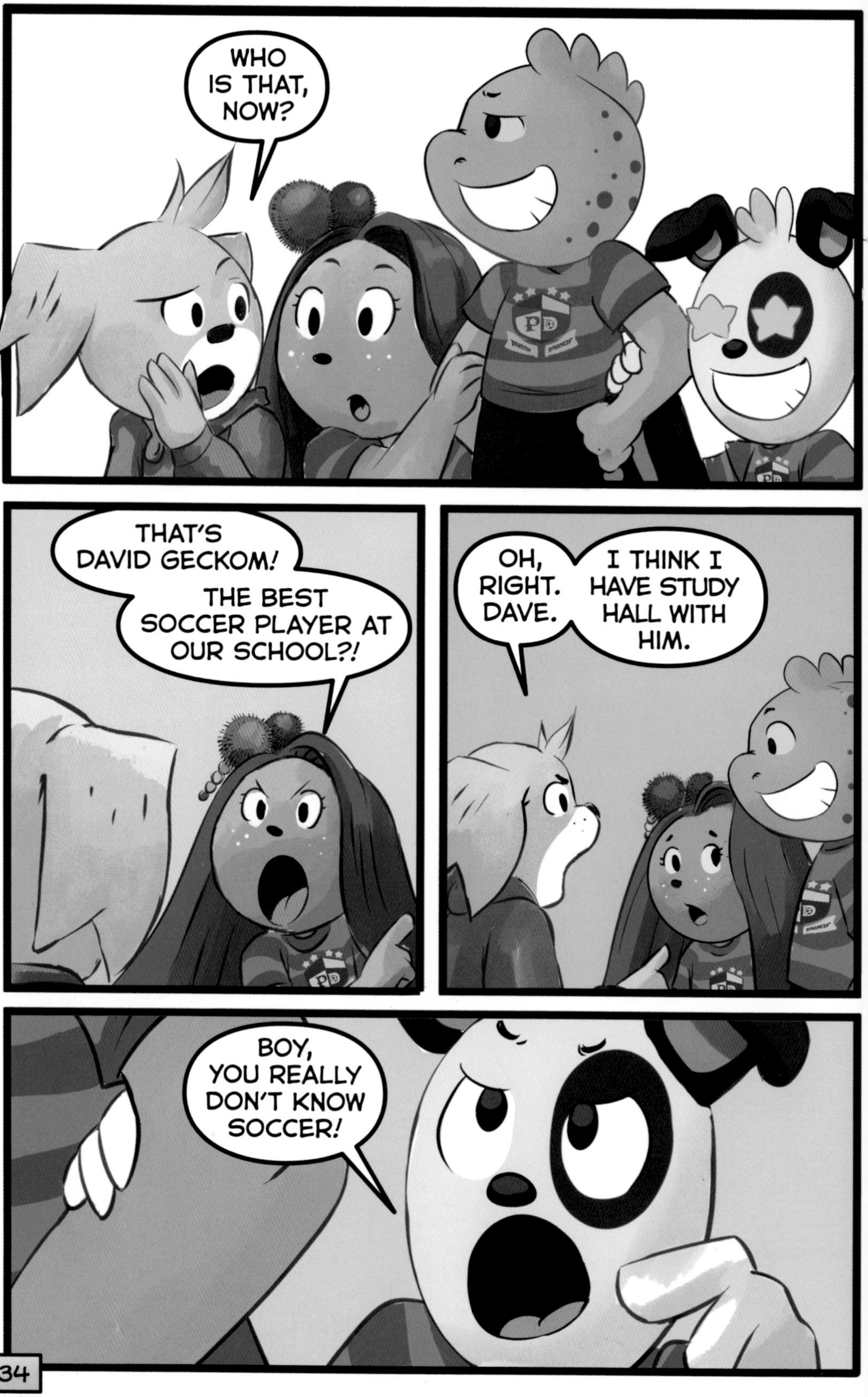
WHO IS THAT, NOW?
THAT'S DAVID GECKOM!
THE BEST SOCCER PLAYER AT OUR SCHOOL?!
OH, RIGHT. DAVE.
I THINK I HAVE STUDY HALL WITH HIM.
BOY, YOU REALLY DON'T KNOW SOCCER!

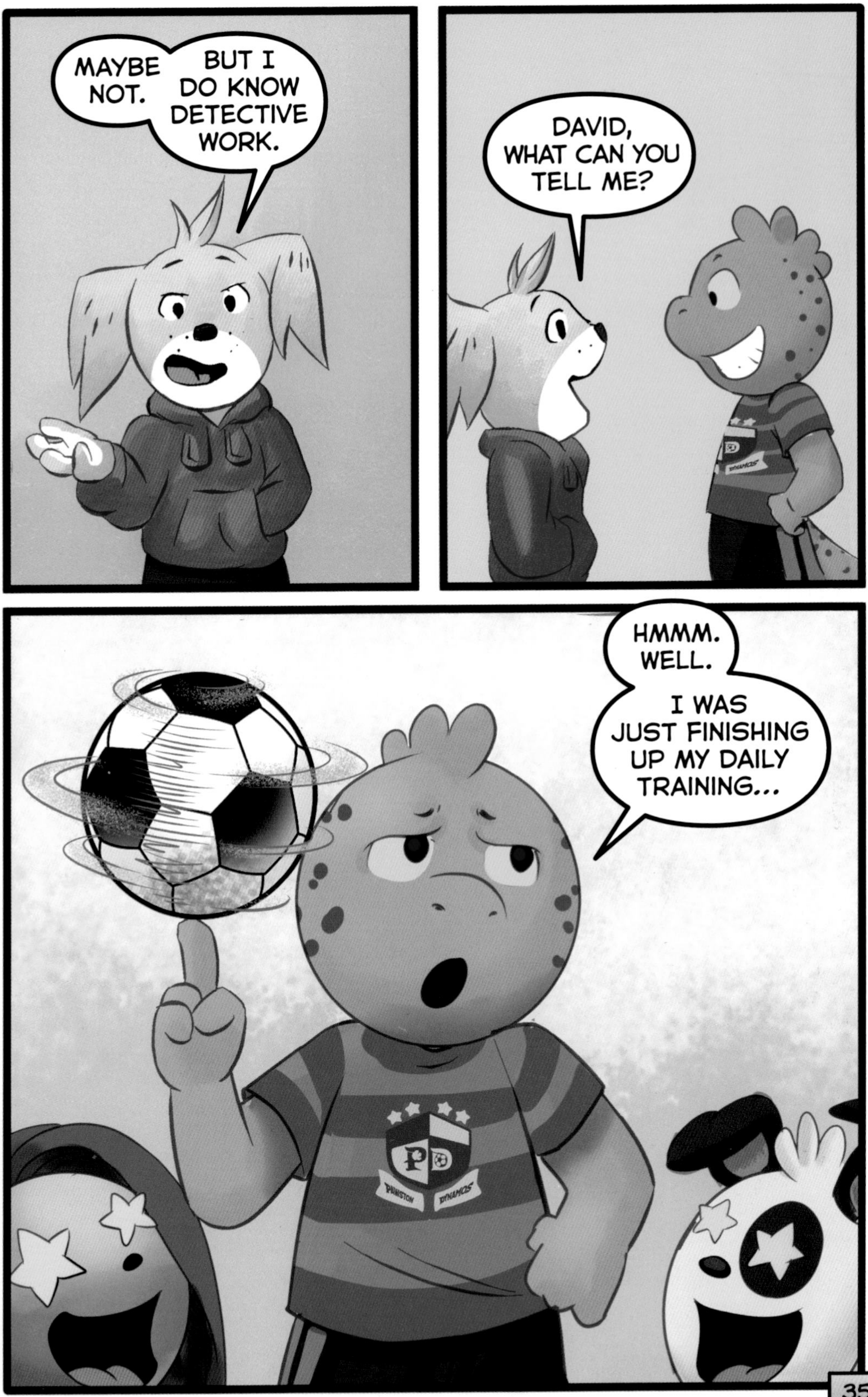
MAYBE NOT.
BUT I DO KNOW DETECTIVE WORK.
DAVID, WHAT CAN YOU TELL ME?
HMMM. WELL.
I WAS JUST FINISHING UP MY DAILY TRAINING...

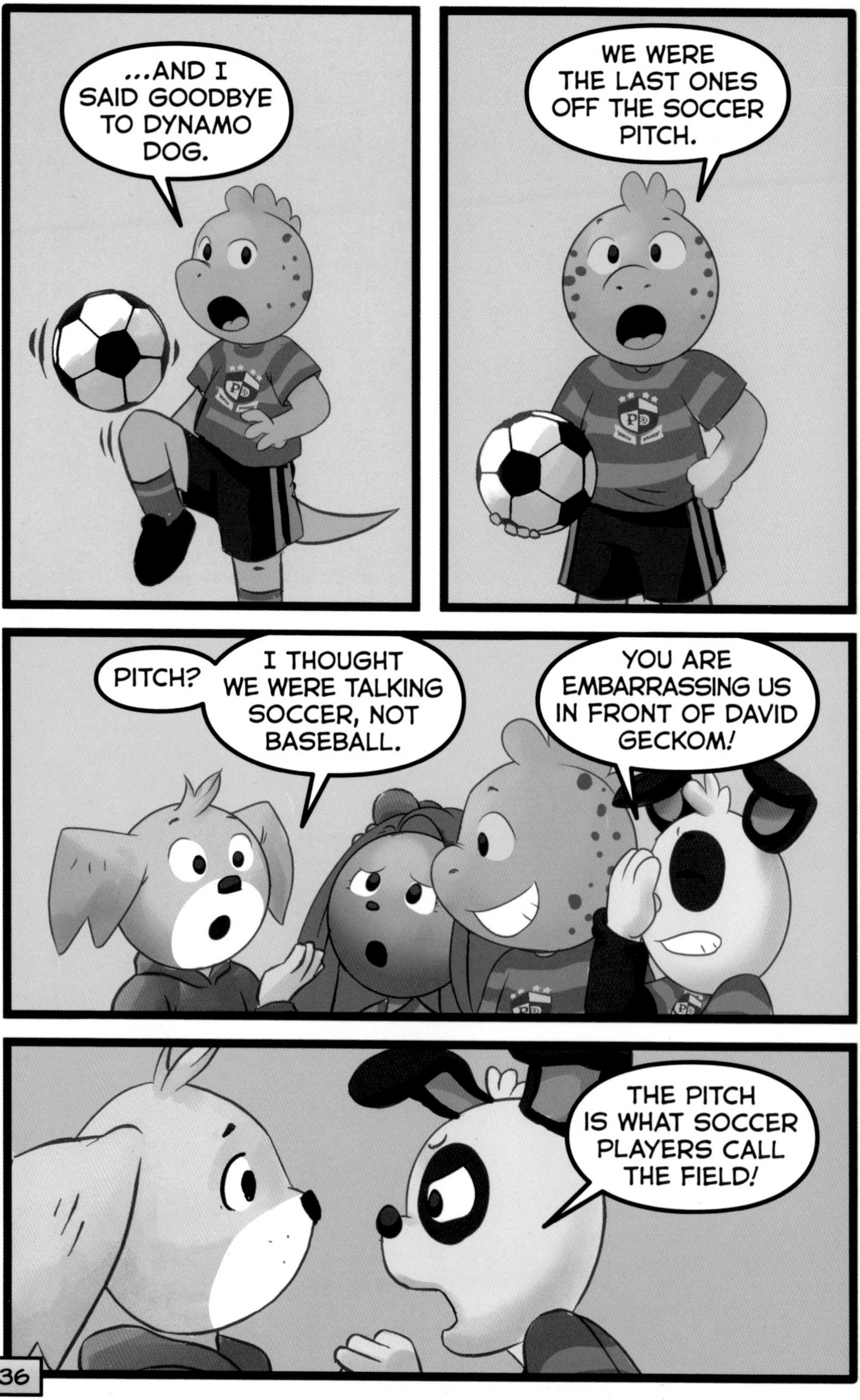
...AND I SAID GOODBYE TO DYNAMO DOG.
WE WERE THE LAST ONES OFF THE SOCCER PITCH.
PITCH?
I THOUGHT WE WERE TALKING SOCCER, NOT BASEBALL.
YOU ARE EMBARRASSING US IN FRONT OF DAVID GECKOM!
THE PITCH IS WHAT SOCCER PLAYERS CALL THE FIELD!

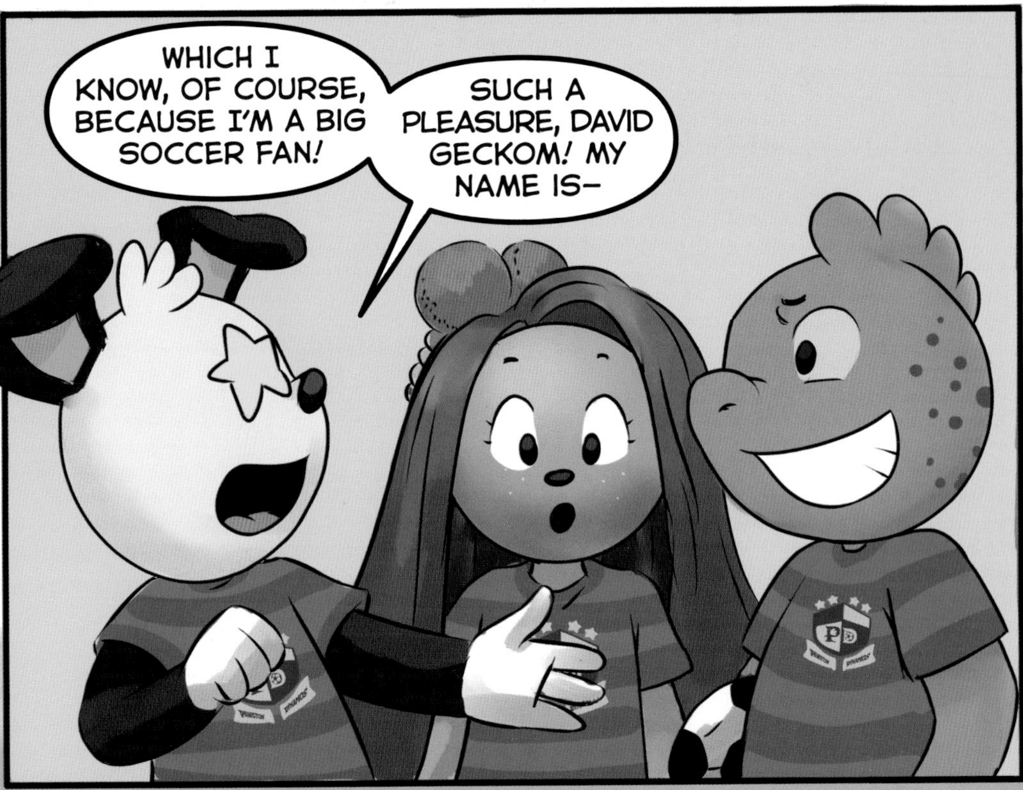
WHICH I KNOW, OF COURSE, BECAUSE I'M A BIG SOCCER FAN!
SUCH A PLEASURE, DAVID GECKOM! MY NAME IS–

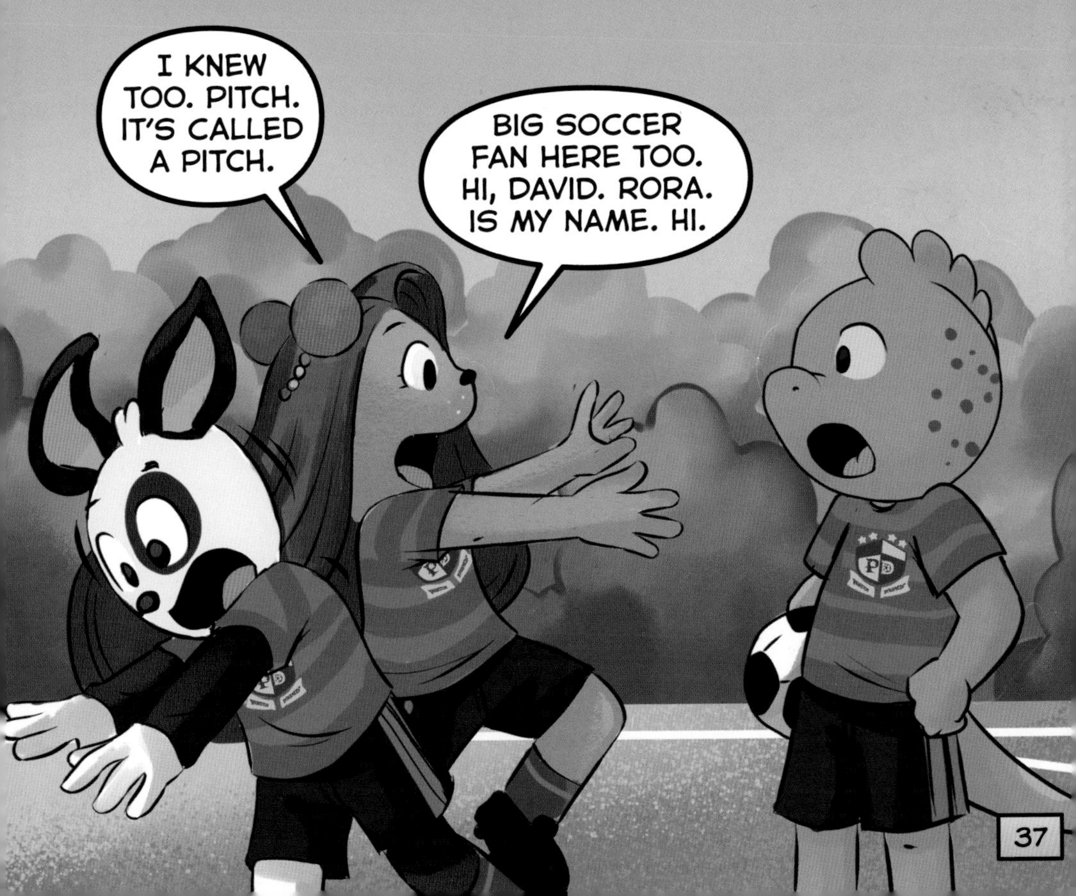
I KNEW TOO. PITCH. IT'S CALLED A PITCH.
BIG SOCCER FAN HERE TOO. HI, DAVID. RORA. IS MY NAME. HI.

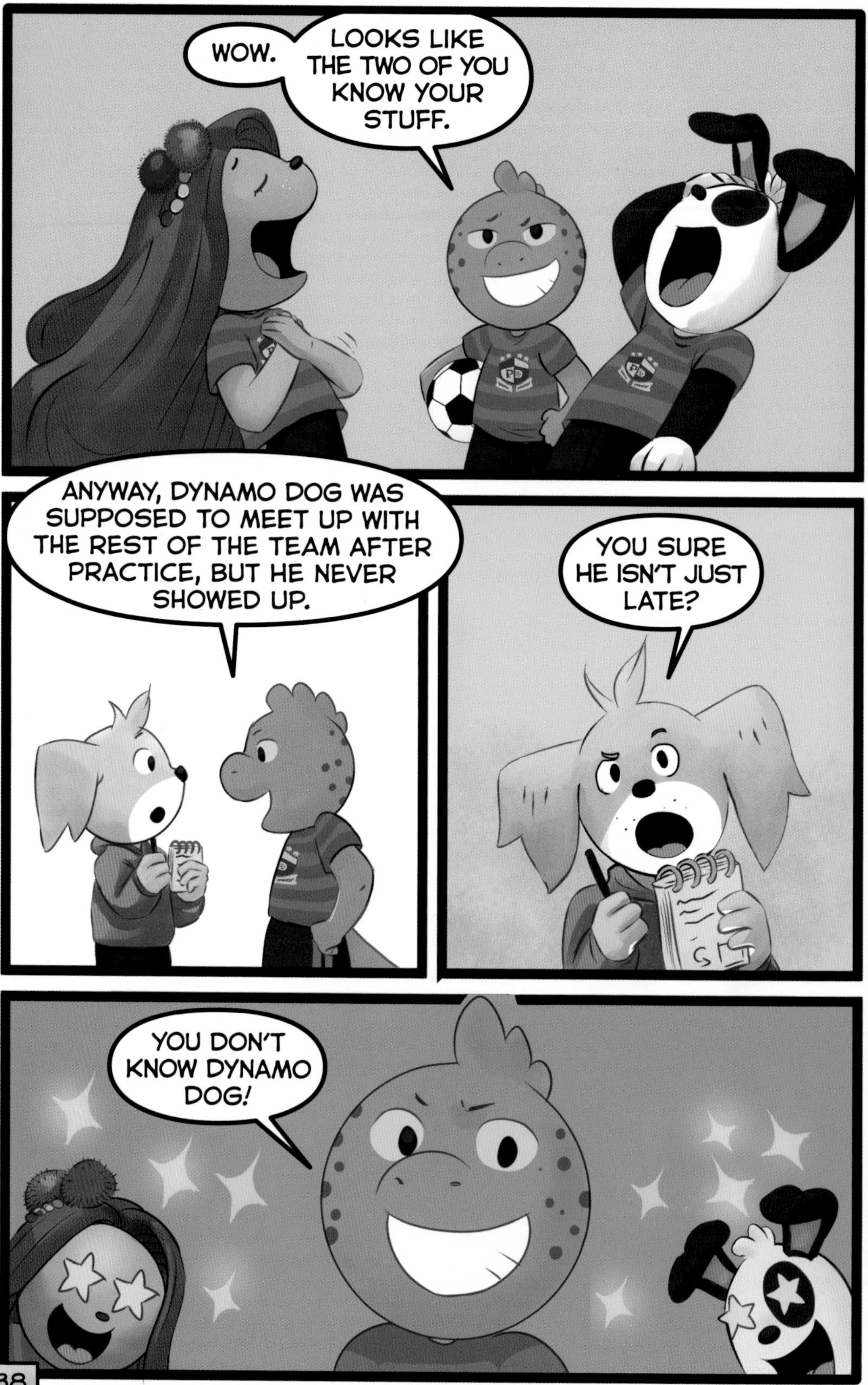
WOW.
LOOKS LIKE THE TWO OF YOU KNOW YOUR STUFF.
ANYWAY, DYNAMO DOG WAS SUPPOSED TO MEET UP WITH THE REST OF THE TEAM AFTER PRACTICE, BUT HE NEVER SHOWED UP.
YOU SURE HE ISN'T JUST LATE?
YOU DON'T KNOW DYNAMO DOG!

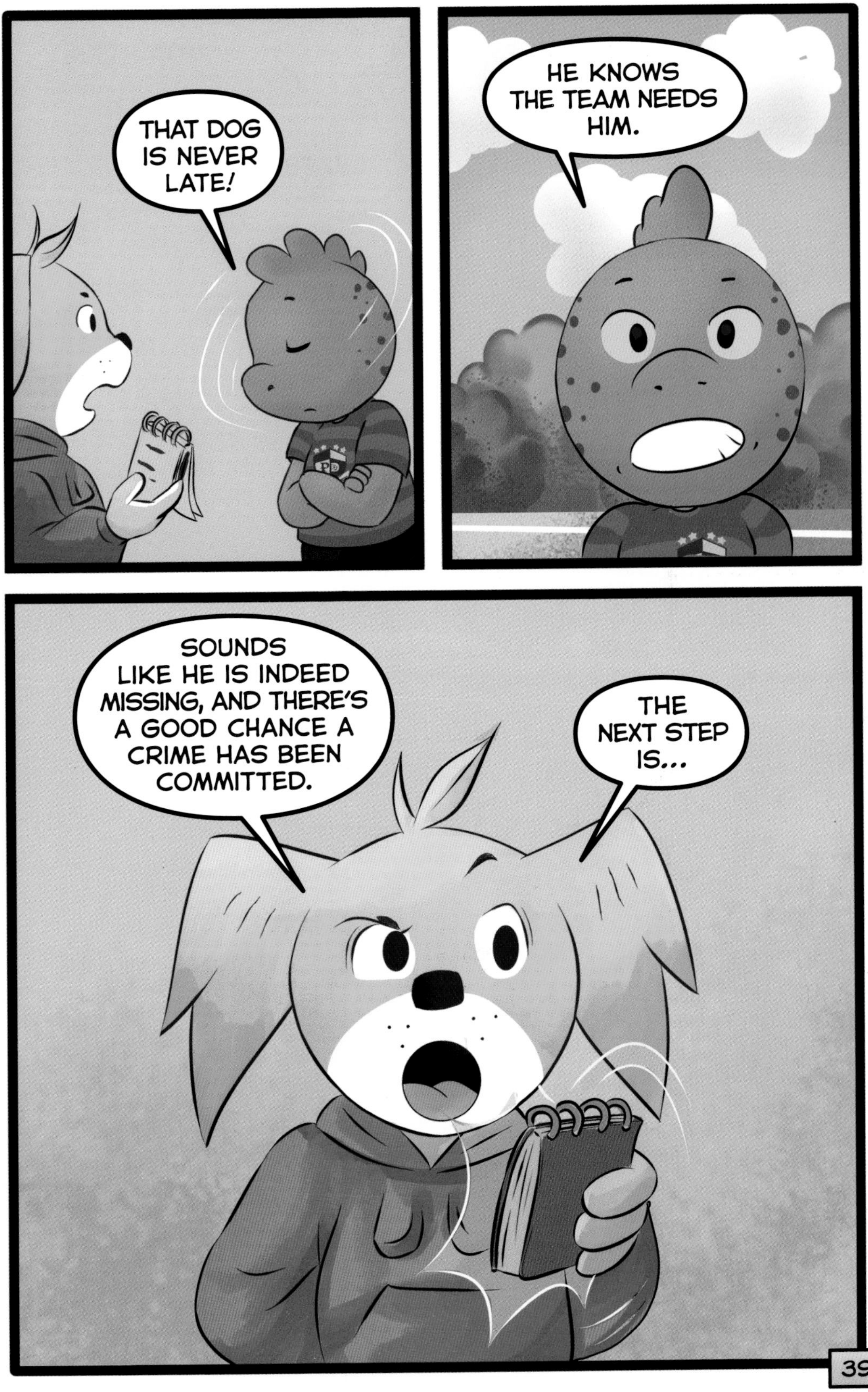
THAT DOG IS NEVER LATE!
HE KNOWS THE TEAM NEEDS HIM.
SOUNDS LIKE HE IS INDEED MISSING, AND THERE'S A GOOD CHANCE A CRIME HAS BEEN COMMITTED.
THE NEXT STEP IS...

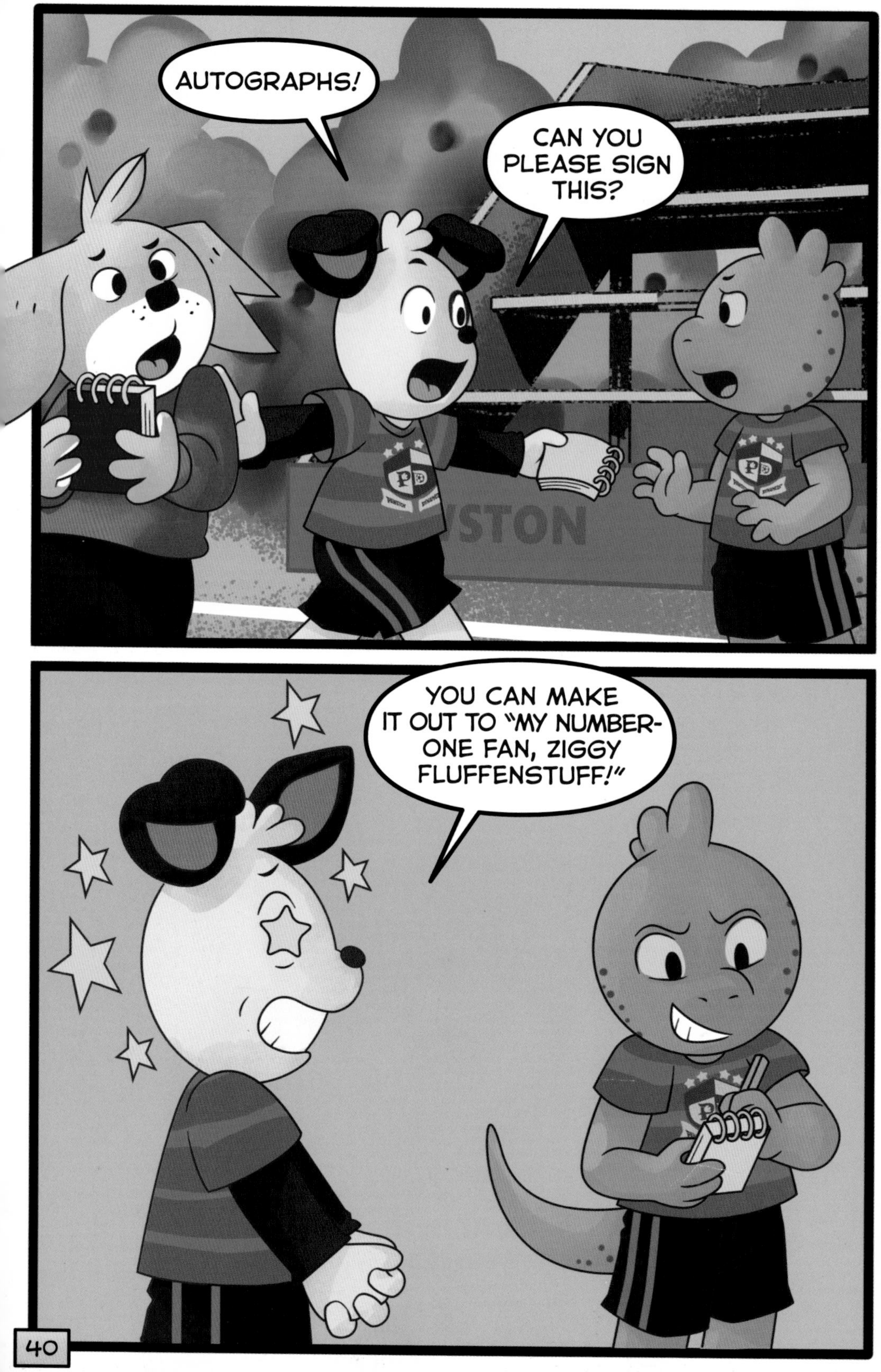
AUTOGRAPHS!
CAN YOU PLEASE SIGN THIS?
YOU CAN MAKE IT OUT TO "MY NUMBER-ONE FAN, ZIGGY FLUFFENSTUFF!"

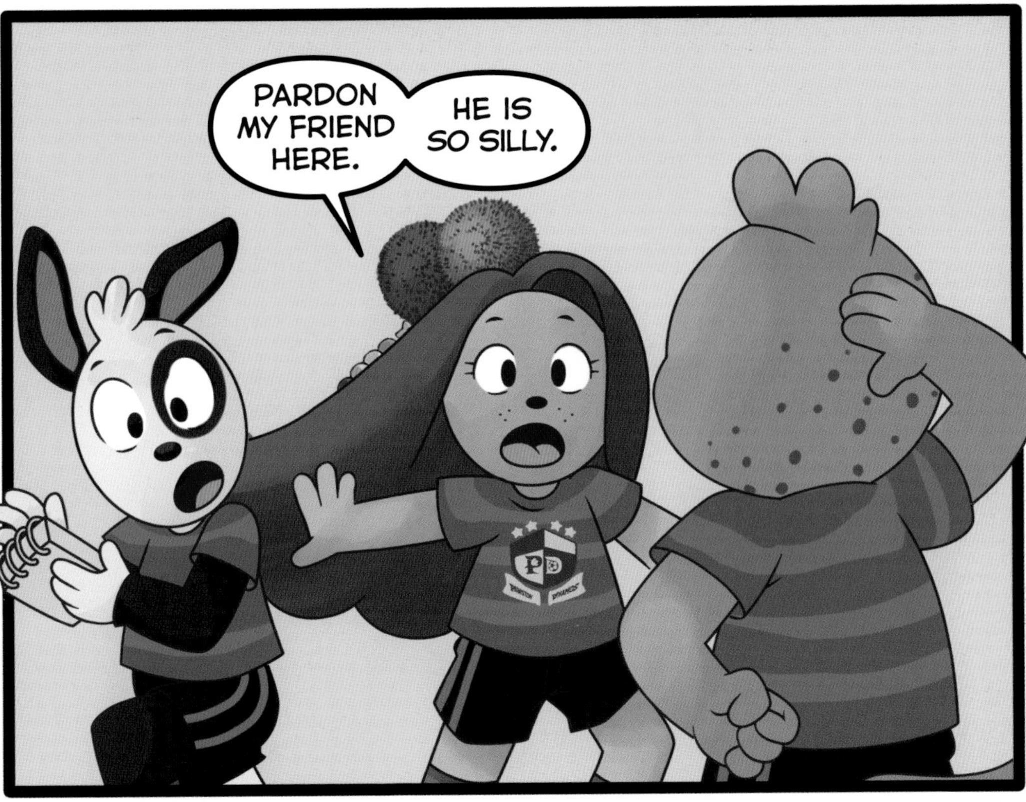
PARDON MY FRIEND HERE.
HE IS SO SILLY.

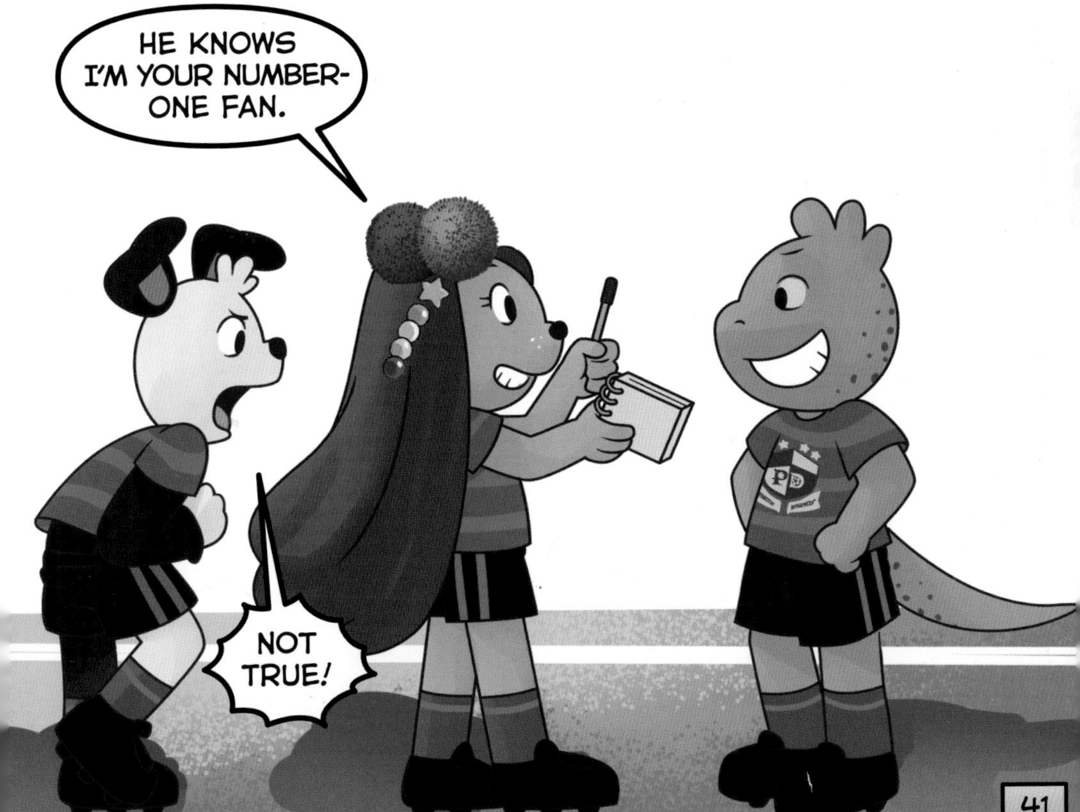
HE KNOWS I'M YOUR NUMBER-ONE FAN.
NOT TRUE!

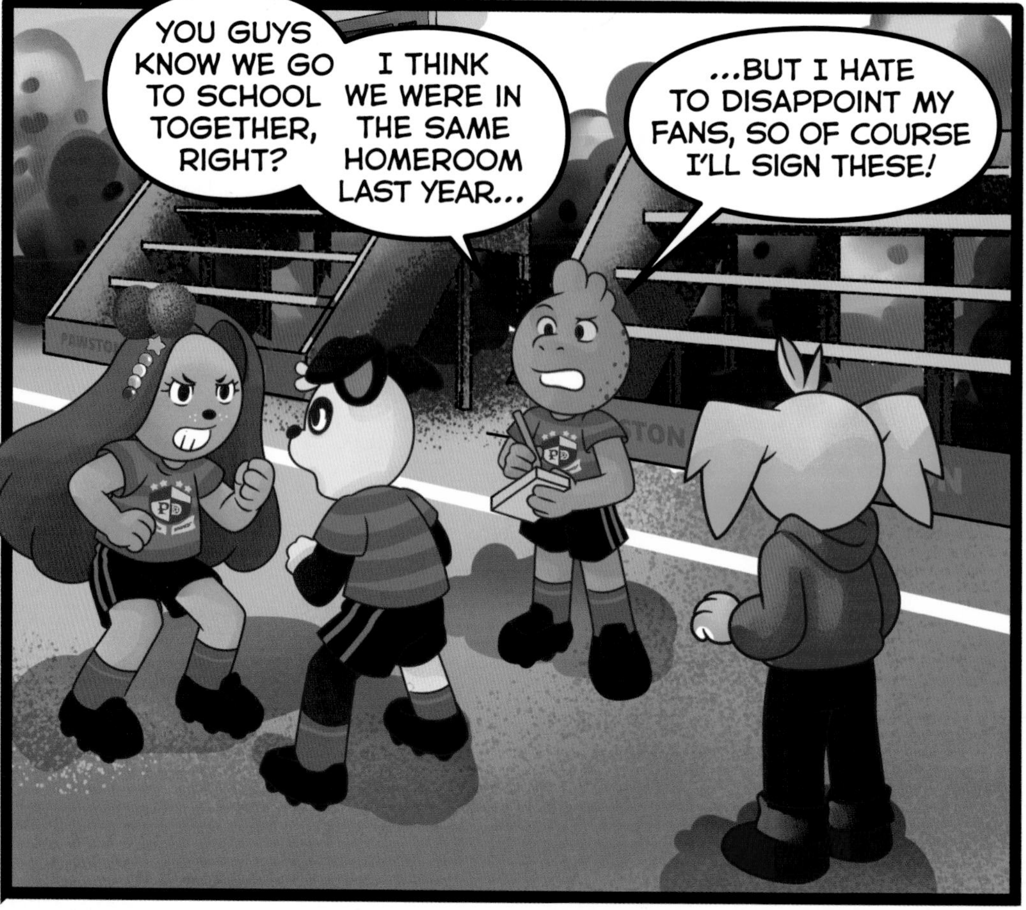
YOU GUYS KNOW WE GO TO SCHOOL TOGETHER, RIGHT?
I THINK WE WERE IN THE SAME HOMEROOM LAST YEAR...
...BUT I HATE TO DISAPPOINT MY FANS, SO OF COURSE I'LL SIGN THESE!

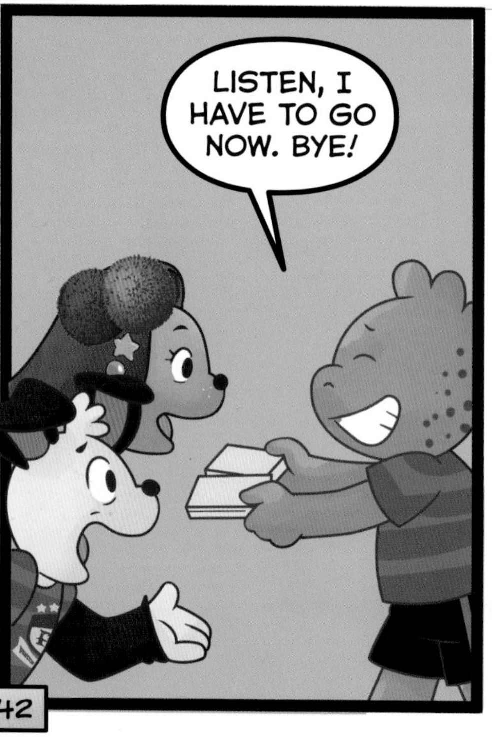
LISTEN, I HAVE TO GO NOW. BYE!

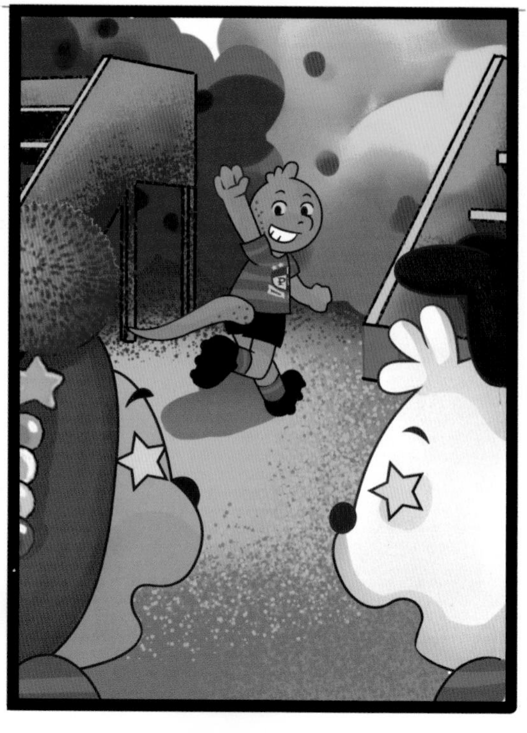

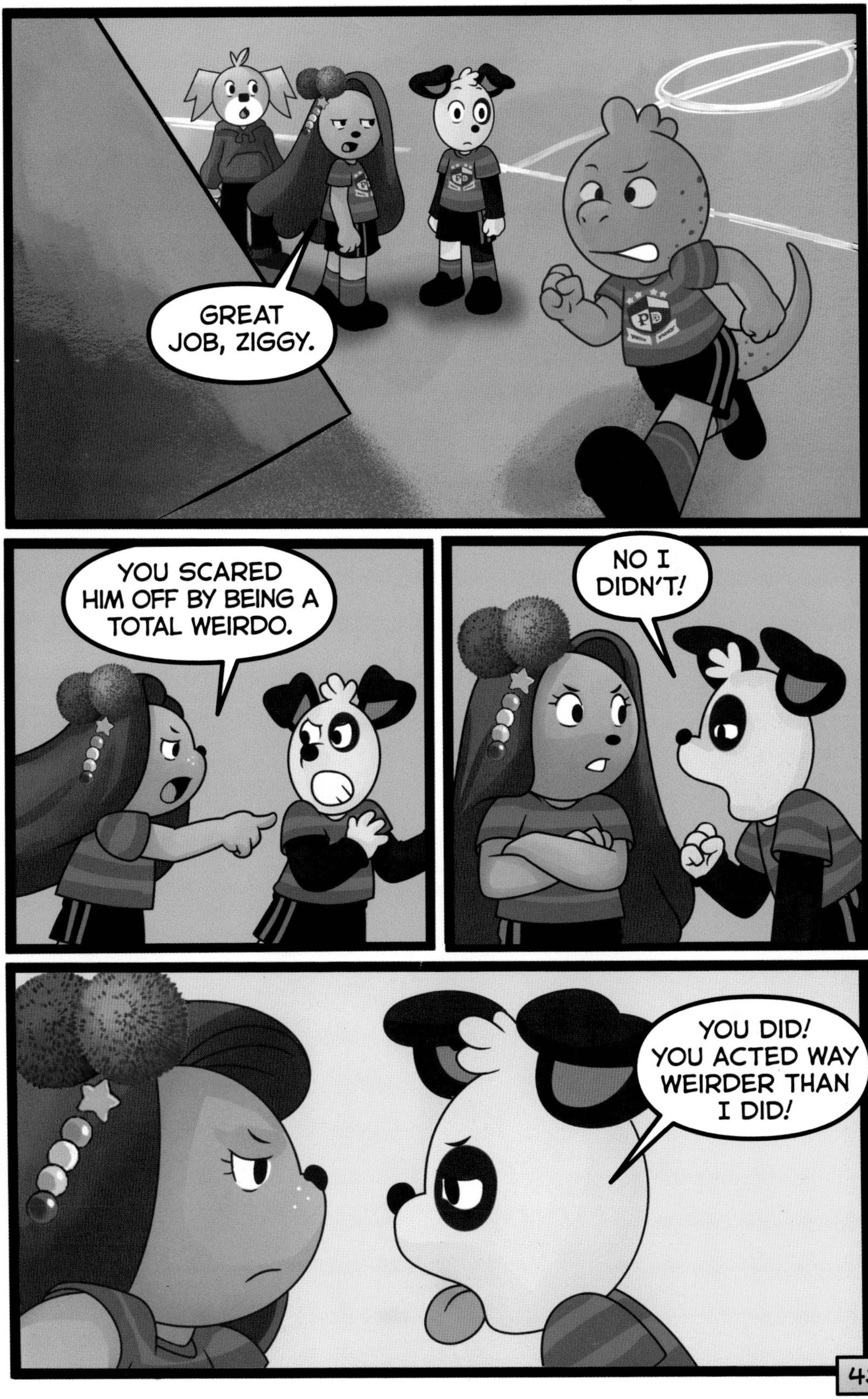
GREAT JOB, ZIGGY.
YOU SCARED HIM OFF BY BEING A TOTAL WEIRDO.
NO I DIDN'T!
YOU DID! YOU ACTED WAY WEIRDER THAN I DID!

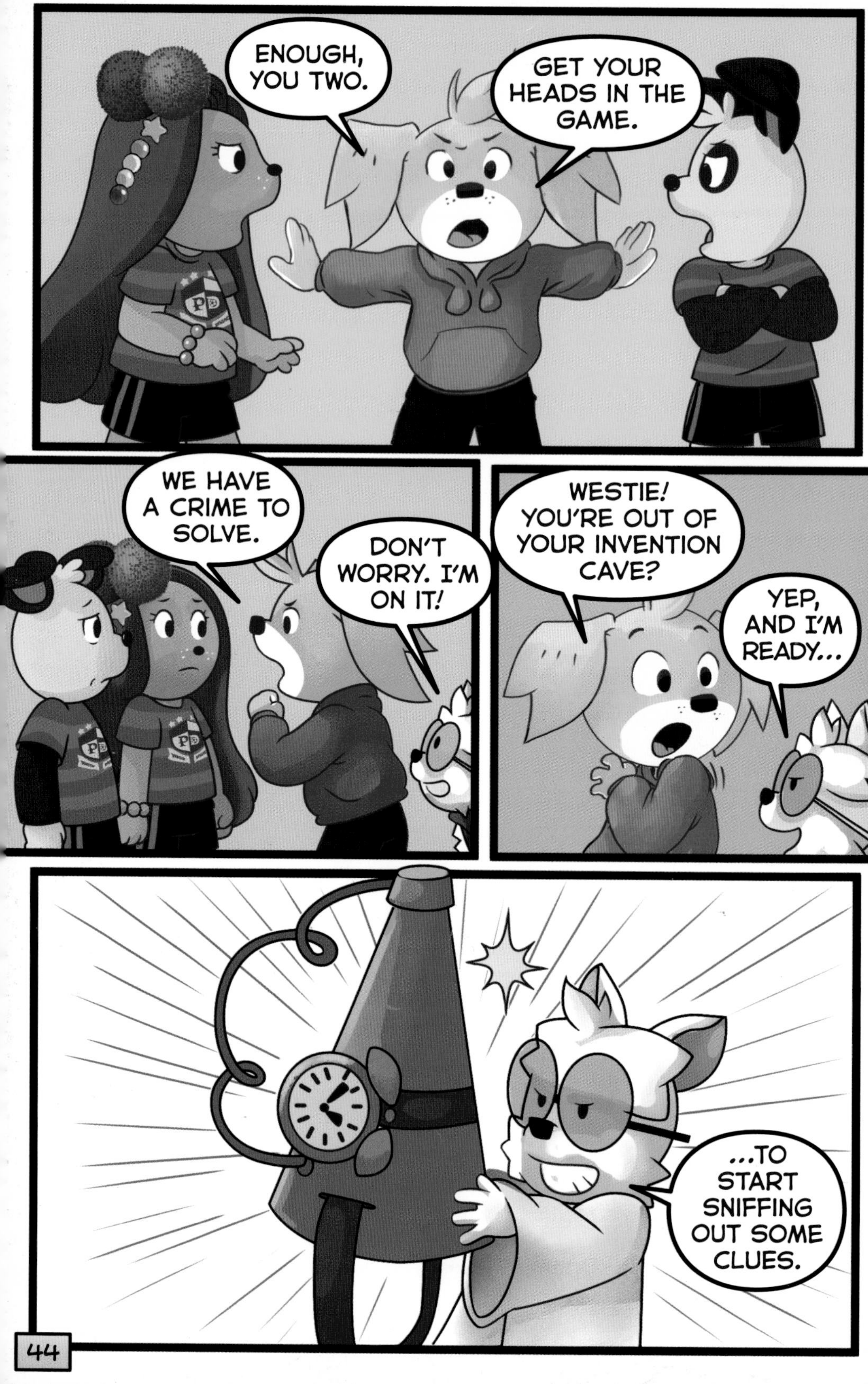
ENOUGH, YOU TWO.
GET YOUR HEADS IN THE GAME.
WE HAVE A CRIME TO SOLVE.
DON'T WORRY. I'M ON IT!
WESTIE! YOU'RE OUT OF YOUR INVENTION CAVE?
YEP, AND I'M READY...
...TO START SNIFFING OUT SOME CLUES.

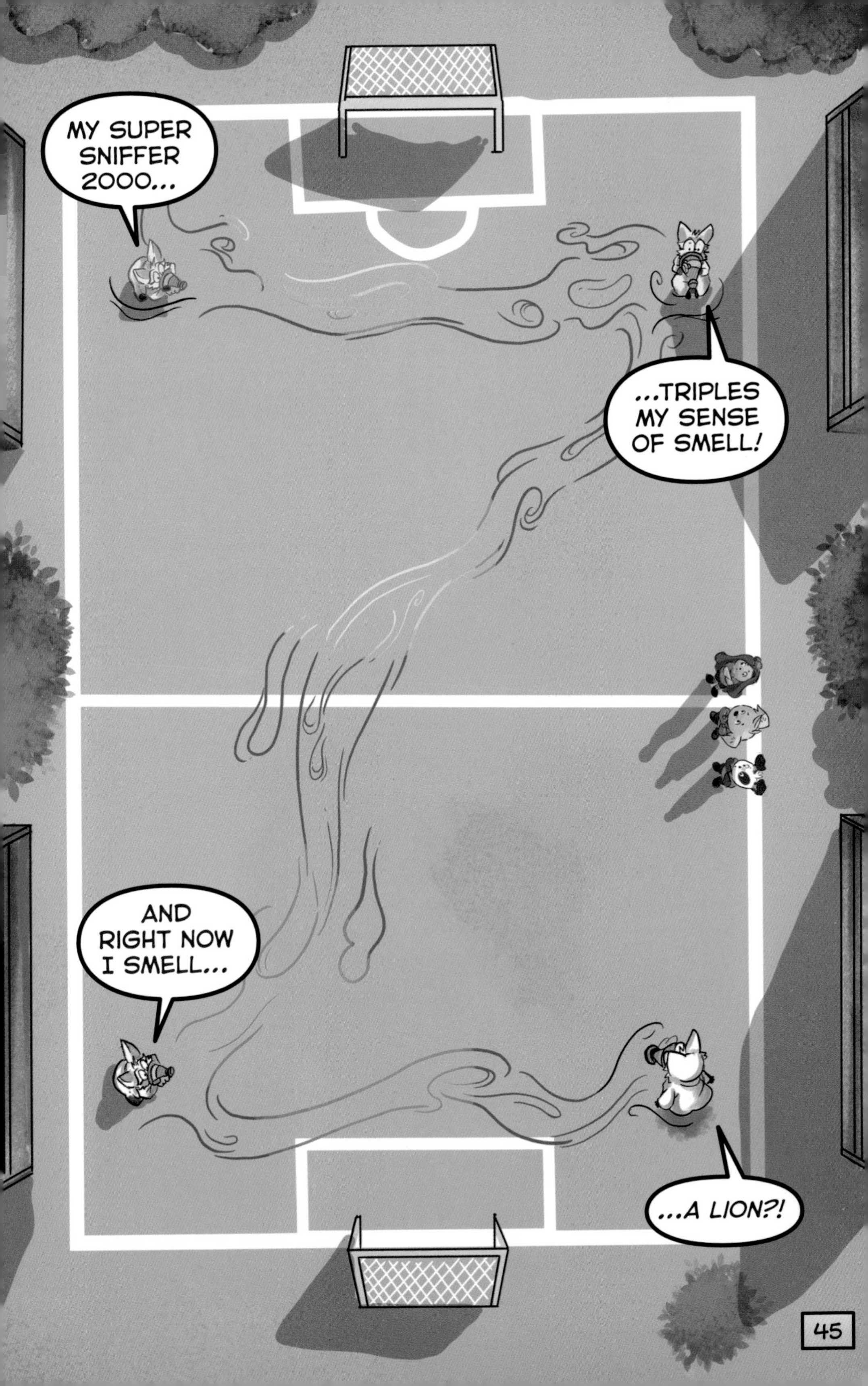
MY SUPER SNIFFER 2000...
...TRIPLES MY SENSE OF SMELL!
AND RIGHT NOW I SMELL...
...A LION?!

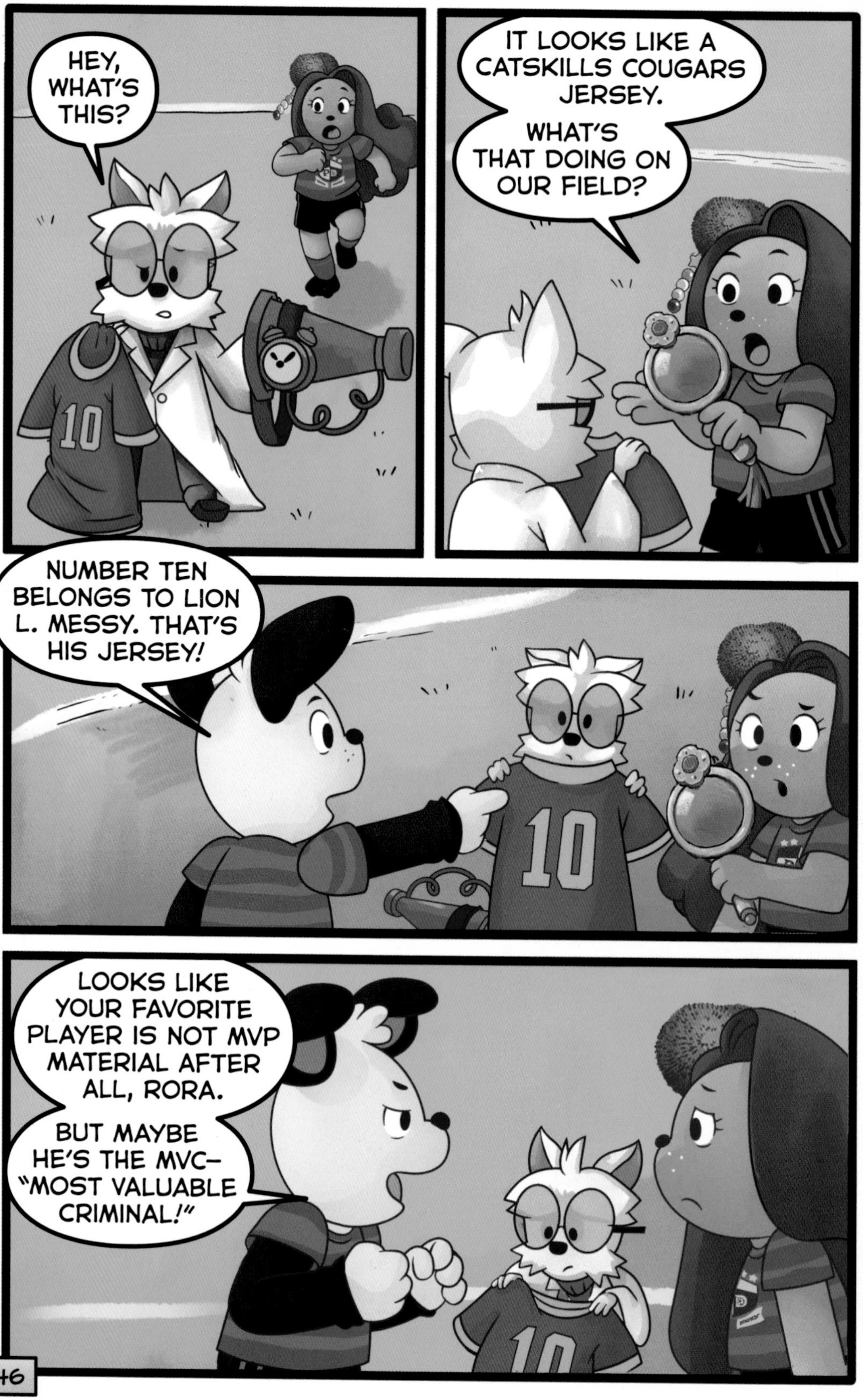
HEY, WHAT'S THIS?
IT LOOKS LIKE A CATSKILLS COUGARS JERSEY.
WHAT'S THAT DOING ON OUR FIELD?
10
NUMBER TEN BELONGS TO LION L. MESSY. THAT'S HIS JERSEY!
10
LOOKS LIKE YOUR FAVORITE PLAYER IS NOT MVP MATERIAL AFTER ALL, RORA.
BUT MAYBE HE'S THE MVC— "MOST VALUABLE CRIMINAL!"

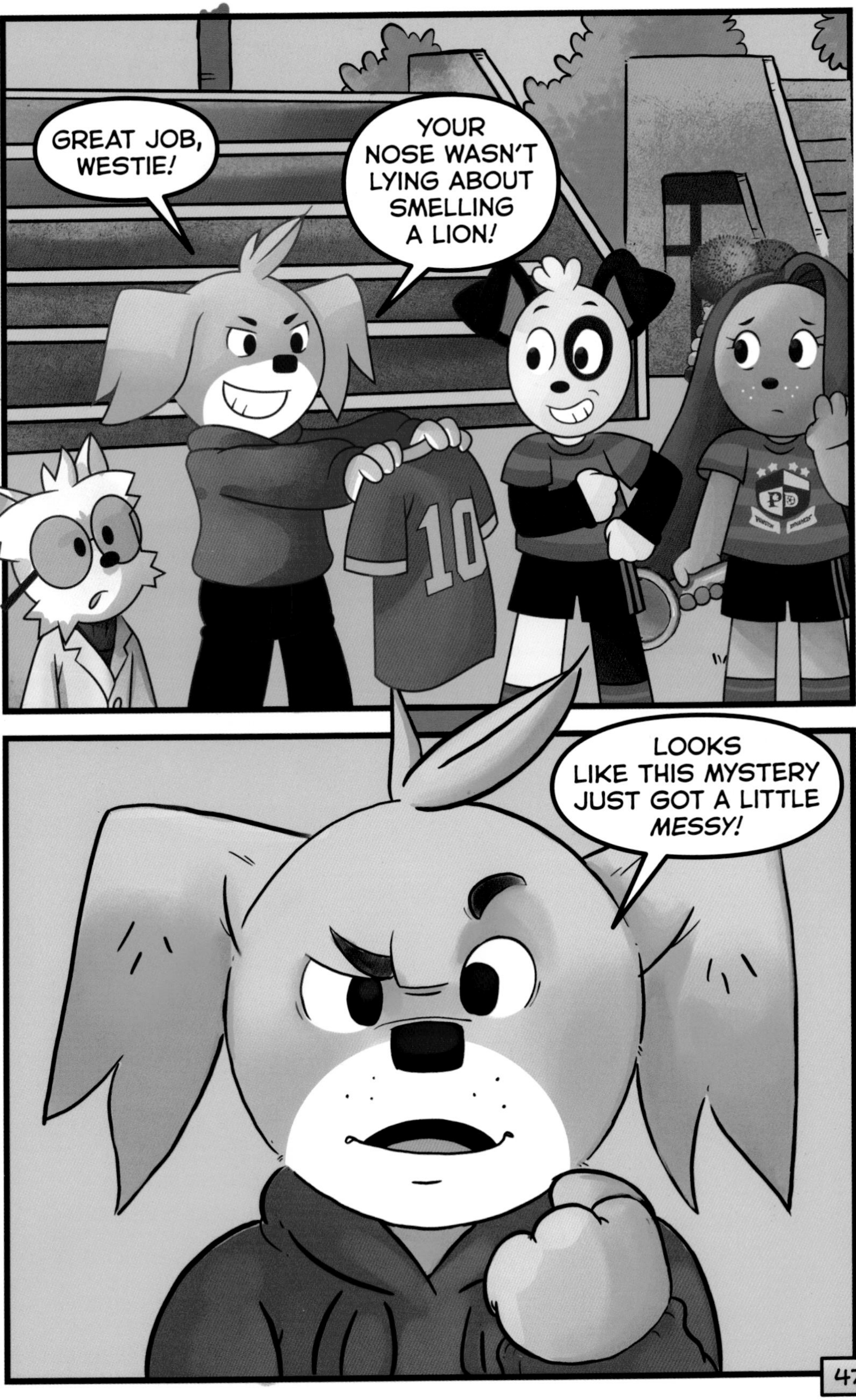
GREAT JOB, WESTIE!
YOUR NOSE WASN'T LYING ABOUT SMELLING A LION!
LOOKS LIKE THIS MYSTERY JUST GOT A LITTLE *MESSY!*

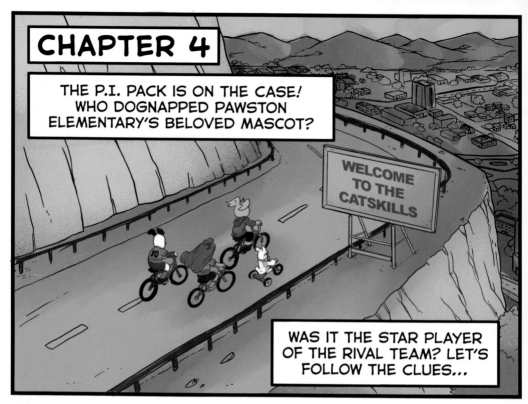

CHAPTER 4

THE P.I. PACK IS ON THE CASE! WHO DOGNAPPED PAWSTON ELEMENTARY'S BELOVED MASCOT?

WELCOME TO THE CATSKILLS

WAS IT THE STAR PLAYER OF THE RIVAL TEAM? LET'S FOLLOW THE CLUES...

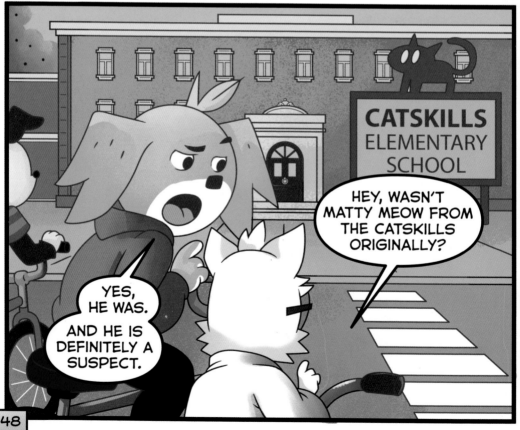

CATSKILLS ELEMENTARY SCHOOL

HEY, WASN'T MATTY MEOW FROM THE CATSKILLS ORIGINALLY?

YES, HE WAS.

AND HE IS DEFINITELY A SUSPECT.

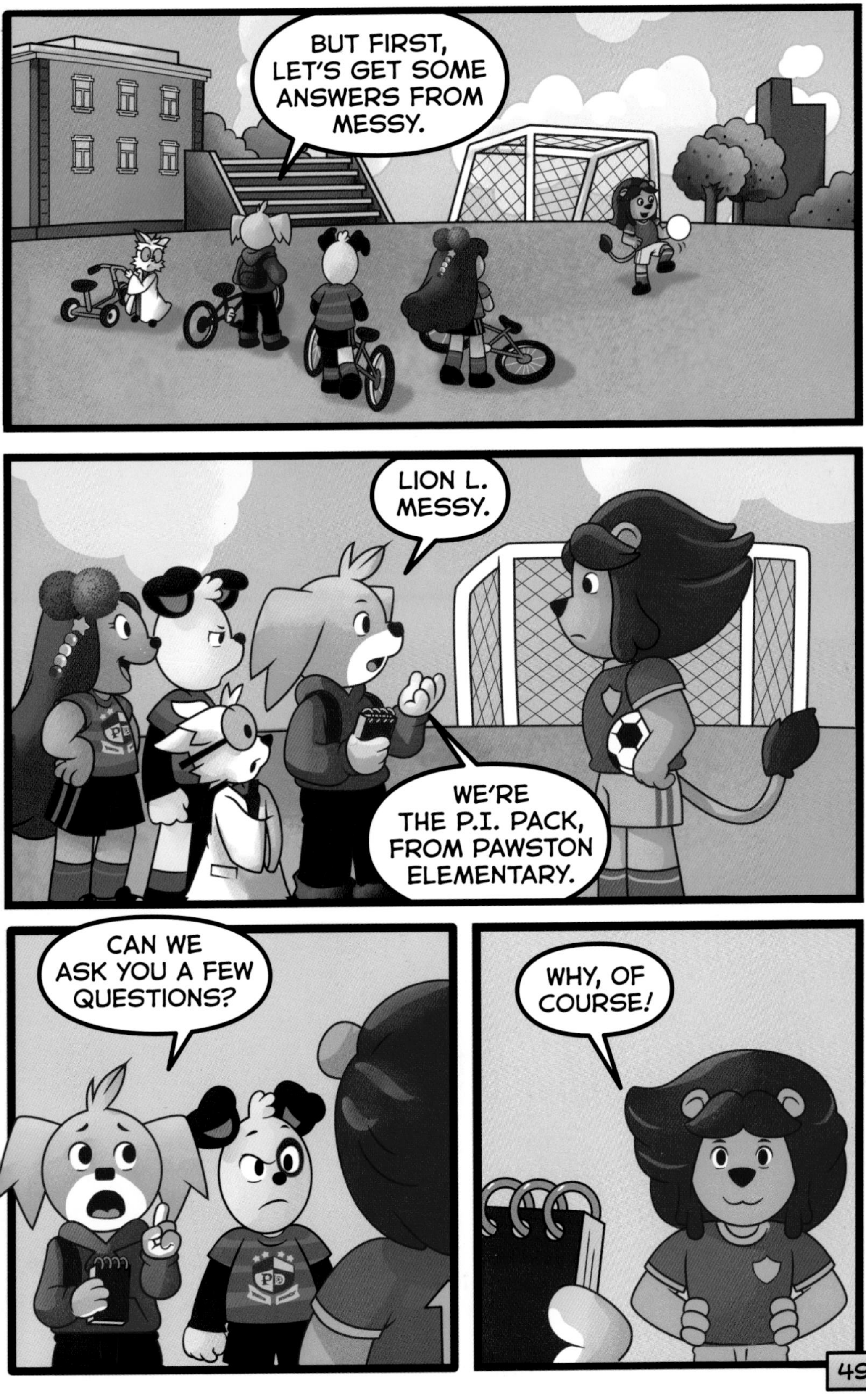
BUT FIRST, LET'S GET SOME ANSWERS FROM MESSY.
LION L. MESSY.
WE'RE THE P.I. PACK, FROM PAWSTON ELEMENTARY.
CAN WE ASK YOU A FEW QUESTIONS?
WHY, OF COURSE!

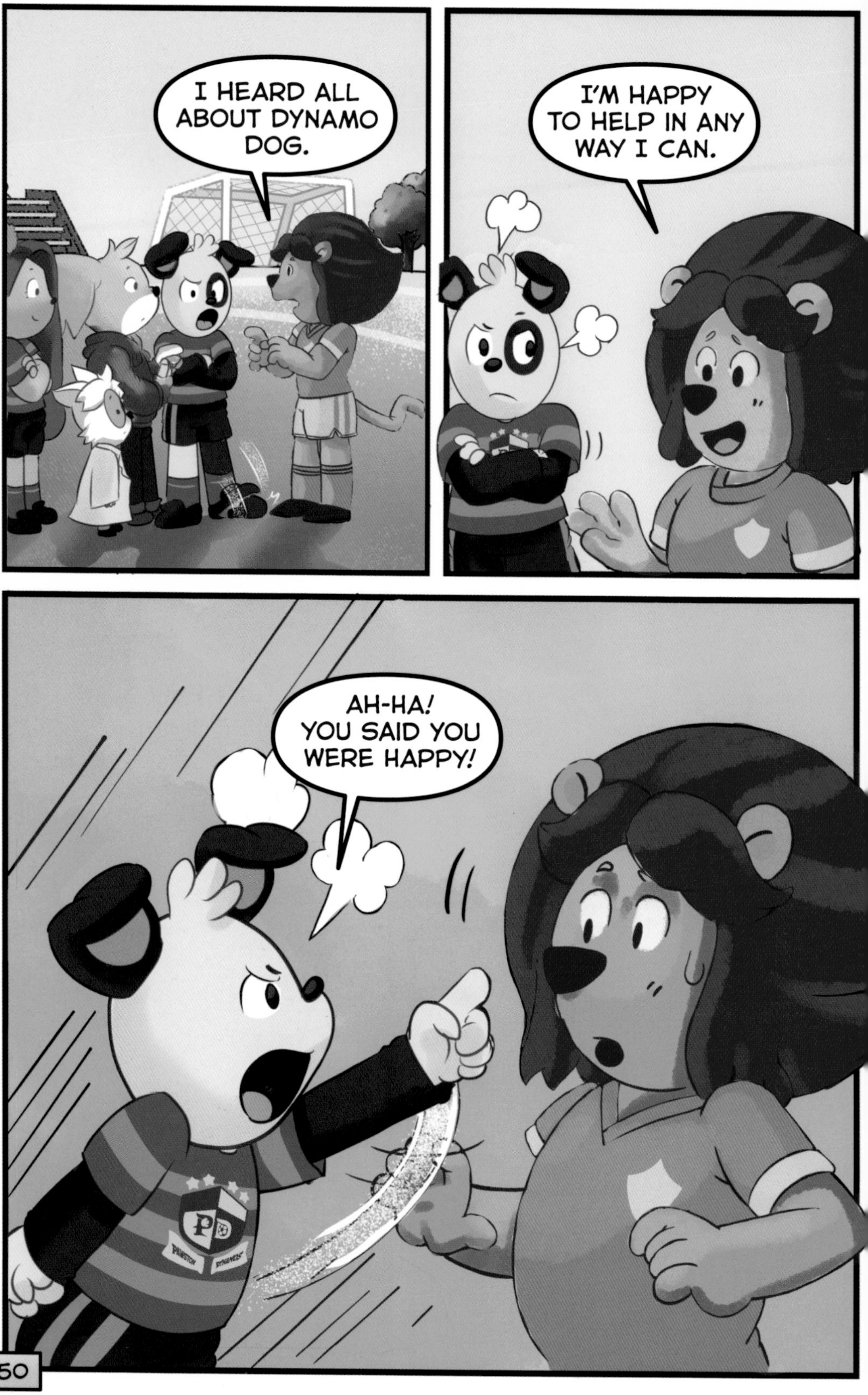
I HEARD ALL ABOUT DYNAMO DOG.
I'M HAPPY TO HELP IN ANY WAY I CAN.
AH-HA! YOU SAID YOU WERE HAPPY!

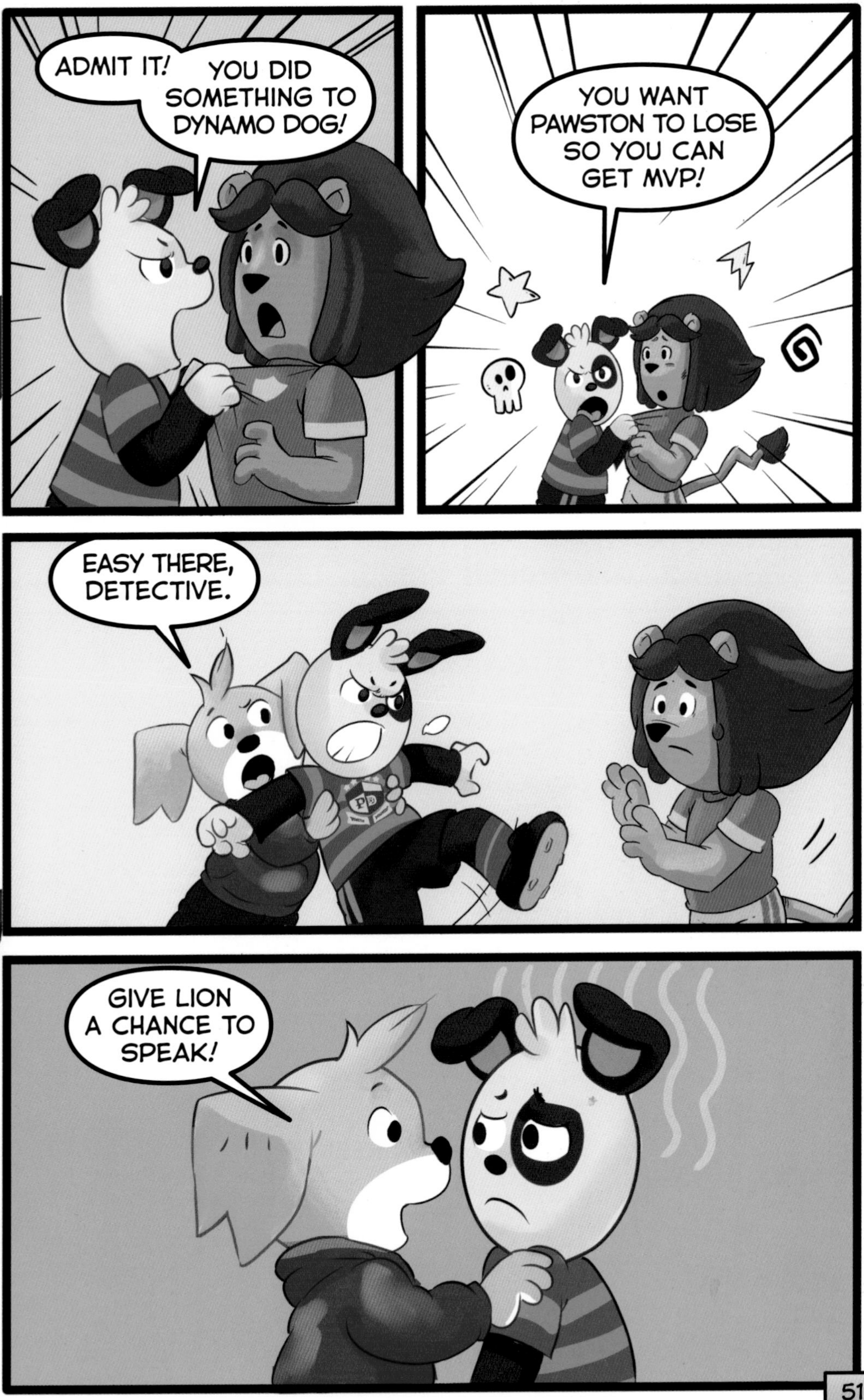
ADMIT IT!
YOU DID SOMETHING TO DYNAMO DOG!
YOU WANT PAWSTON TO LOSE SO YOU CAN GET MVP!
EASY THERE, DETECTIVE.
GIVE LION A CHANCE TO SPEAK!

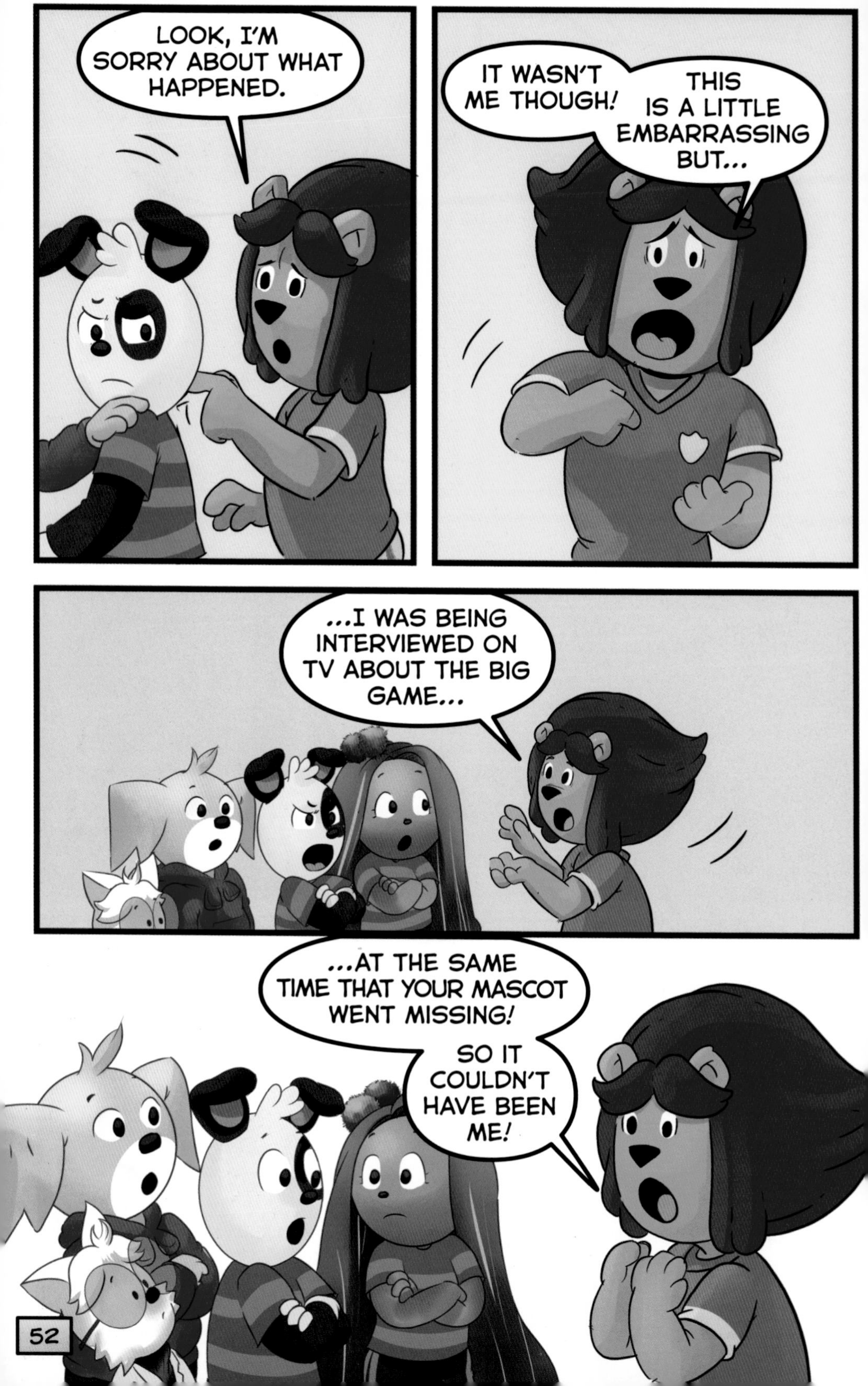
LOOK, I'M SORRY ABOUT WHAT HAPPENED.
IT WASN'T ME THOUGH!
THIS IS A LITTLE EMBARRASSING BUT...
...I WAS BEING INTERVIEWED ON TV ABOUT THE BIG GAME...
...AT THE SAME TIME THAT YOUR MASCOT WENT MISSING!
SO IT COULDN'T HAVE BEEN ME!

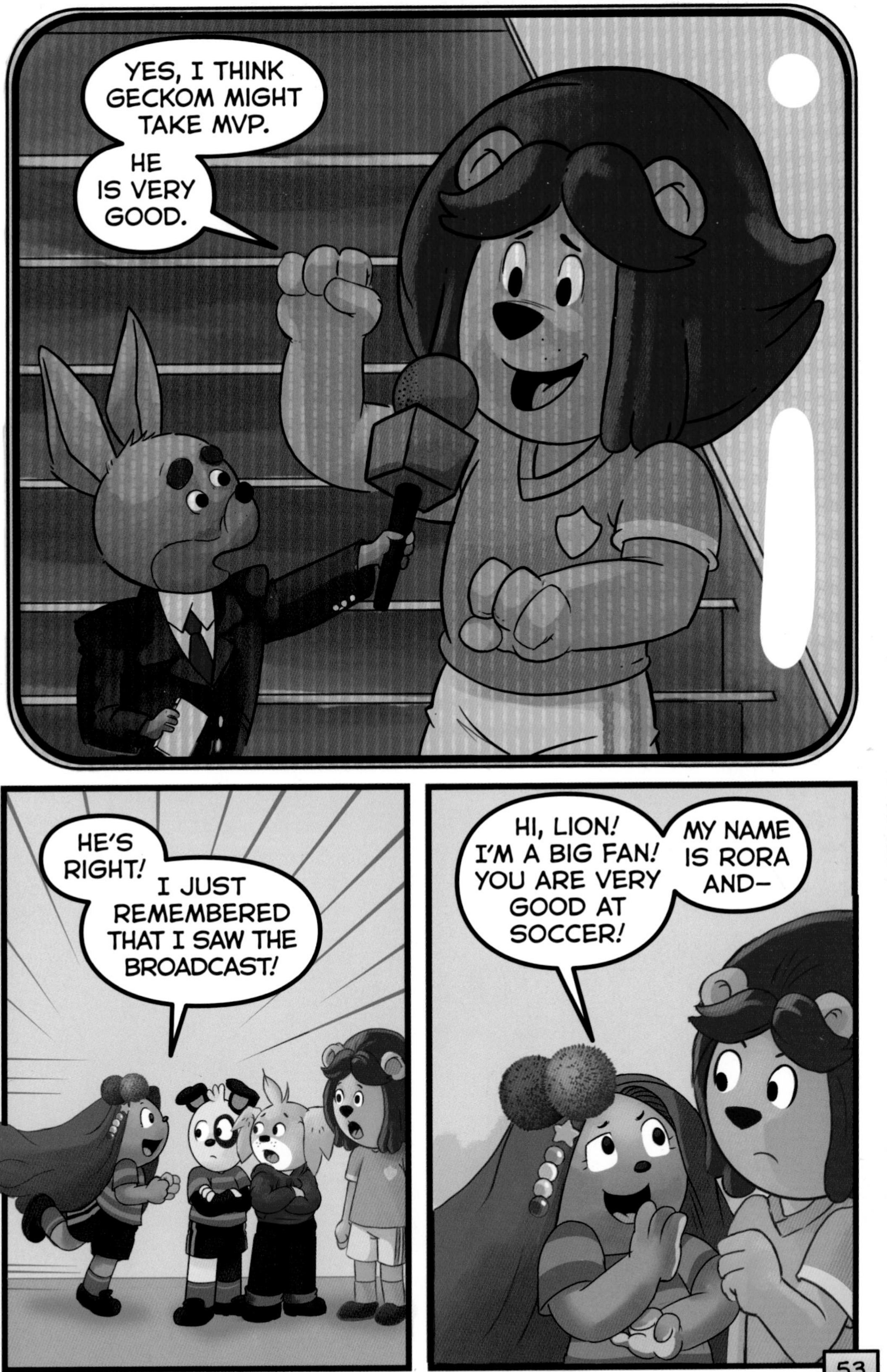
YES, I THINK GECKOM MIGHT TAKE MVP.
HE IS VERY GOOD.
HE'S RIGHT!
I JUST REMEMBERED THAT I SAW THE BROADCAST!
HI, LION! I'M A BIG FAN! YOU ARE VERY GOOD AT SOCCER!
MY NAME IS RORA AND–

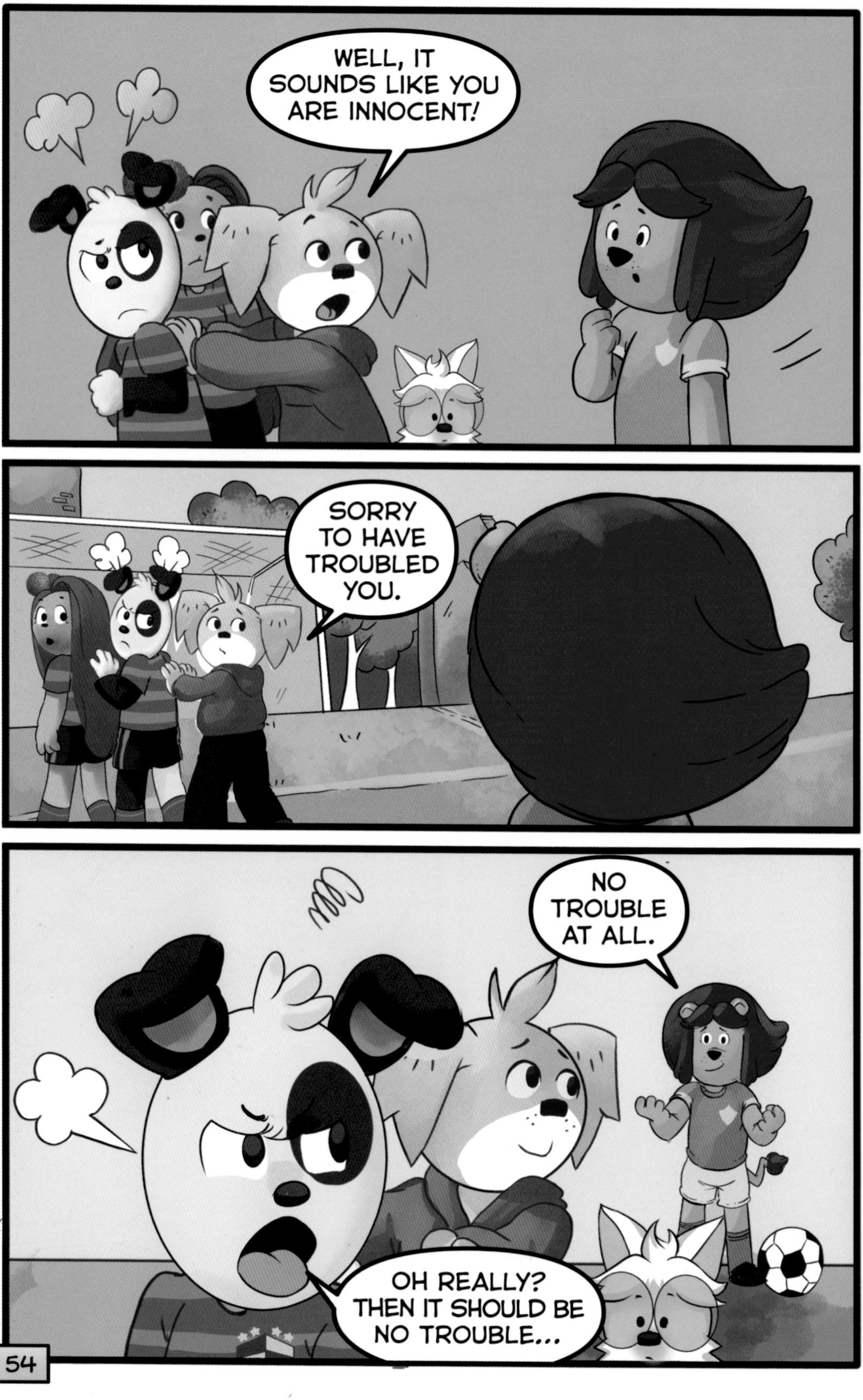
WELL, IT SOUNDS LIKE YOU ARE INNOCENT!
SORRY TO HAVE TROUBLED YOU.
NO TROUBLE AT ALL.
OH REALLY? THEN IT SHOULD BE NO TROUBLE...

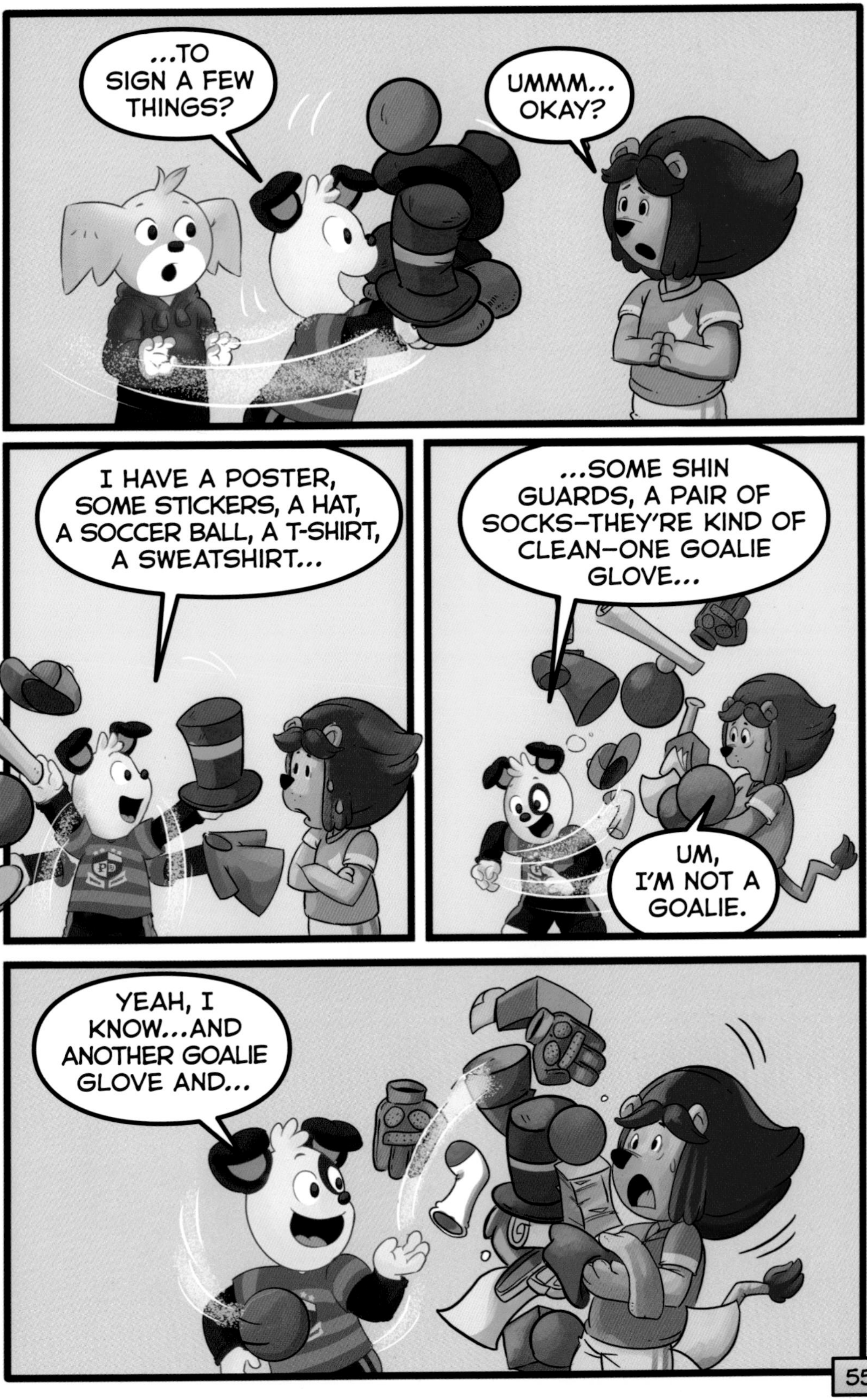
...TO SIGN A FEW THINGS?
UMMM... OKAY?
I HAVE A POSTER, SOME STICKERS, A HAT, A SOCCER BALL, A T-SHIRT, A SWEATSHIRT...
...SOME SHIN GUARDS, A PAIR OF SOCKS—THEY'RE KIND OF CLEAN—ONE GOALIE GLOVE...
UM, I'M NOT A GOALIE.
YEAH, I KNOW...AND ANOTHER GOALIE GLOVE AND...

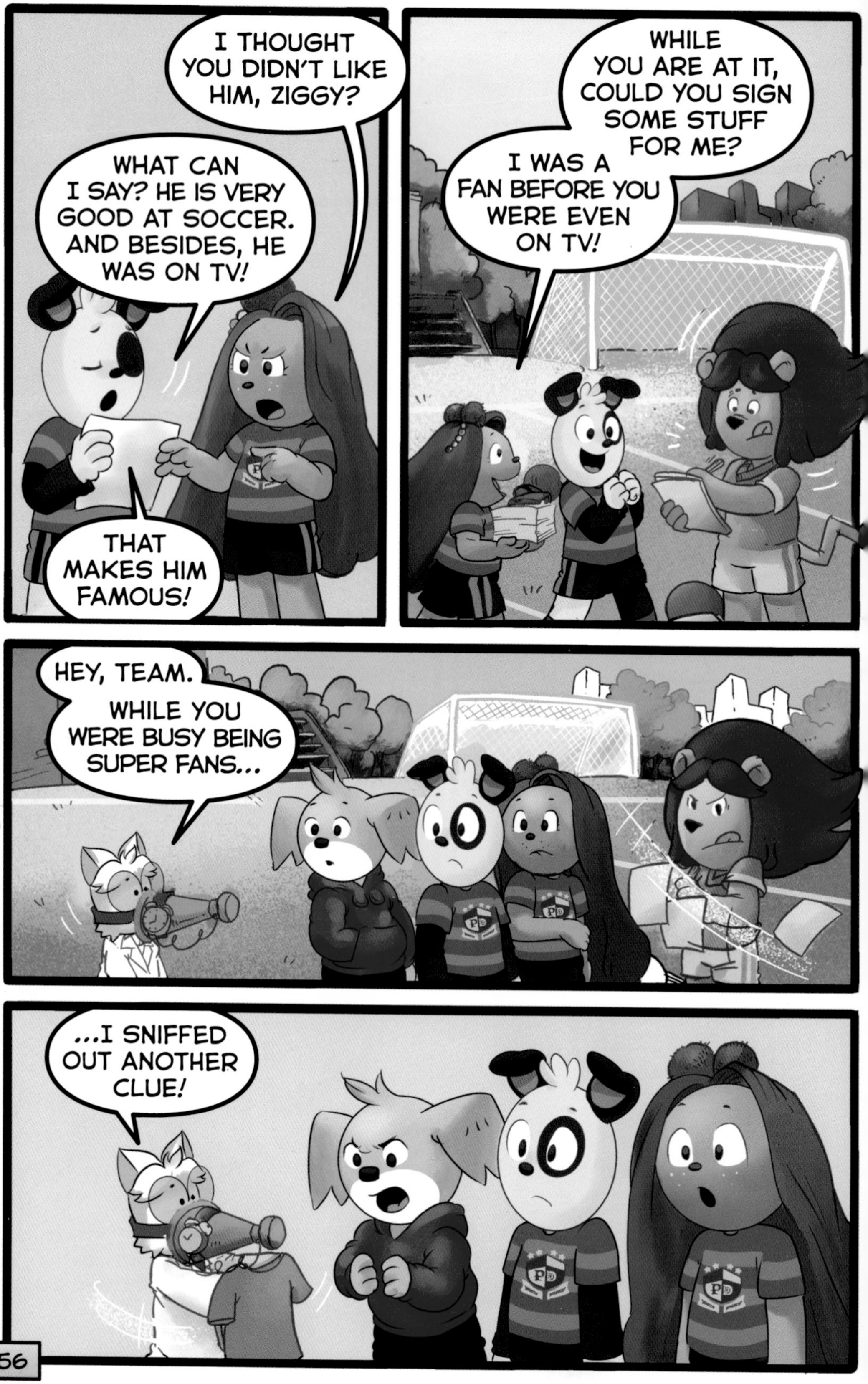
I THOUGHT YOU DIDN'T LIKE HIM, ZIGGY?
WHAT CAN I SAY? HE IS VERY GOOD AT SOCCER. AND BESIDES, HE WAS ON TV!
THAT MAKES HIM FAMOUS!
WHILE YOU ARE AT IT, COULD YOU SIGN SOME STUFF FOR ME?
I WAS A FAN BEFORE YOU WERE EVEN ON TV!
HEY, TEAM.
WHILE YOU WERE BUSY BEING SUPER FANS...
...I SNIFFED OUT ANOTHER CLUE!

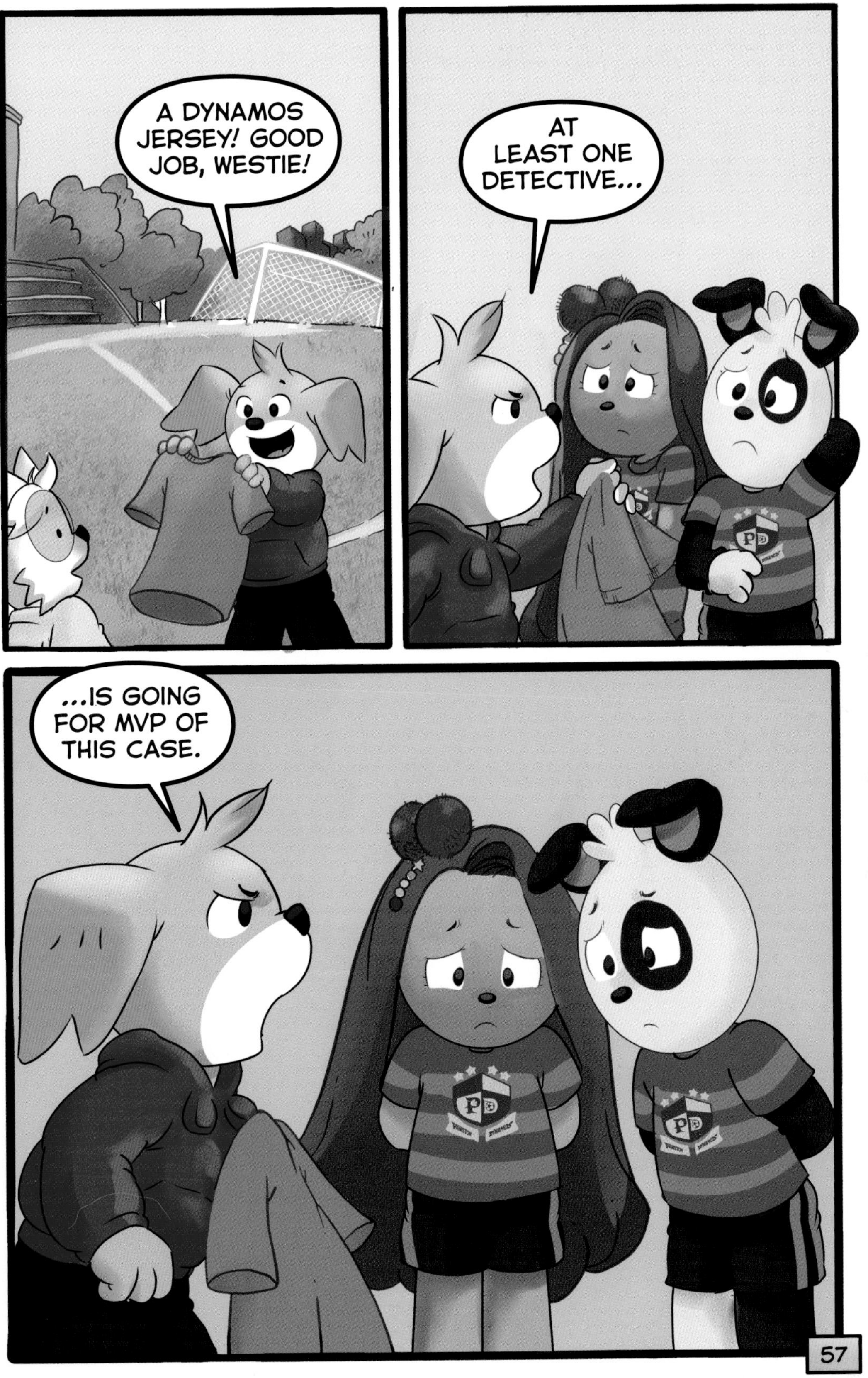
A DYNAMOS JERSEY! GOOD JOB, WESTIE!
AT LEAST ONE DETECTIVE...
...IS GOING FOR MVP OF THIS CASE.

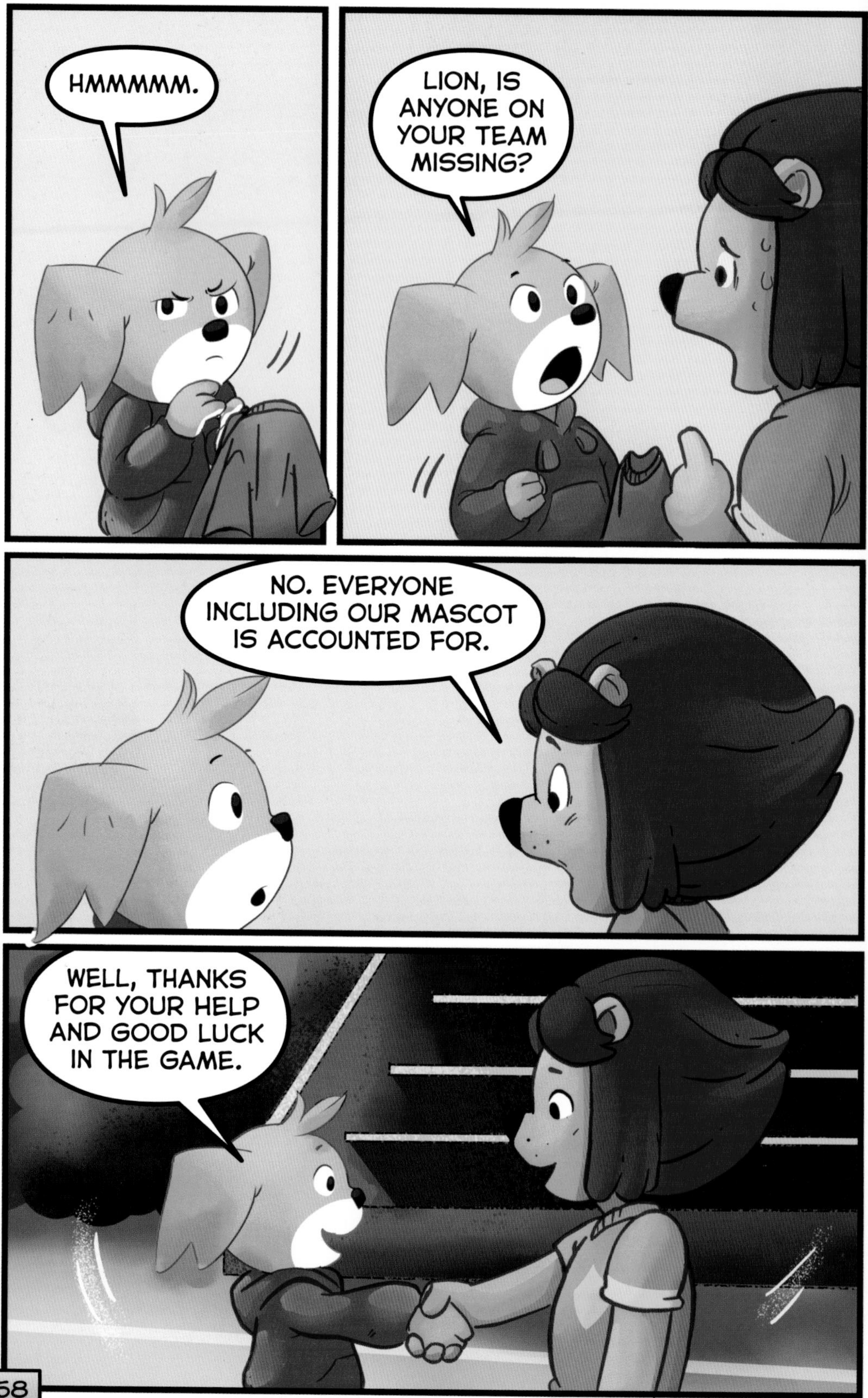
HMMMMM.
LION, IS ANYONE ON YOUR TEAM MISSING?
NO. EVERYONE INCLUDING OUR MASCOT IS ACCOUNTED FOR.
WELL, THANKS FOR YOUR HELP AND GOOD LUCK IN THE GAME.

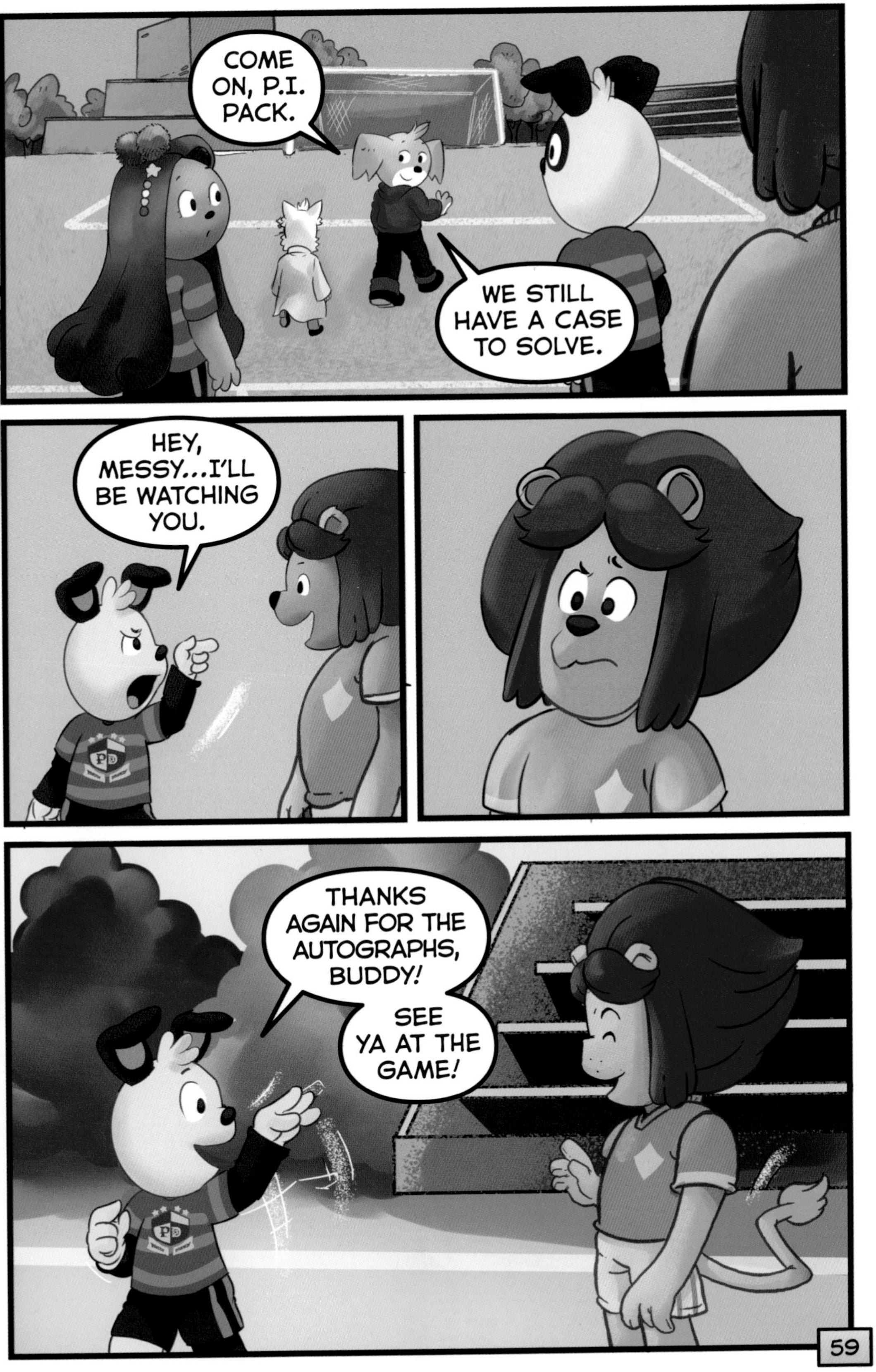
COME ON, P.I. PACK.
WE STILL HAVE A CASE TO SOLVE.
HEY, MESSY...I'LL BE WATCHING YOU.
THANKS AGAIN FOR THE AUTOGRAPHS, BUDDY!
SEE YA AT THE GAME!

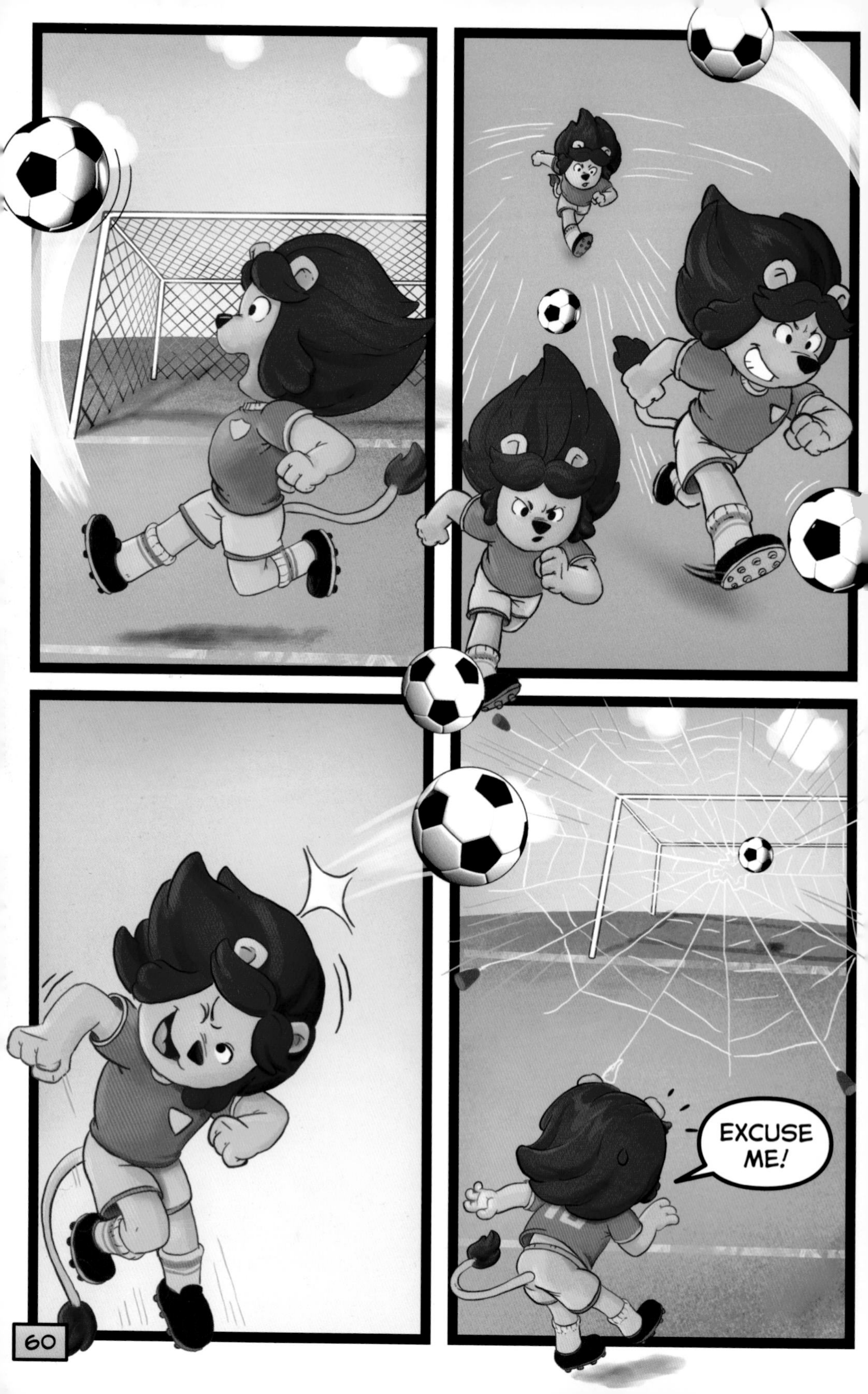
EXCUSE ME!

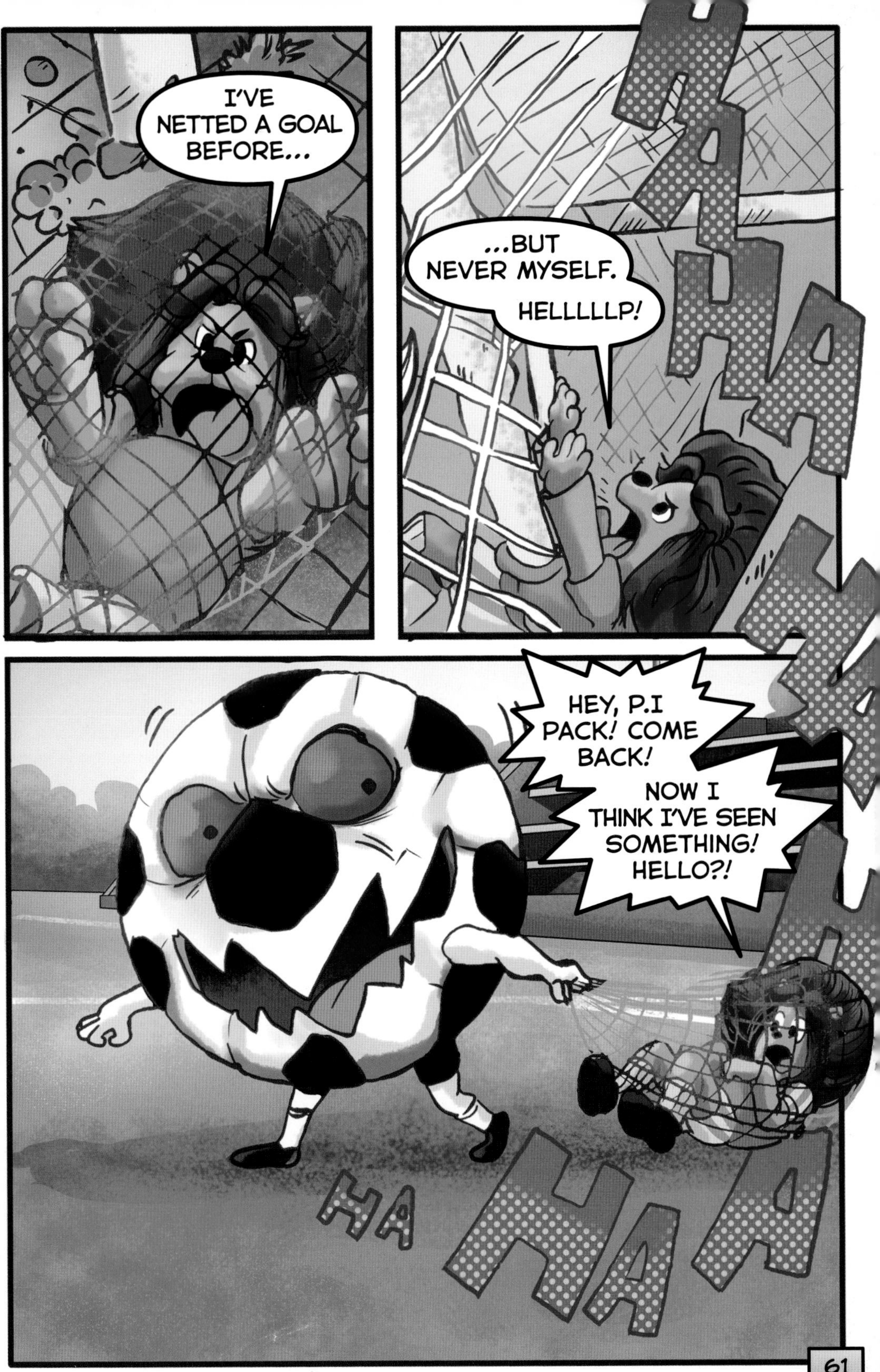
I'VE NETTED A GOAL BEFORE...
...BUT NEVER MYSELF.
HELLLLLP!
HAHAHAHA
HEY, P.I PACK! COME BACK!
NOW I THINK I'VE SEEN SOMETHING! HELLO?!
HA
HAHA

CHAPTER 5

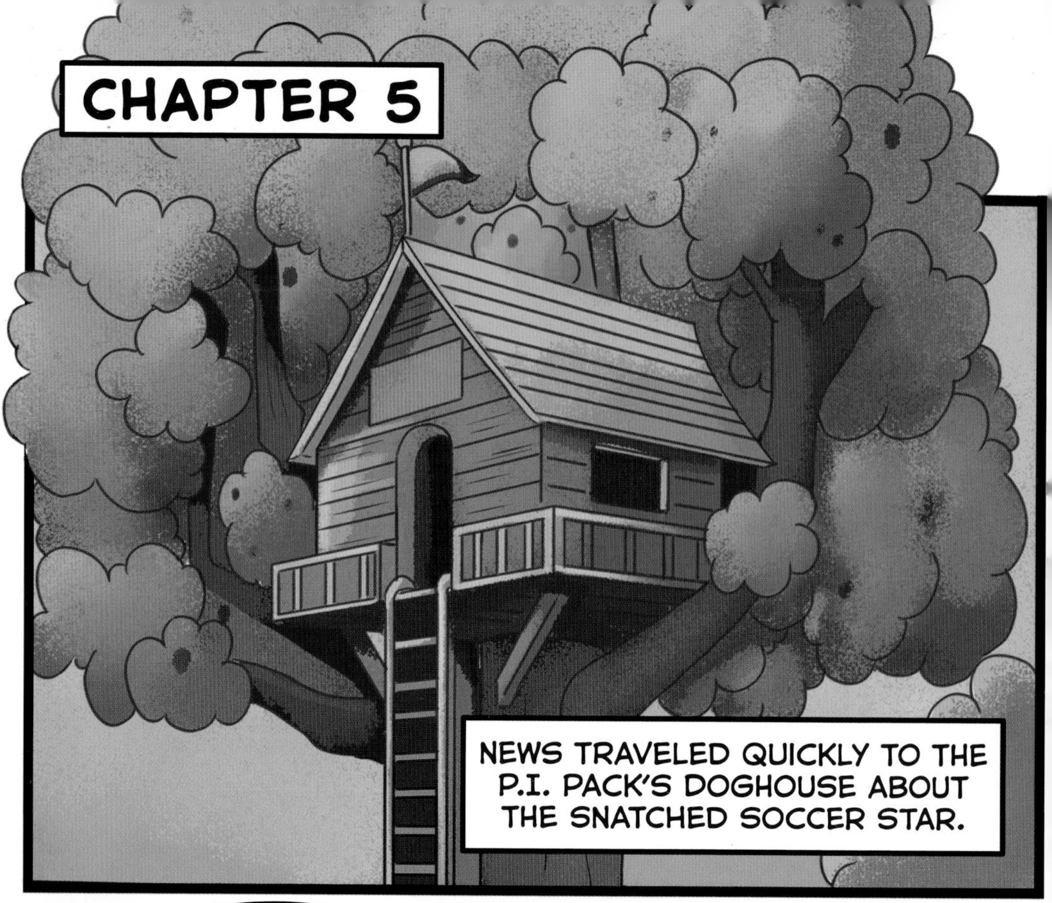
NEWS TRAVELED QUICKLY TO THE P.I. PACK'S DOGHOUSE ABOUT THE SNATCHED SOCCER STAR.

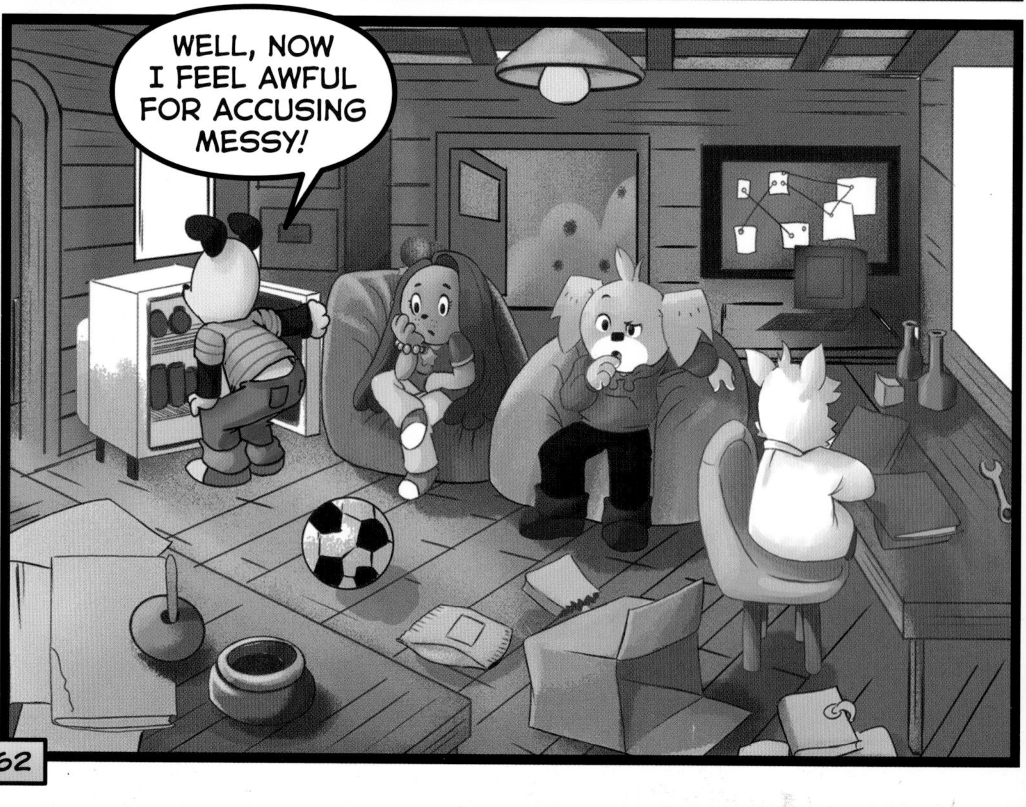
WELL, NOW I FEEL AWFUL FOR ACCUSING MESSY!

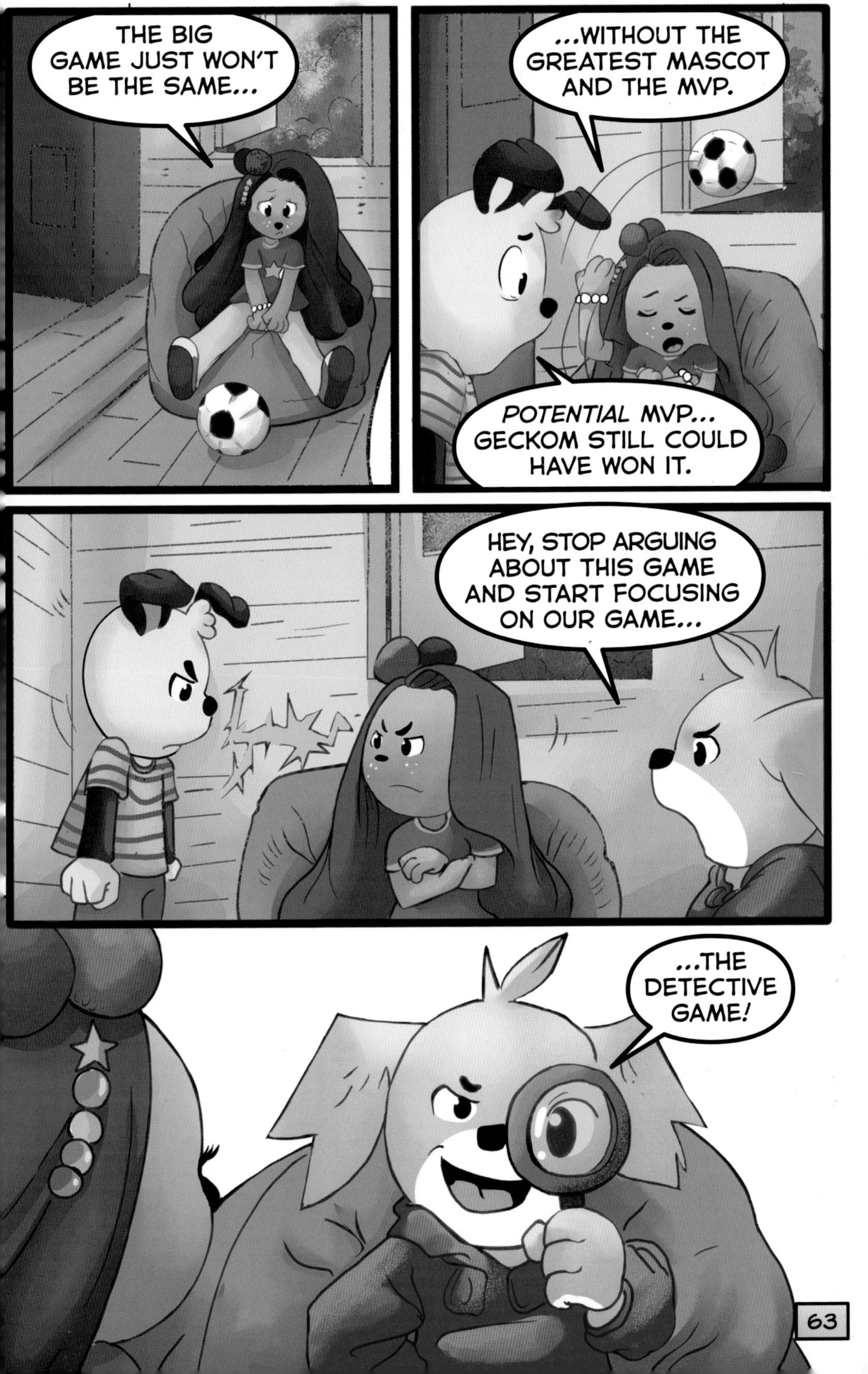
THE BIG GAME JUST WON'T BE THE SAME...
...WITHOUT THE GREATEST MASCOT AND THE MVP.
POTENTIAL MVP... GECKOM STILL COULD HAVE WON IT.
HEY, STOP ARGUING ABOUT THIS GAME AND START FOCUSING ON OUR GAME...
...THE DETECTIVE GAME!

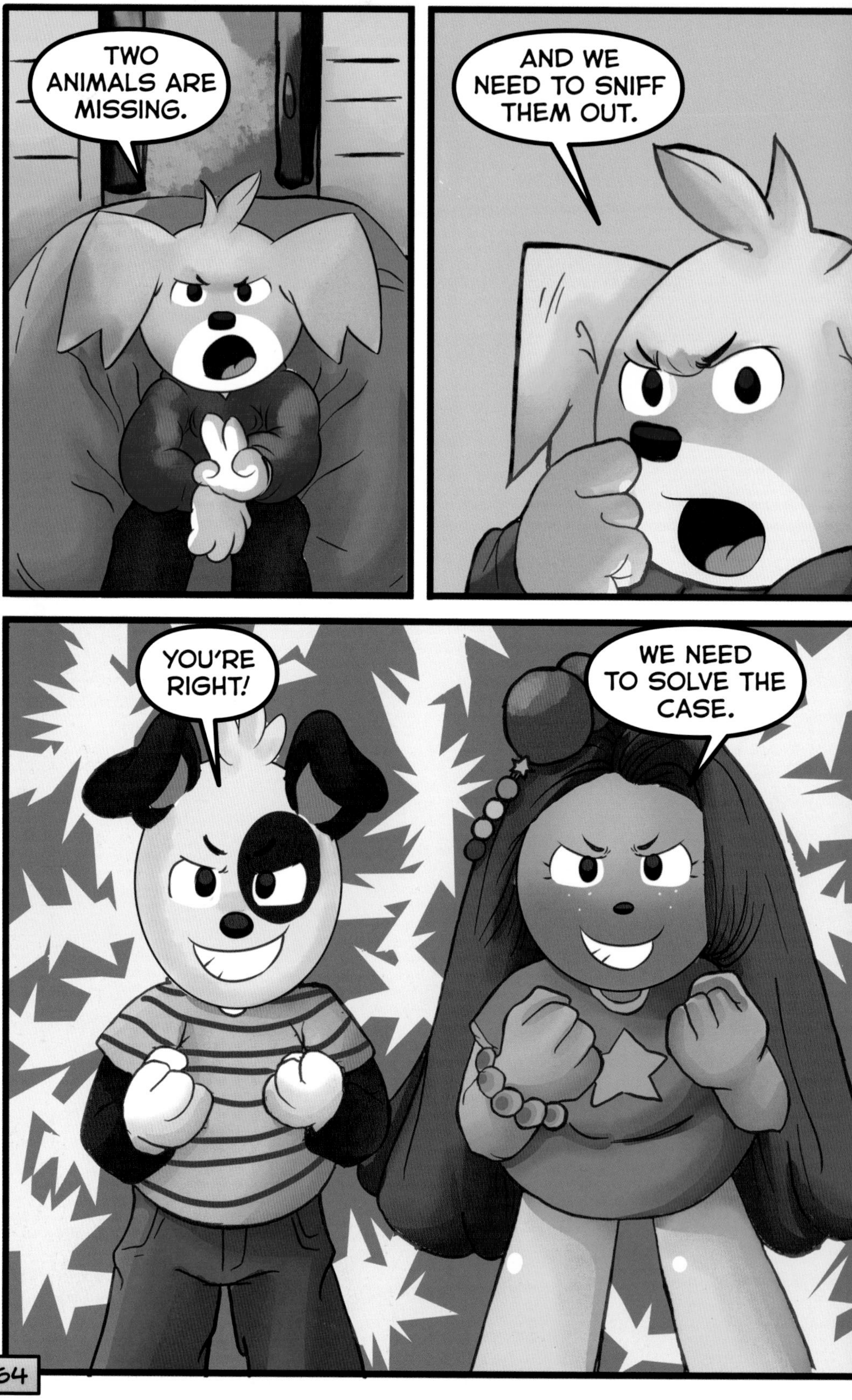
TWO ANIMALS ARE MISSING.
AND WE NEED TO SNIFF THEM OUT.
YOU'RE RIGHT!
WE NEED TO SOLVE THE CASE.

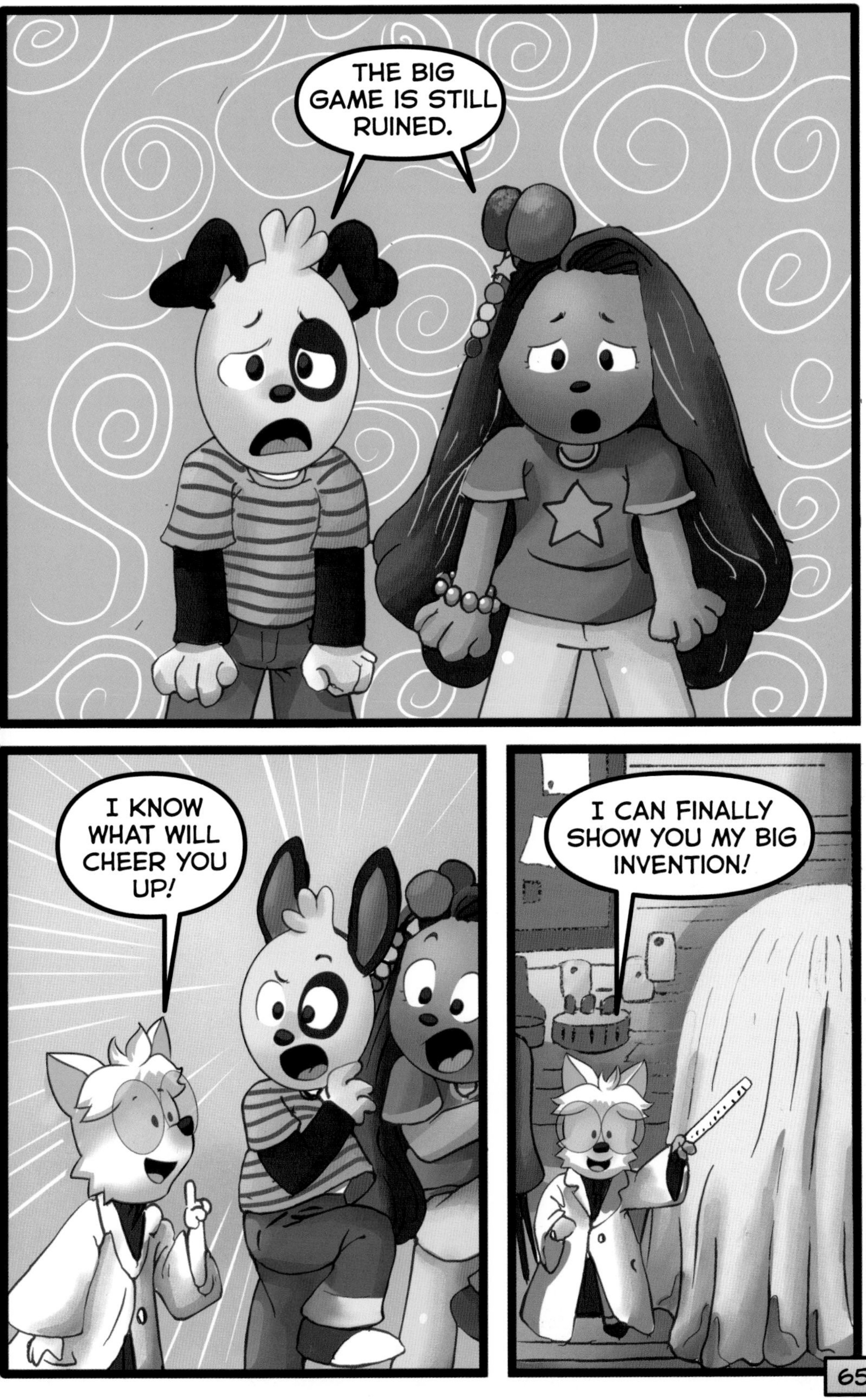
THE BIG GAME IS STILL RUINED.
I KNOW WHAT WILL CHEER YOU UP!
I CAN FINALLY SHOW YOU MY BIG INVENTION!

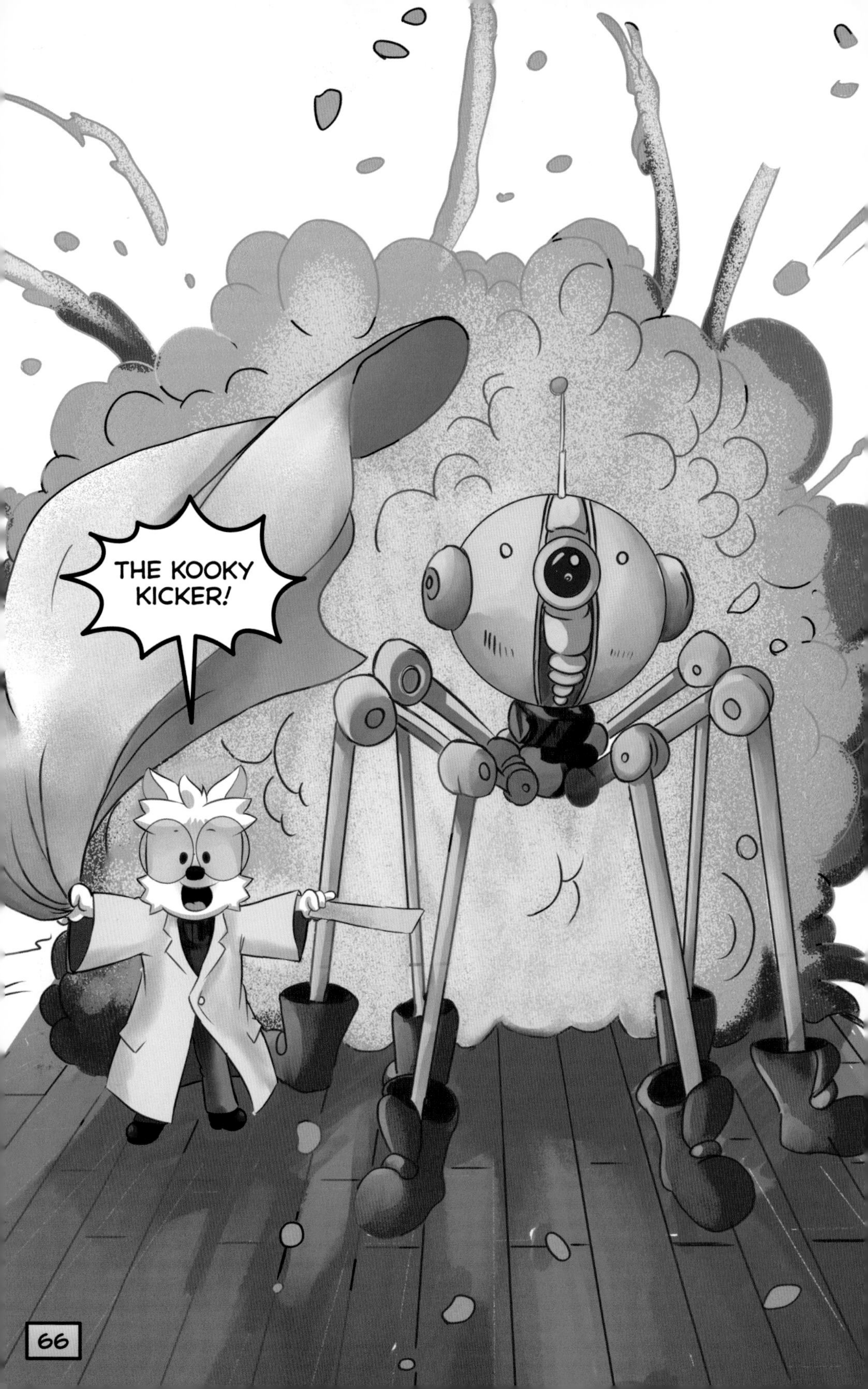
THE KOOKY KICKER!

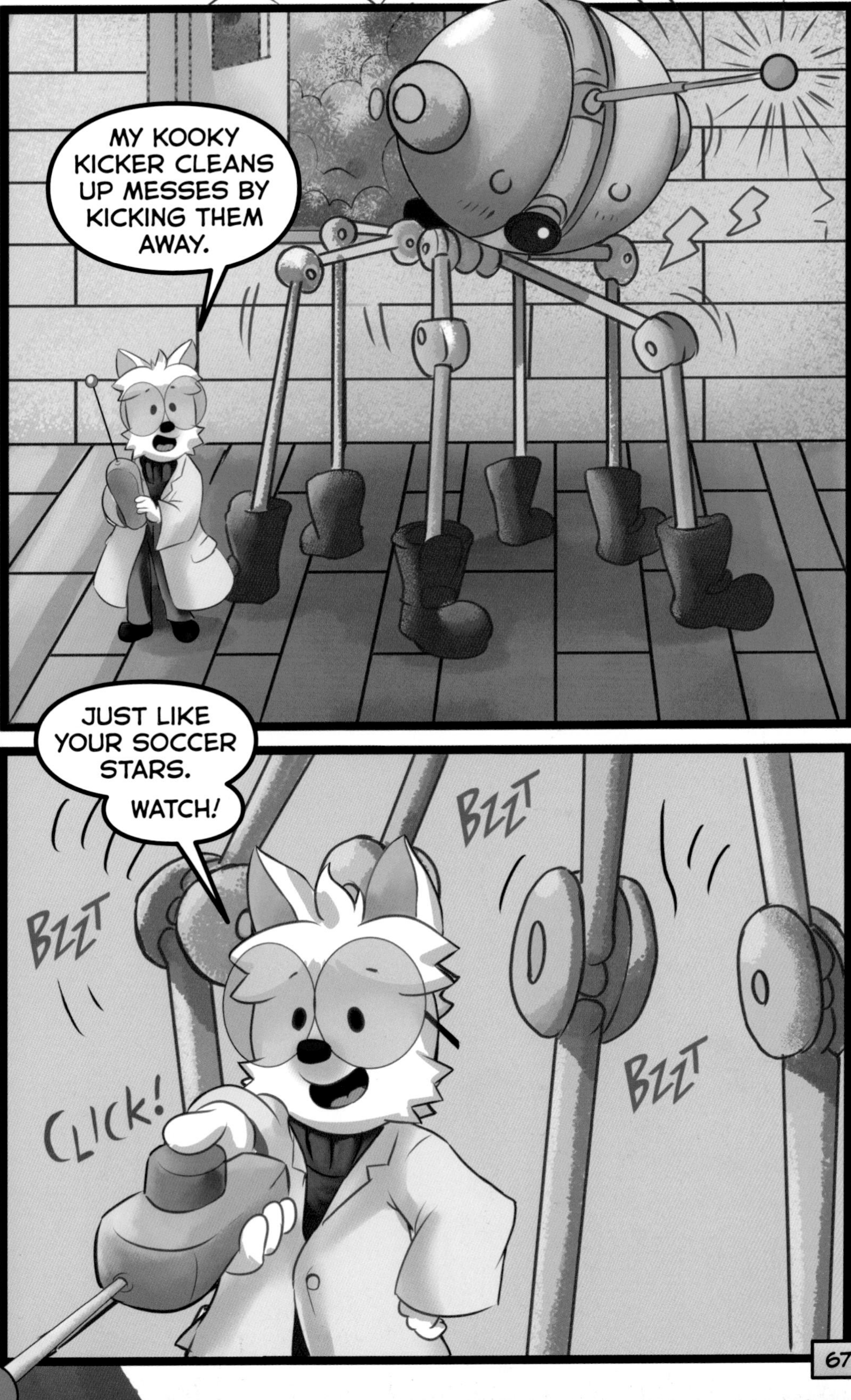
MY KOOKY KICKER CLEANS UP MESSES BY KICKING THEM AWAY.
JUST LIKE YOUR SOCCER STARS.
WATCH!
BZZT
BZZT
BZZT
CLICK!

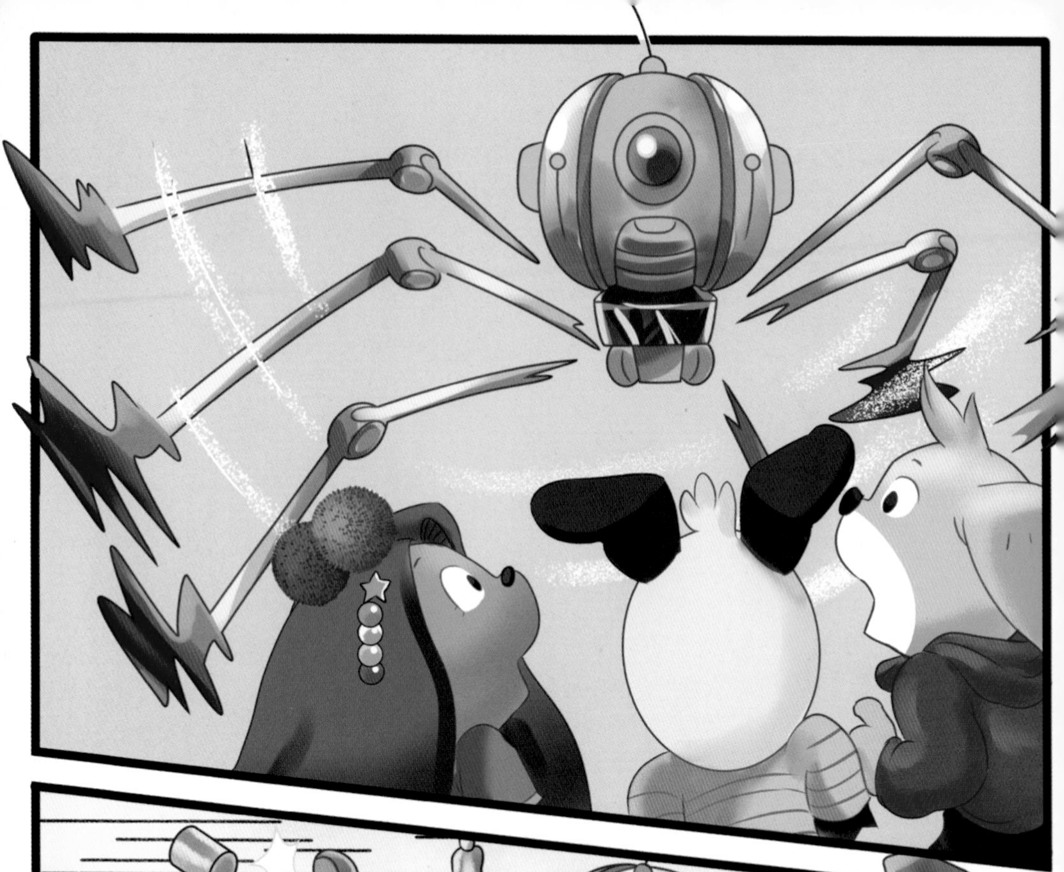

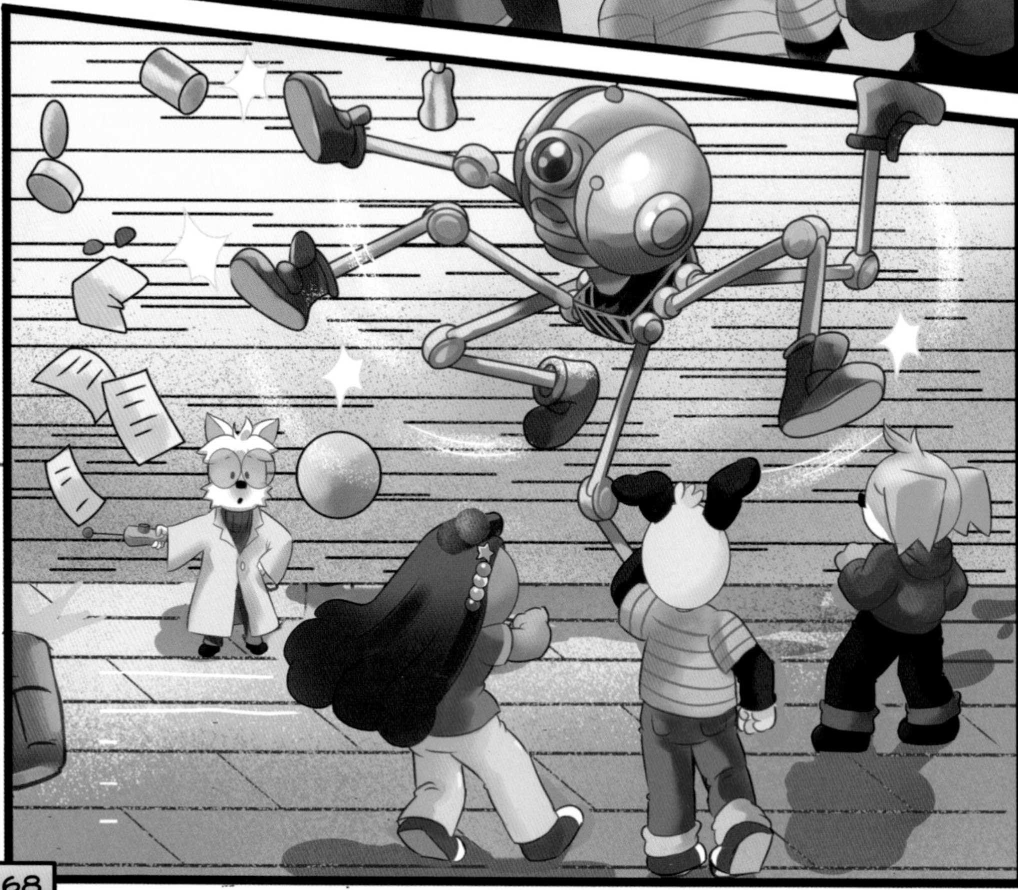

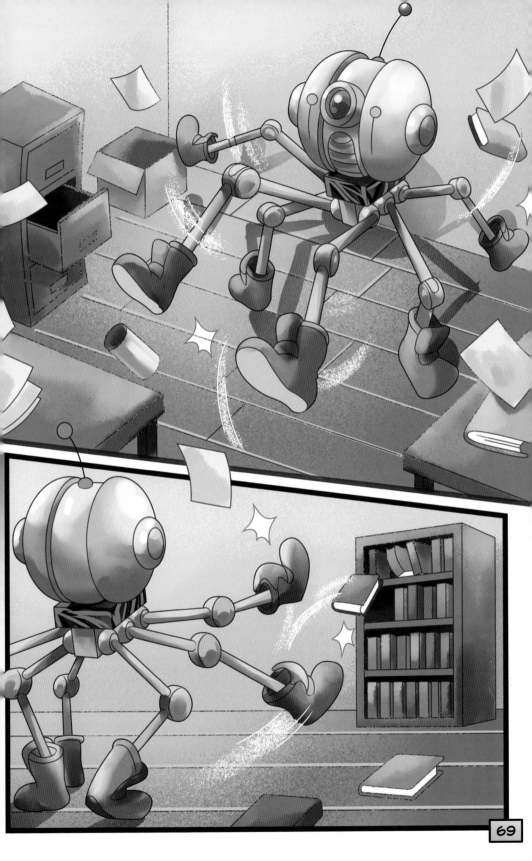

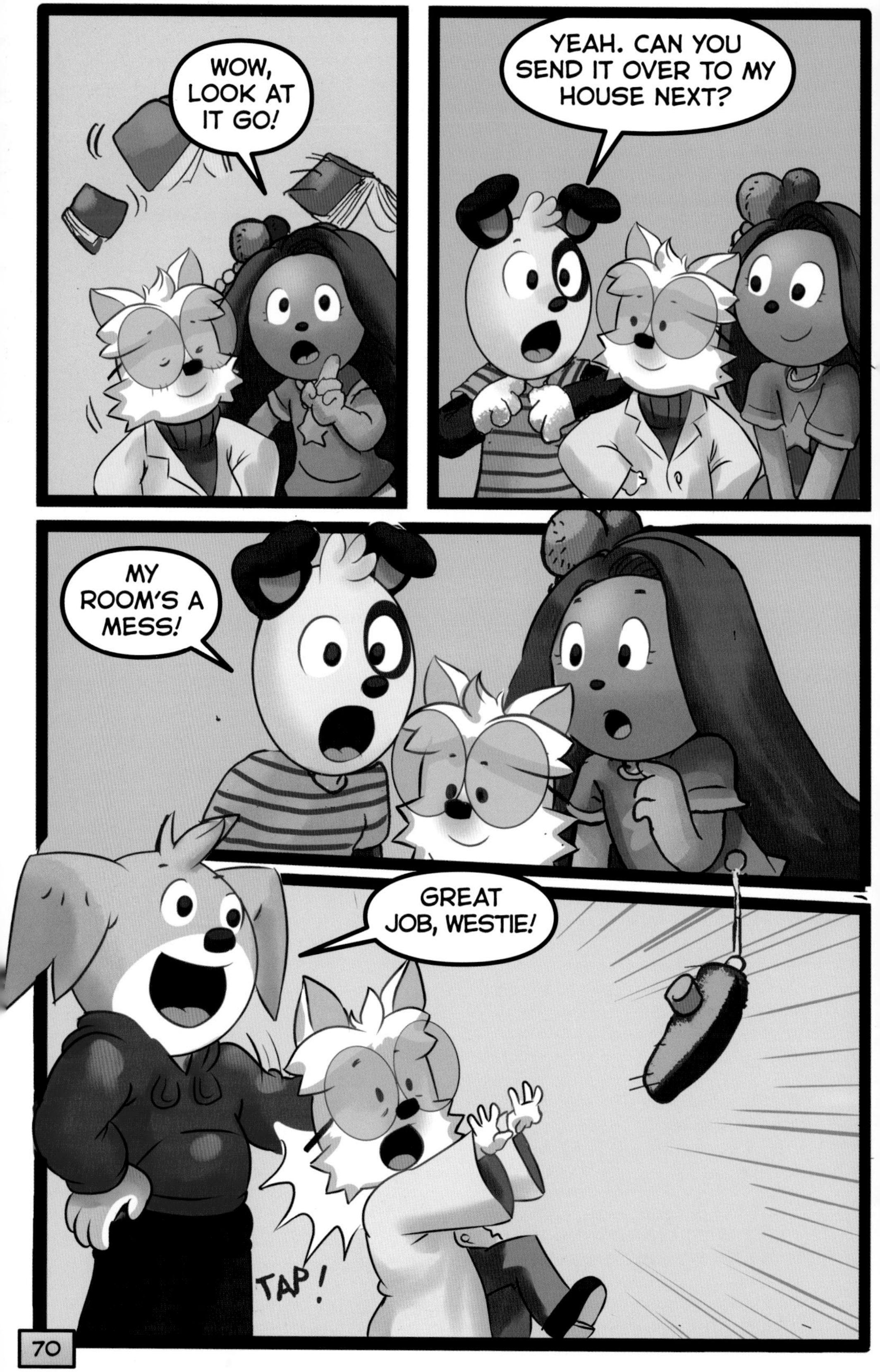
WOW, LOOK AT IT GO!
YEAH. CAN YOU SEND IT OVER TO MY HOUSE NEXT?
MY ROOM'S A MESS!
GREAT JOB, WESTIE!
TAP!

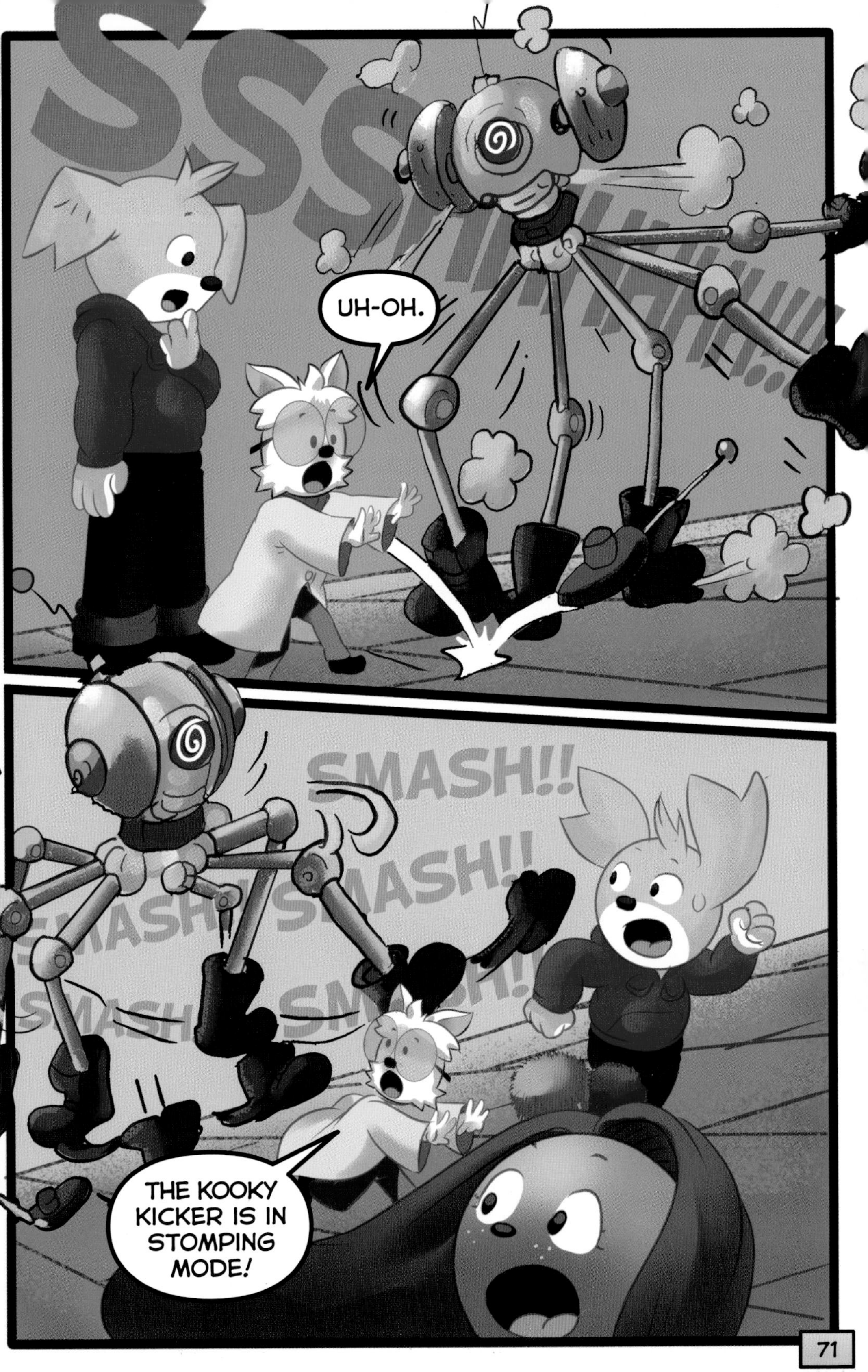
UH-OH.
SMASH!!
SMASH!!
SMASH!!
SMASH!!
SMASH!!
THE KOOKY KICKER IS IN STOMPING MODE!

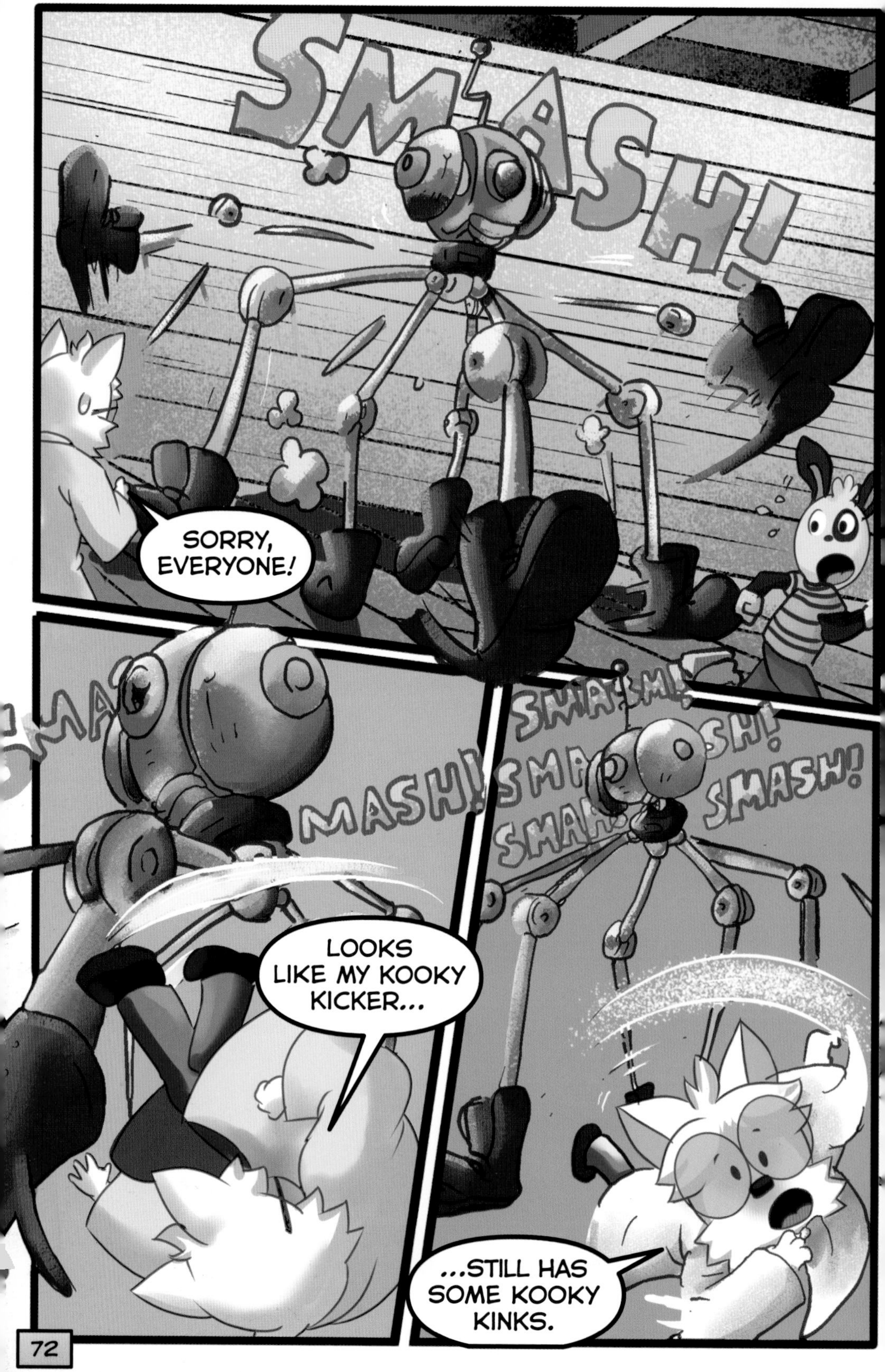
SMASH!
SORRY, EVERYONE!
MASH!
LOOKS LIKE MY KOOKY KICKER...
SMASH!
...STILL HAS SOME KOOKY KINKS.

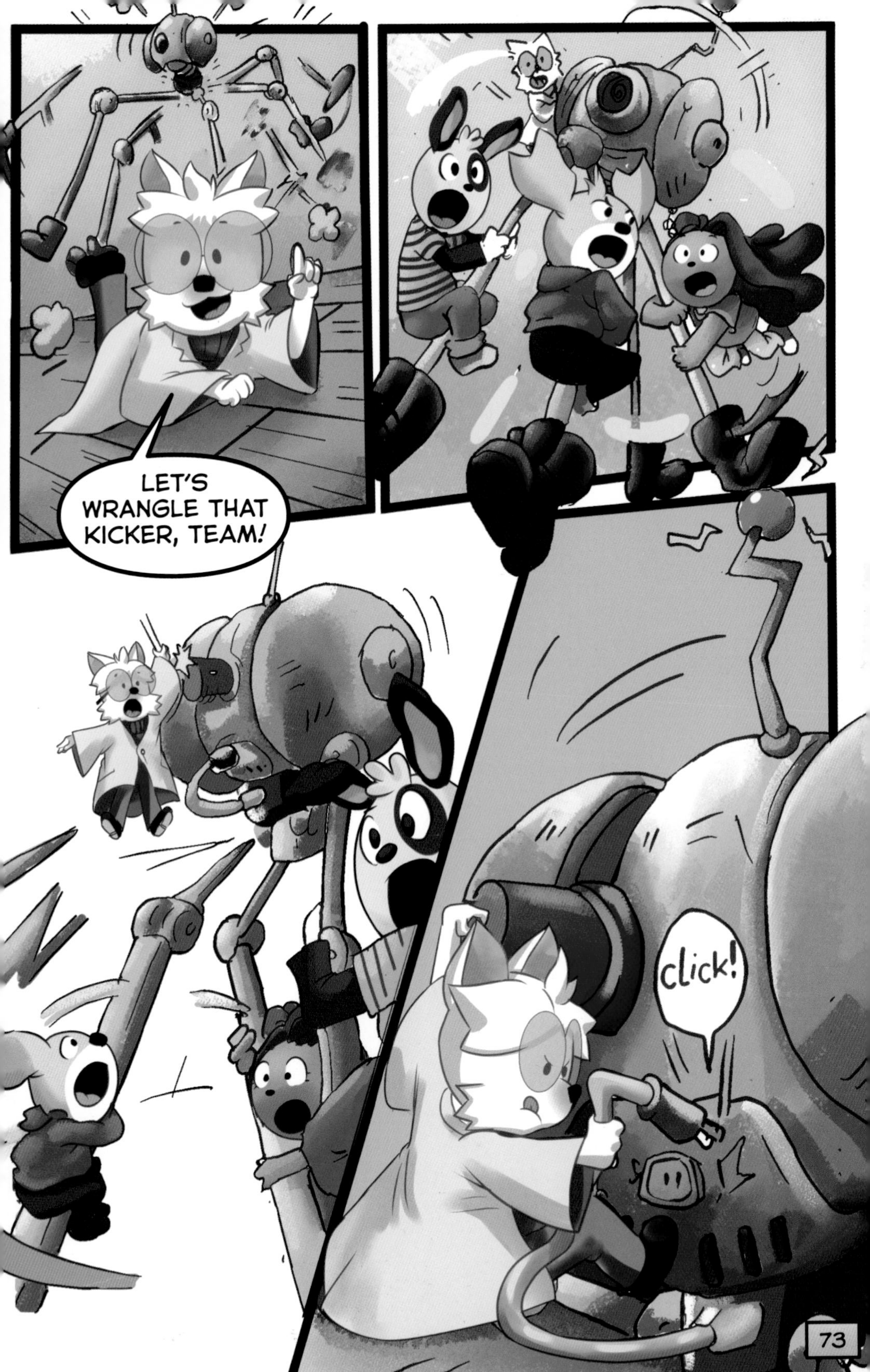
LET'S WRANGLE THAT KICKER, TEAM!
click!

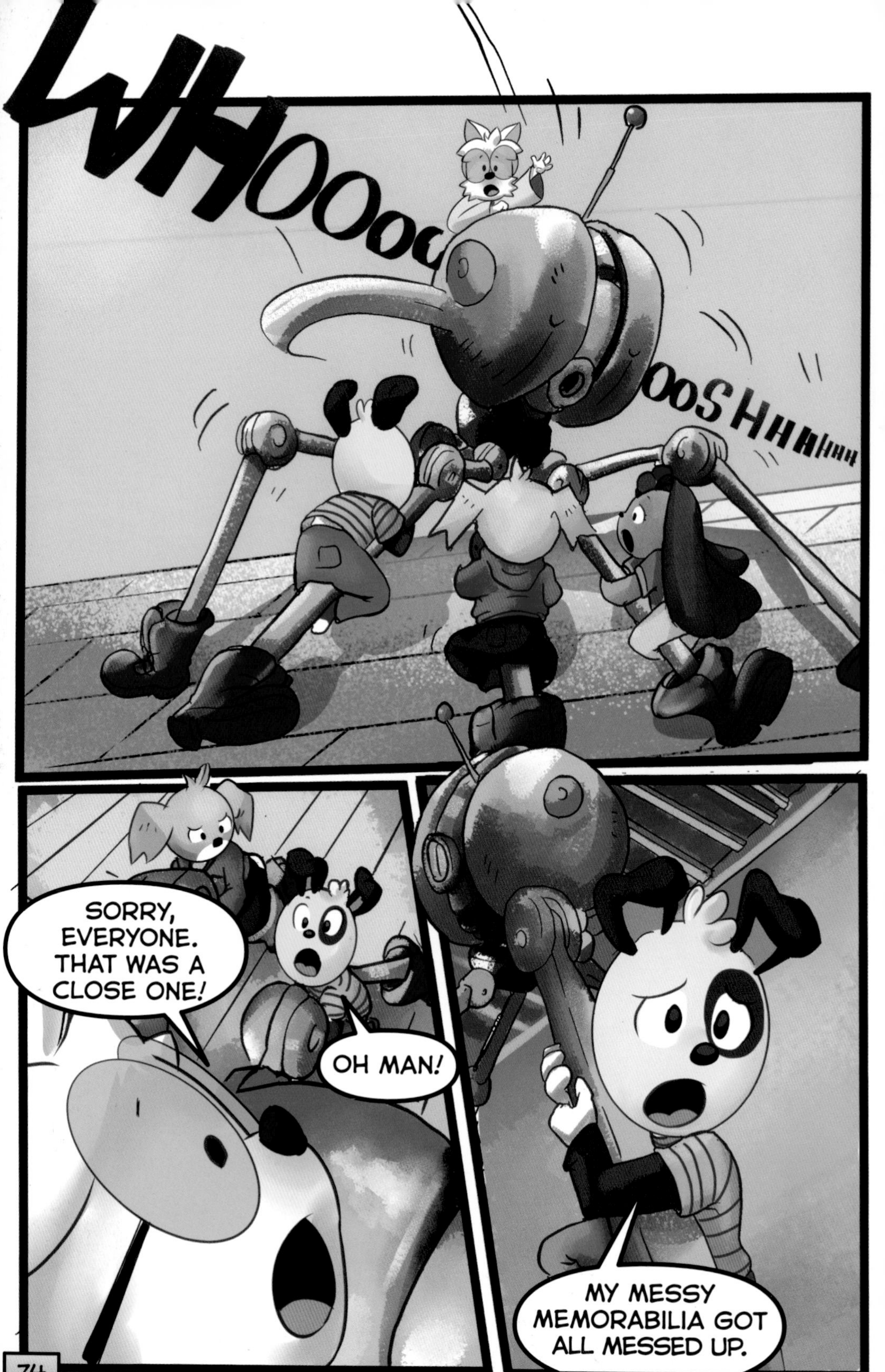
WHOOOOOOOSHHHHHHH
SORRY, EVERYONE. THAT WAS A CLOSE ONE!
OH MAN!
MY MESSY MEMORABILIA GOT ALL MESSED UP.

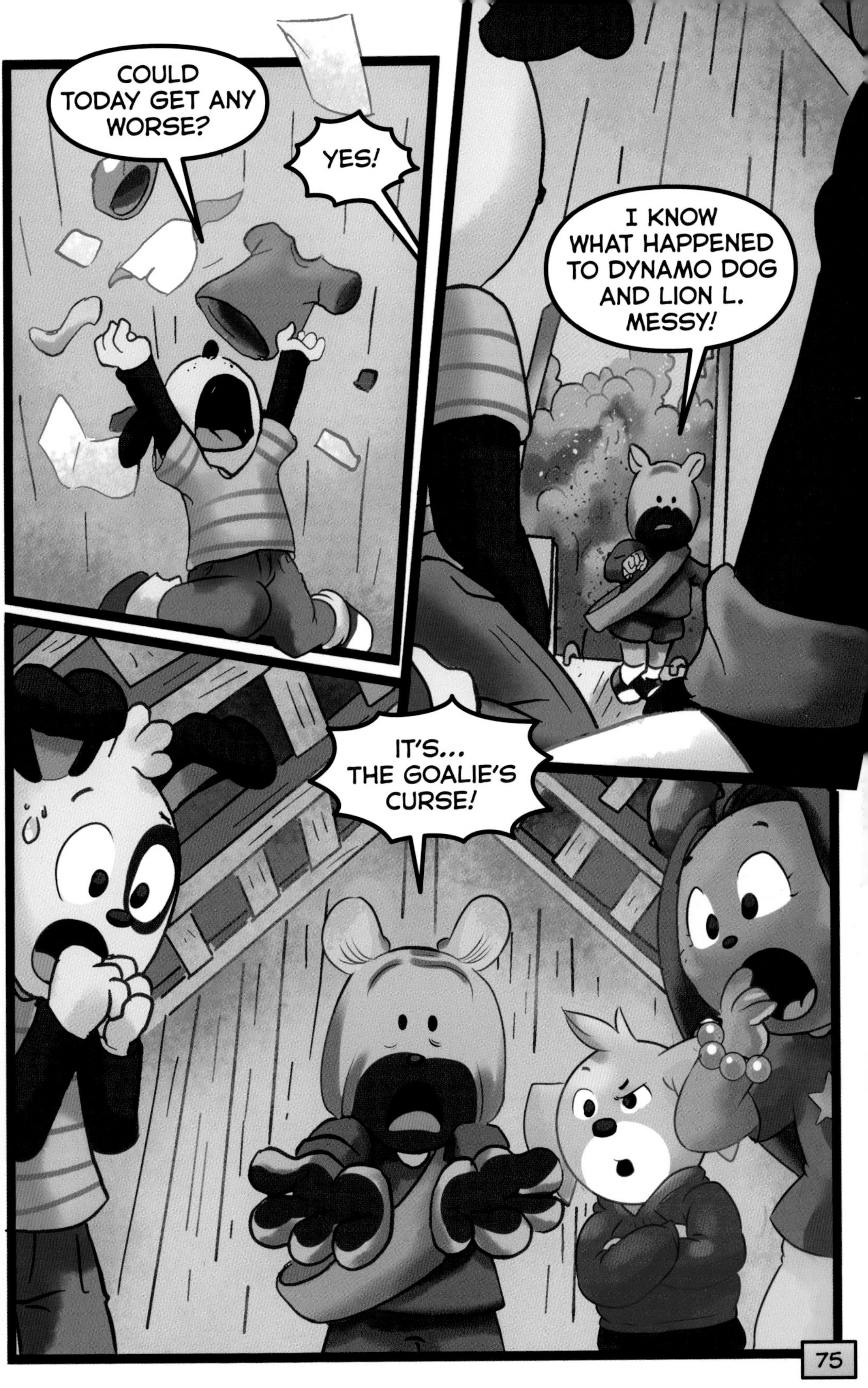
COULD TODAY GET ANY WORSE?
YES!
I KNOW WHAT HAPPENED TO DYNAMO DOG AND LION L. MESSY!
IT'S... THE GOALIE'S CURSE!

CHAPTER 6

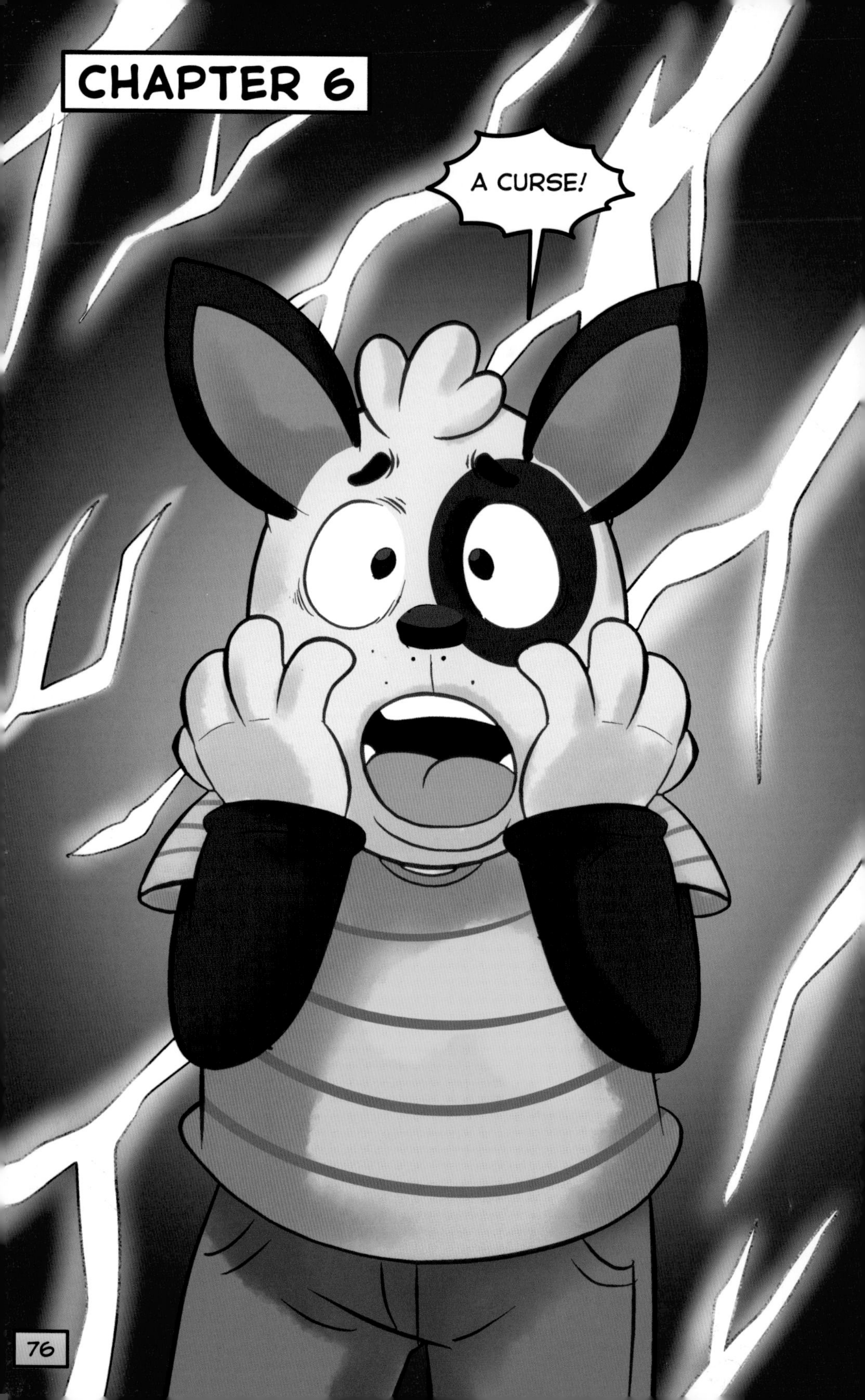
A CURSE!

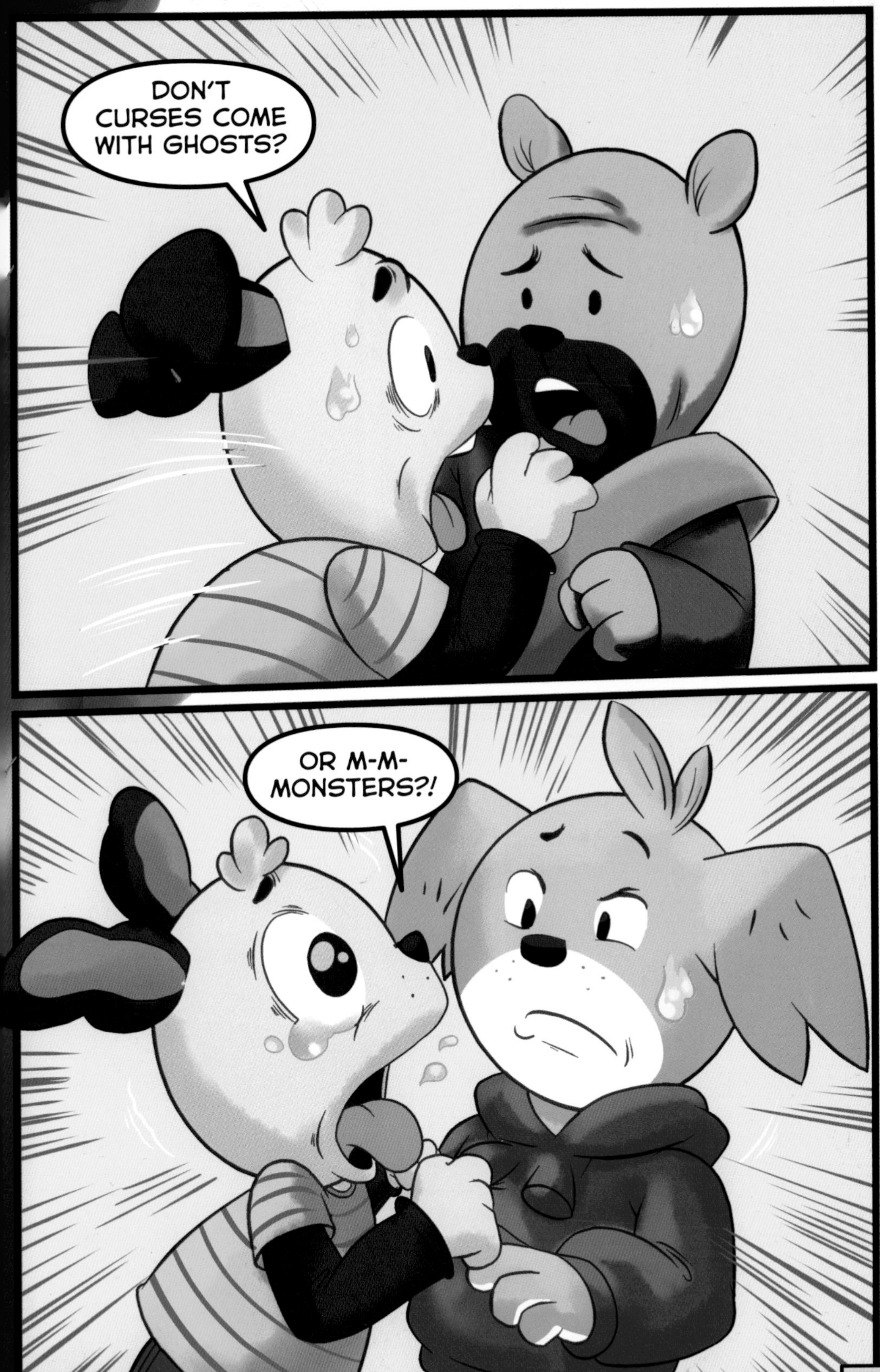
DON'T CURSES COME WITH GHOSTS?
OR M-M-MONSTERS?!

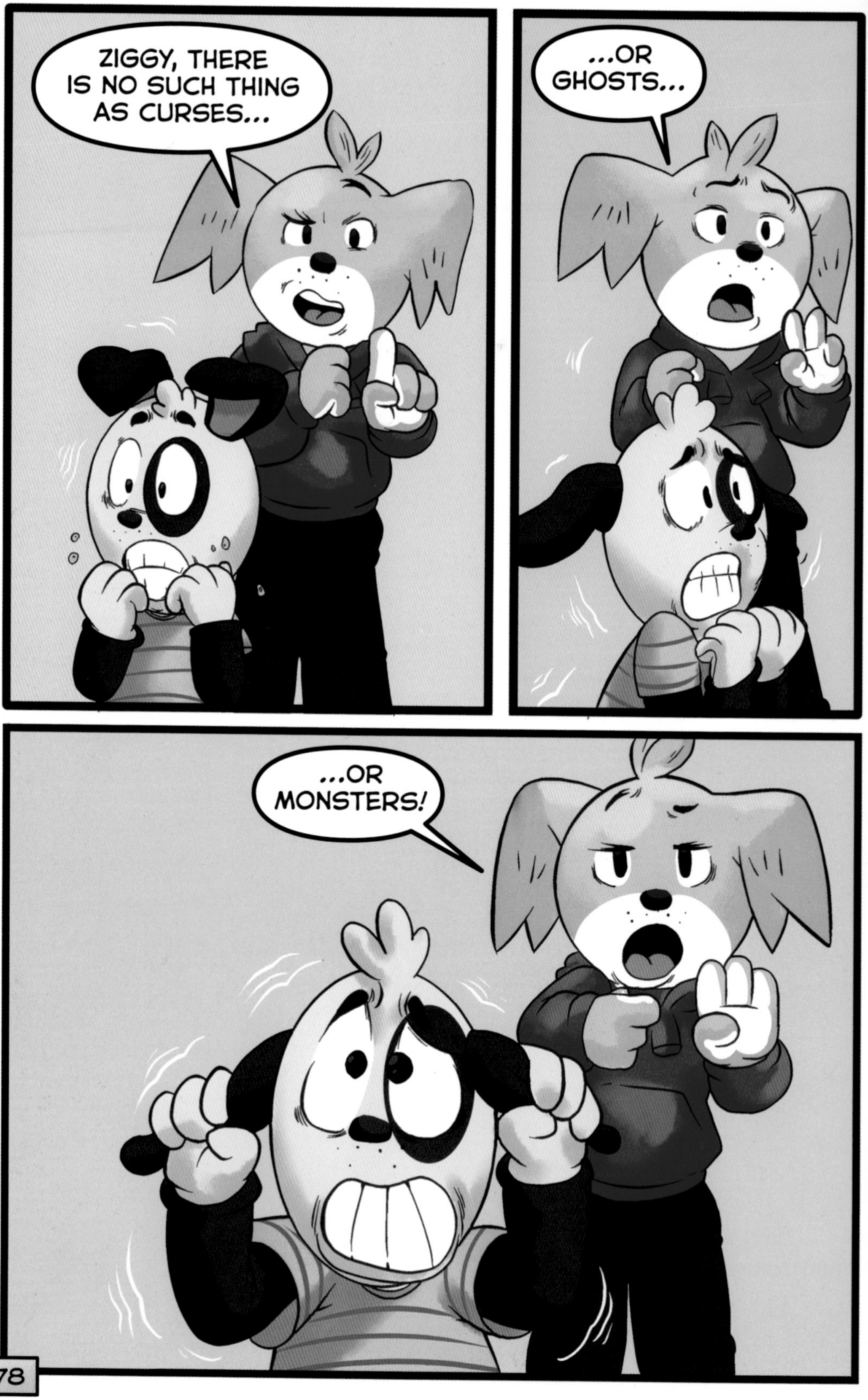
ZIGGY, THERE IS NO SUCH THING AS CURSES...
...OR GHOSTS...
...OR MONSTERS!

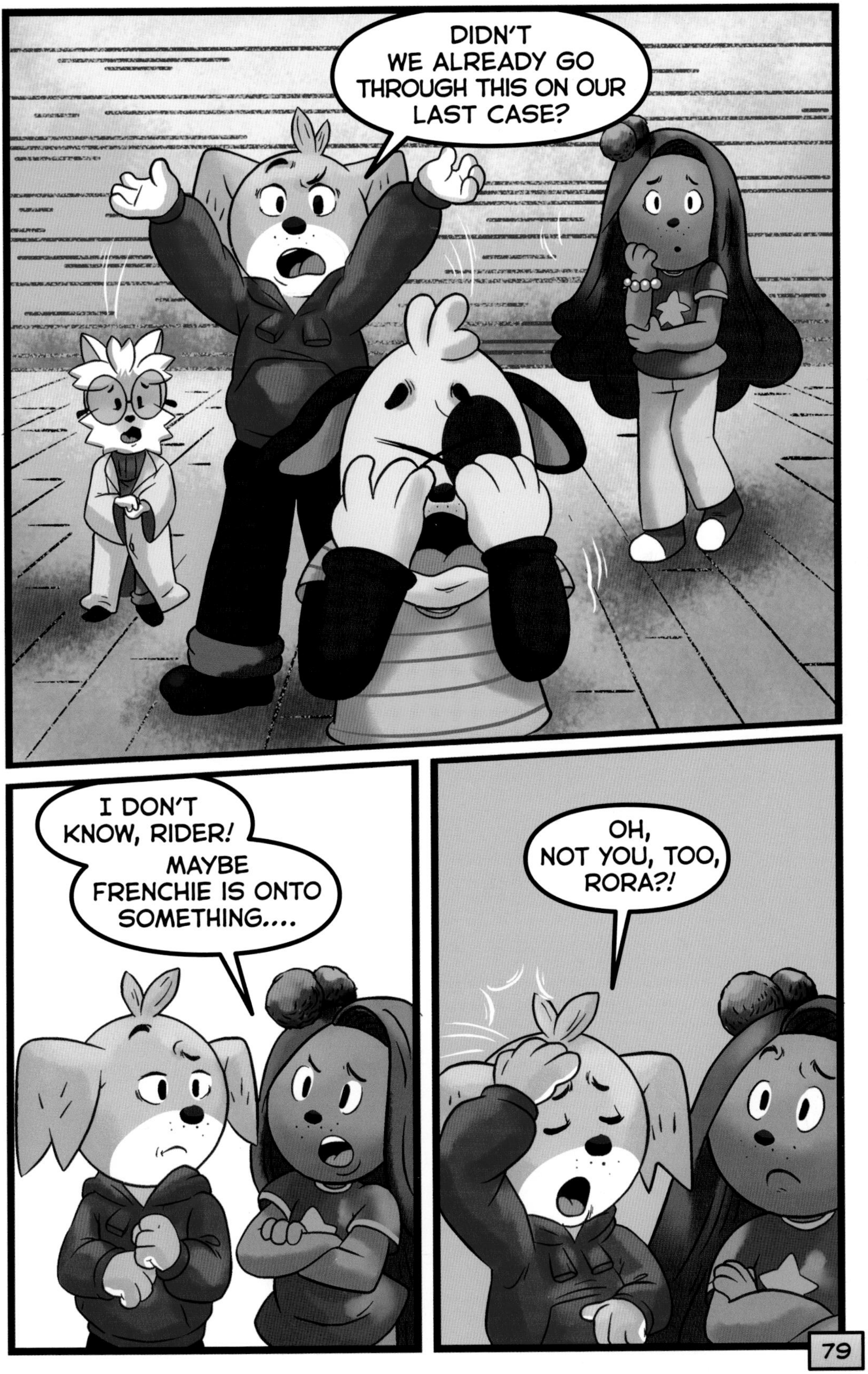
DIDN'T WE ALREADY GO THROUGH THIS ON OUR LAST CASE?
I DON'T KNOW, RIDER!
MAYBE FRENCHIE IS ONTO SOMETHING....
OH, NOT YOU, TOO, RORA?!

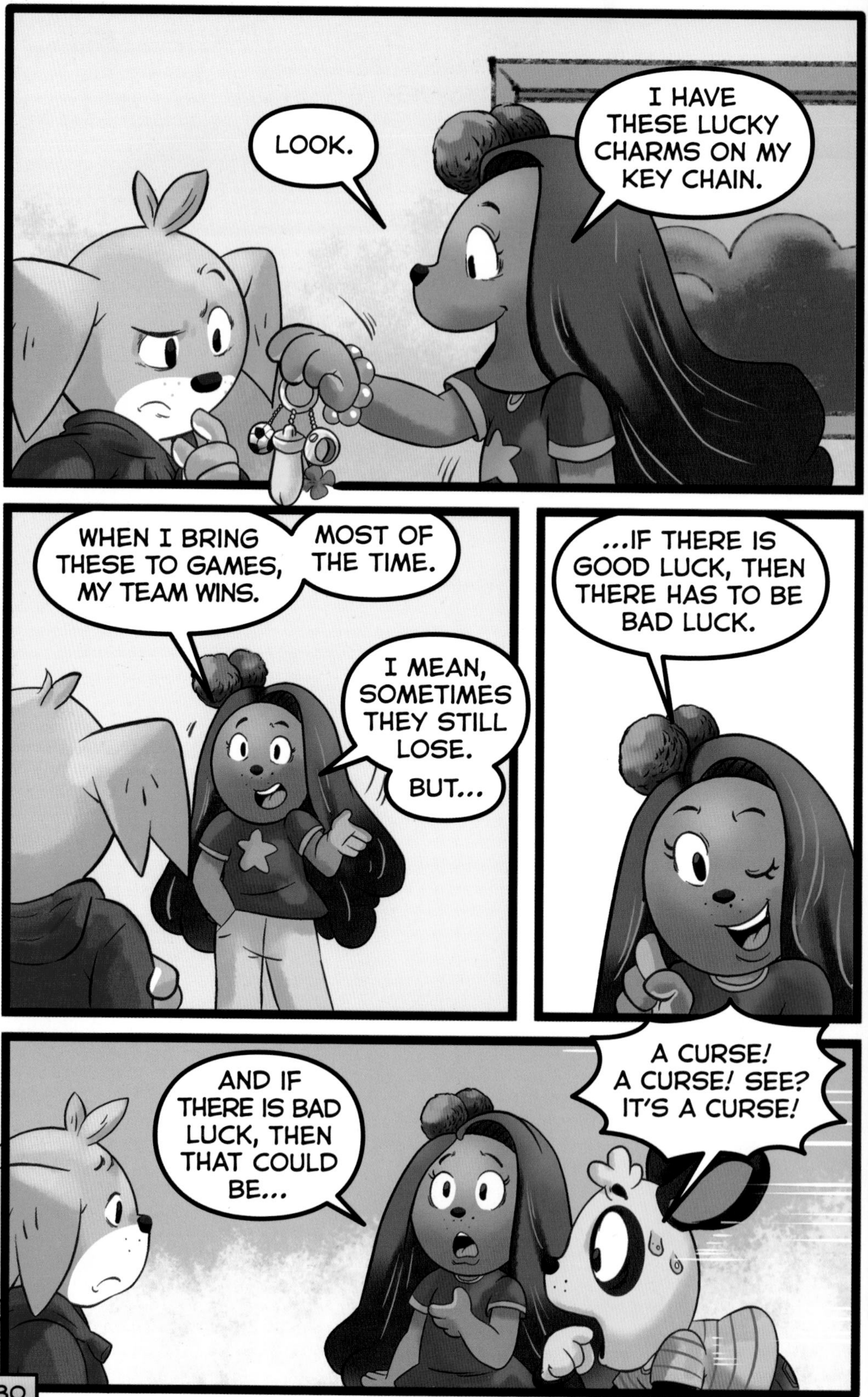
LOOK.
I HAVE THESE LUCKY CHARMS ON MY KEY CHAIN.
WHEN I BRING THESE TO GAMES, MY TEAM WINS.
MOST OF THE TIME.
I MEAN, SOMETIMES THEY STILL LOSE.
BUT...
...IF THERE IS GOOD LUCK, THEN THERE HAS TO BE BAD LUCK.
AND IF THERE IS BAD LUCK, THEN THAT COULD BE...
A CURSE! A CURSE! SEE? IT'S A CURSE!

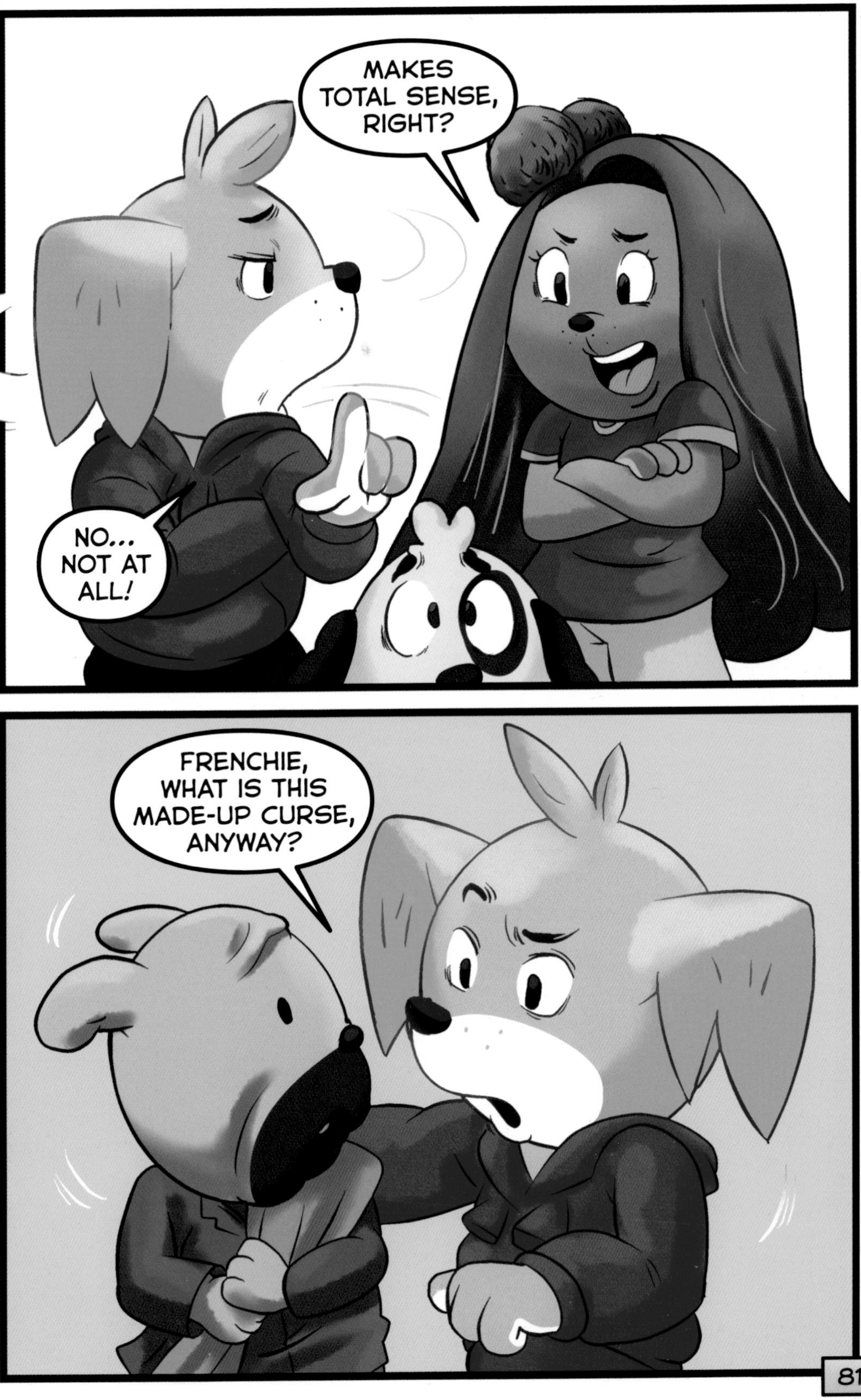
MAKES TOTAL SENSE, RIGHT?
NO... NOT AT ALL!
FRENCHIE, WHAT IS THIS MADE-UP CURSE, ANYWAY?

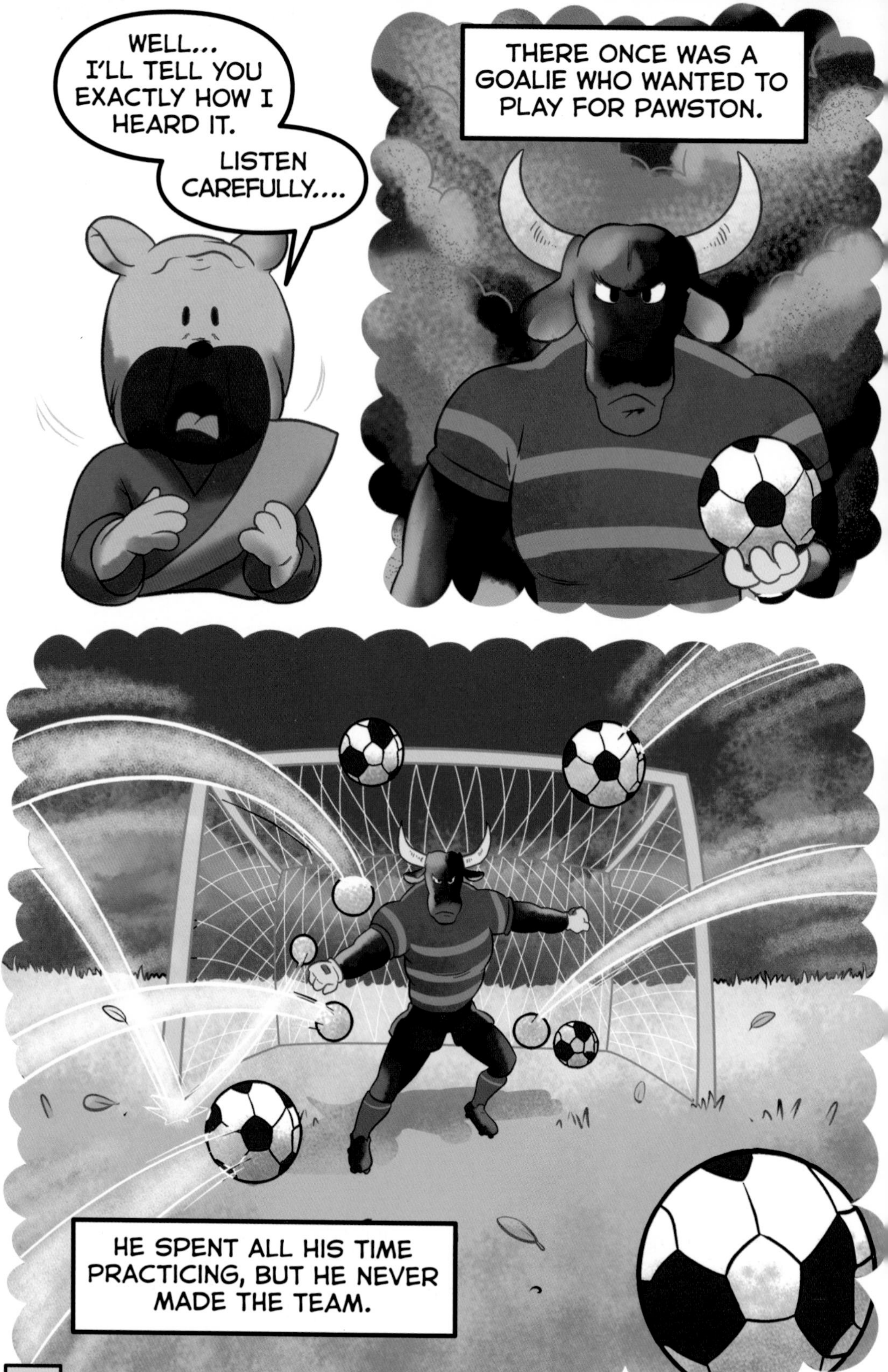
WELL... I'LL TELL YOU EXACTLY HOW I HEARD IT.
LISTEN CAREFULLY....
THERE ONCE WAS A GOALIE WHO WANTED TO PLAY FOR PAWSTON.
HE SPENT ALL HIS TIME PRACTICING, BUT HE NEVER MADE THE TEAM.

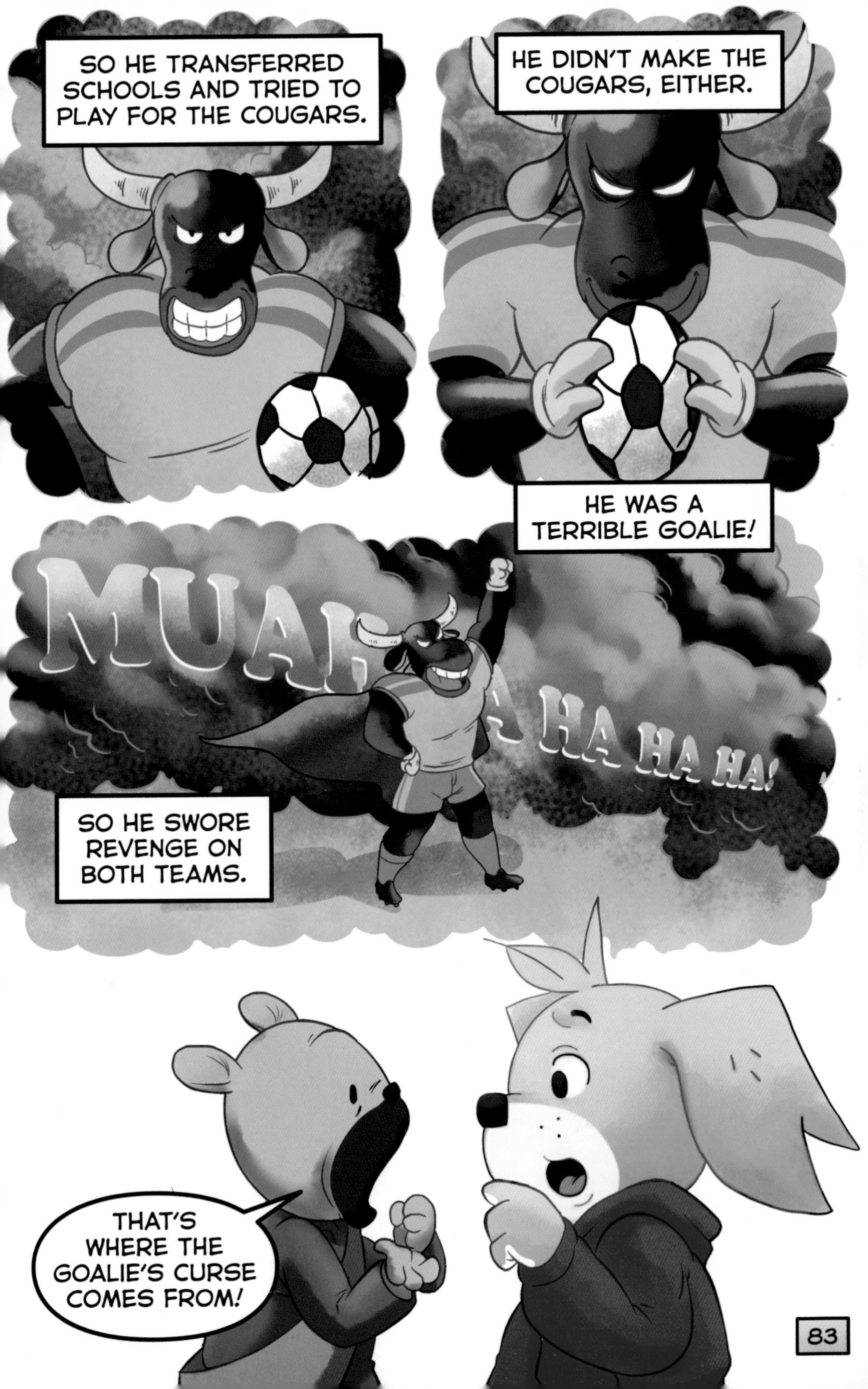
SO HE TRANSFERRED SCHOOLS AND TRIED TO PLAY FOR THE COUGARS.
HE DIDN'T MAKE THE COUGARS, EITHER.
HE WAS A TERRIBLE GOALIE!
MUAHA HA HA HA HA!
SO HE SWORE REVENGE ON BOTH TEAMS.
THAT'S WHERE THE GOALIE'S CURSE COMES FROM!

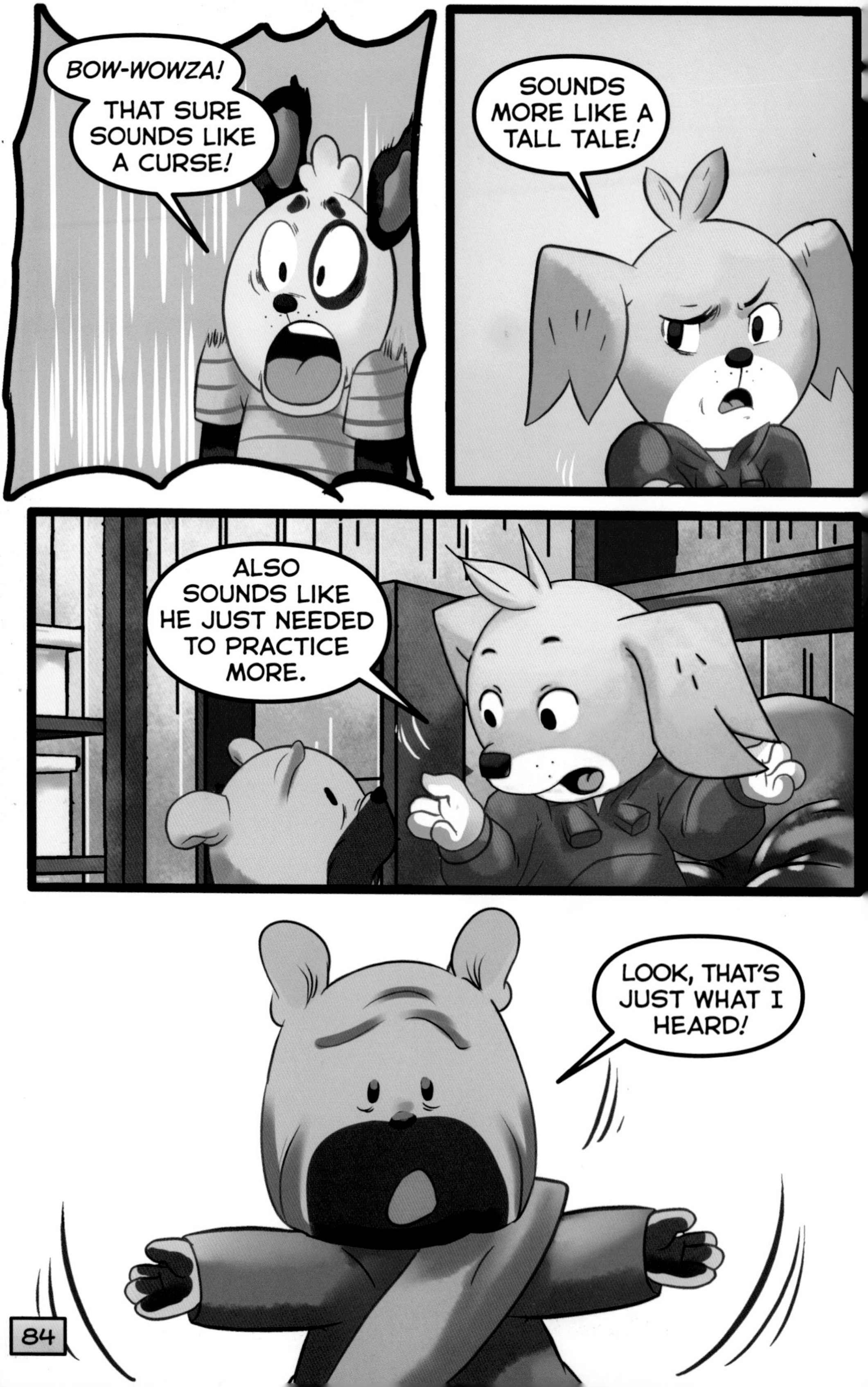
BOW-WOWZA! THAT SURE SOUNDS LIKE A CURSE!
SOUNDS MORE LIKE A TALL TALE!
ALSO SOUNDS LIKE HE JUST NEEDED TO PRACTICE MORE.
LOOK, THAT'S JUST WHAT I HEARD!

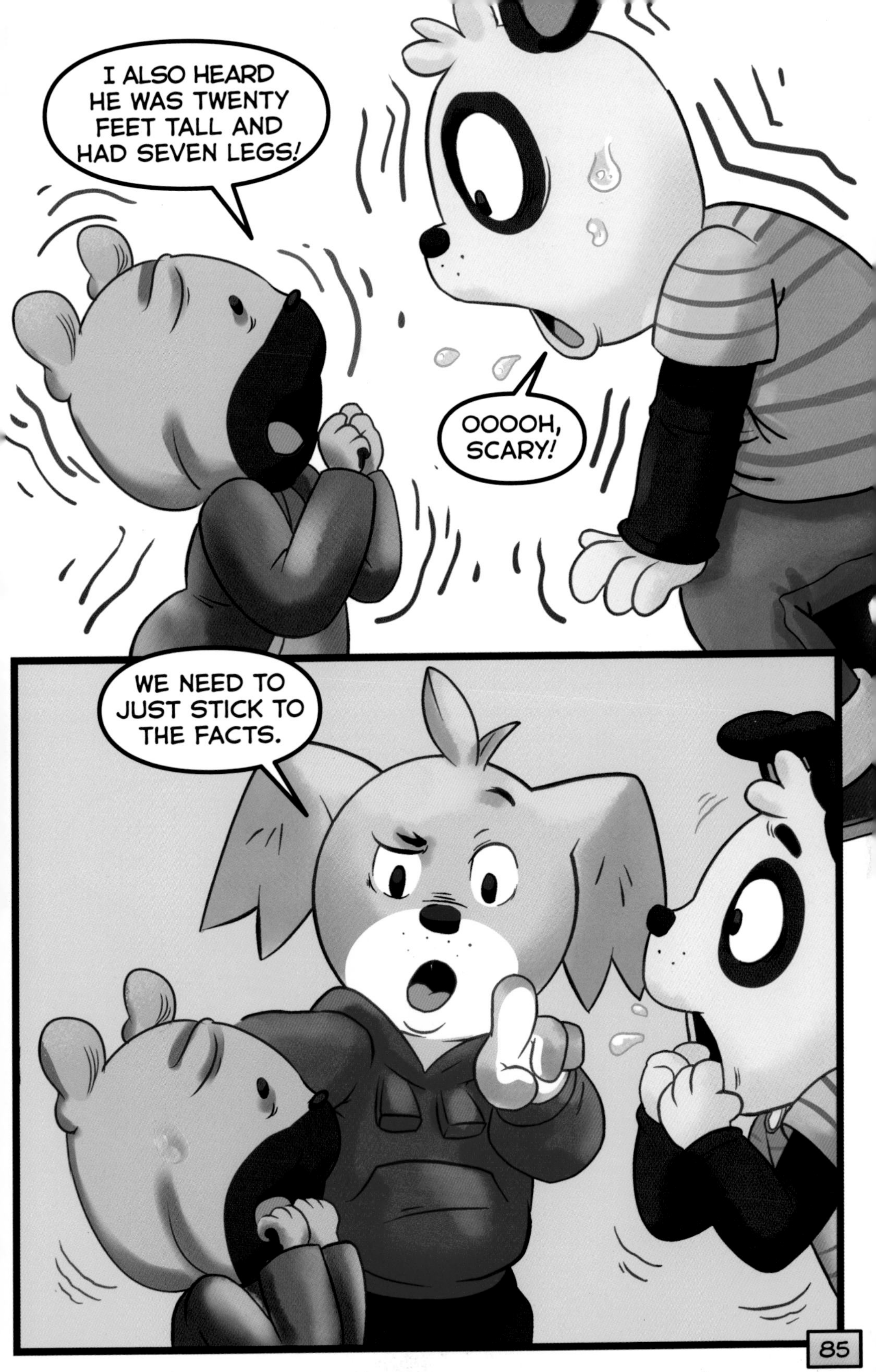
I ALSO HEARD HE WAS TWENTY FEET TALL AND HAD SEVEN LEGS!
OOOOH, SCARY!
WE NEED TO JUST STICK TO THE FACTS.

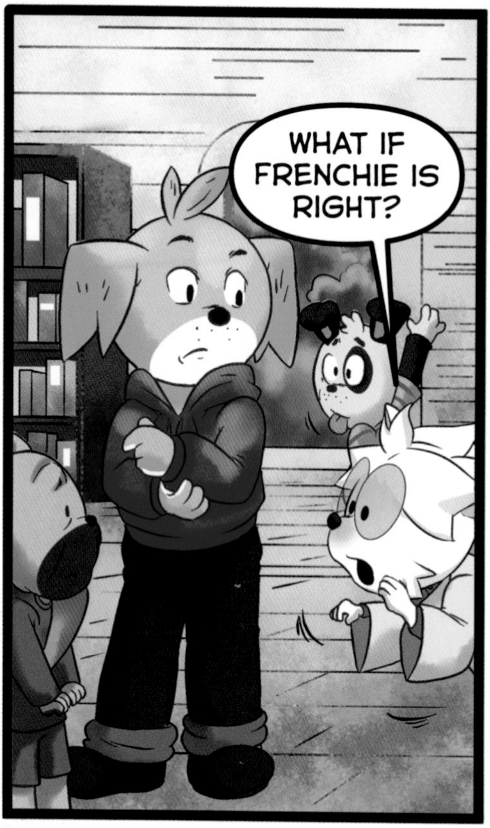
WHAT IF FRENCHIE IS RIGHT?

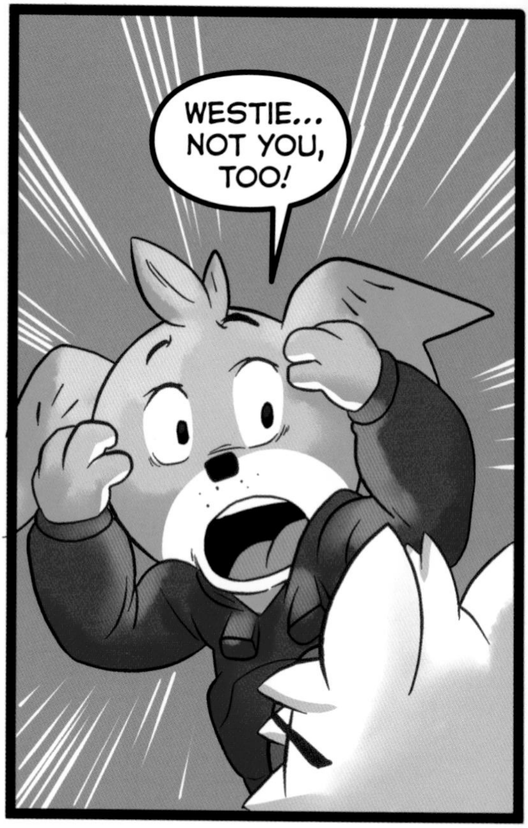
WESTIE... NOT YOU, TOO!

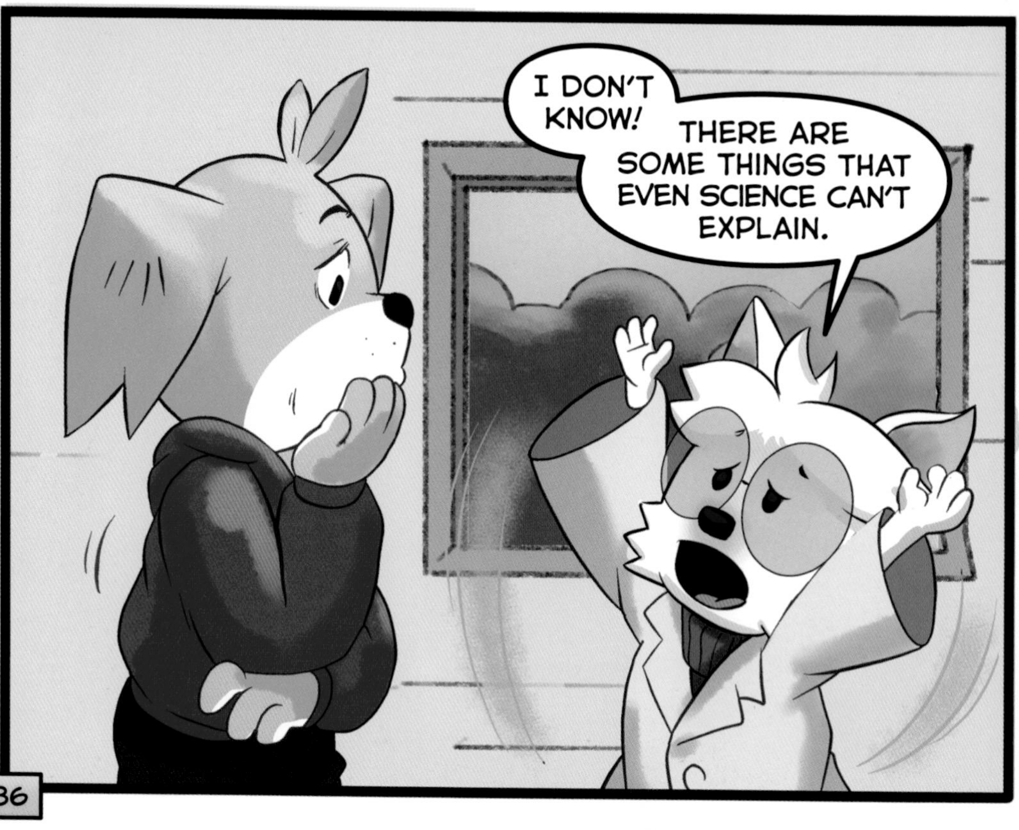
I DON'T KNOW!
THERE ARE SOME THINGS THAT EVEN SCIENCE CAN'T EXPLAIN.

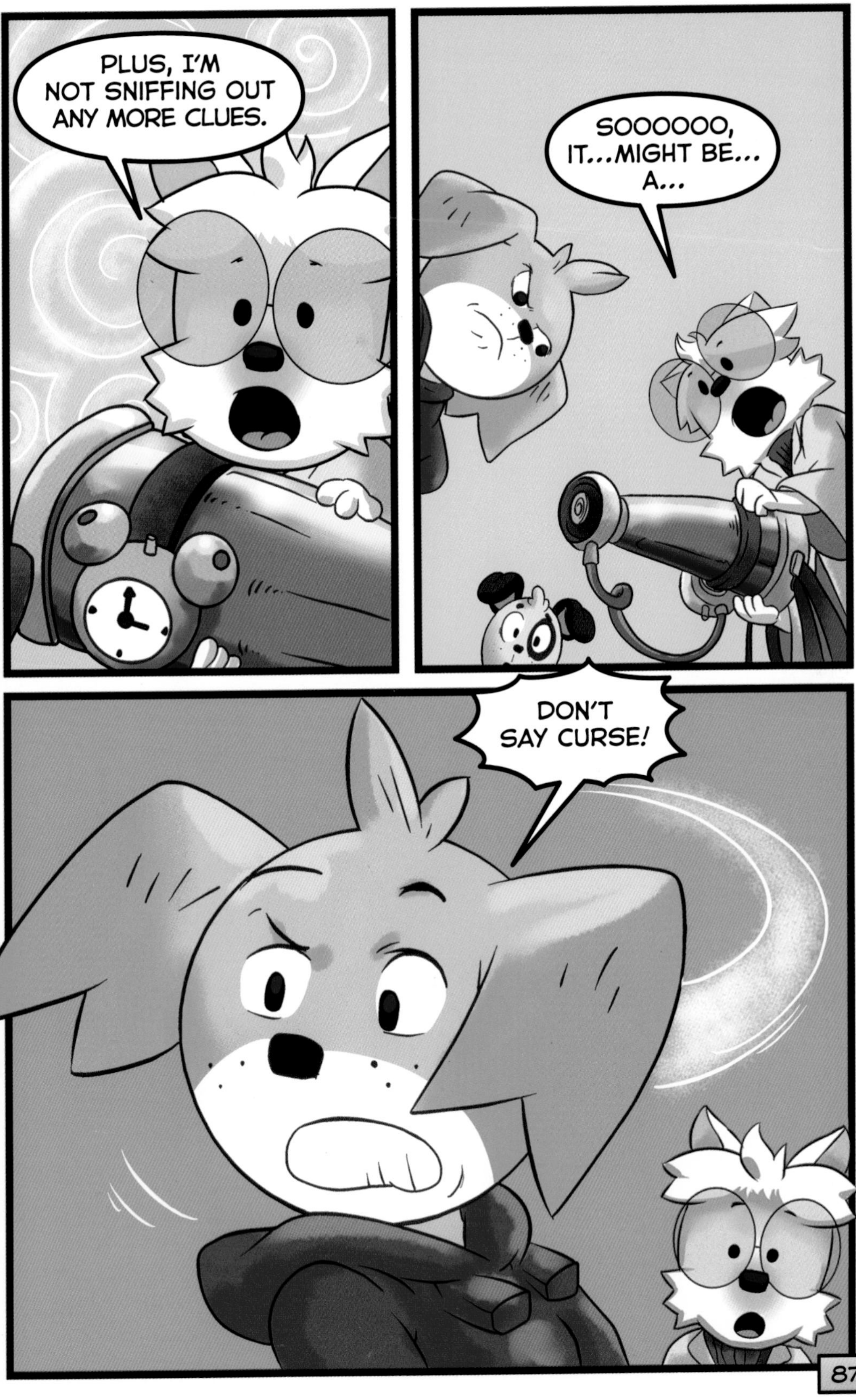
PLUS, I'M NOT SNIFFING OUT ANY MORE CLUES.
SOOOOOO, IT...MIGHT BE... A...
DON'T SAY CURSE!

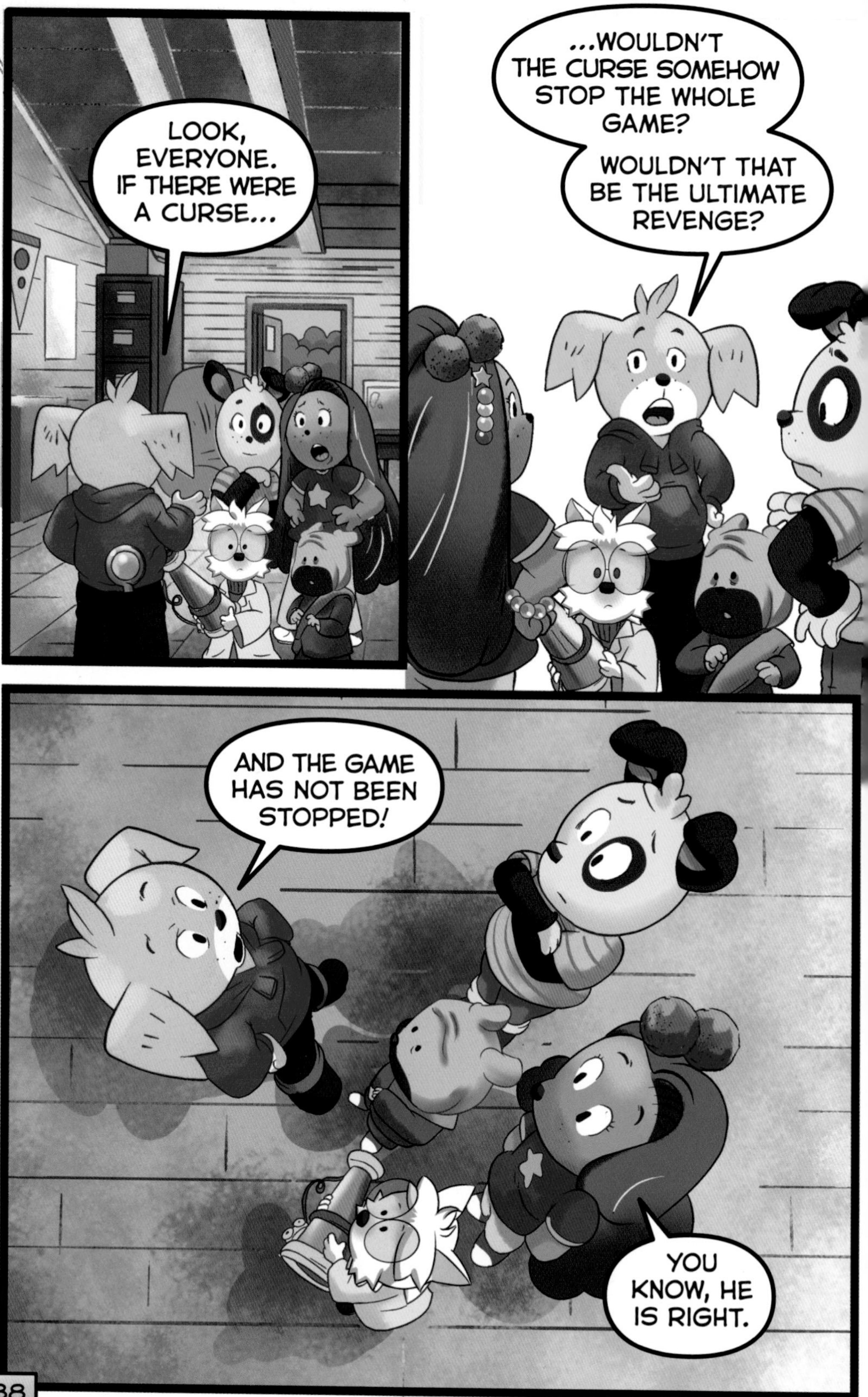
LOOK, EVERYONE. IF THERE WERE A CURSE...
...WOULDN'T THE CURSE SOMEHOW STOP THE WHOLE GAME?
WOULDN'T THAT BE THE ULTIMATE REVENGE?
AND THE GAME HAS NOT BEEN STOPPED!
YOU KNOW, HE IS RIGHT.

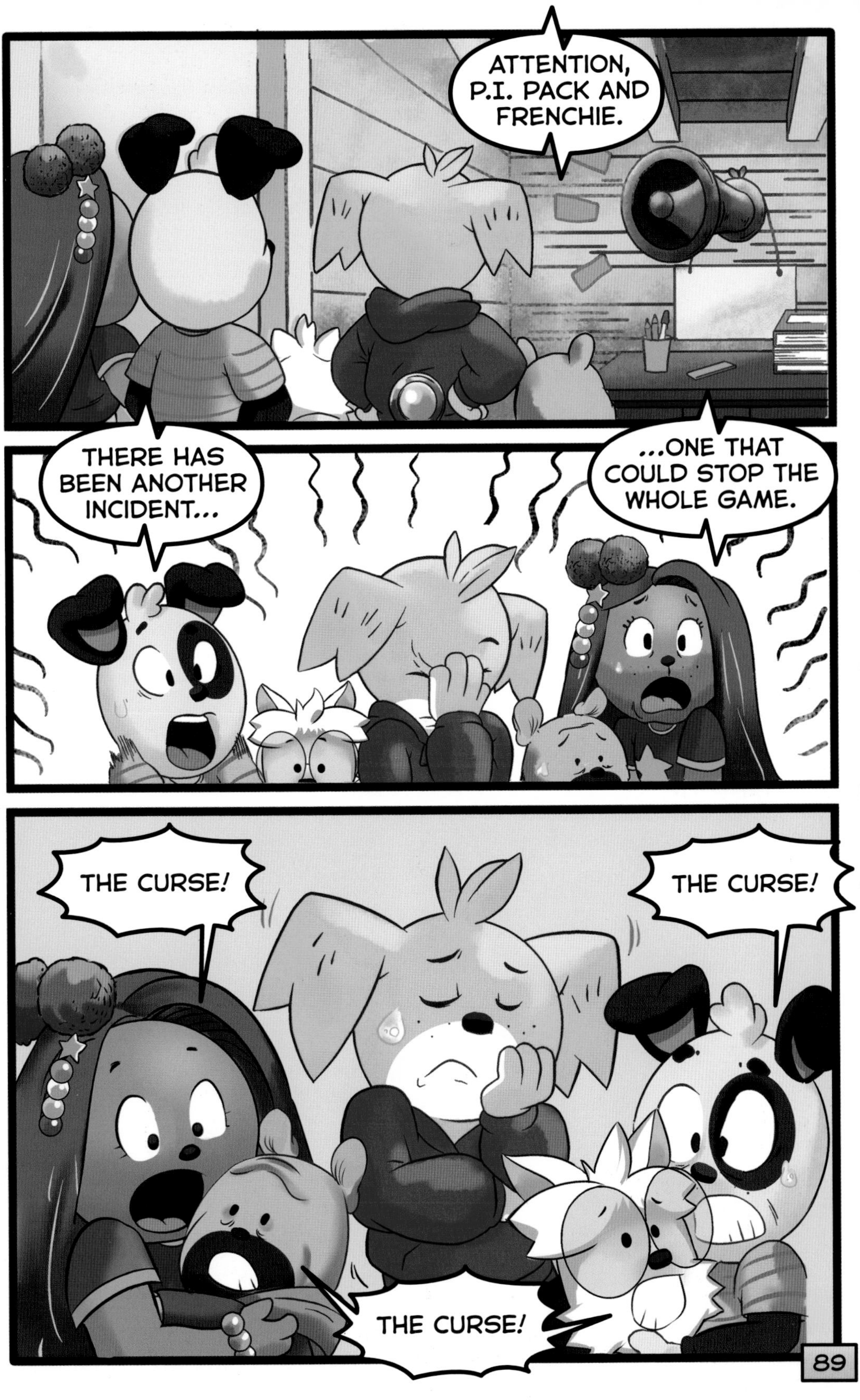
ATTENTION, P.I. PACK AND FRENCHIE.
THERE HAS BEEN ANOTHER INCIDENT...
...ONE THAT COULD STOP THE WHOLE GAME.
THE CURSE!
THE CURSE!
THE CURSE!

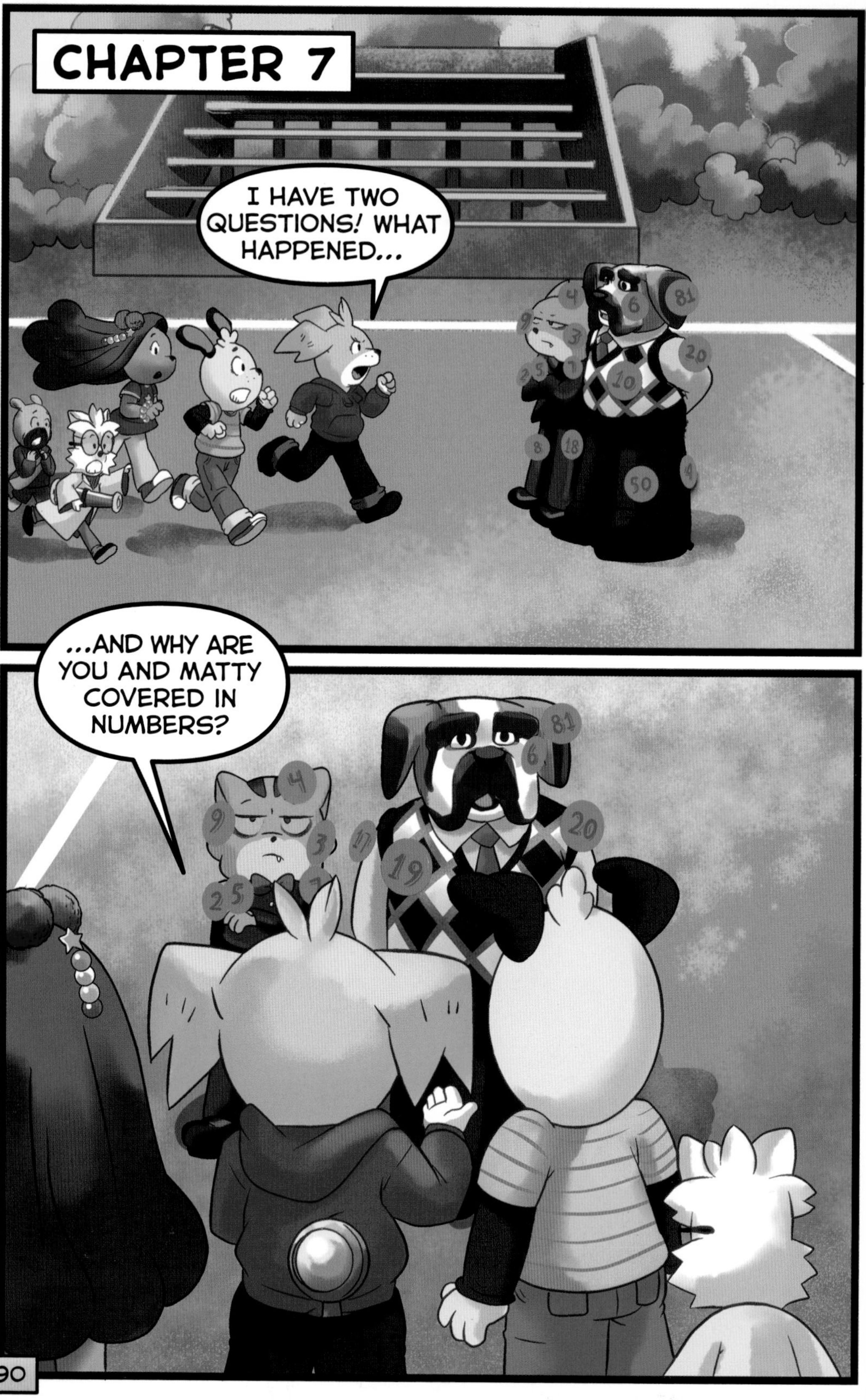
CHAPTER 7
I HAVE TWO QUESTIONS! WHAT HAPPENED...
...AND WHY ARE YOU AND MATTY COVERED IN NUMBERS?

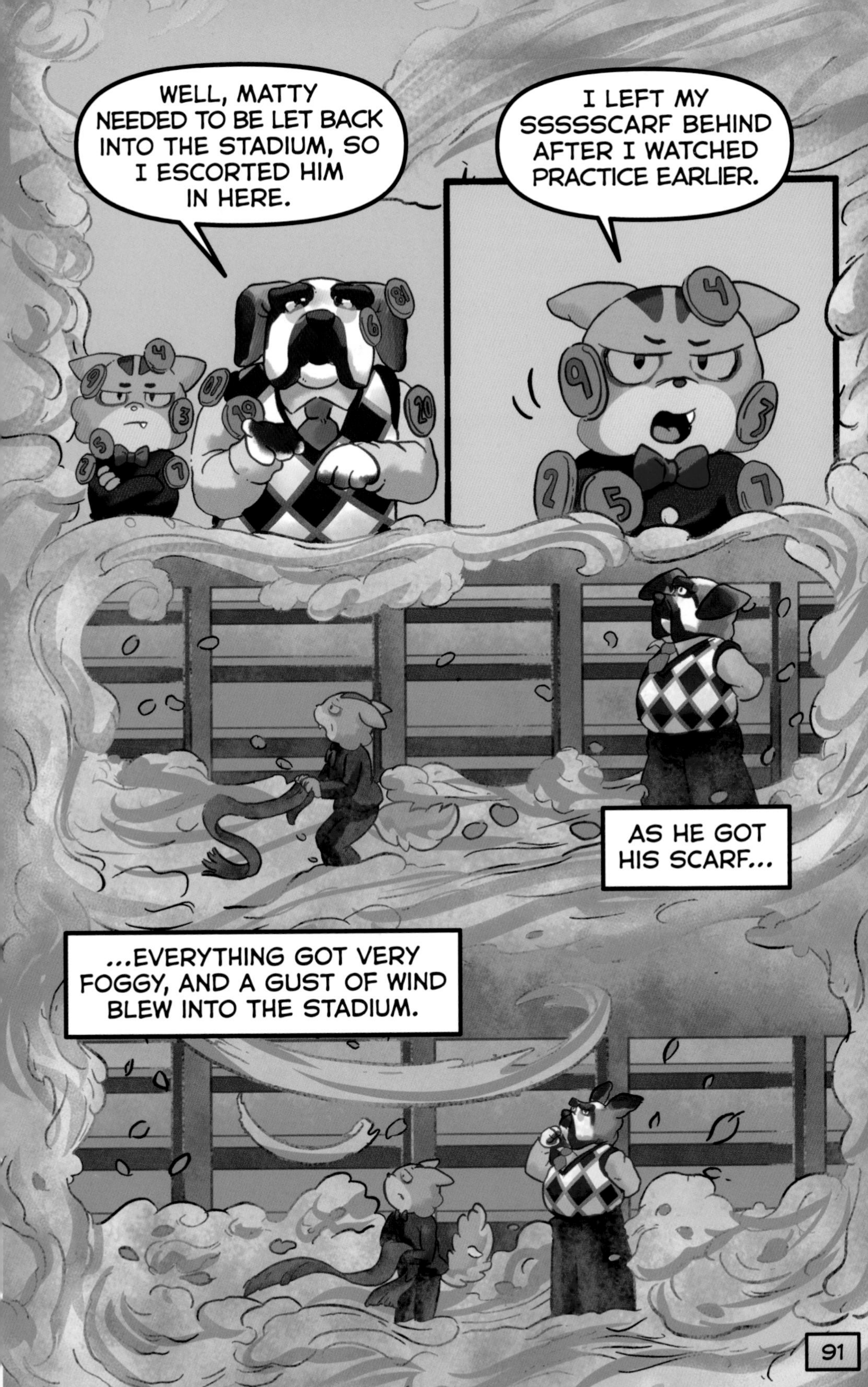
WELL, MATTY NEEDED TO BE LET BACK INTO THE STADIUM, SO I ESCORTED HIM IN HERE.
I LEFT MY SSSSSCARF BEHIND AFTER I WATCHED PRACTICE EARLIER.
AS HE GOT HIS SCARF...
...EVERYTHING GOT VERY FOGGY, AND A GUST OF WIND BLEW INTO THE STADIUM.

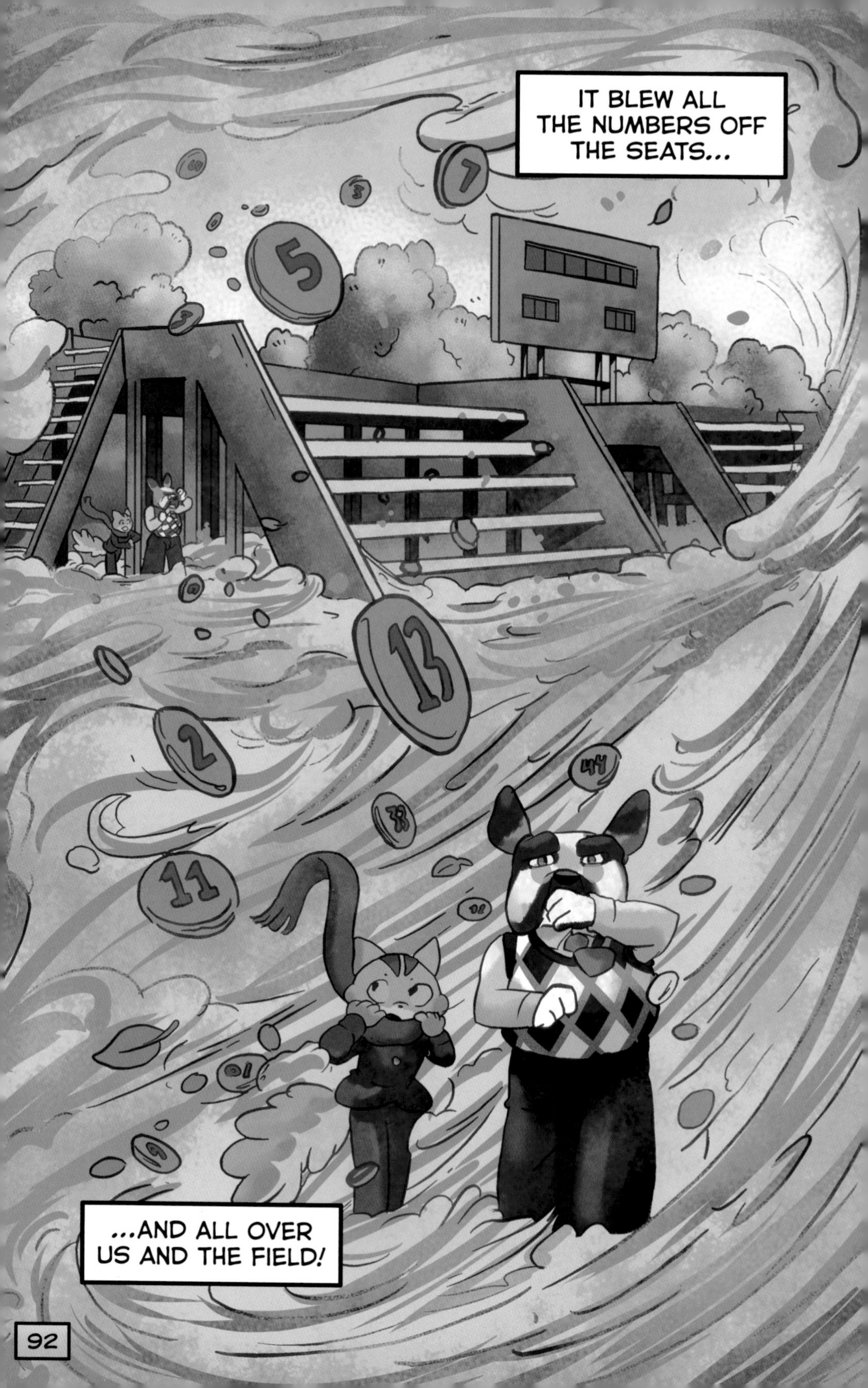
IT BLEW ALL THE NUMBERS OFF THE SEATS...
...AND ALL OVER US AND THE FIELD!

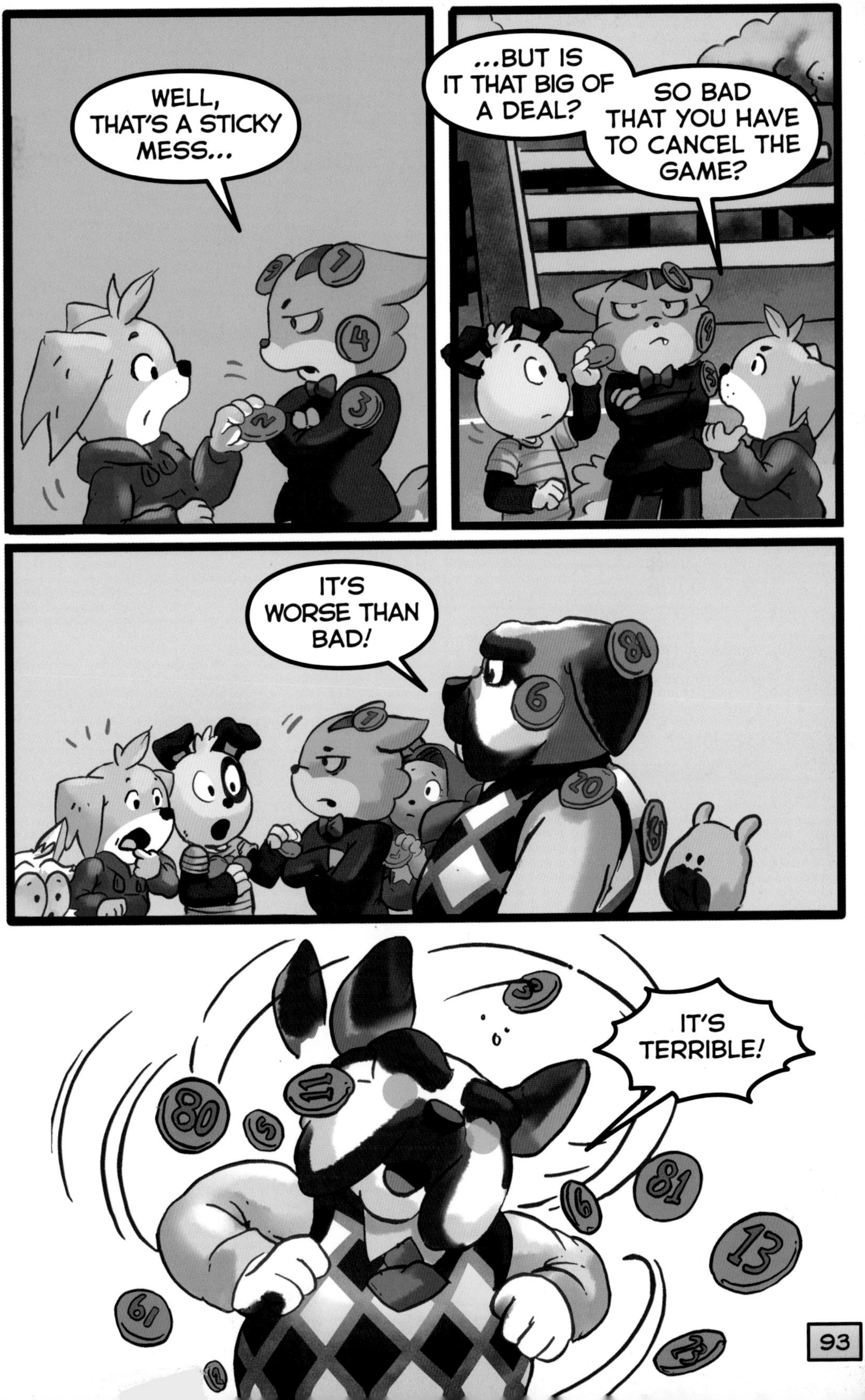
WELL, THAT'S A STICKY MESS...
...BUT IS IT THAT BIG OF A DEAL?
SO BAD THAT YOU HAVE TO CANCEL THE GAME?
IT'S WORSE THAN BAD!
IT'S TERRIBLE!

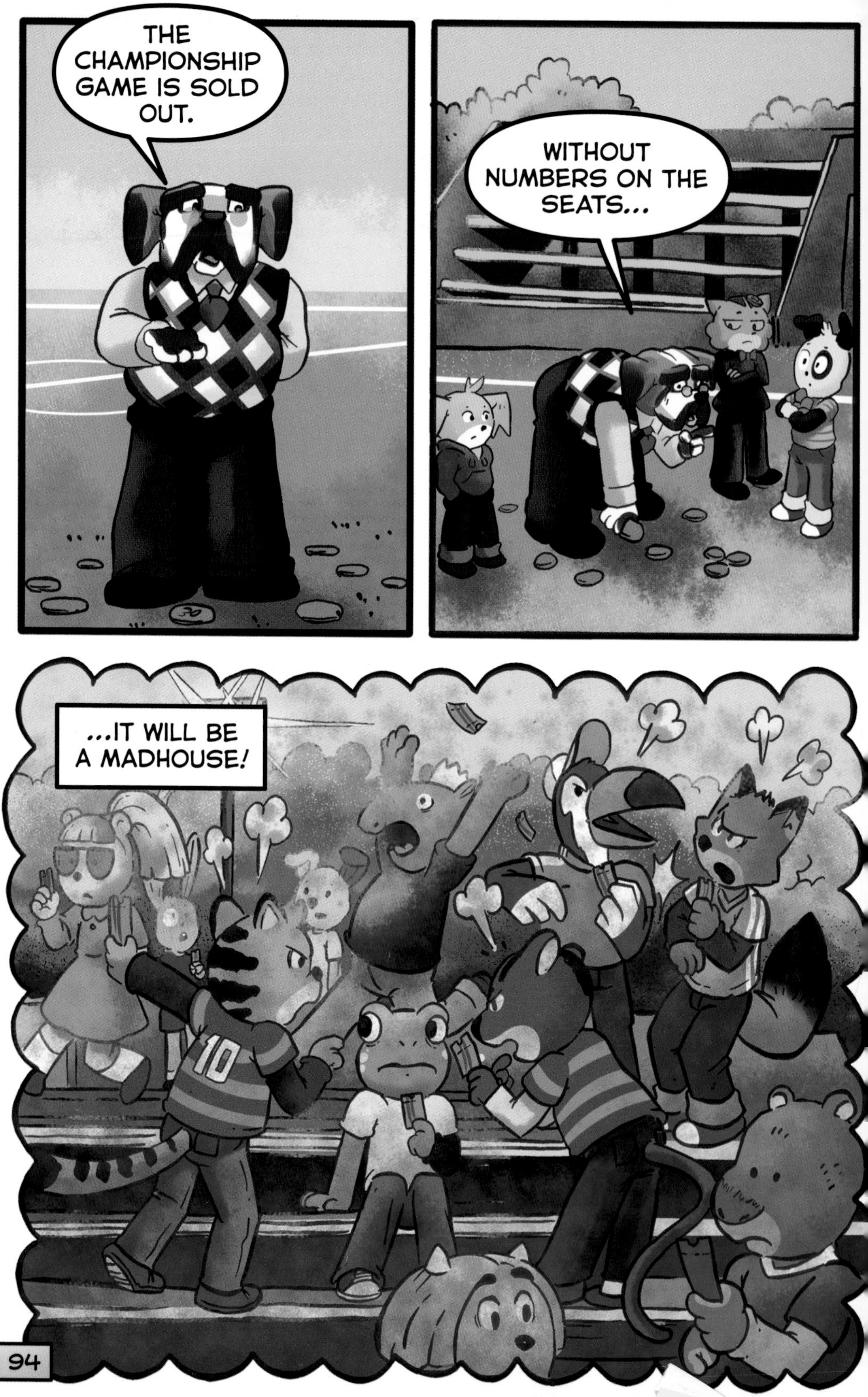
THE CHAMPIONSHIP GAME IS SOLD OUT.
WITHOUT NUMBERS ON THE SEATS...
...IT WILL BE A MADHOUSE!
10

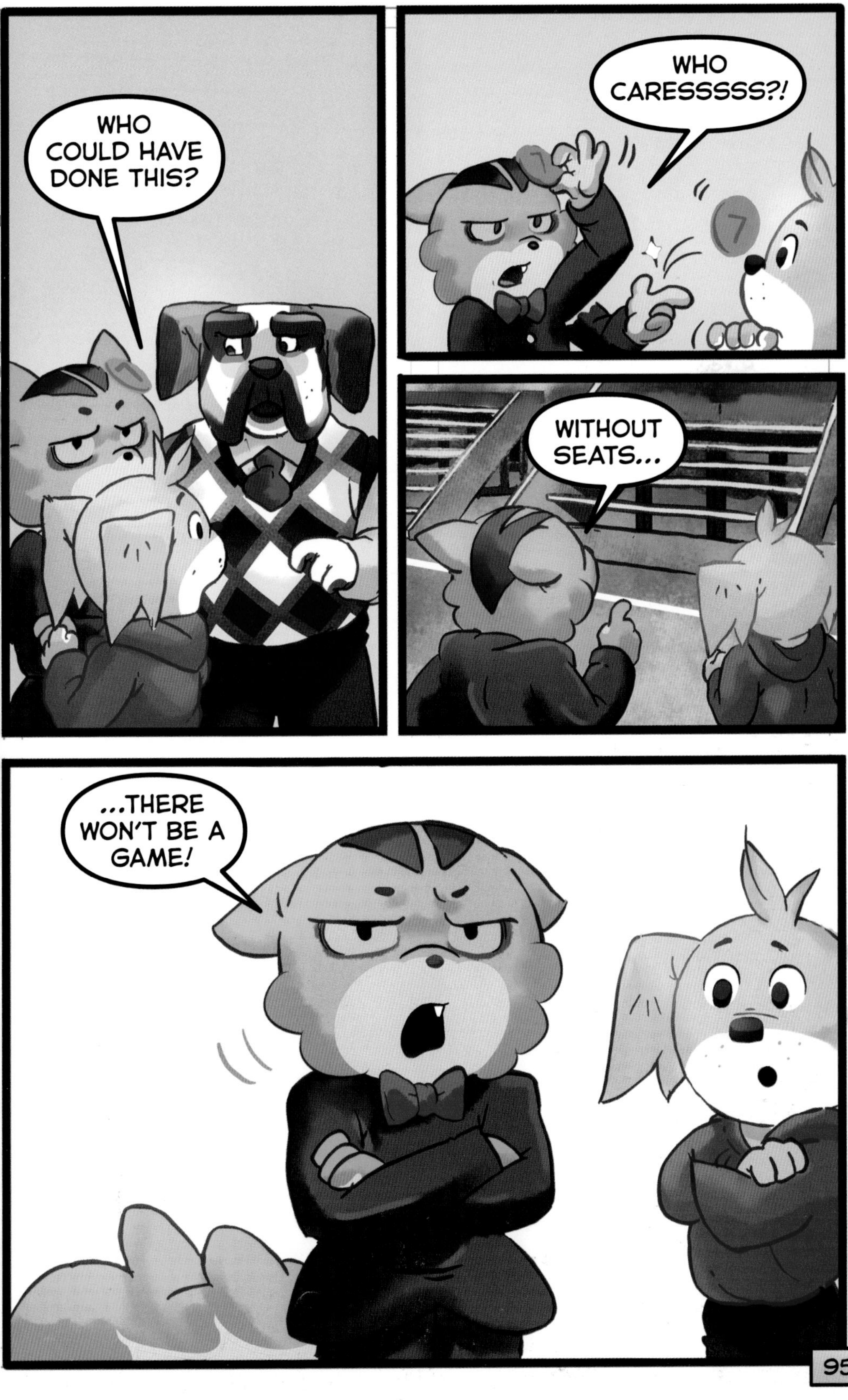
WHO COULD HAVE DONE THIS?
WHO CARESSSSS?!
WITHOUT SEATS...
...THERE WON'T BE A GAME!

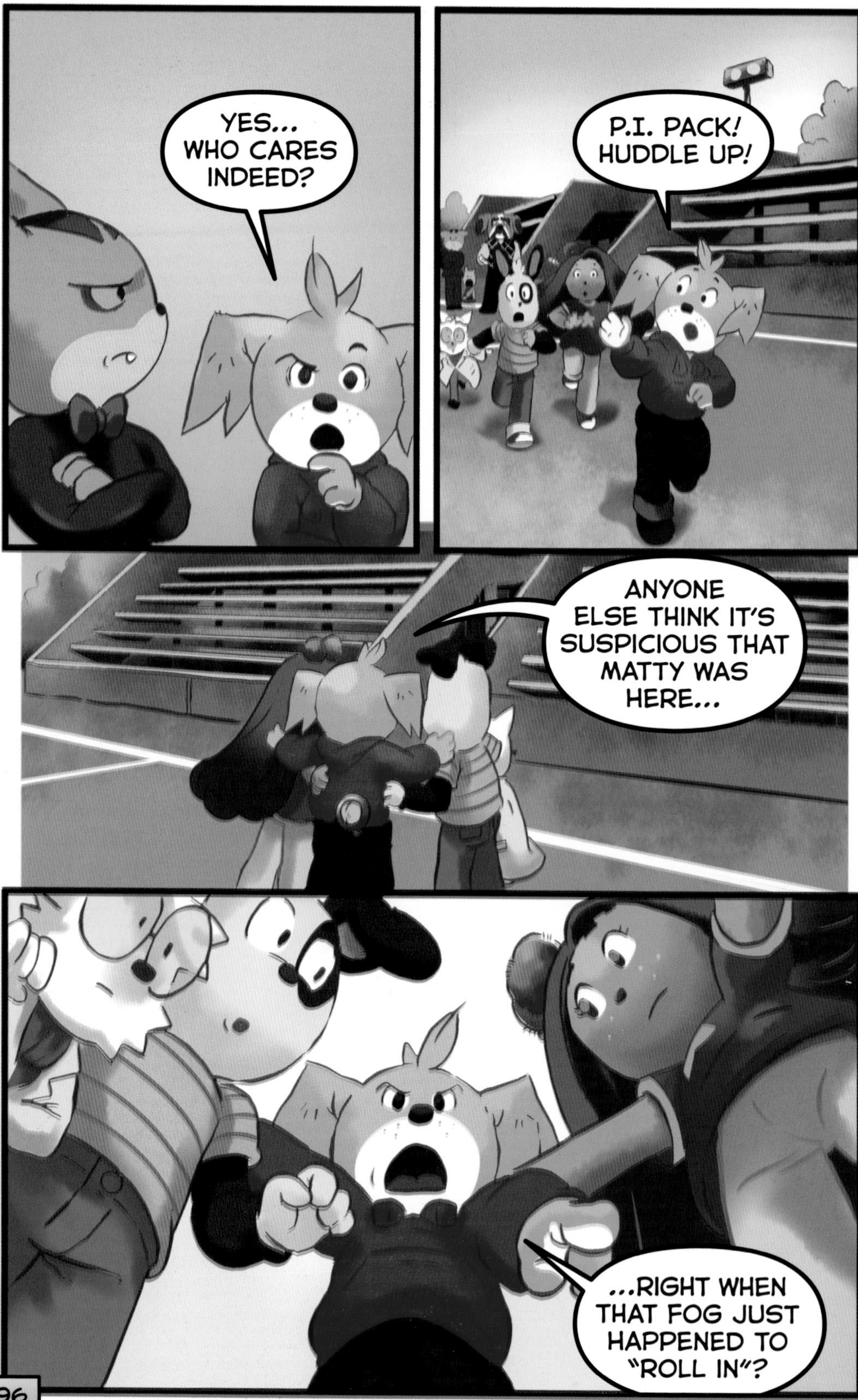
YES... WHO CARES INDEED?
P.I. PACK! HUDDLE UP!
ANYONE ELSE THINK IT'S SUSPICIOUS THAT MATTY WAS HERE...
...RIGHT WHEN THAT FOG JUST HAPPENED TO "ROLL IN"?

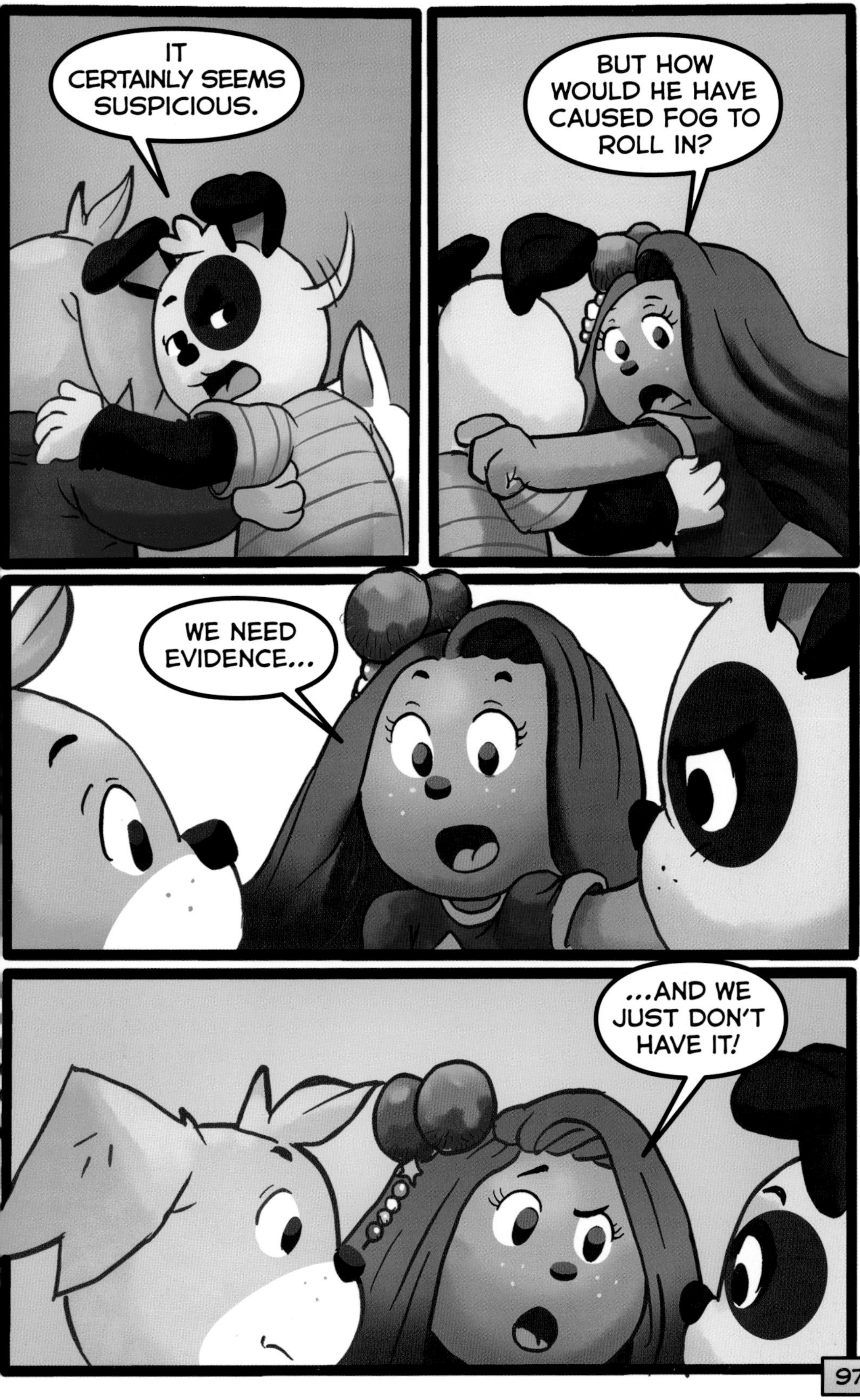
IT CERTAINLY SEEMS SUSPICIOUS.
BUT HOW WOULD HE HAVE CAUSED FOG TO ROLL IN?
WE NEED EVIDENCE...
...AND WE JUST DON'T HAVE IT!

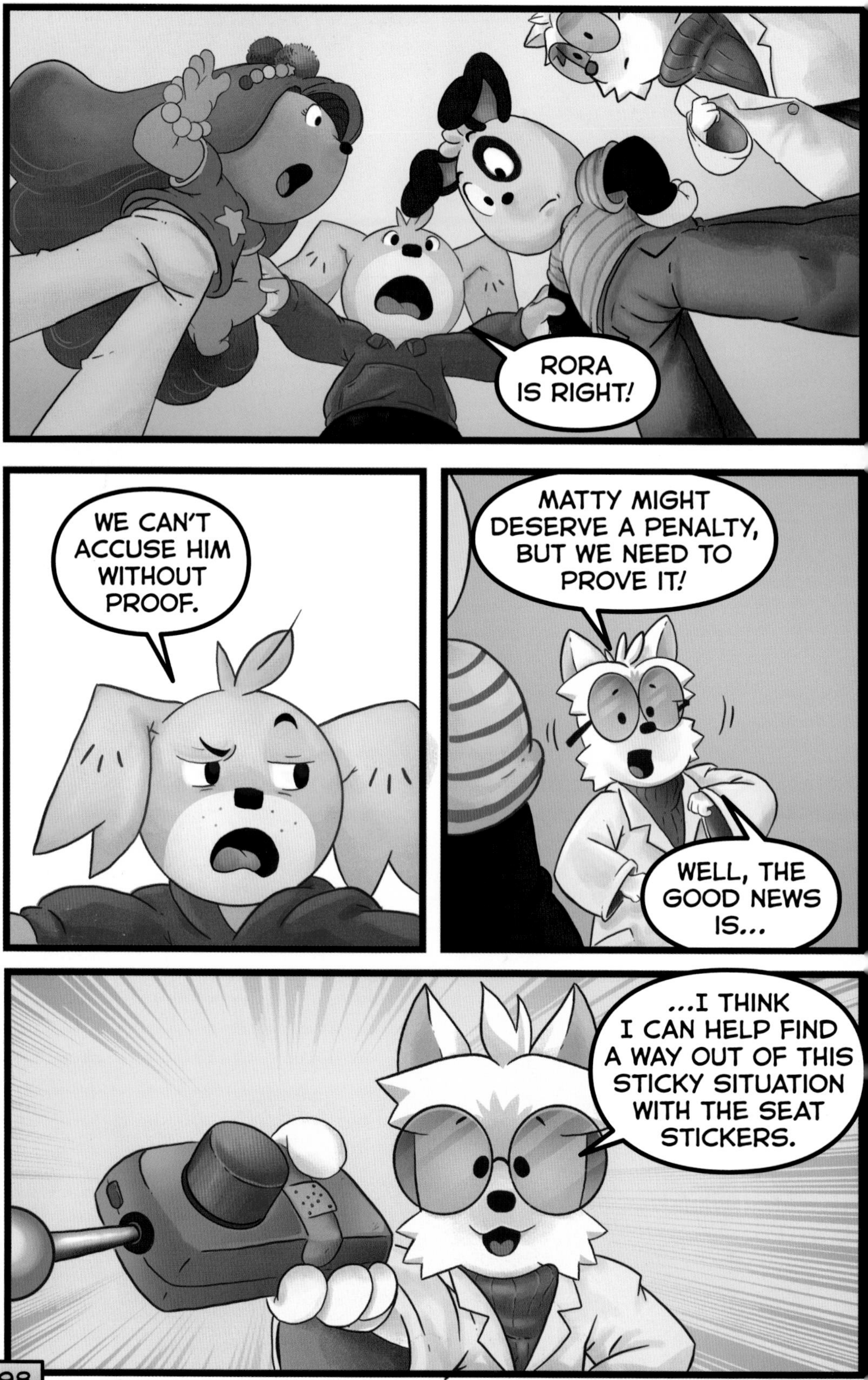
RORA IS RIGHT!
WE CAN'T ACCUSE HIM WITHOUT PROOF.
MATTY MIGHT DESERVE A PENALTY, BUT WE NEED TO PROVE IT!
WELL, THE GOOD NEWS IS...
...I THINK I CAN HELP FIND A WAY OUT OF THIS STICKY SITUATION WITH THE SEAT STICKERS.

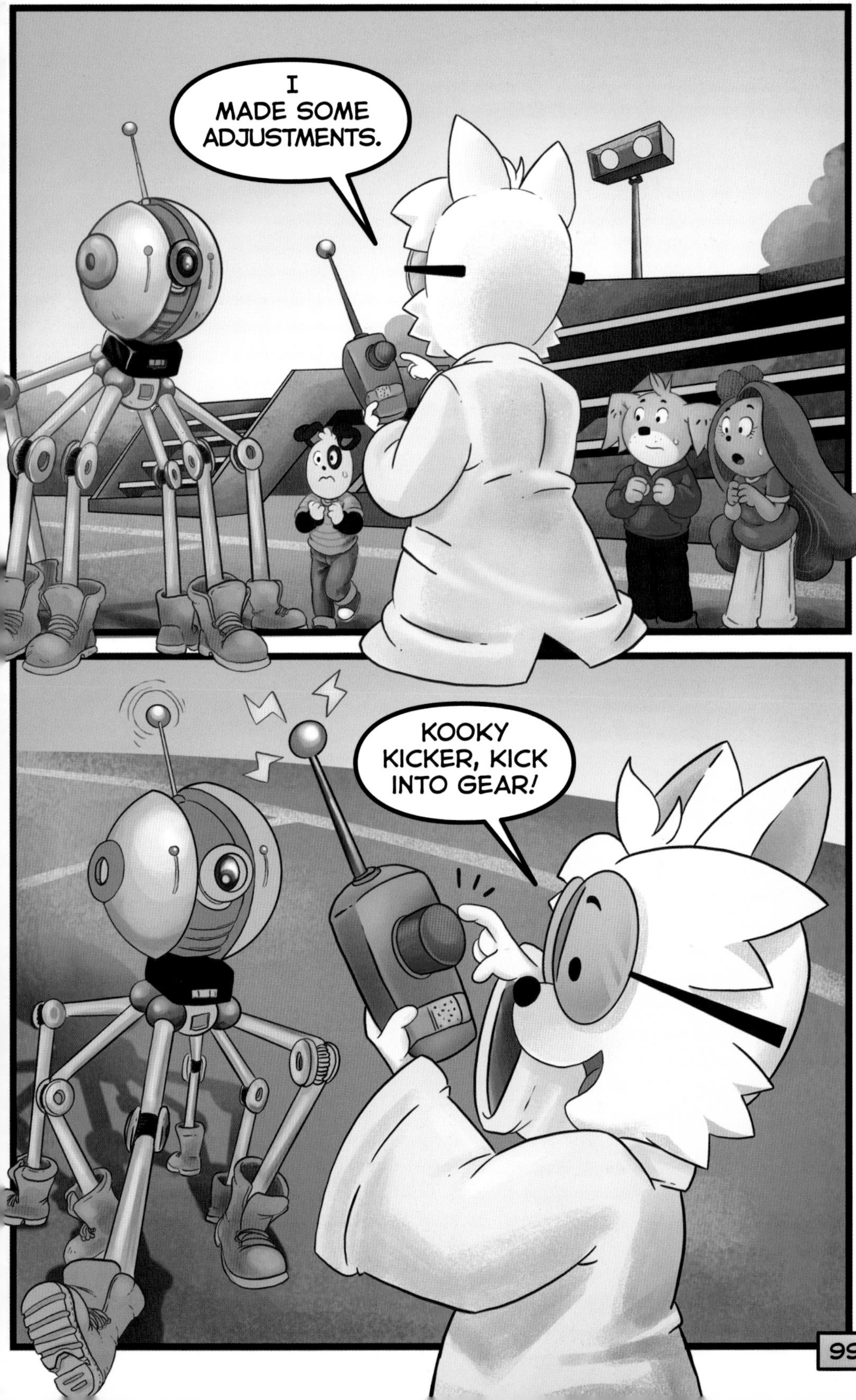
I MADE SOME ADJUSTMENTS.
KOOKY KICKER, KICK INTO GEAR!

CHAPTER 8

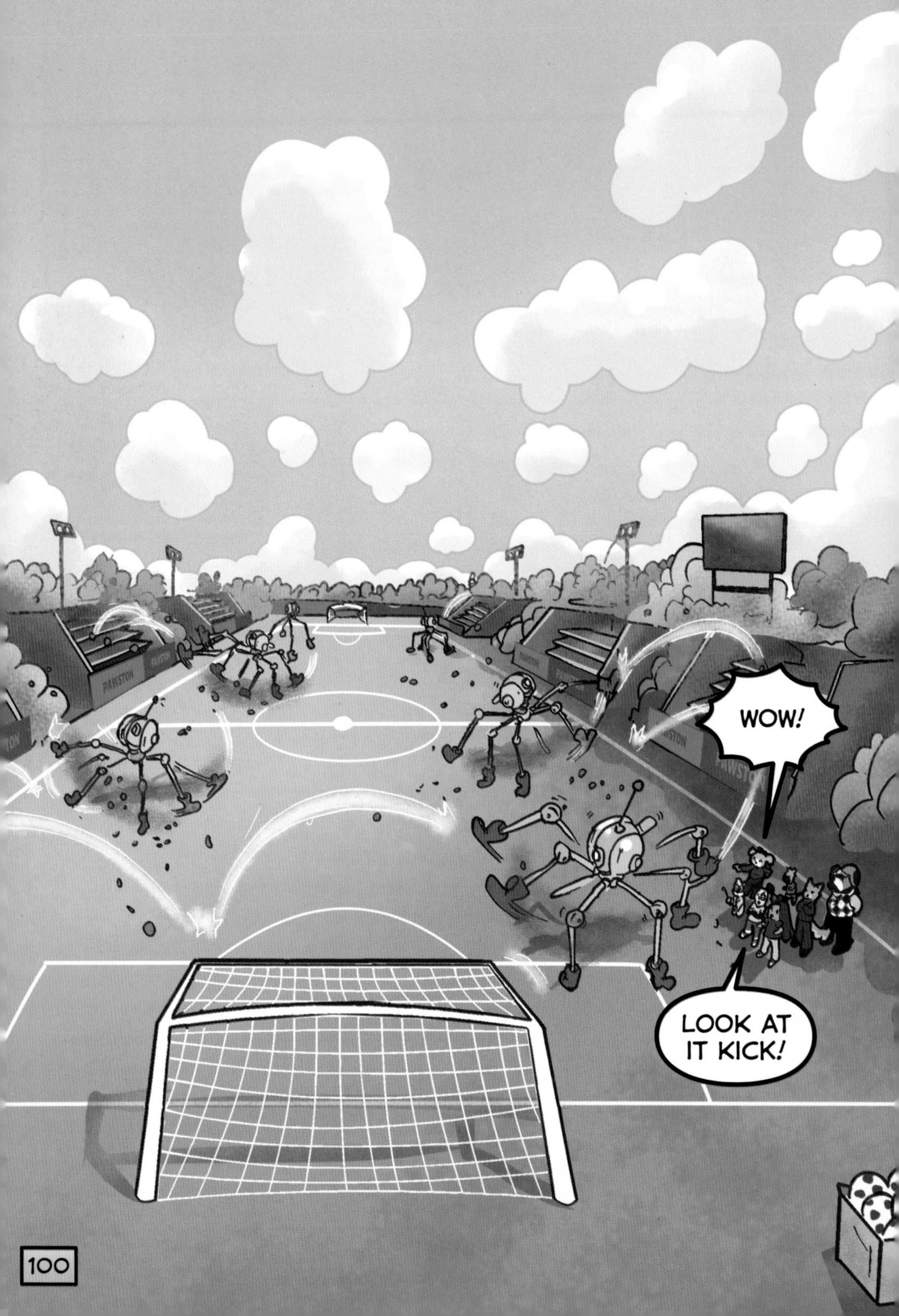
PAWSTON
WOW!
LOOK AT IT KICK!

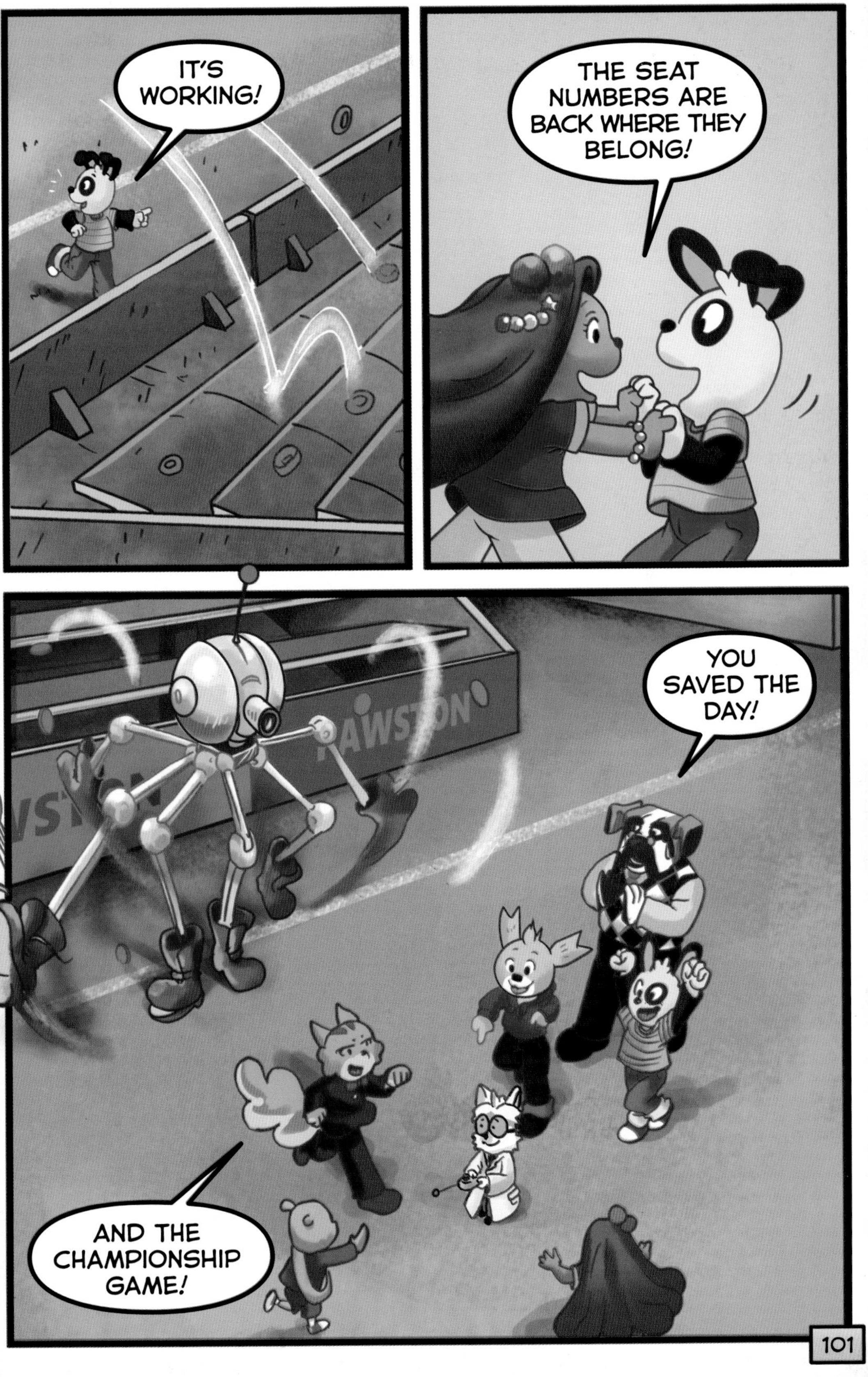
IT'S WORKING!
THE SEAT NUMBERS ARE BACK WHERE THEY BELONG!
YOU SAVED THE DAY!
AND THE CHAMPIONSHIP GAME!

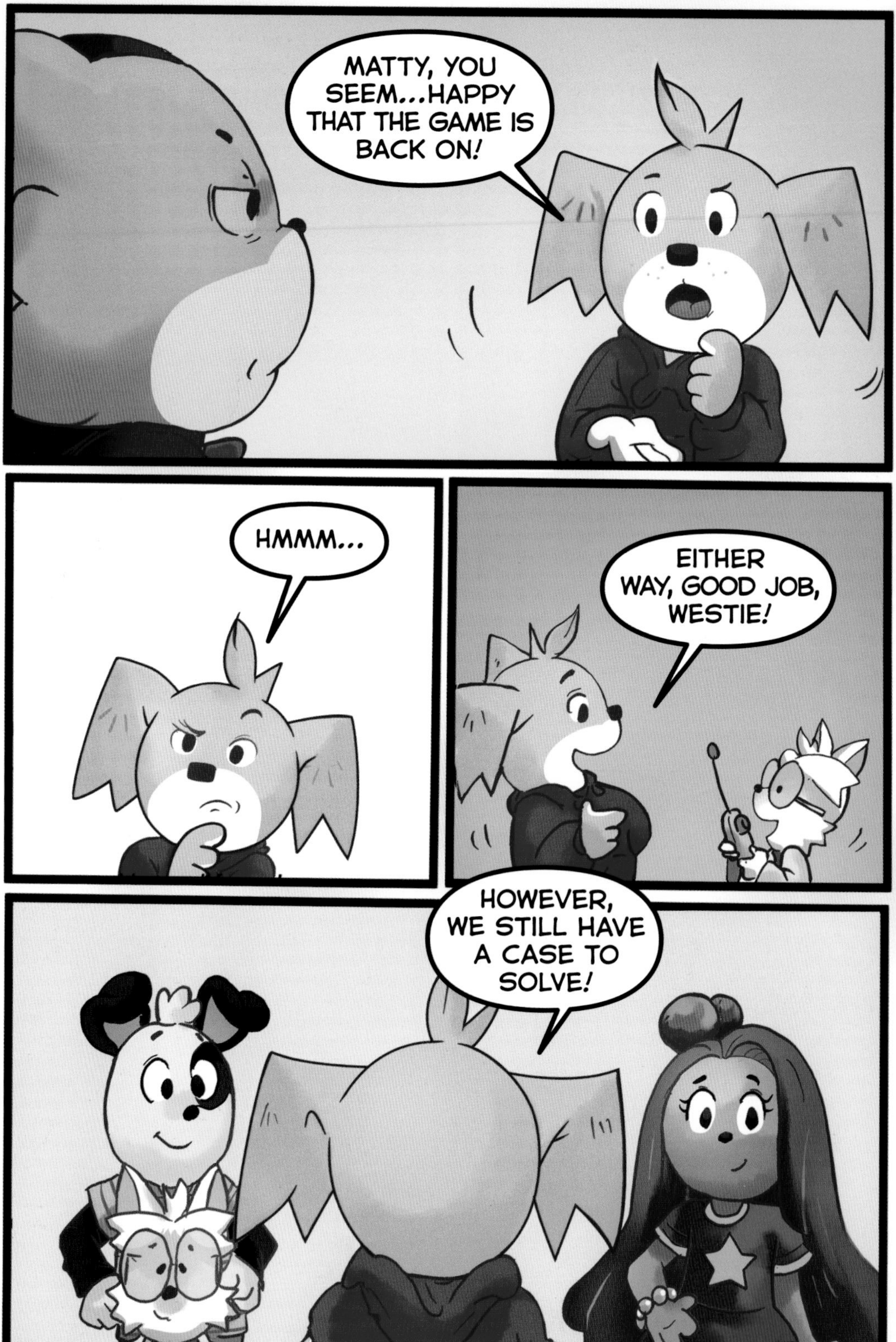
MATTY, YOU SEEM...HAPPY THAT THE GAME IS BACK ON!
HMMM...
EITHER WAY, GOOD JOB, WESTIE!
HOWEVER, WE STILL HAVE A CASE TO SOLVE!

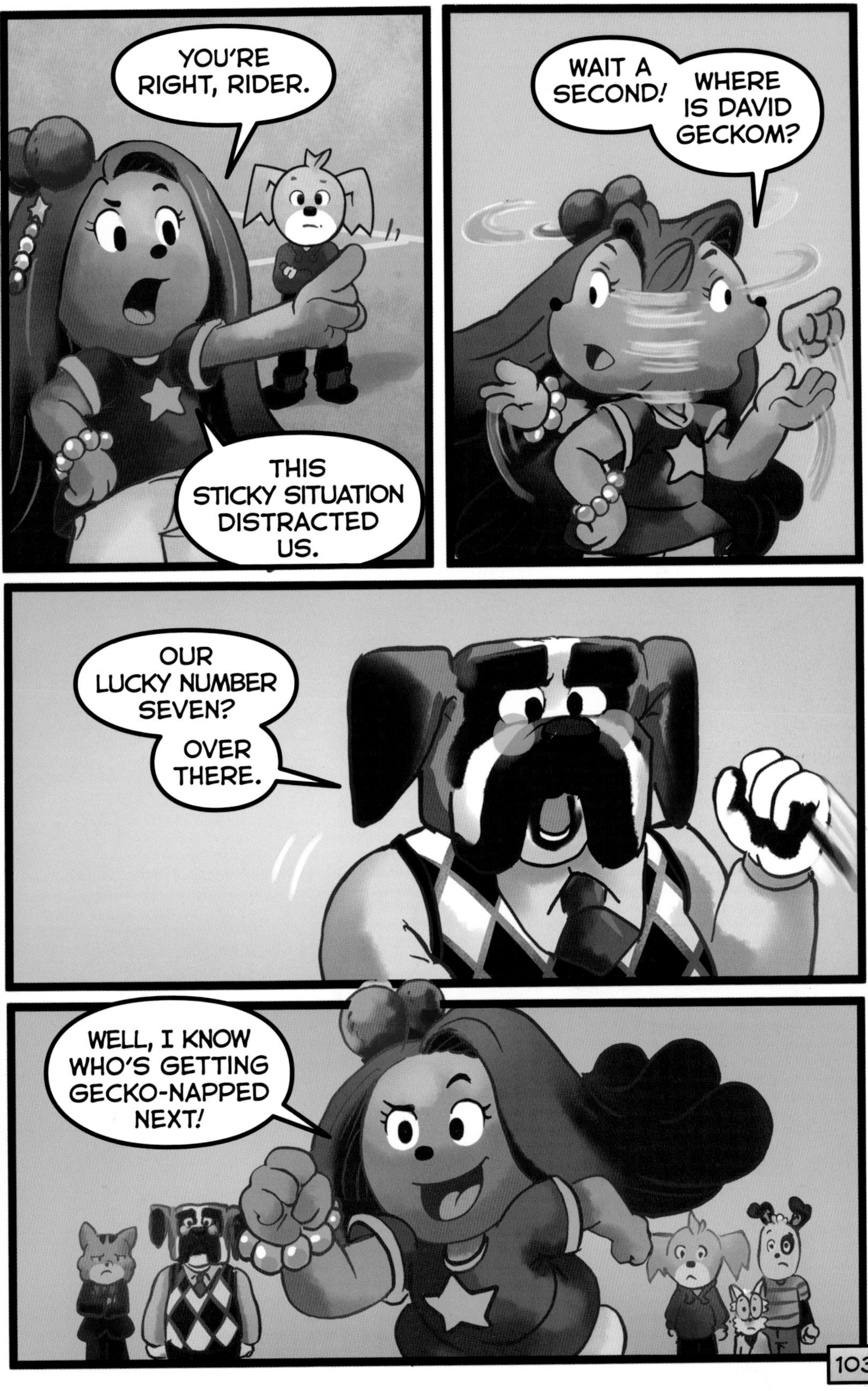
YOU'RE RIGHT, RIDER.
THIS STICKY SITUATION DISTRACTED US.
WAIT A SECOND!
WHERE IS DAVID GECKOM?
OUR LUCKY NUMBER SEVEN?
OVER THERE.
WELL, I KNOW WHO'S GETTING GECKO-NAPPED NEXT!

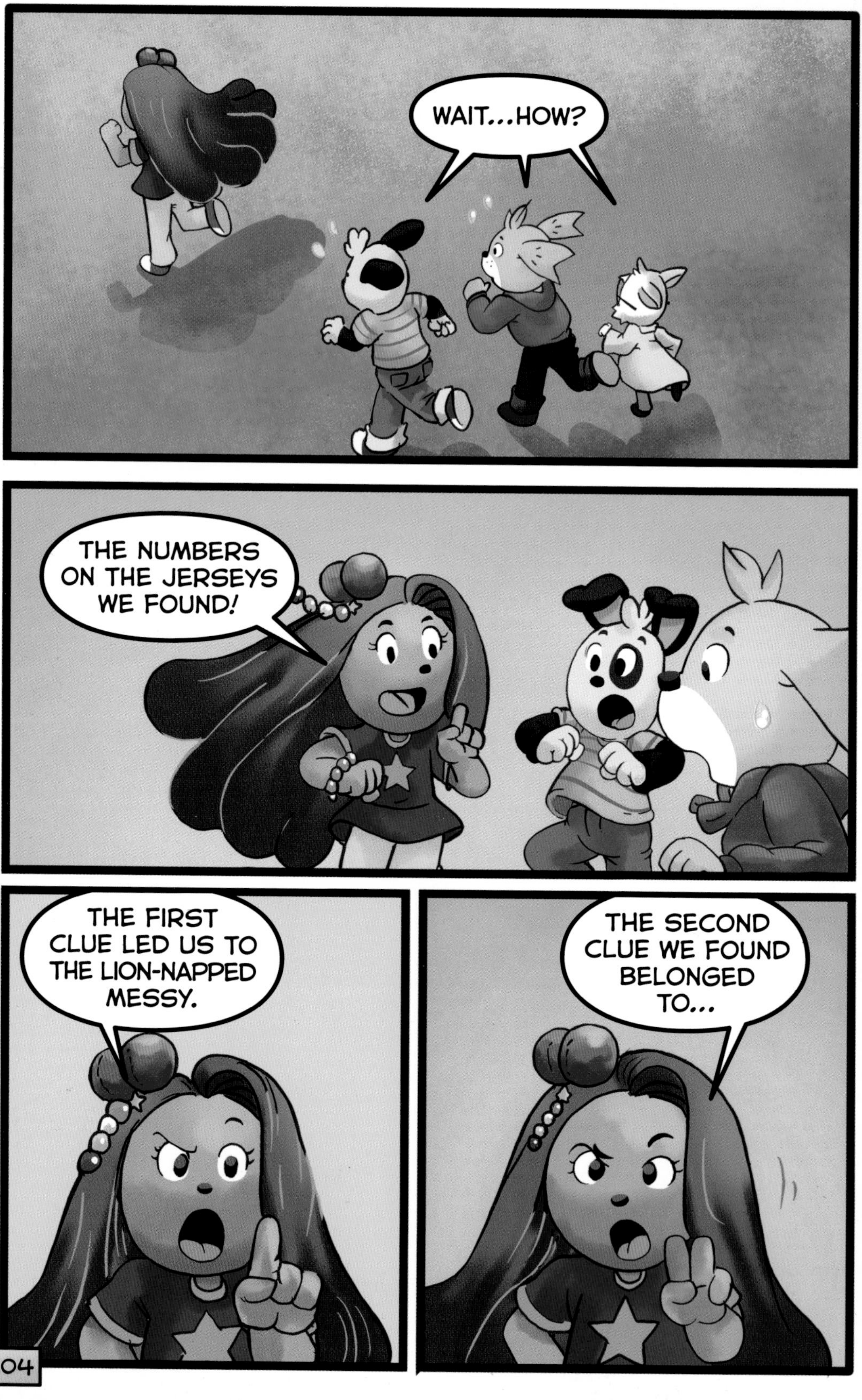
WAIT...HOW?
THE NUMBERS ON THE JERSEYS WE FOUND!
THE FIRST CLUE LED US TO THE LION-NAPPED MESSY.
THE SECOND CLUE WE FOUND BELONGED TO...

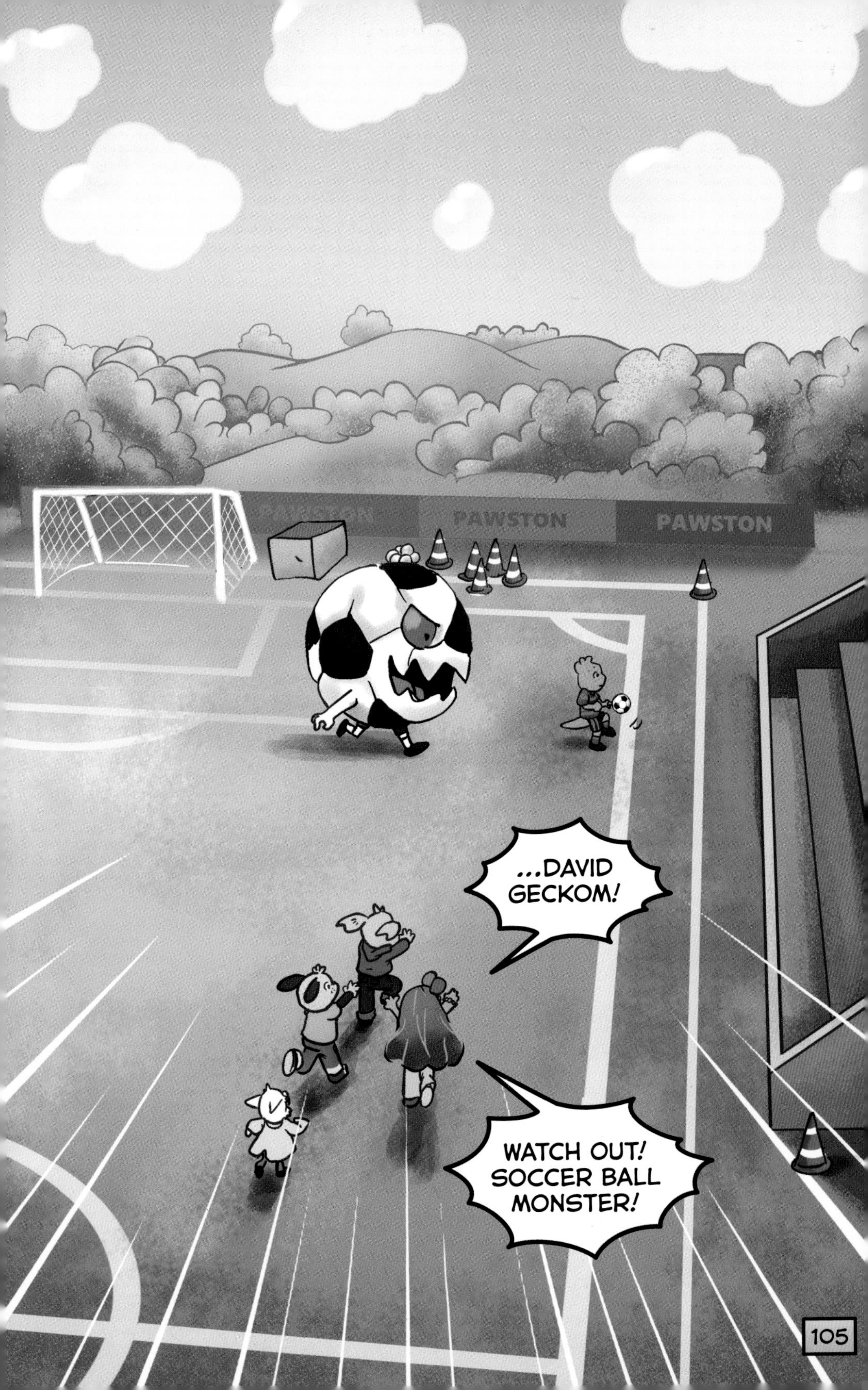
PAWSTON
PAWSTON
PAWSTON
...DAVID GECKOM!
WATCH OUT! SOCCER BALL MONSTER!

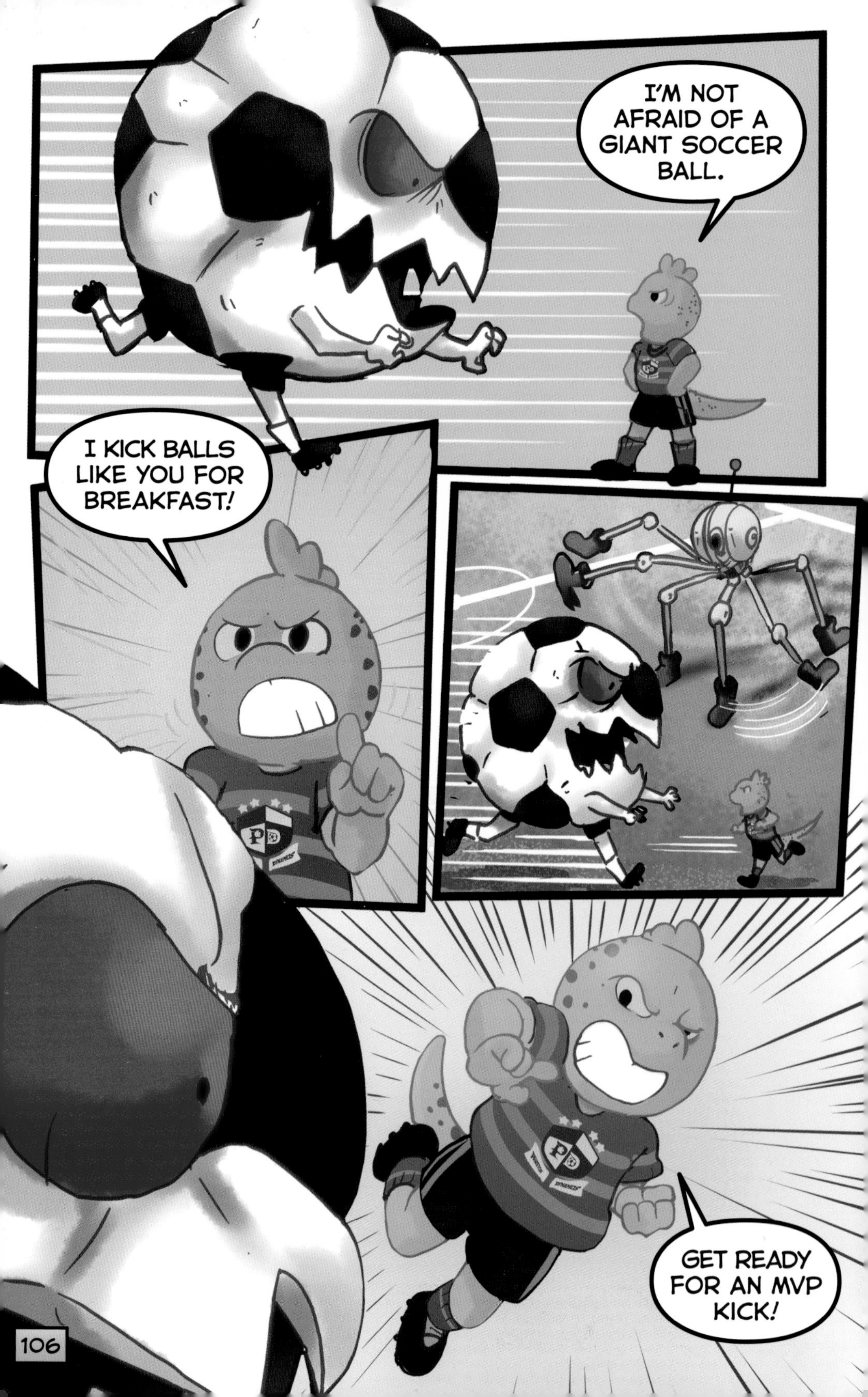
I'M NOT AFRAID OF A GIANT SOCCER BALL.
I KICK BALLS LIKE YOU FOR BREAKFAST!
GET READY FOR AN MVP KICK!

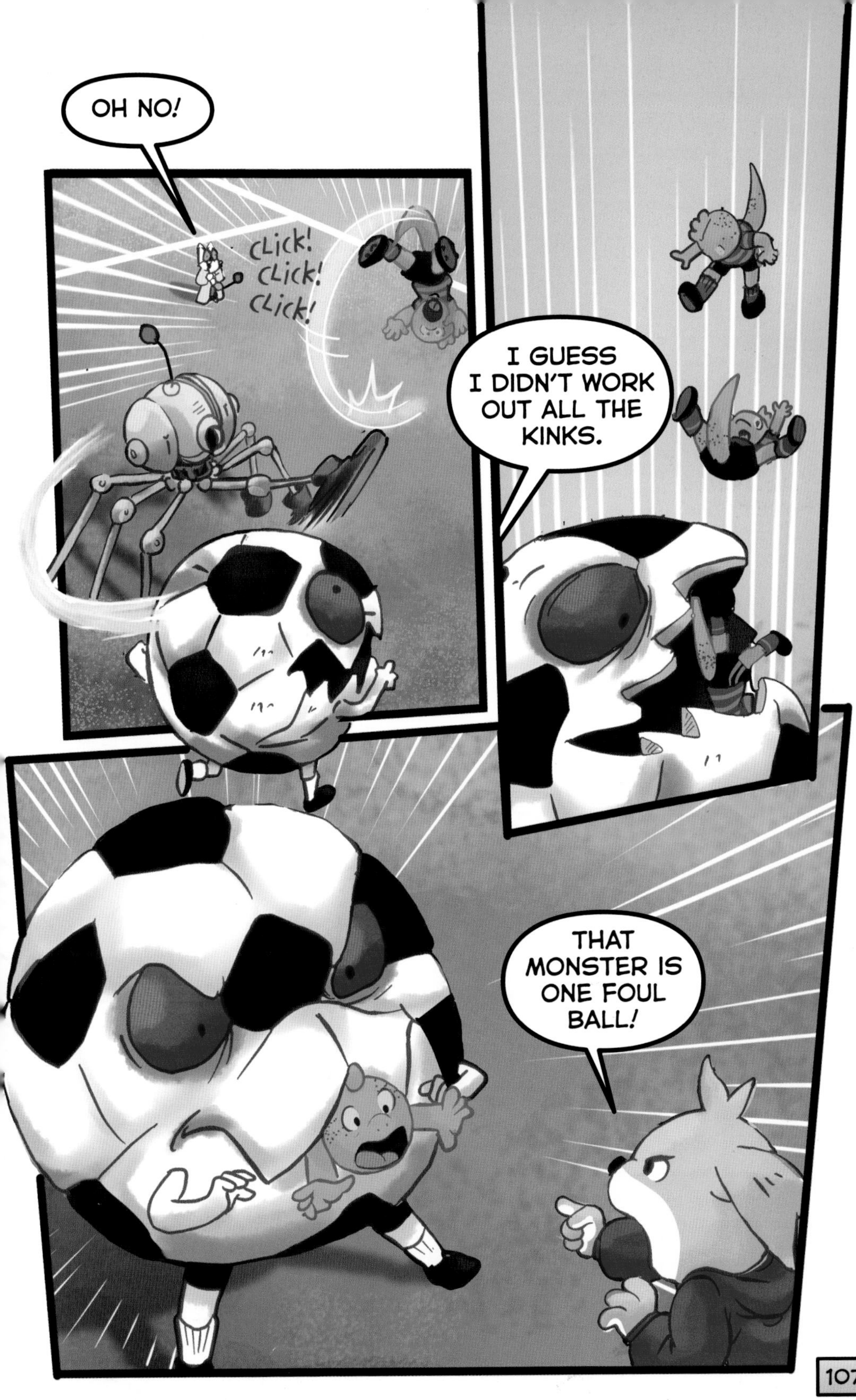
OH NO!
CLICK! CLICK! CLICK!
I GUESS I DIDN'T WORK OUT ALL THE KINKS.
THAT MONSTER IS ONE FOUL BALL!

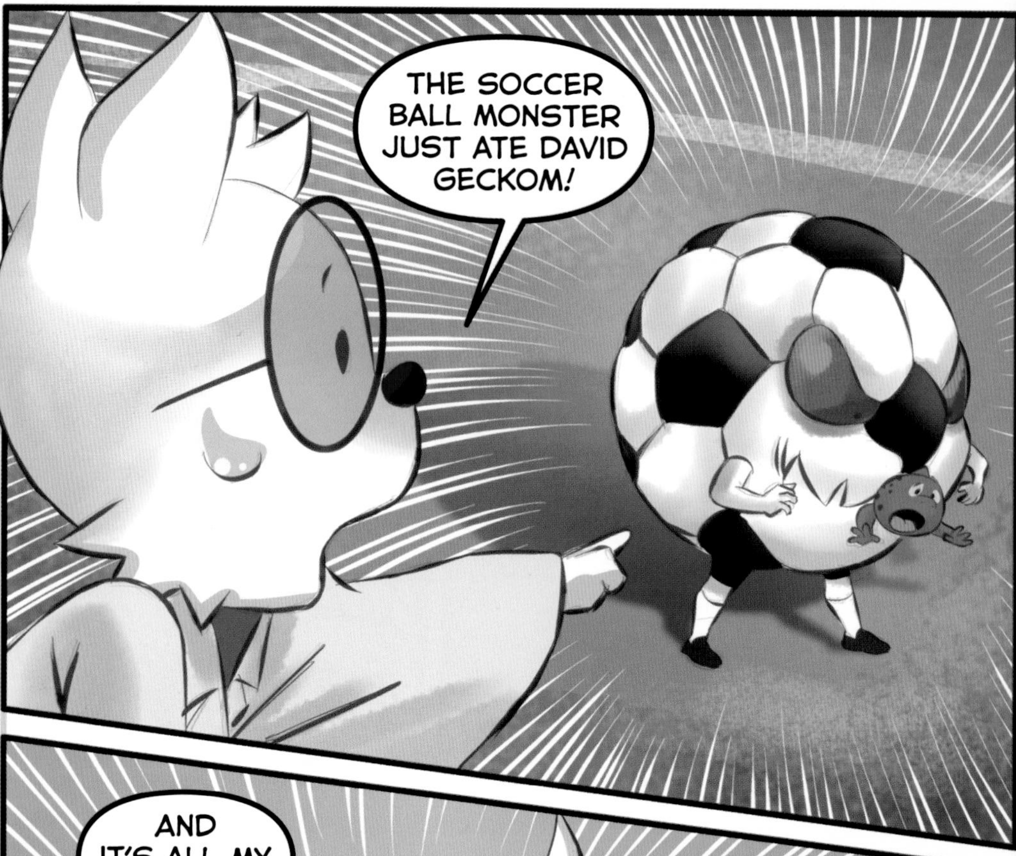
THE SOCCER BALL MONSTER JUST ATE DAVID GECKOM!

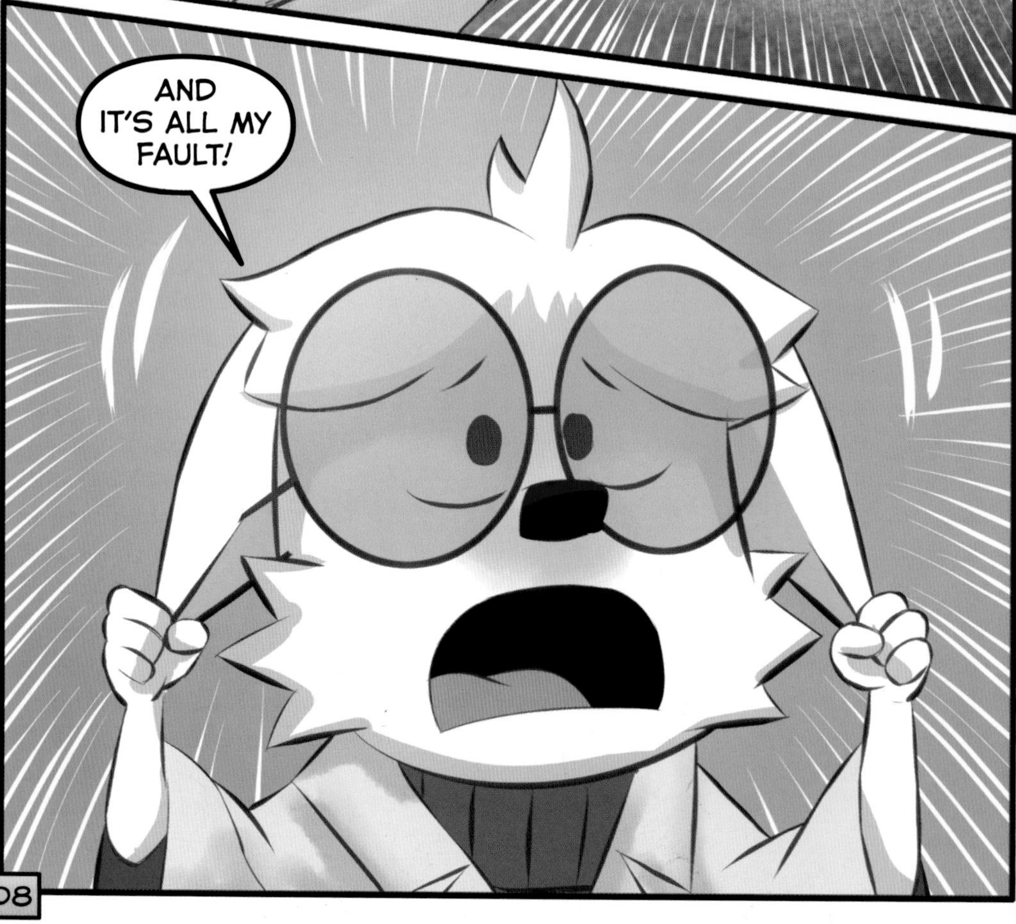
AND IT'S ALL MY FAULT!

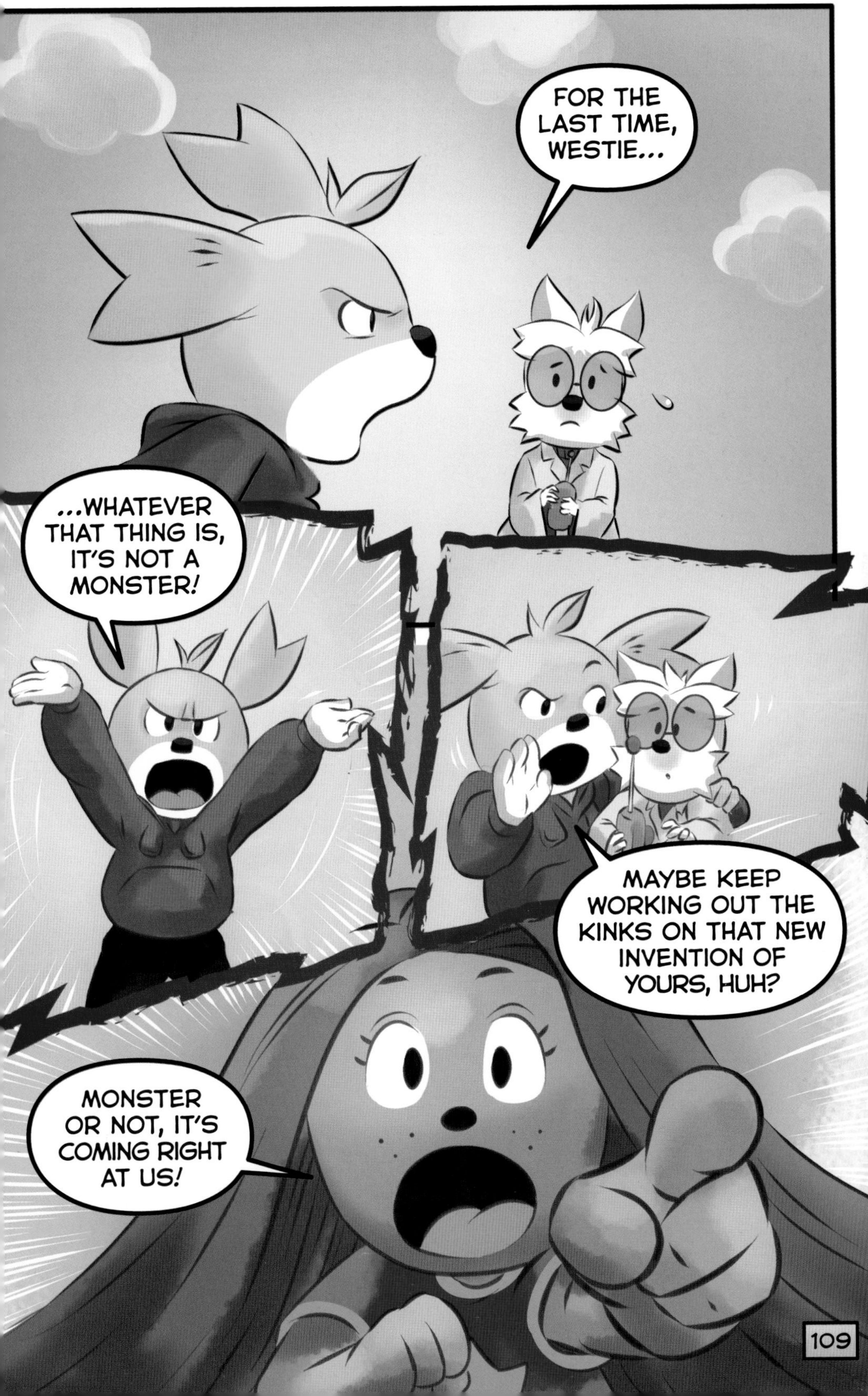
FOR THE LAST TIME, WESTIE...
...WHATEVER THAT THING IS, IT'S NOT A MONSTER!
MAYBE KEEP WORKING OUT THE KINKS ON THAT NEW INVENTION OF YOURS, HUH?
MONSTER OR NOT, IT'S COMING RIGHT AT US!

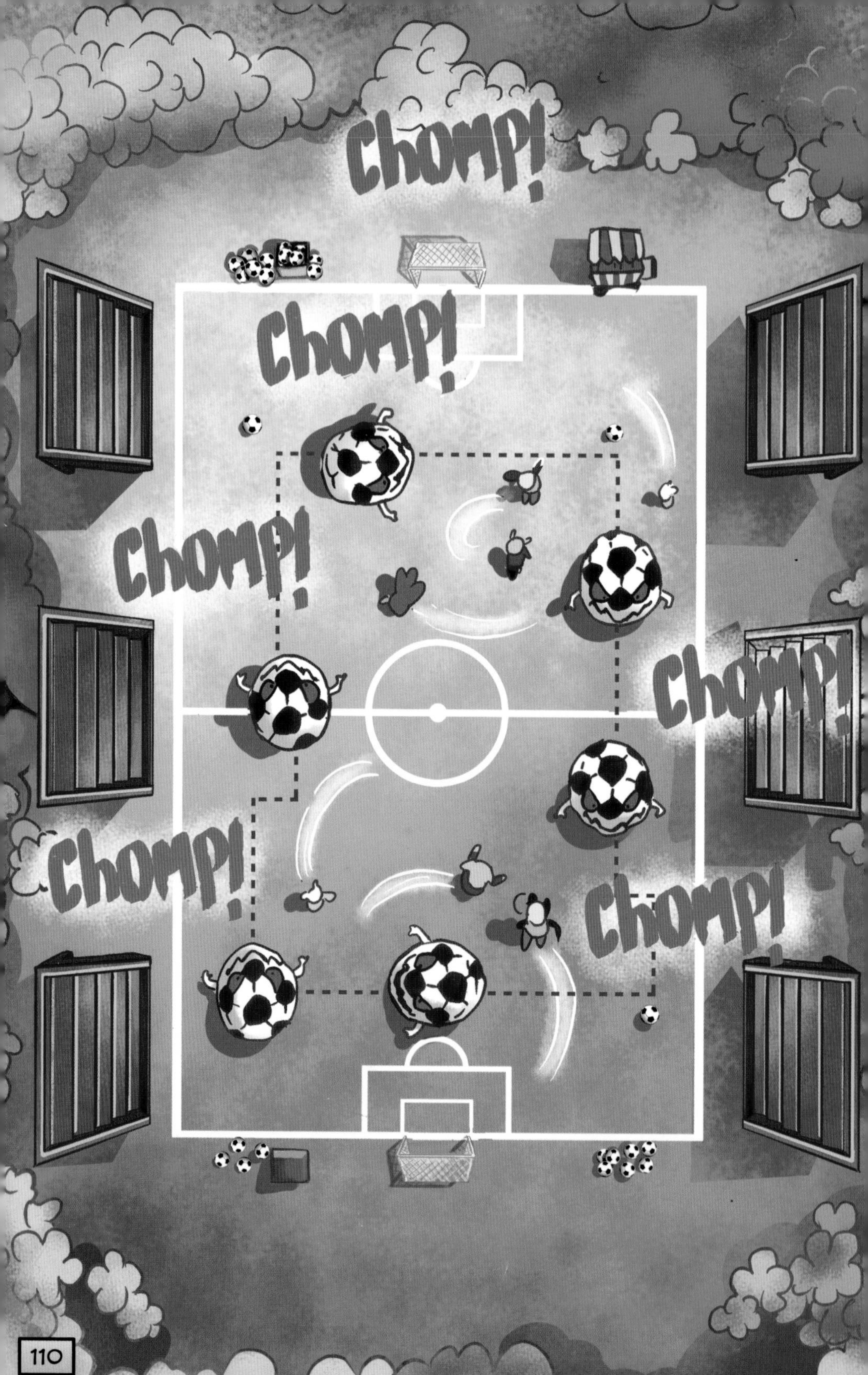
CHOMP!
CHOMP!
CHOMP!
CHOMP!
CHOMP!
CHOMP!

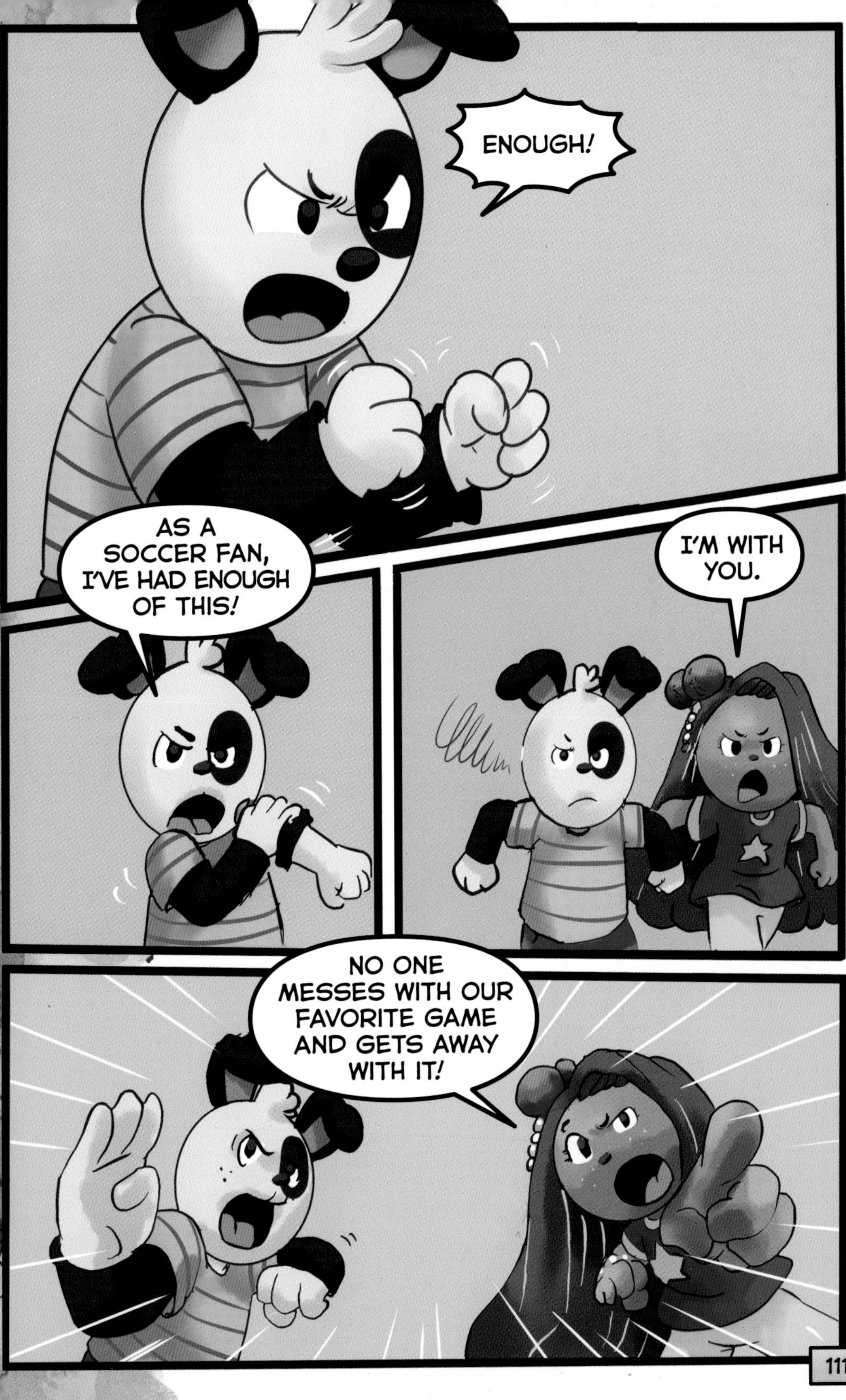
ENOUGH!
AS A SOCCER FAN, I'VE HAD ENOUGH OF THIS!
I'M WITH YOU.
NO ONE MESSES WITH OUR FAVORITE GAME AND GETS AWAY WITH IT!

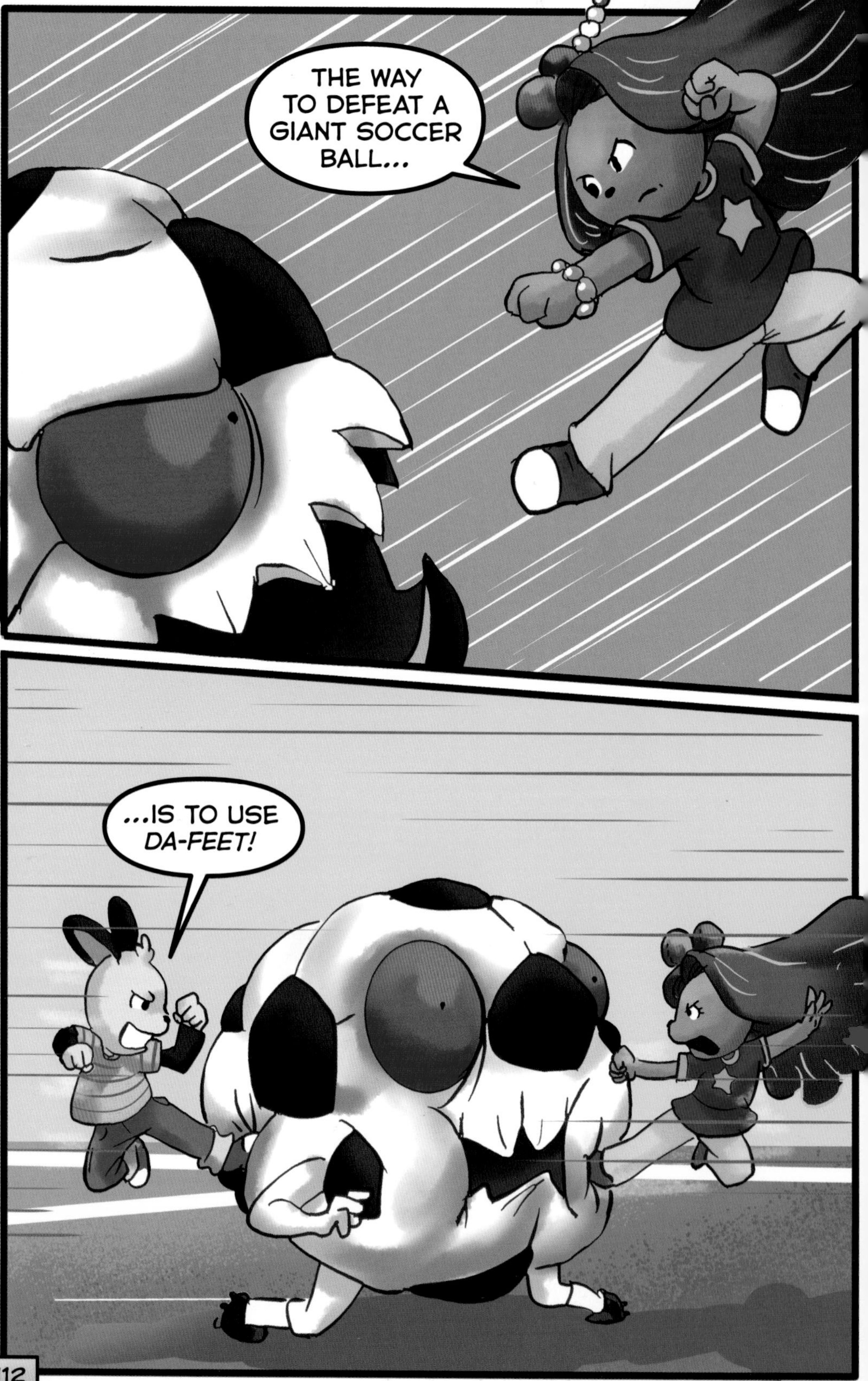
THE WAY TO DEFEAT A GIANT SOCCER BALL...
...IS TO USE DA-FEET!

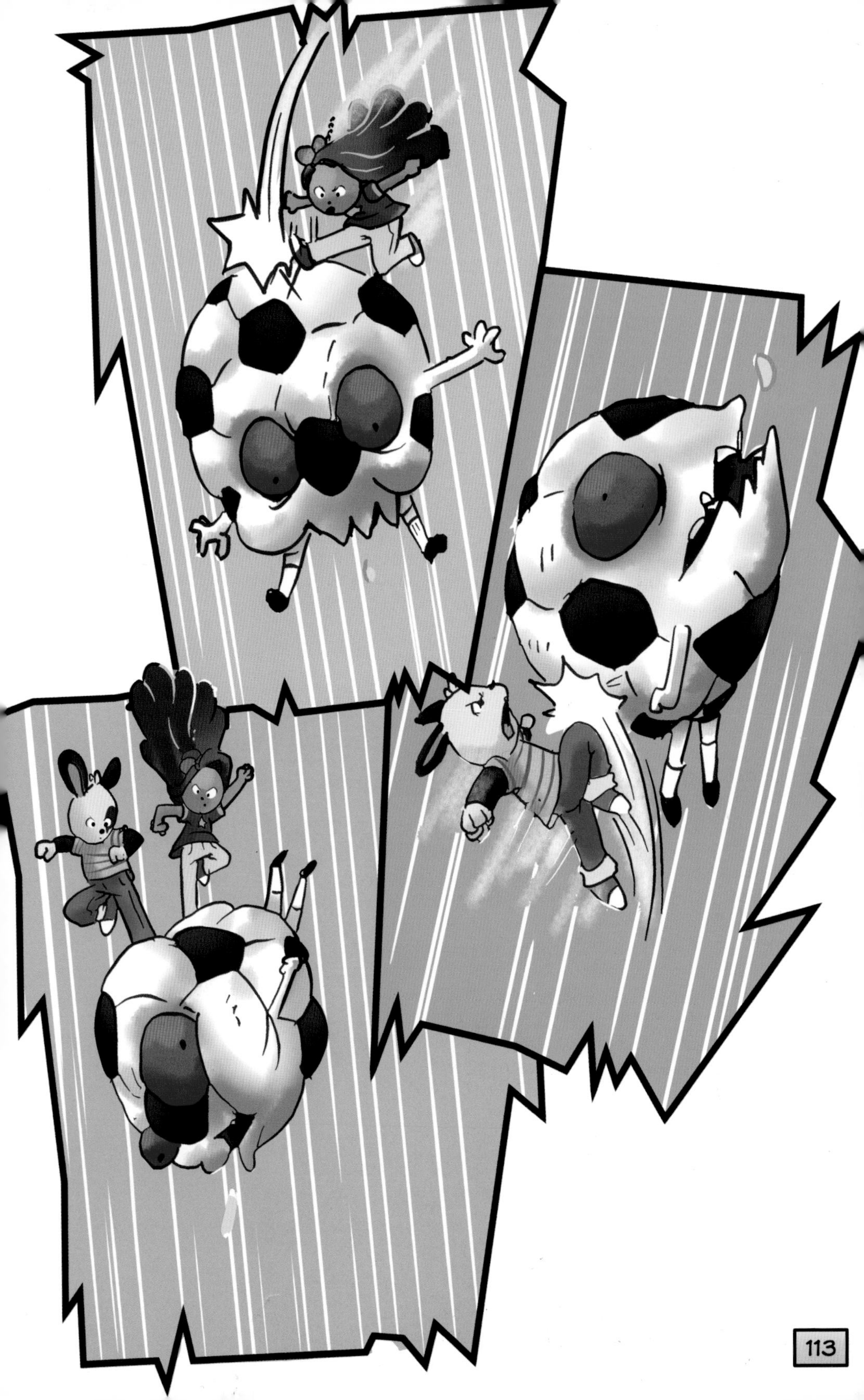

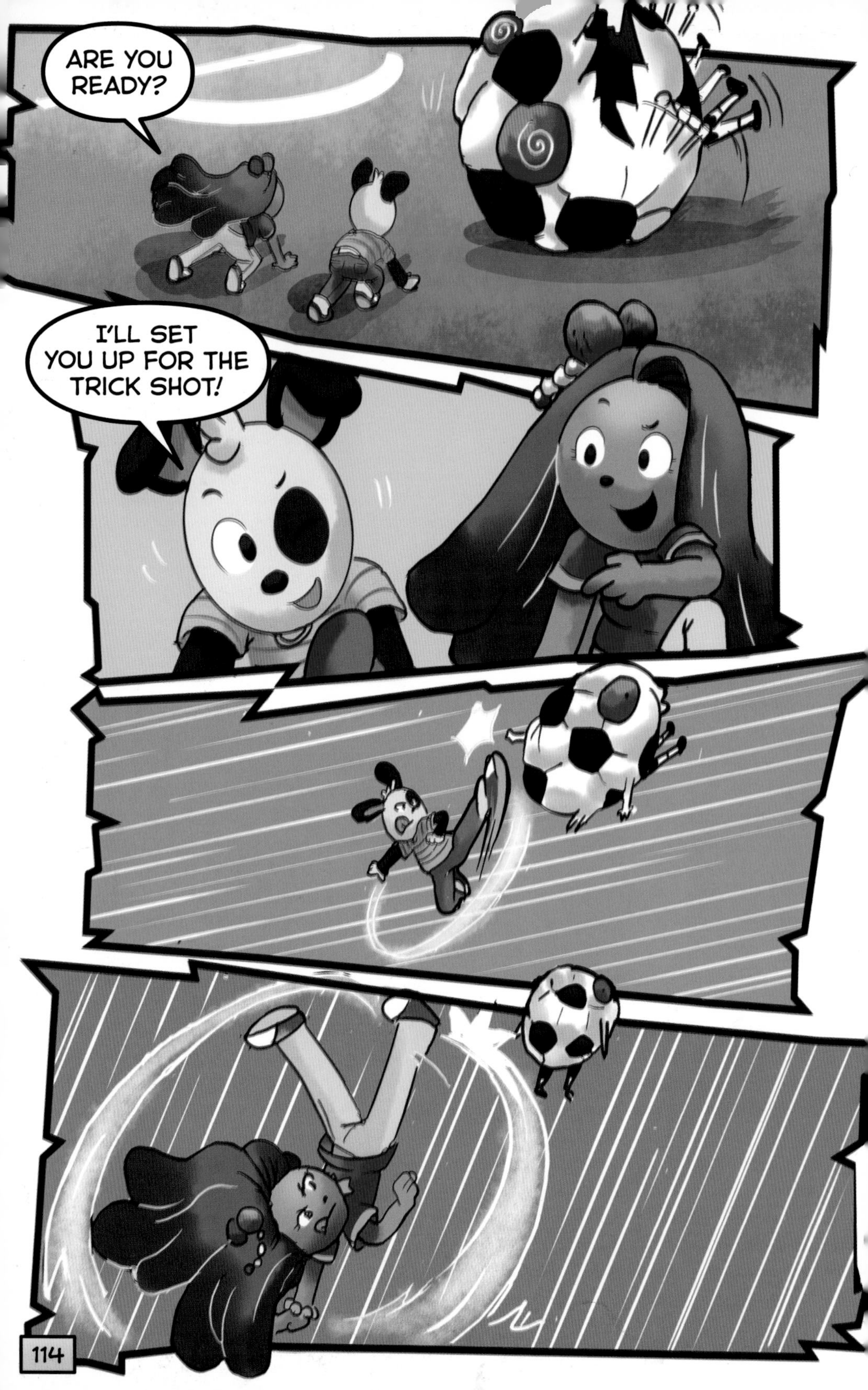
ARE YOU READY?
I'LL SET YOU UP FOR THE TRICK SHOT!

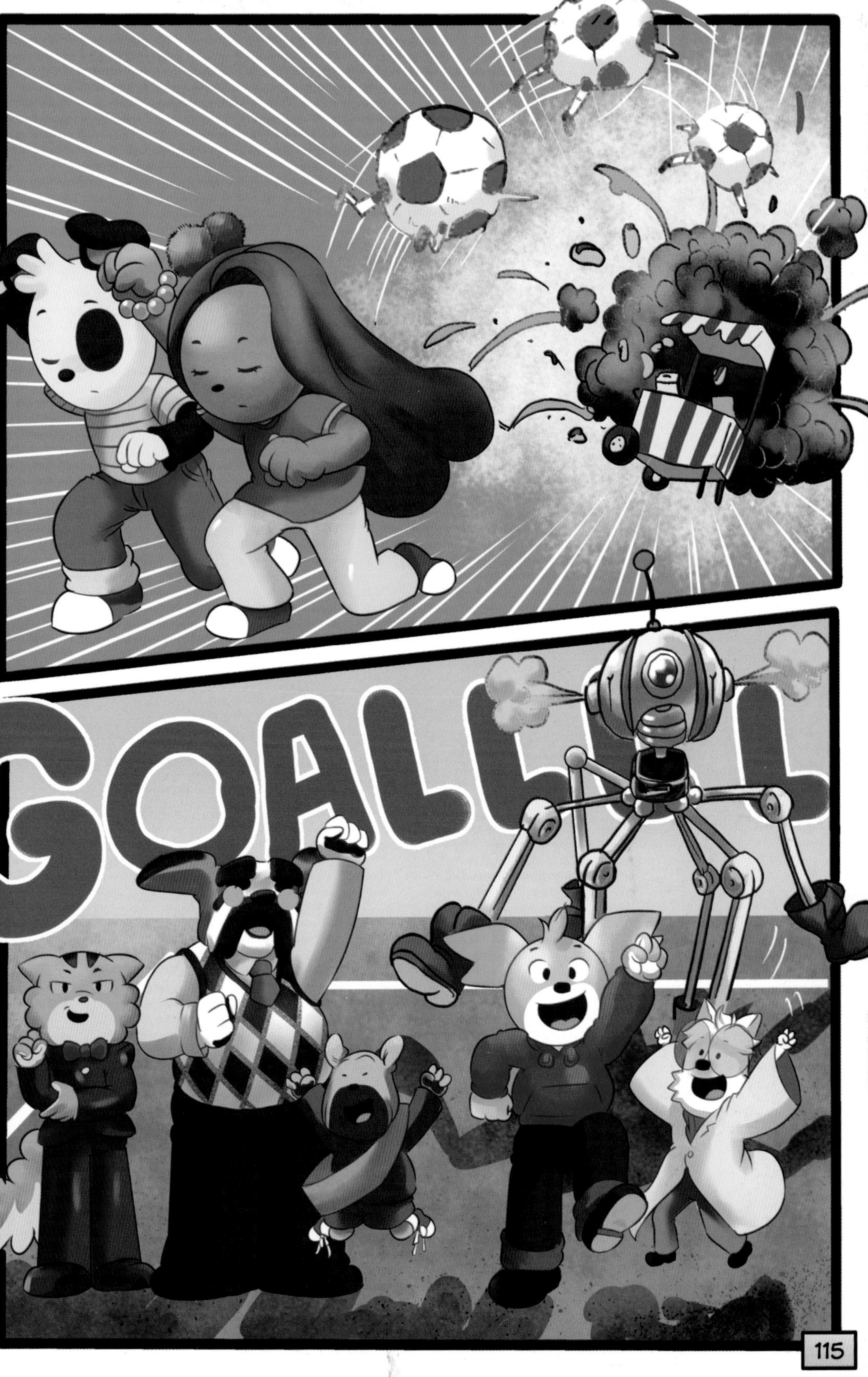
GOALLLL

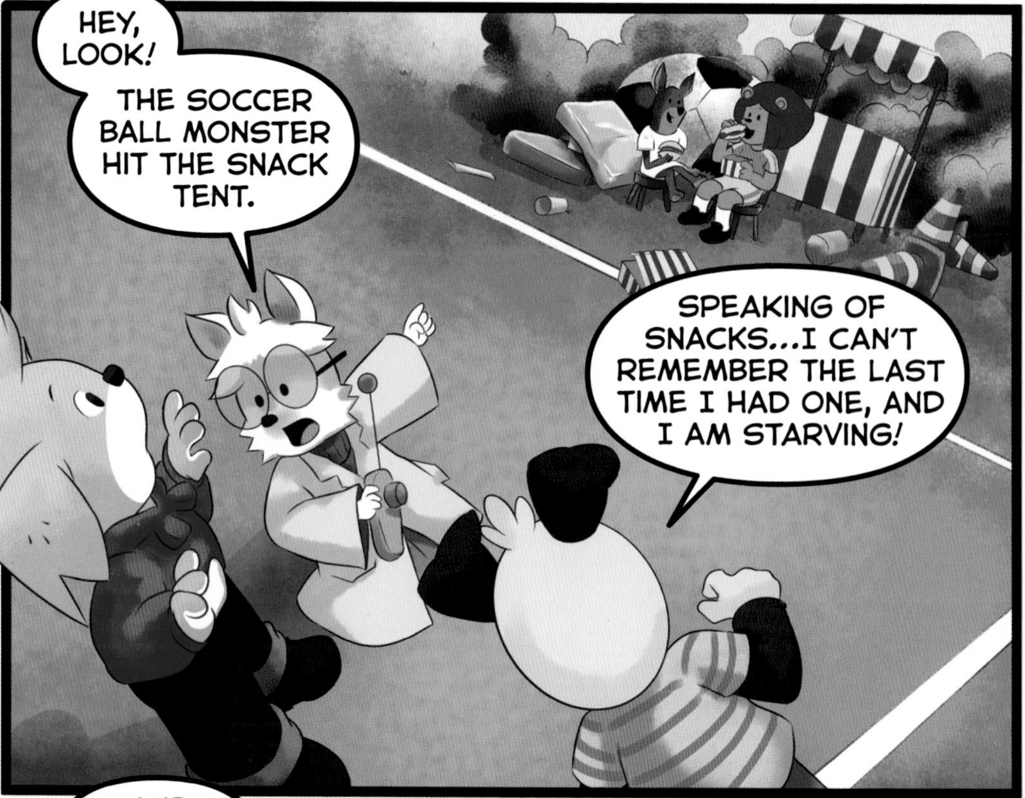
HEY, LOOK!
THE SOCCER BALL MONSTER HIT THE SNACK TENT.
SPEAKING OF SNACKS...I CAN'T REMEMBER THE LAST TIME I HAD ONE, AND I AM STARVING!

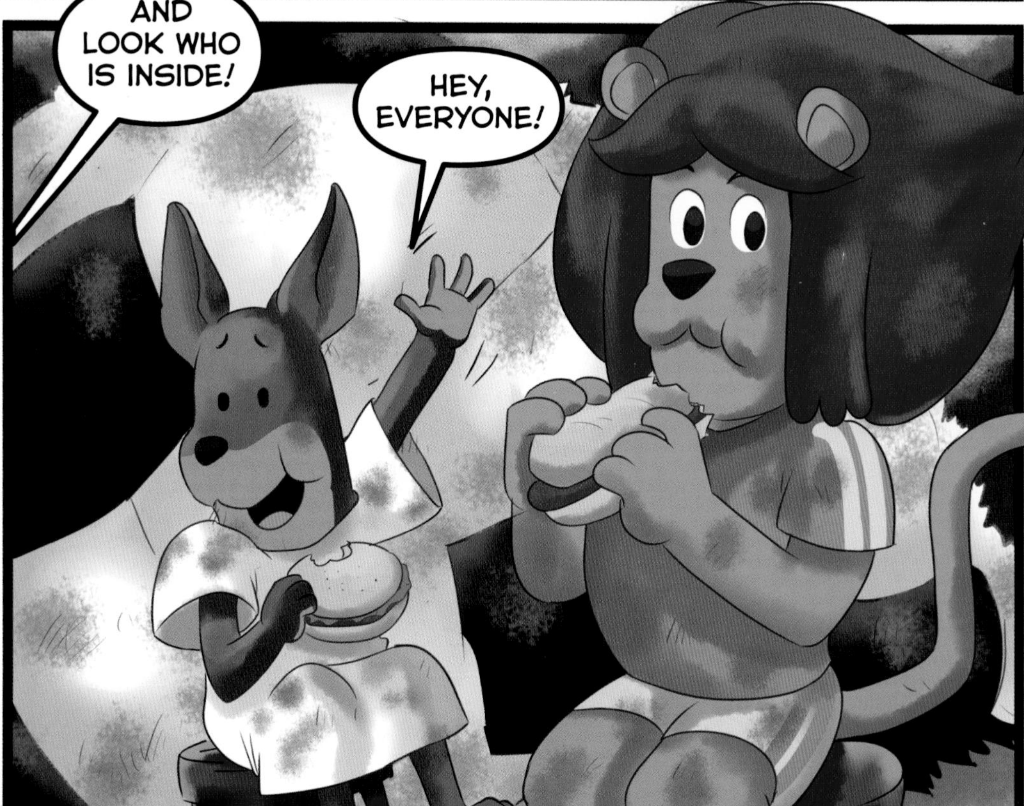
AND LOOK WHO IS INSIDE!
HEY, EVERYONE!

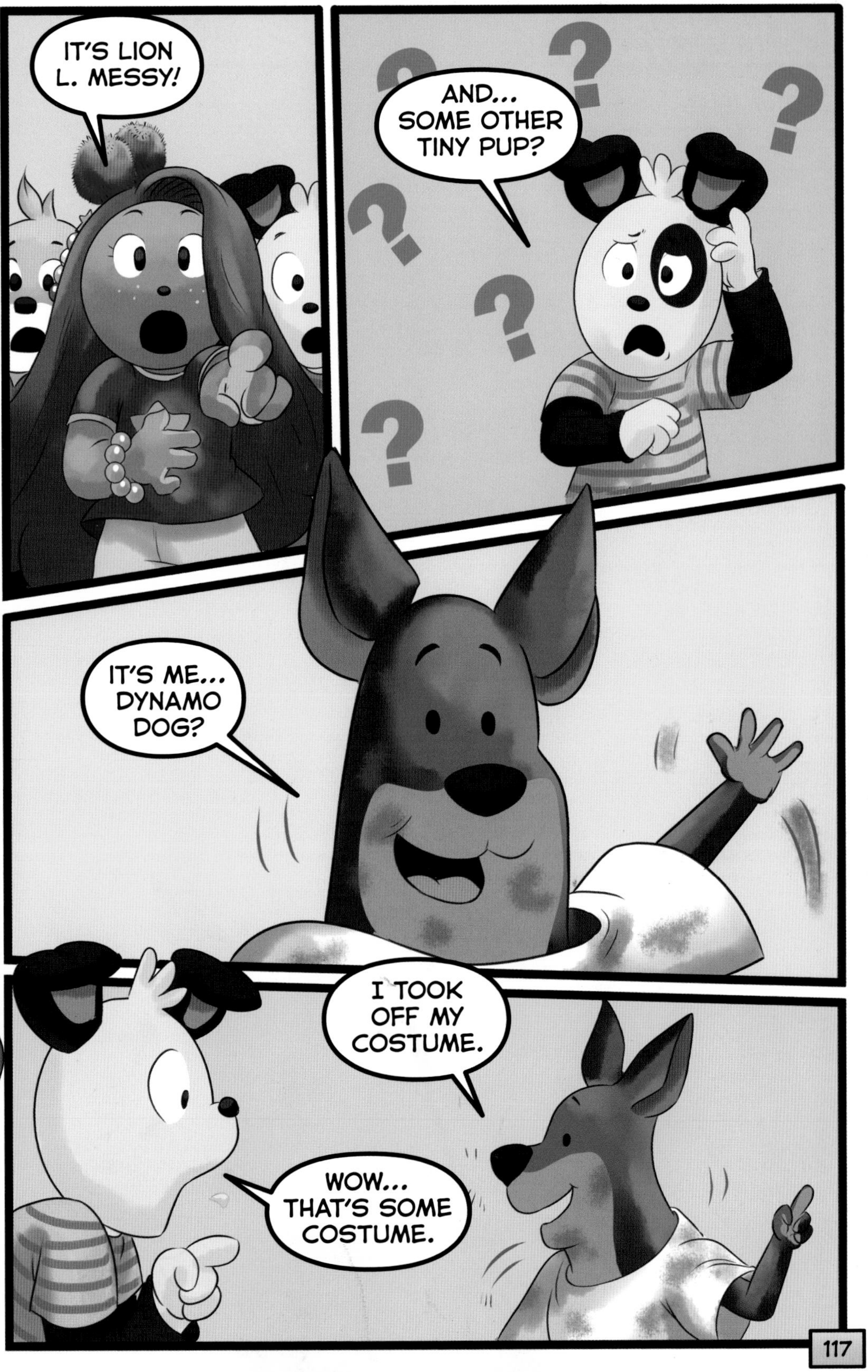
IT'S LION L. MESSY!
AND... SOME OTHER TINY PUP?
IT'S ME... DYNAMO DOG?
I TOOK OFF MY COSTUME.
WOW... THAT'S SOME COSTUME.

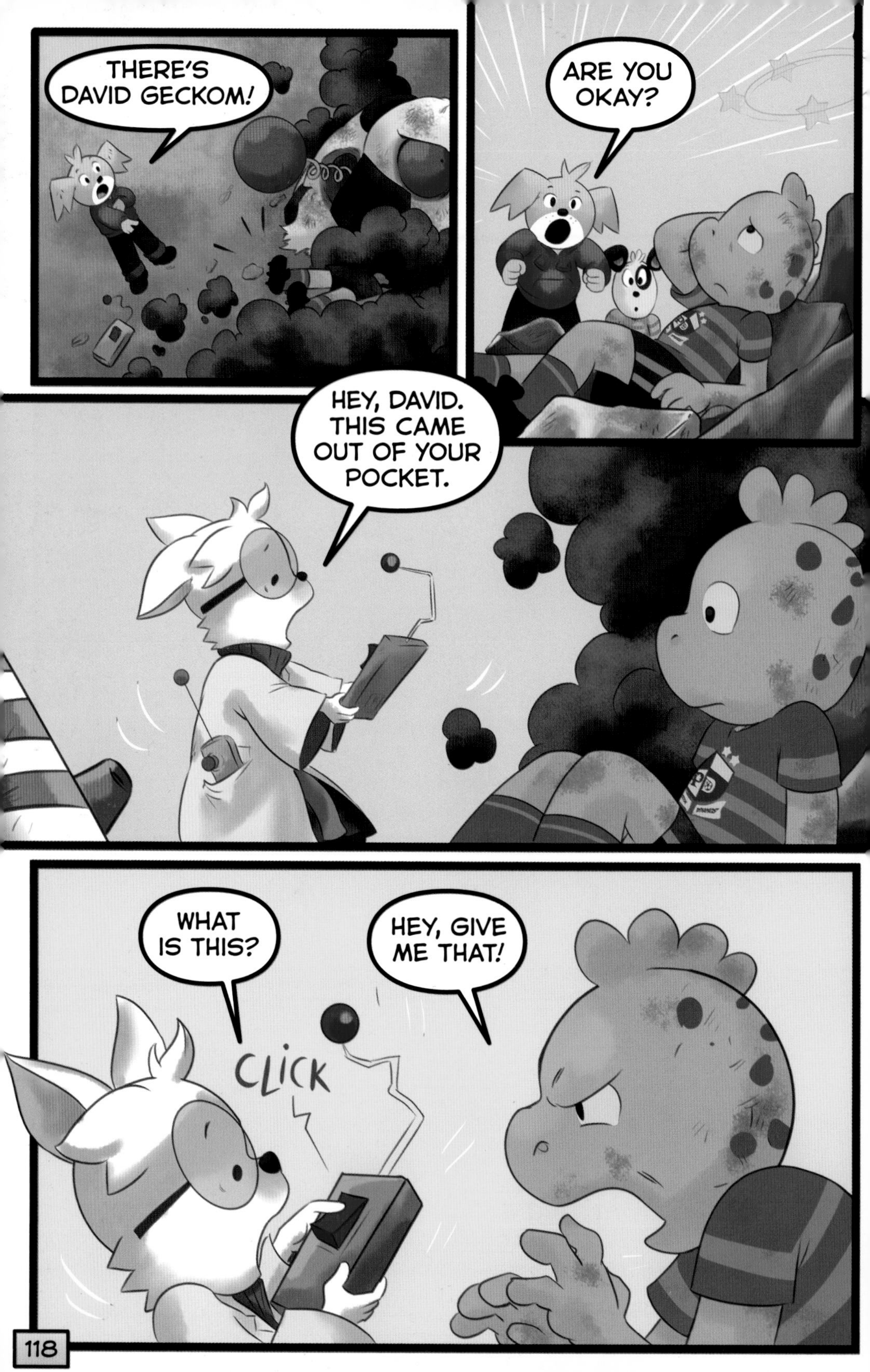
THERE'S DAVID GECKOM!
ARE YOU OKAY?
HEY, DAVID. THIS CAME OUT OF YOUR POCKET.
WHAT IS THIS?
HEY, GIVE ME THAT!
CLICK

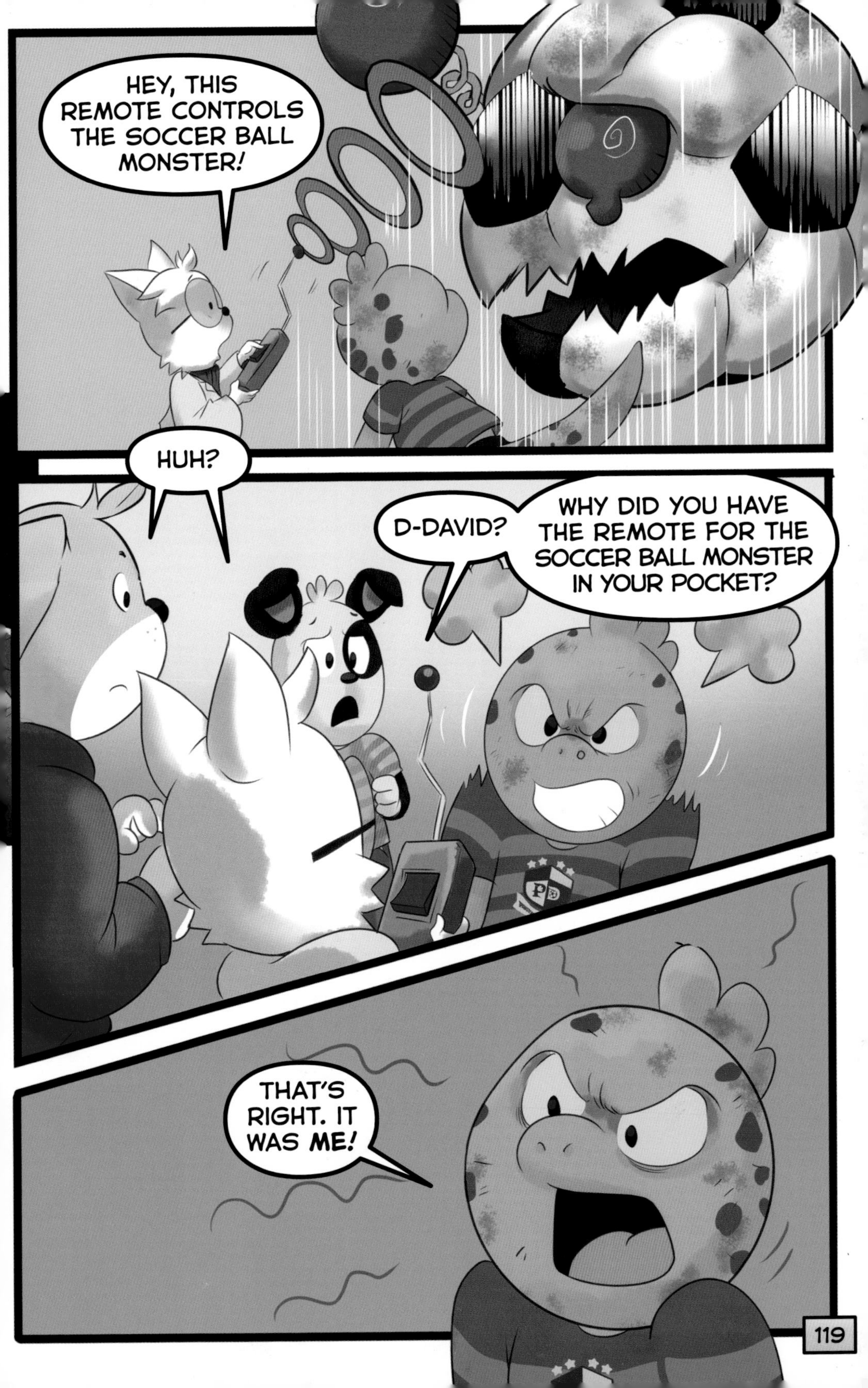
HEY, THIS REMOTE CONTROLS THE SOCCER BALL MONSTER!
HUH?
D-DAVID?
WHY DID YOU HAVE THE REMOTE FOR THE SOCCER BALL MONSTER IN YOUR POCKET?
THAT'S RIGHT. IT WAS ME!

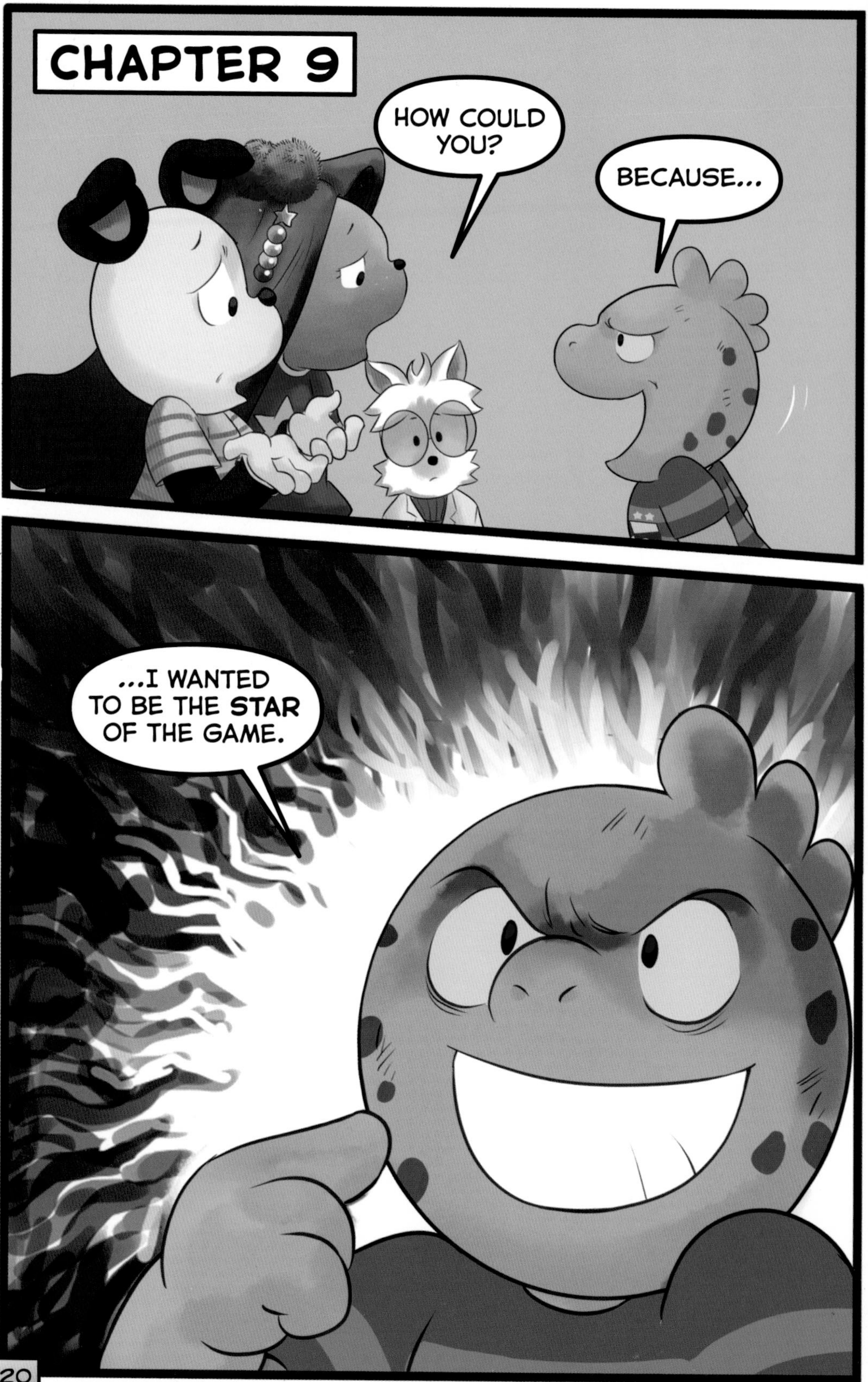
CHAPTER 9
HOW COULD YOU?
BECAUSE...
...I WANTED TO BE THE STAR OF THE GAME.

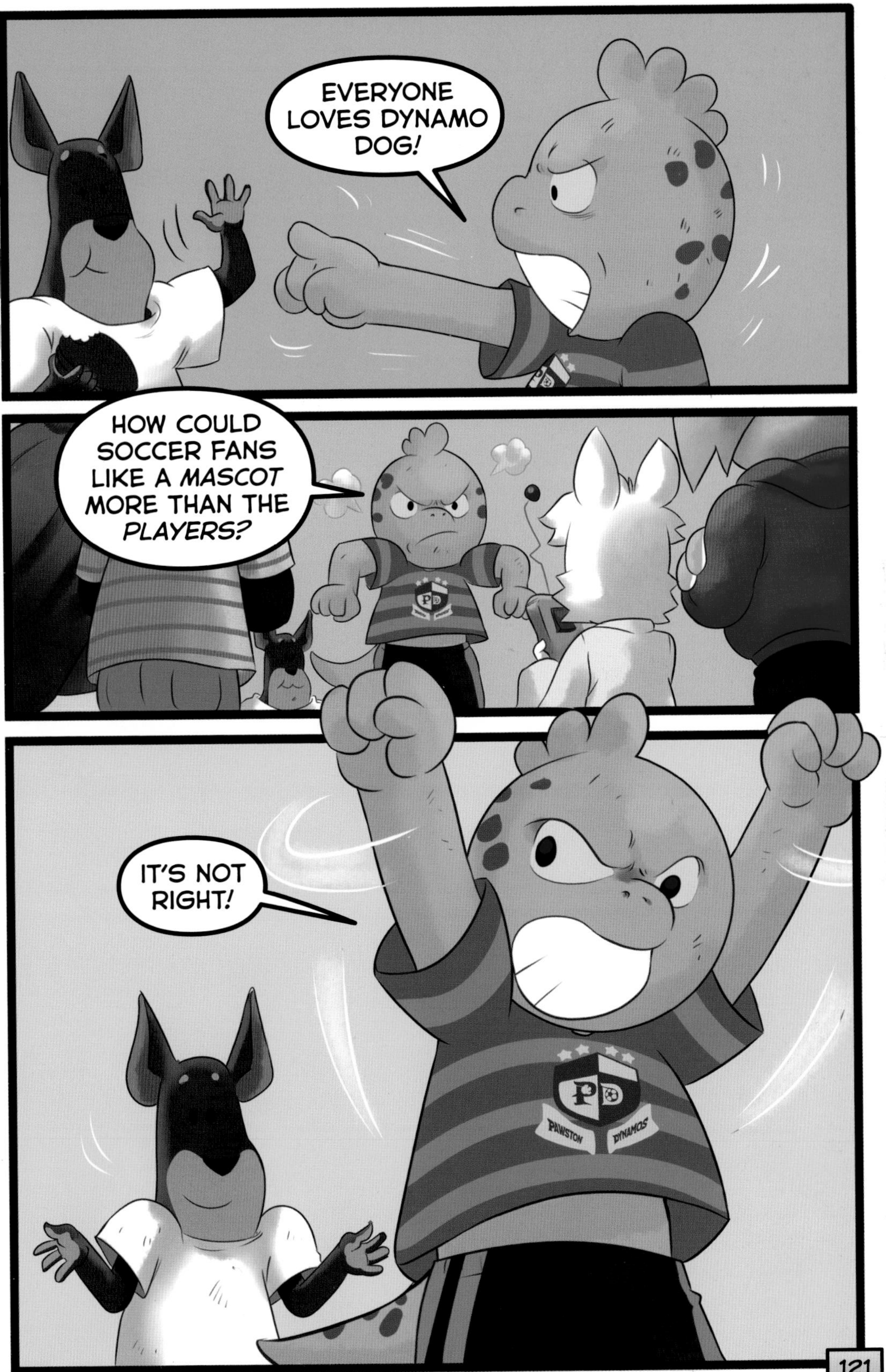
EVERYONE LOVES DYNAMO DOG!
HOW COULD SOCCER FANS LIKE A *MASCOT* MORE THAN THE *PLAYERS?*
PAWSTON DYNAMOS
IT'S NOT RIGHT!

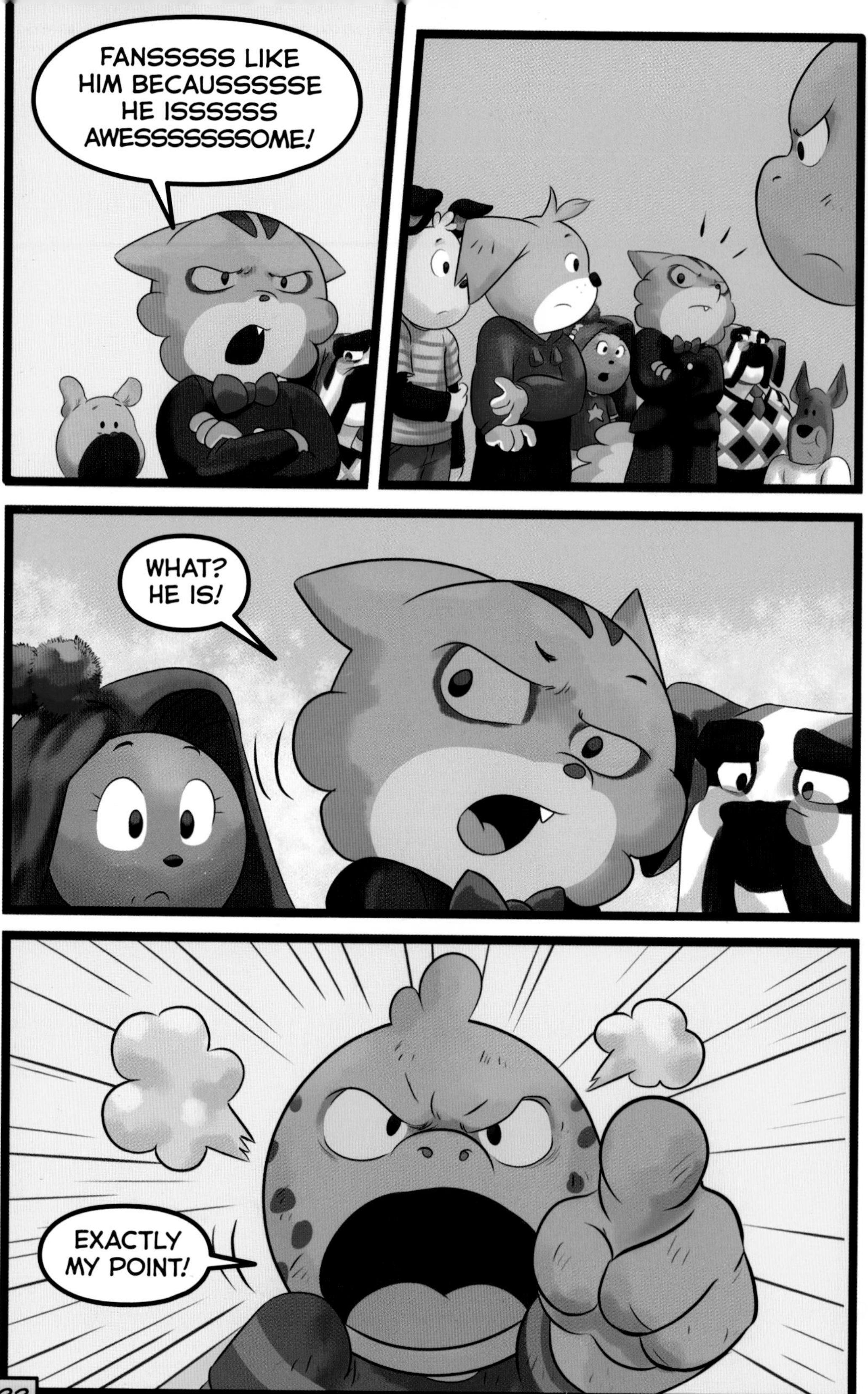
FANSSSSS LIKE HIM BECAUSSSSSE HE ISSSSSS AWESSSSSSSSOME!
WHAT? HE IS!
EXACTLY MY POINT!

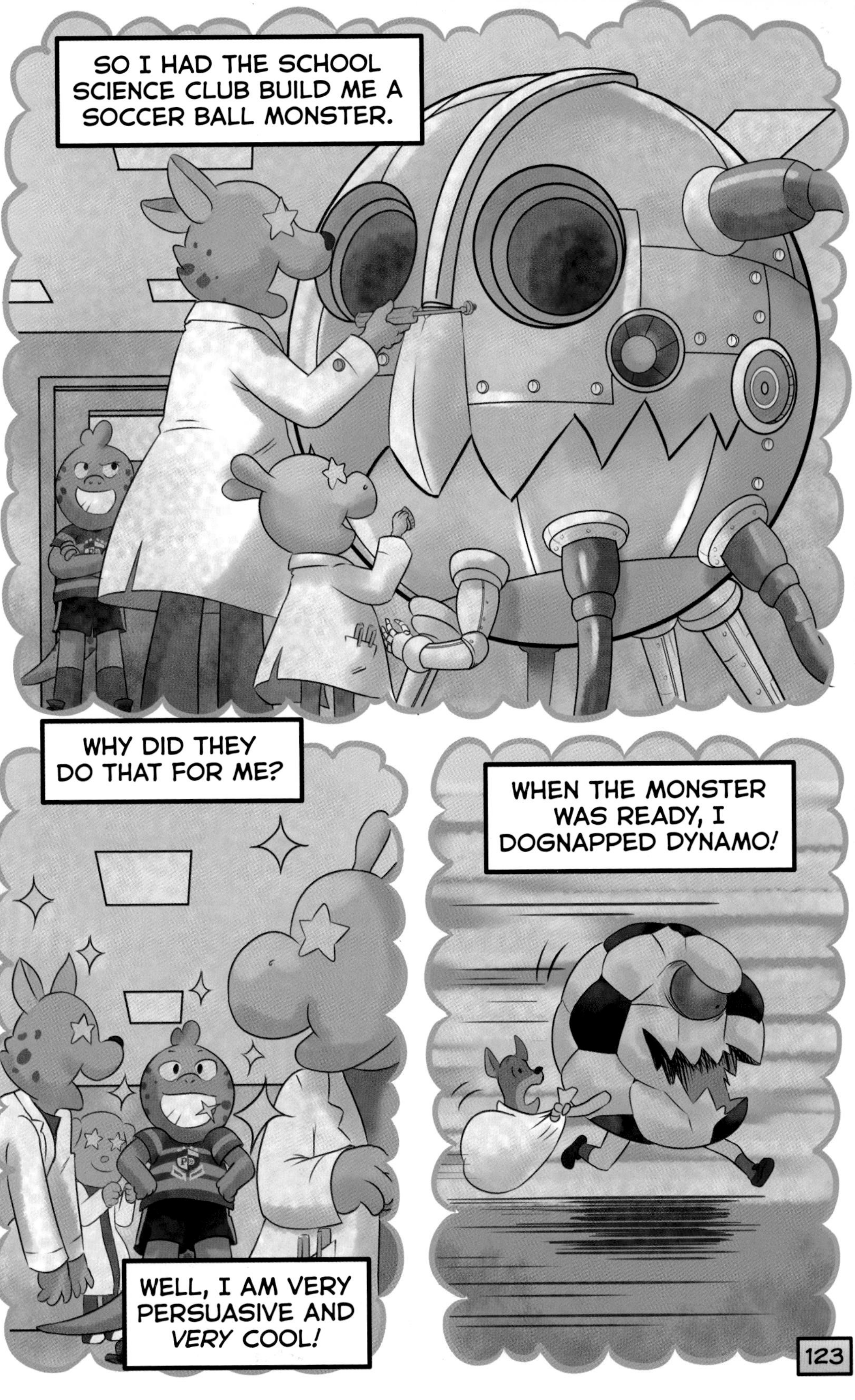
SO I HAD THE SCHOOL SCIENCE CLUB BUILD ME A SOCCER BALL MONSTER.
WHY DID THEY DO THAT FOR ME?
WELL, I AM VERY PERSUASIVE AND *VERY* COOL!
WHEN THE MONSTER WAS READY, I DOGNAPPED DYNAMO!

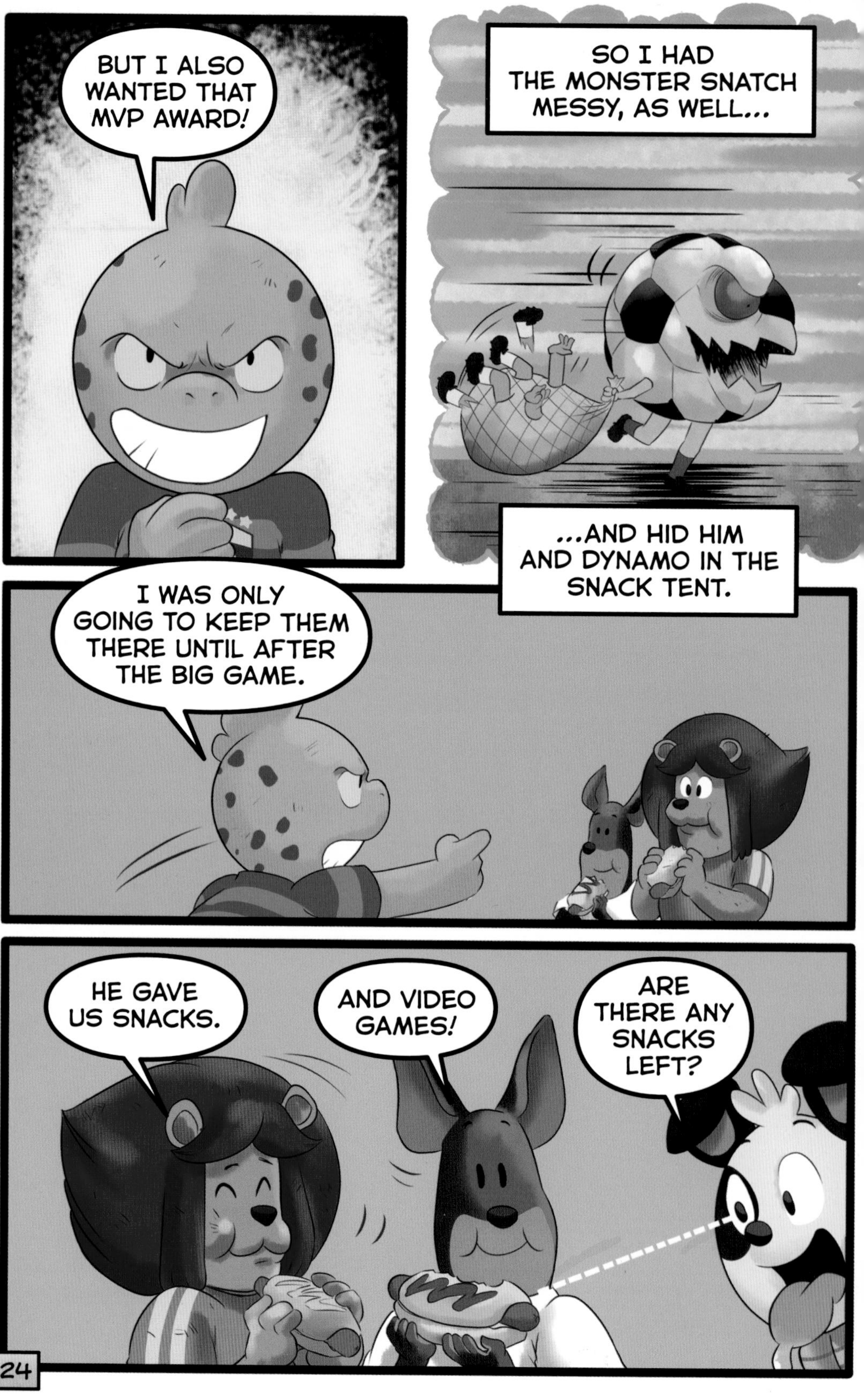

BUT I ALSO WANTED THAT MVP AWARD!
SO I HAD THE MONSTER SNATCH MESSY, AS WELL...
...AND HID HIM AND DYNAMO IN THE SNACK TENT.
I WAS ONLY GOING TO KEEP THEM THERE UNTIL AFTER THE BIG GAME.
HE GAVE US SNACKS.
AND VIDEO GAMES!
ARE THERE ANY SNACKS LEFT?

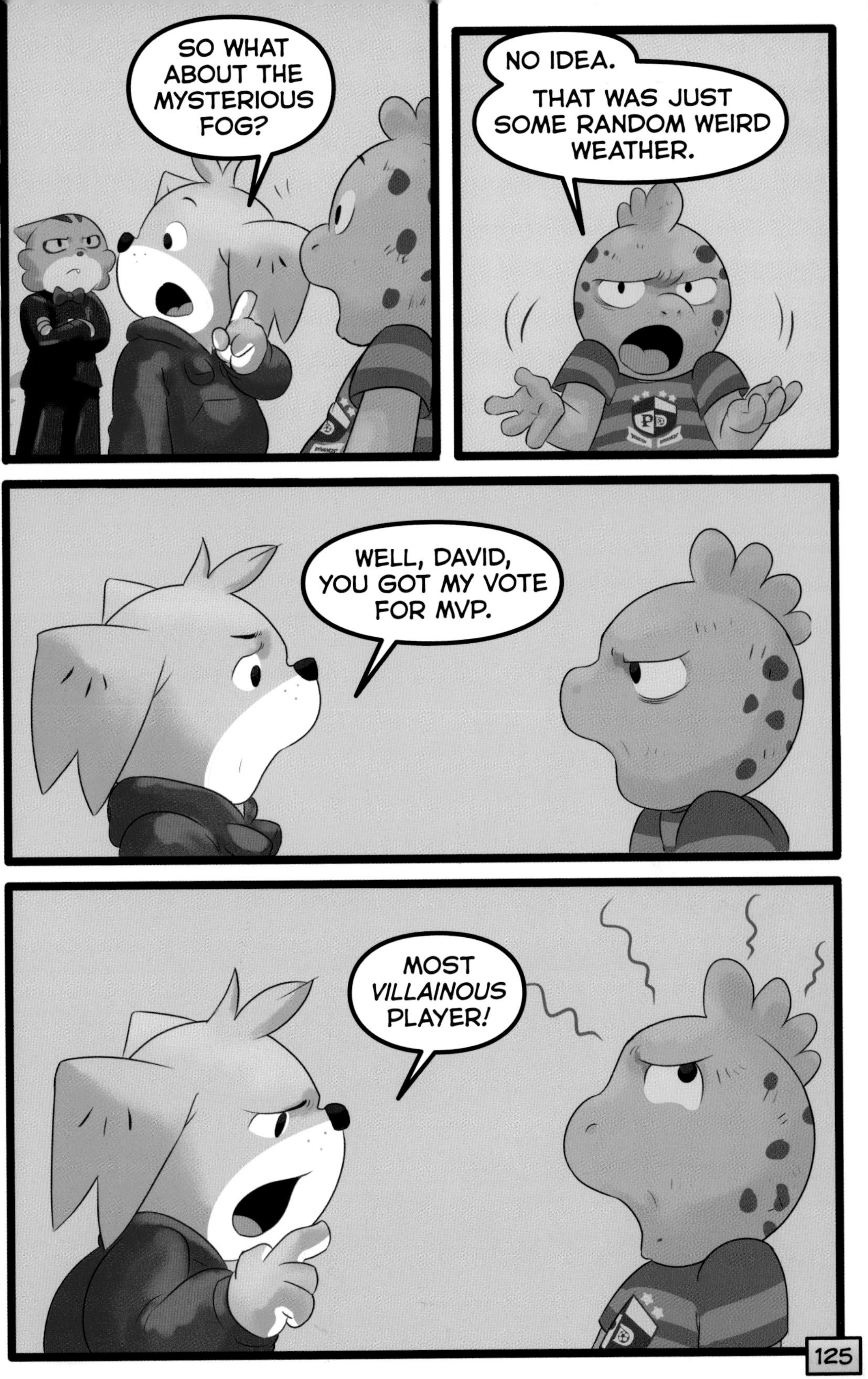
SO WHAT ABOUT THE MYSTERIOUS FOG?
NO IDEA.
THAT WAS JUST SOME RANDOM WEIRD WEATHER.
WELL, DAVID, YOU GOT MY VOTE FOR MVP.
MOST VILLAINOUS PLAYER!

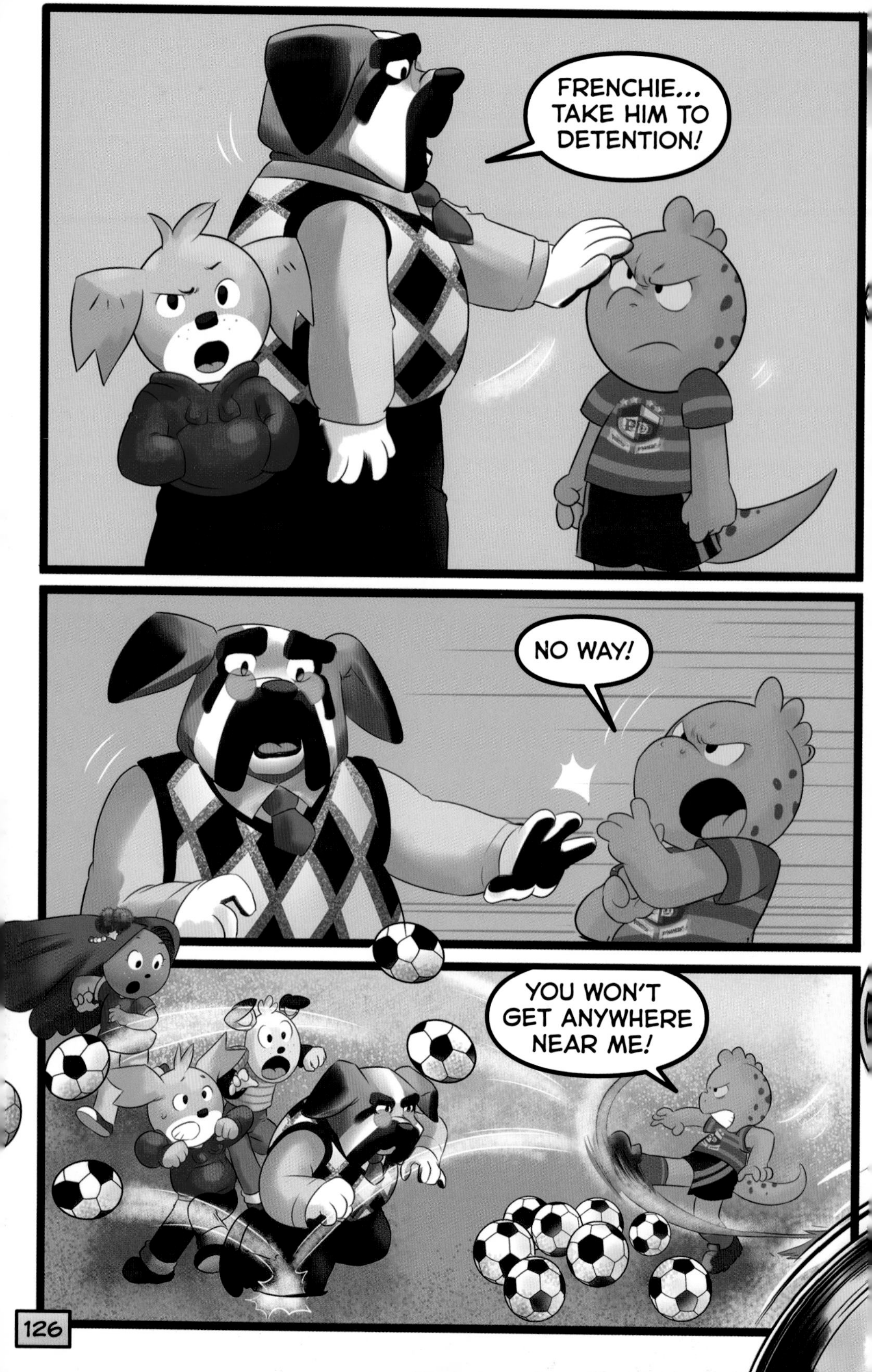
FRENCHIE... TAKE HIM TO DETENTION!
NO WAY!
YOU WON'T GET ANYWHERE NEAR ME!

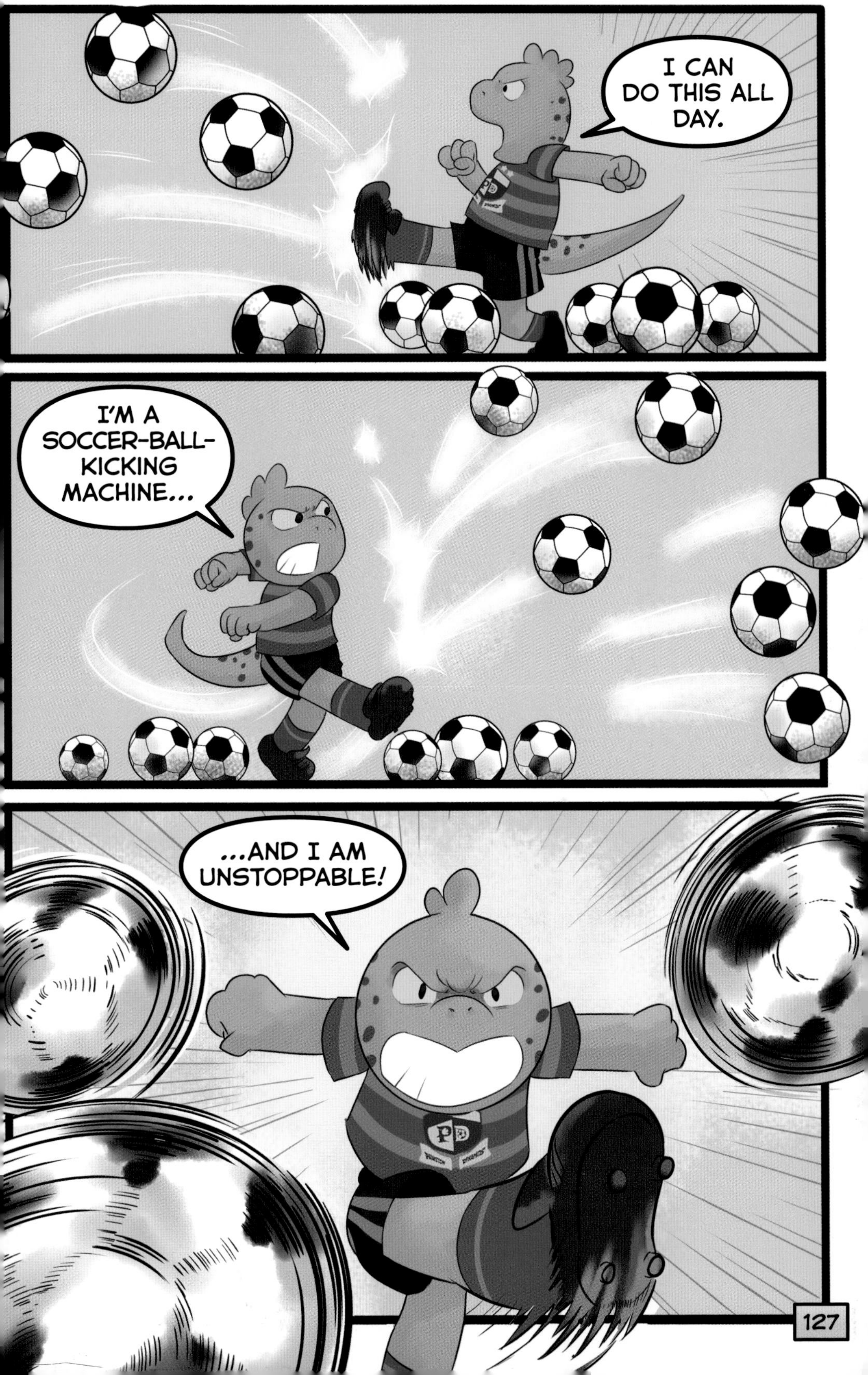
I CAN DO THIS ALL DAY.
I'M A SOCCER-BALL-KICKING MACHINE...
...AND I AM UNSTOPPABLE!

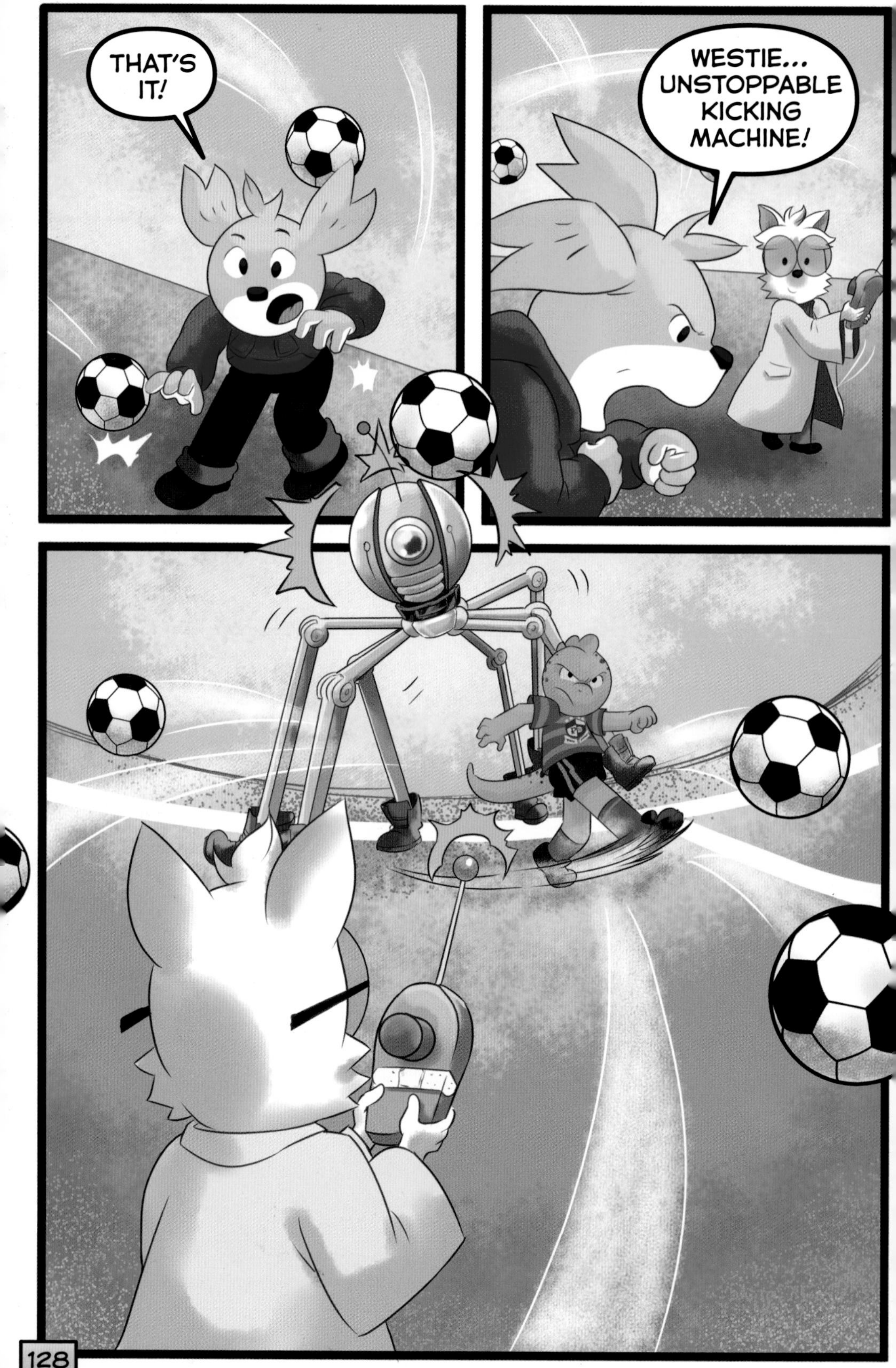
THAT'S IT!
WESTIE... UNSTOPPABLE KICKING MACHINE!

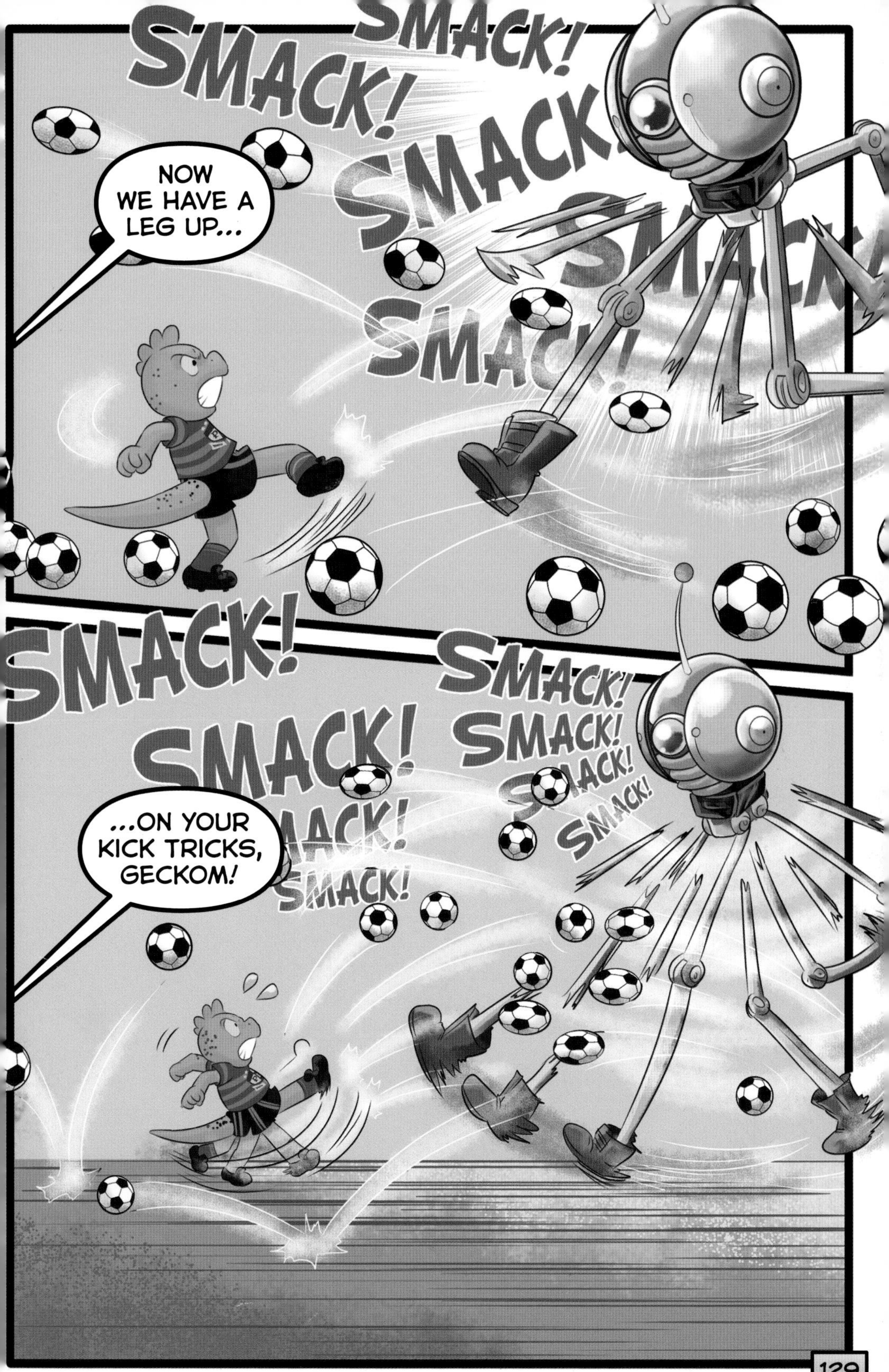
SMACK!
SMACK!
SMACK!
SMACK!
NOW WE HAVE A LEG UP...
SMACK!
SMACK!
SMACK!
SMACK!
SMACK!
SMACK!
SMACK!
SMACK!
...ON YOUR KICK TRICKS, GECKOM!
SMACK!

CHAPTER 10

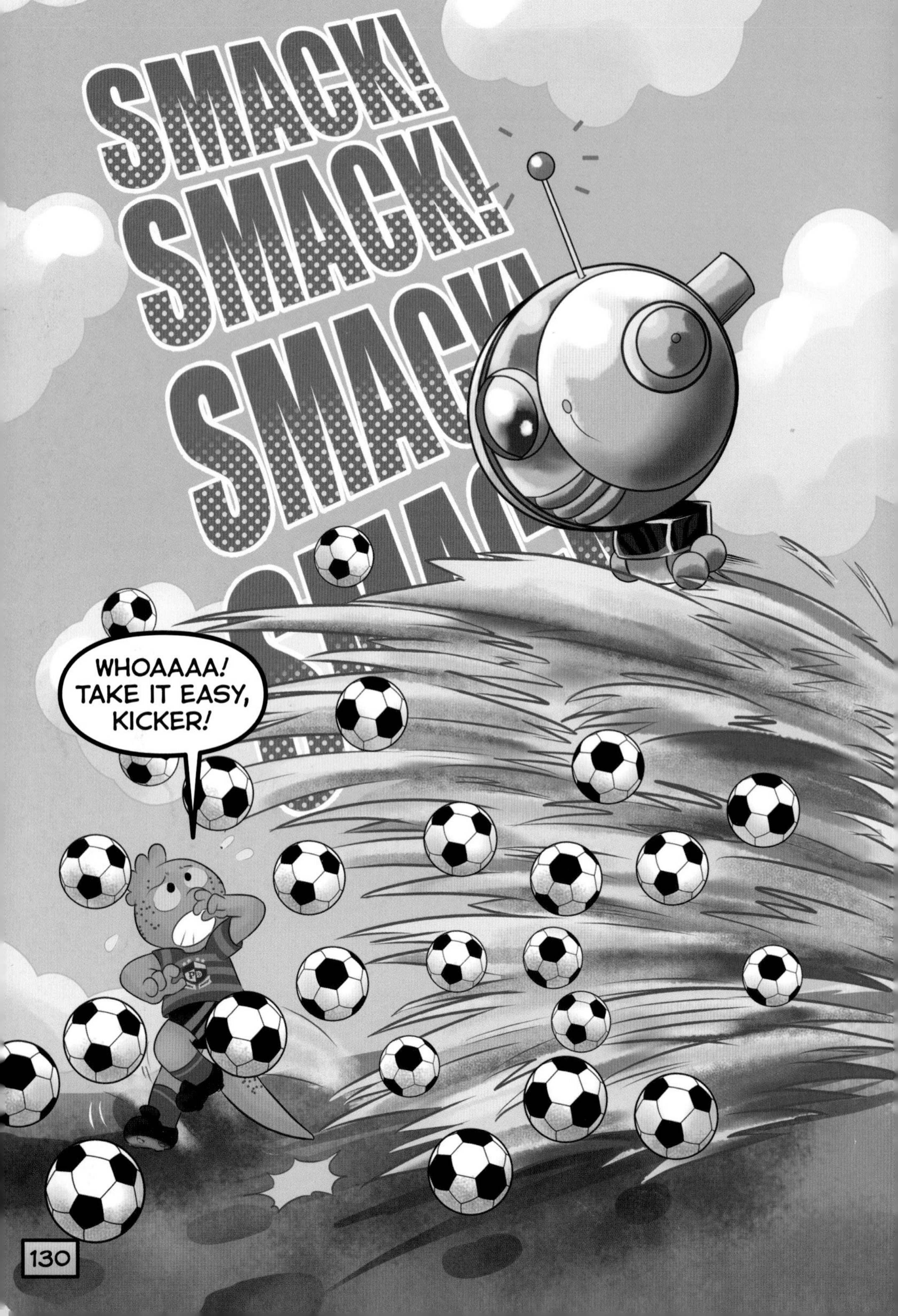
SMACK!
SMACK!
SMACK!
WHOAAAA! TAKE IT EASY, KICKER!

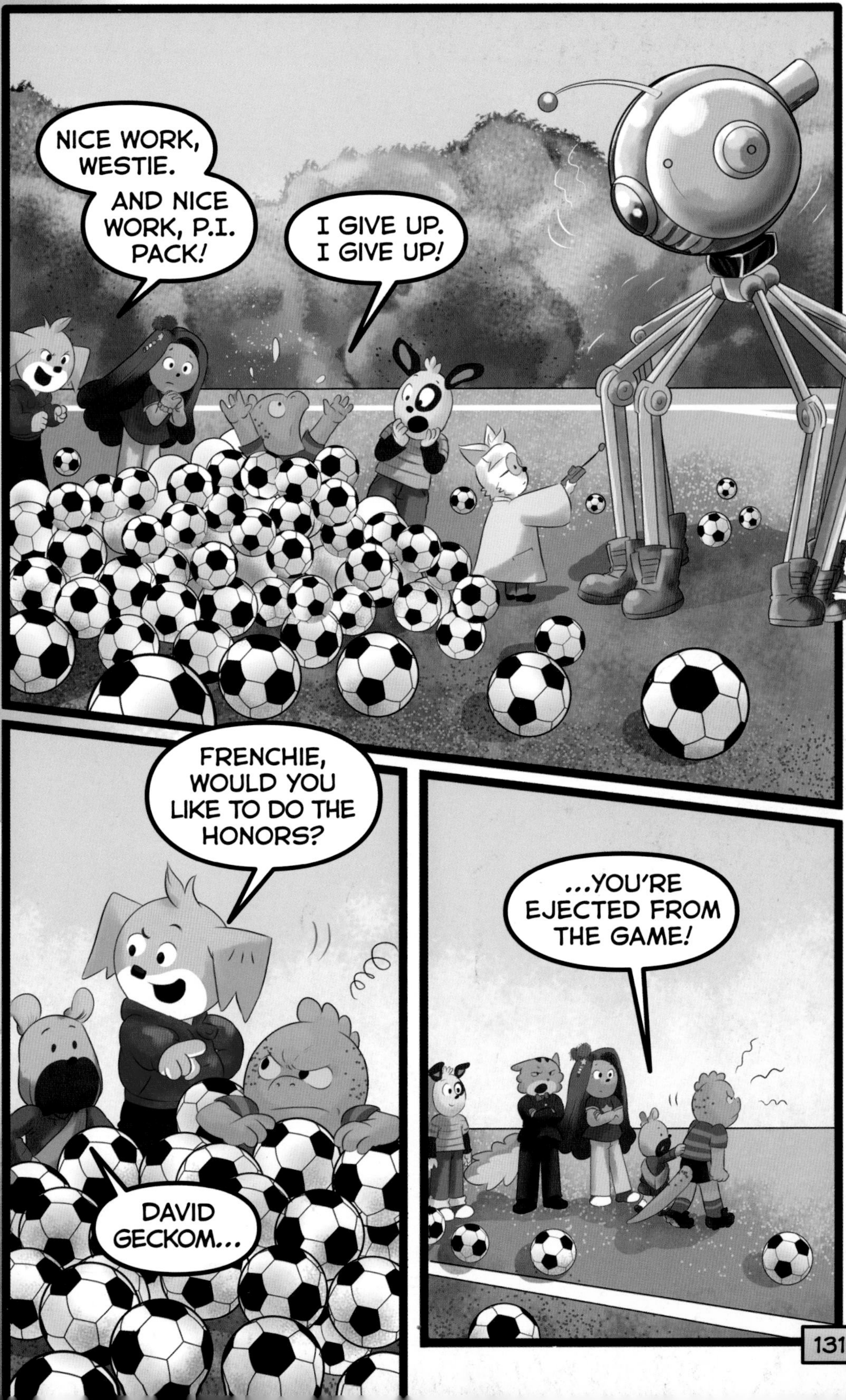
NICE WORK, WESTIE.
AND NICE WORK, P.I. PACK!
I GIVE UP. I GIVE UP!
FRENCHIE, WOULD YOU LIKE TO DO THE HONORS?
DAVID GECKOM...
...YOU'RE EJECTED FROM THE GAME!

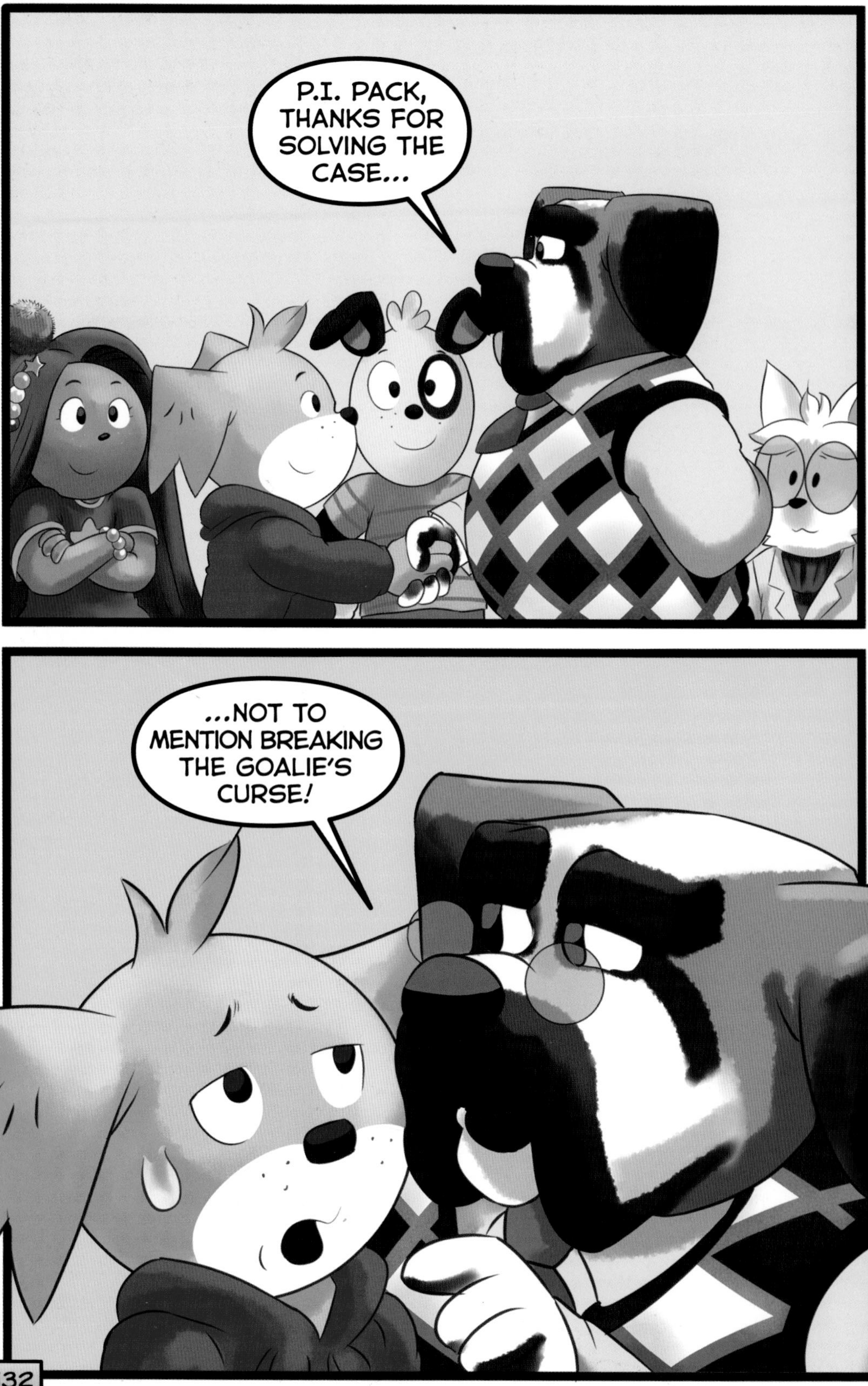
P.I. PACK, THANKS FOR SOLVING THE CASE...
...NOT TO MENTION BREAKING THE GOALIE'S CURSE!

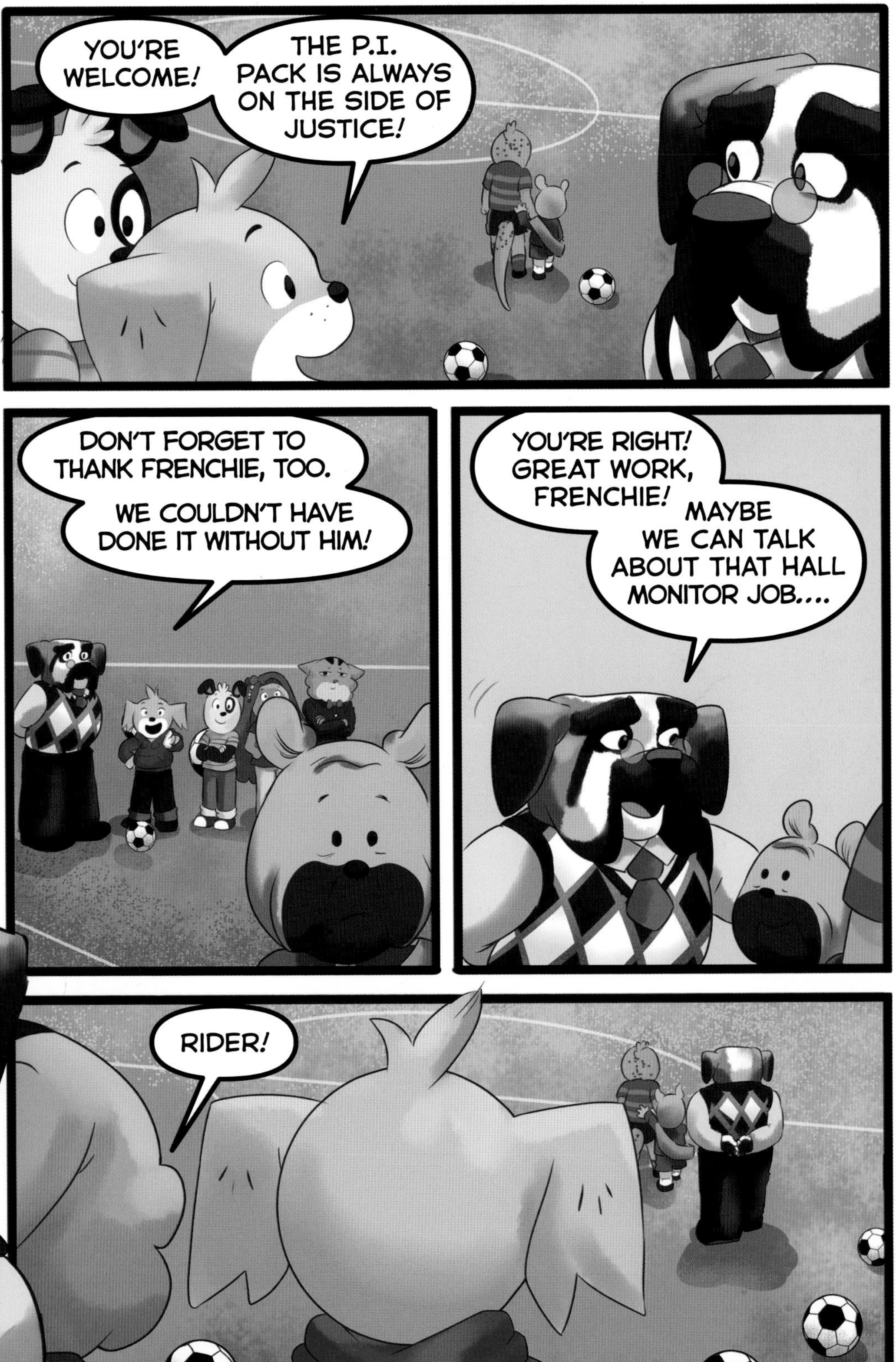
YOU'RE WELCOME!
THE P.I. PACK IS ALWAYS ON THE SIDE OF JUSTICE!
DON'T FORGET TO THANK FRENCHIE, TOO.
WE COULDN'T HAVE DONE IT WITHOUT HIM!
YOU'RE RIGHT! GREAT WORK, FRENCHIE!
MAYBE WE CAN TALK ABOUT THAT HALL MONITOR JOB....
RIDER!

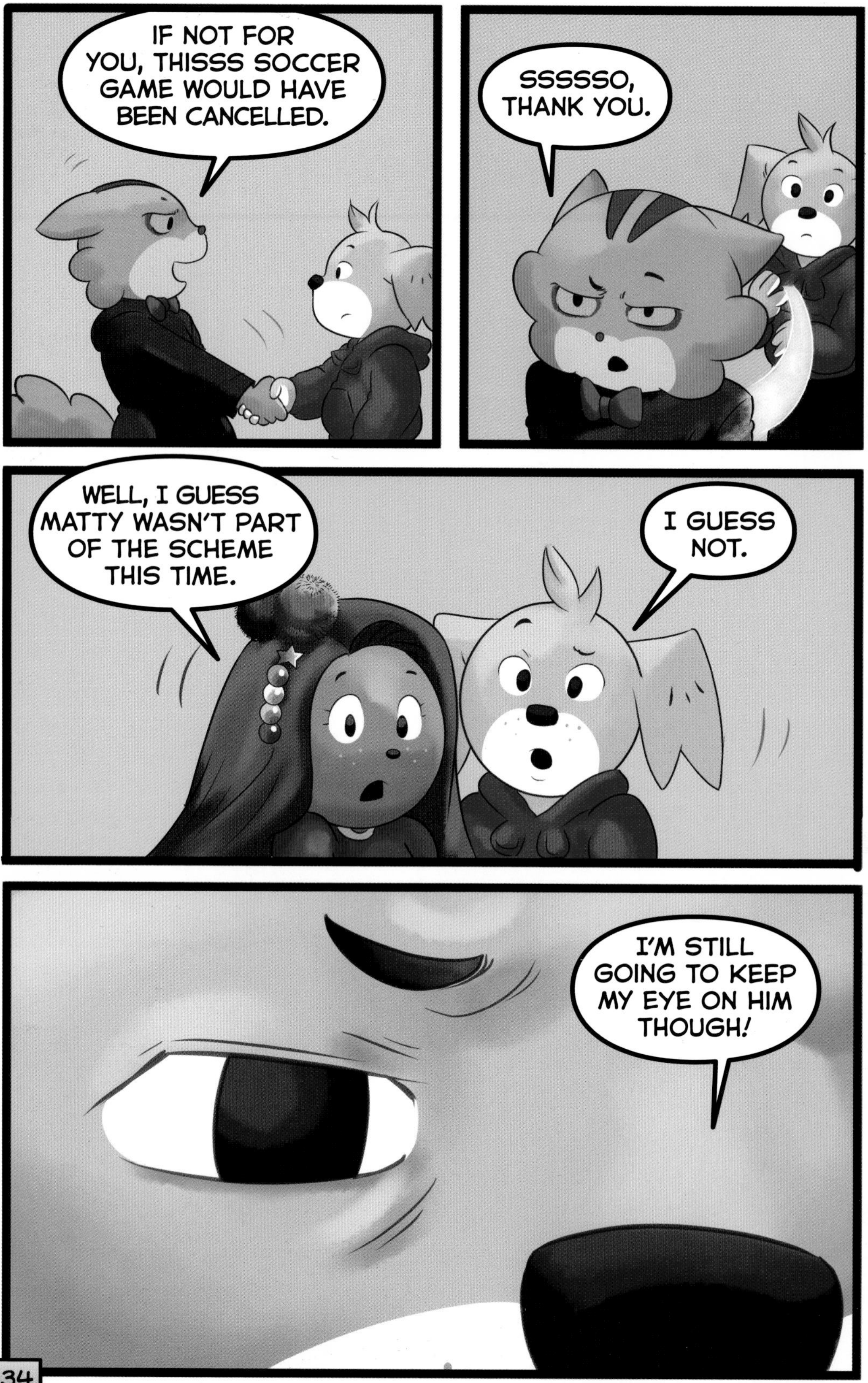
IF NOT FOR YOU, THISSS SOCCER GAME WOULD HAVE BEEN CANCELLED.
SSSSSO, THANK YOU.
WELL, I GUESS MATTY WASN'T PART OF THE SCHEME THIS TIME.
I GUESS NOT.
I'M STILL GOING TO KEEP MY EYE ON HIM THOUGH!

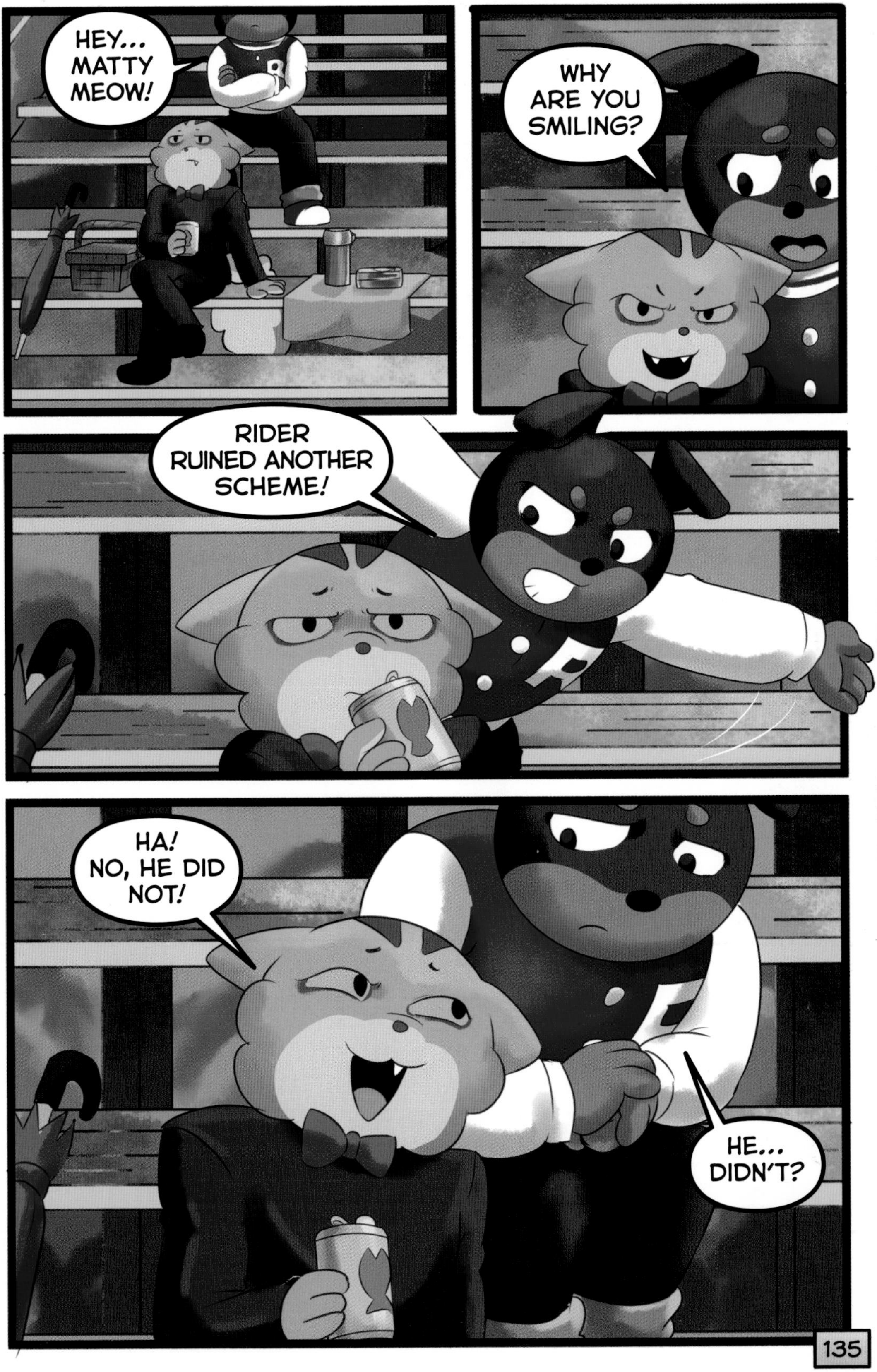
HEY... MATTY MEOW!
WHY ARE YOU SMILING?
RIDER RUINED ANOTHER SCHEME!
HA! NO, HE DID NOT!
HE... DIDN'T?

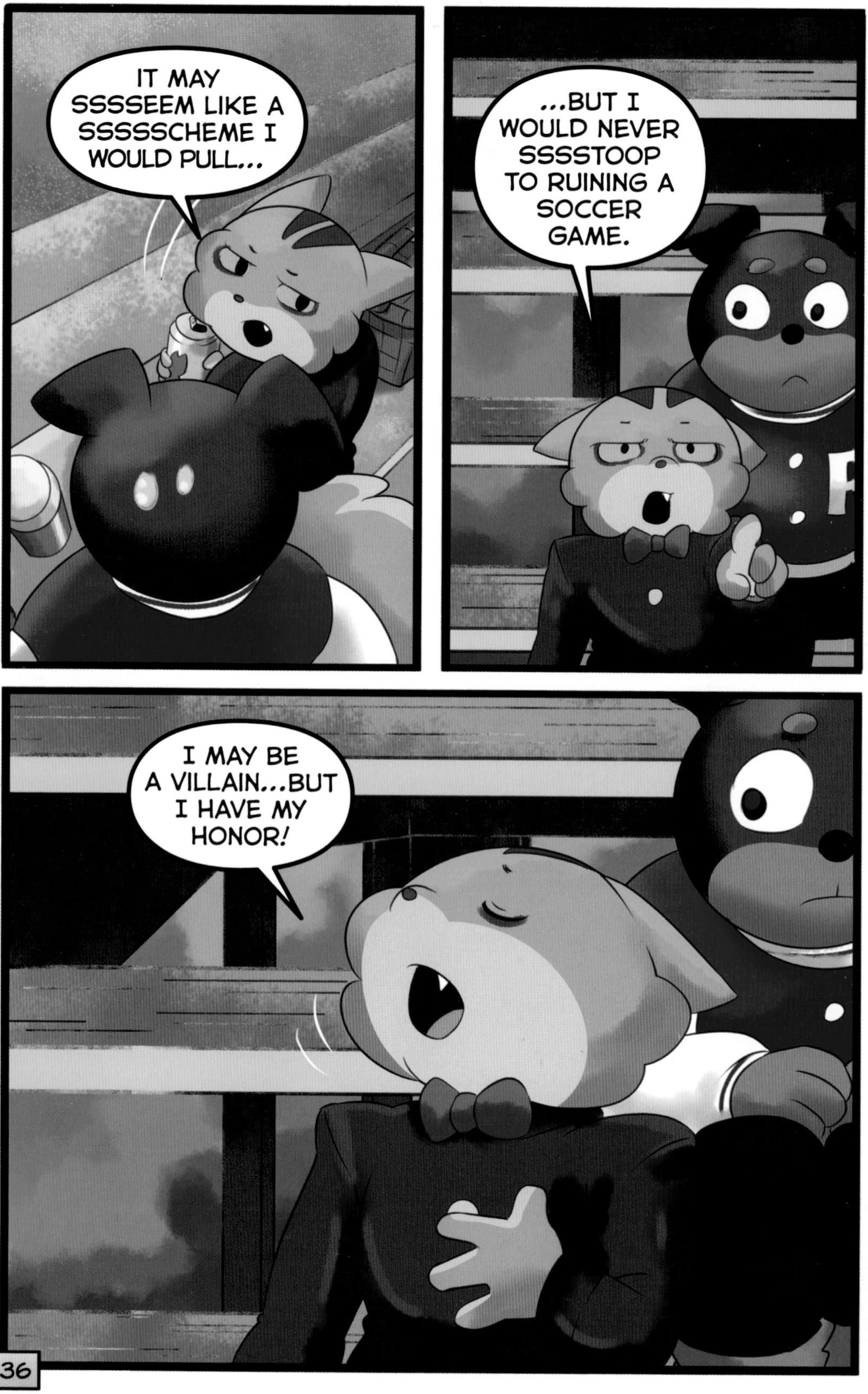
IT MAY SSSSEEM LIKE A SSSSSCHEME I WOULD PULL...
...BUT I WOULD NEVER SSSSTOOP TO RUINING A SOCCER GAME.
I MAY BE A VILLAIN...BUT I HAVE MY HONOR!

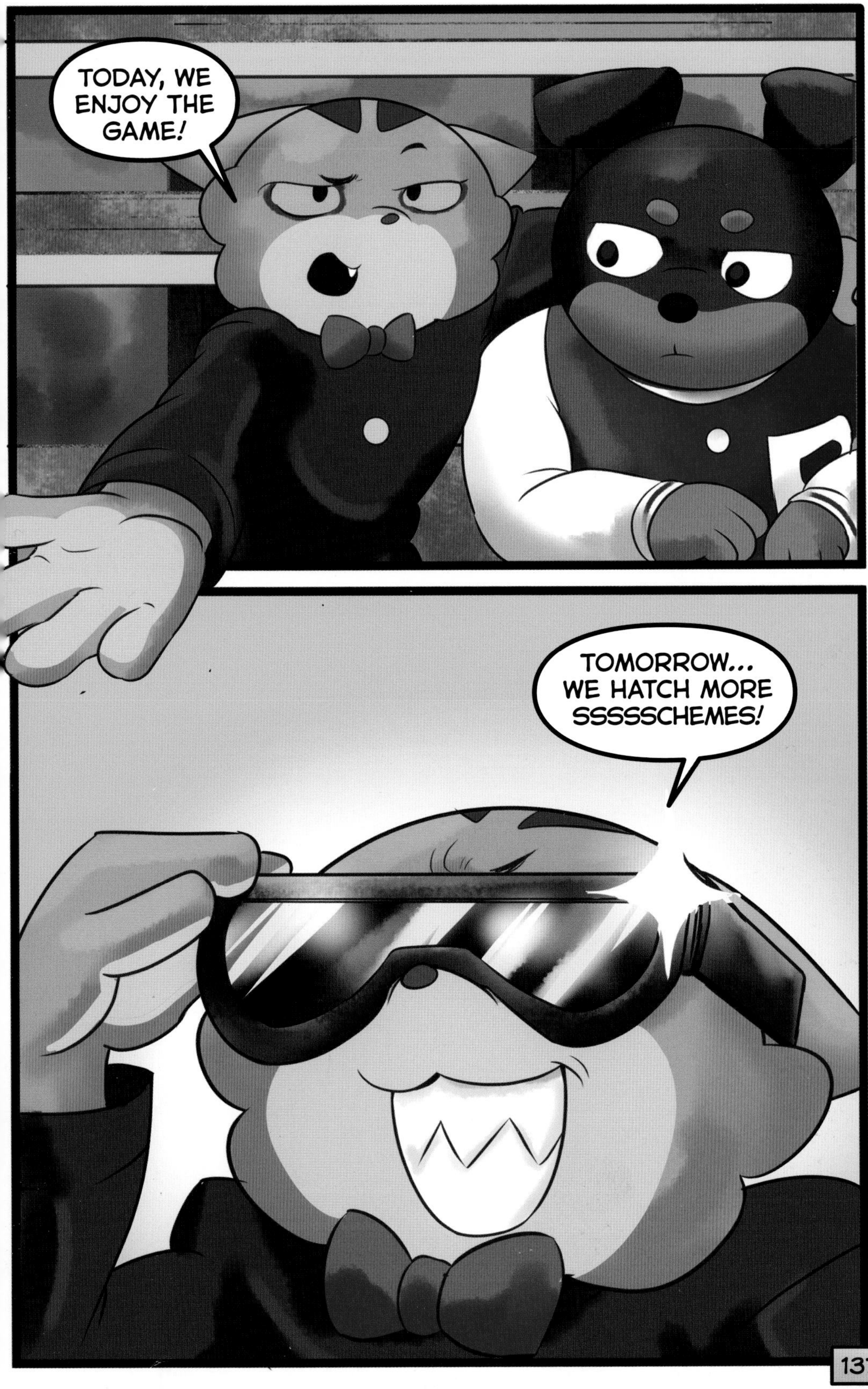
TODAY, WE ENJOY THE GAME!
TOMORROW... WE HATCH MORE SSSSSCHEMES!

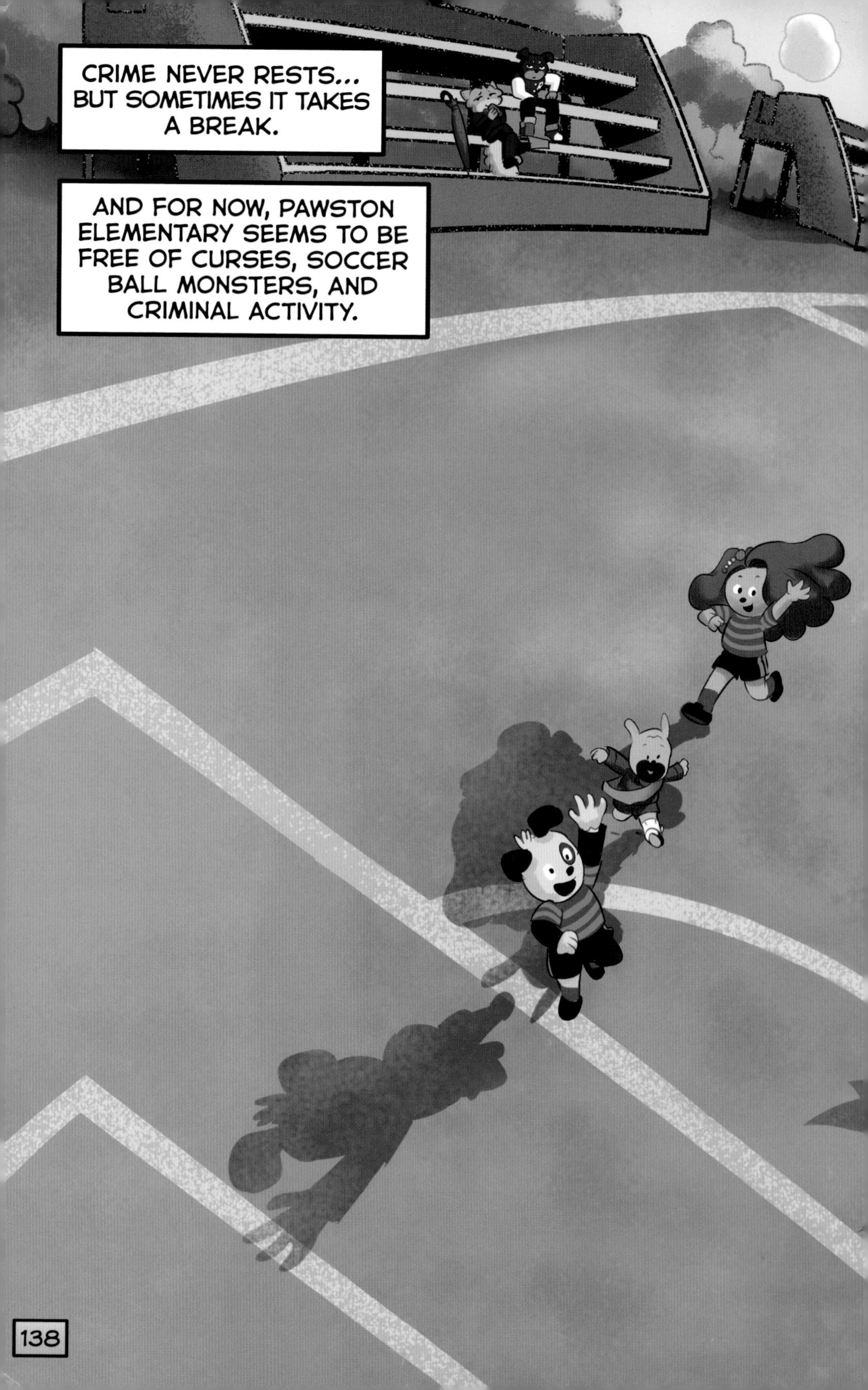
CRIME NEVER RESTS...
BUT SOMETIMES IT TAKES
A BREAK.
AND FOR NOW, PAWSTON
ELEMENTARY SEEMS TO BE
FREE OF CURSES, SOCCER
BALL MONSTERS, AND
CRIMINAL ACTIVITY.

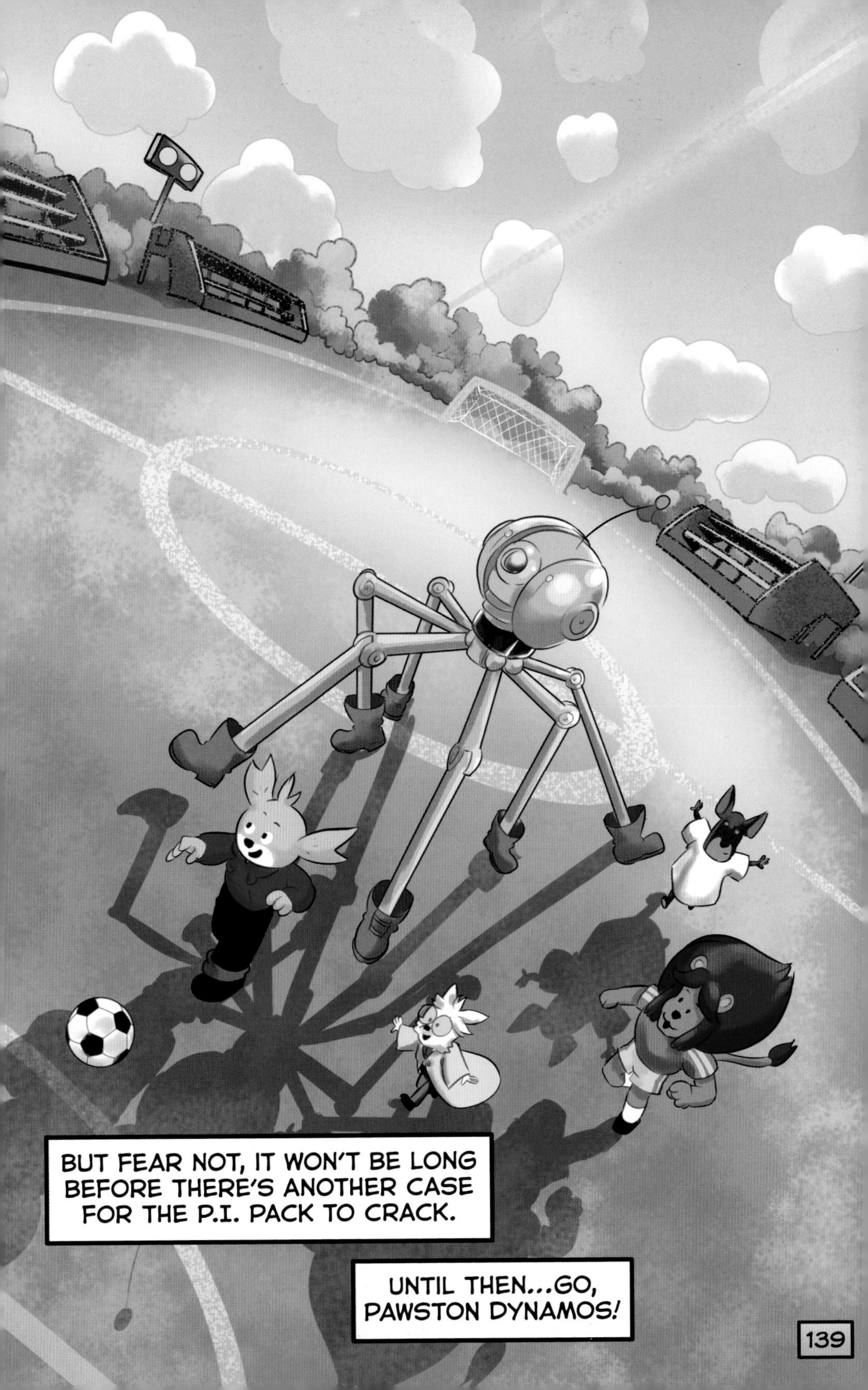
BUT FEAR NOT, IT WON'T BE LONG BEFORE THERE'S ANOTHER CASE FOR THE P.I. PACK TO CRACK.
UNTIL THEN...GO, PAWSTON DYNAMOS!

A NEW CASE AWAITS IN THE NEXT INSTALLMENT OF

Graphic Novel
PUP DETECTIVES
FEATURING...
GHOSTS, GOBLINS, AND NINJAS!
SENSEI
GOBLIN
NINJAS
PAWSTON ELEMENTARY · P.I. Pack · #004
4

TURN THE PAGE FOR A SNEAK PEEK...

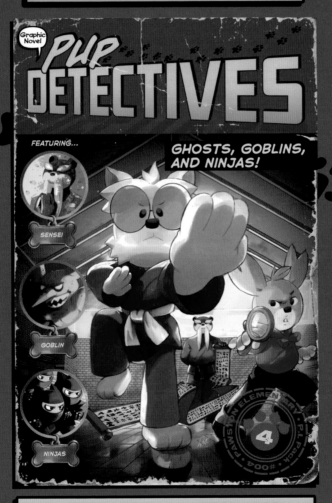

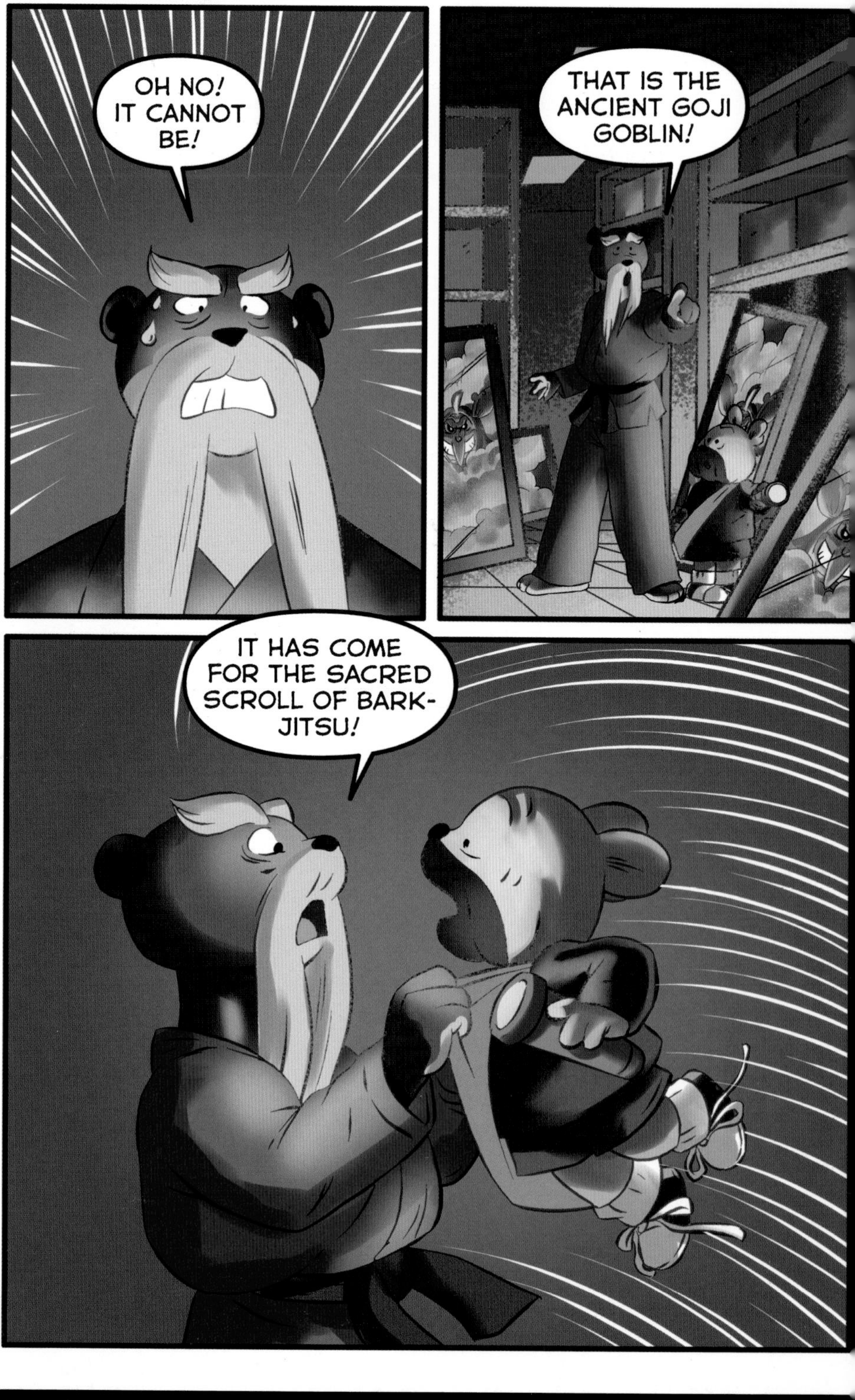
OH NO! IT CANNOT BE!
THAT IS THE ANCIENT GOJI GOBLIN!
IT HAS COME FOR THE SACRED SCROLL OF BARK-JITSU!

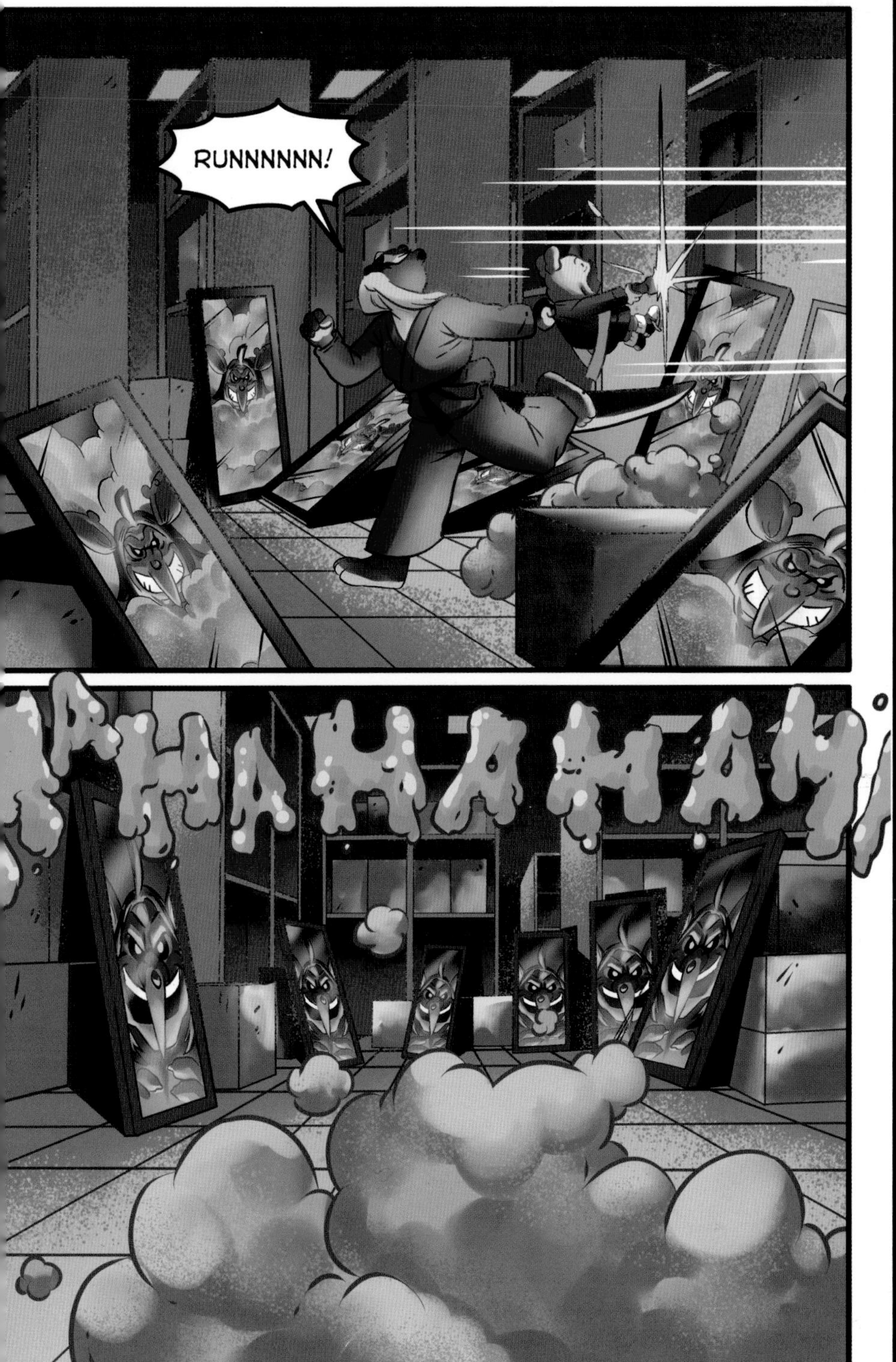
RUNNNNNN!
HAHAHAHA